Dallas

"I see we have a new student with us today — Tex Dobson."

"Yes, sir," the new boy in the front row said, his voice low, almost shy. He was tall, so tall that his lean legs in faded jeans and old cowboy boots stuck out into the aisle. The girl several seats behind him was unable to see his face, but the back of his neck was a ruddy brown, crisscrossed with the weather marks of hot suns and strong winds. Big-shouldered, hunched over the small desk, he might have been an older man, someone just visiting the classroom, but his words were young, respectful, and carefully courteous.

"I've been called Tex, sir," he said. "And I guess my father might have registered me that way, but now that I'm here, and back in school, I'd like to go by my given name."

"All right. What's that?" Mr. Engel asked.

"I was christened 'Dallas,'" the boy said.

**Other Point paperbacks
you will want to read:**

point

ACTS OF LOVE

Maureen Daly

SCHOLASTIC INC.
New York Toronto London Auckland Sydney

ISBN 0-590-40708-2

12 11 10 9 8 7 6 5 4 3 2 1   8   7 8 9/8 0 1 2/9

With thoughts of Megan, always. And with special thanks to Jan and Ken Stelter of the Arriba Arabian Stud and Equestrian Center of Thousand Palms, California, for their information and for coming to Dallas Dobson's help when he needed them most.

ACTS OF LOVE

. . . that best portion of a good man's life,
His little, nameless, unremembered, acts
Of kindness and of love.

William Wordsworth

Chapter
1

M ost important things don't happen overnight, at least the things that change lives. Henrietta Caldwell didn't know that. And her mother, if she did know, chose not to say anything, at least not until near the end.

With the new highway, there had been flags of warning, the first surveyors' stakes stuck into the ground, slim wooden shafts tied at one end with a little flutter of red cloth. Those telltale stakes traced a pathway through the woods and meadows, almost cutting the Caldwell lands in half. They started at the property line down behind the pond and ended at the top of the meadow near the big dead oak, a split, gray tree that had been struck by winter lightning some years ago.

It took the young girl more than three hours, that early spring day she had first sighted the red flags. Snow was still on the ground, but there was the sound of water just beginning to run under the thick brook ice.

Anger gave her energy. With wet, cold hands, Retta pulled out every stake, dumping armload after armload on the front terrace. How had someone dared to walk over those fields and lay claim to land that belonged only to the Caldwells?

Ever since the days when William Penn was the first governor of Pennsylvania, a Caldwell had built and lived on that property — a span of almost three hundred years. The present Caldwell family still owned more than forty acres, and Henrietta and her young brother were familiar with every rocky mica pit and ivy-covered fence on the property. No one had to tell them at what side of the brook the first green-leafed arum broke through crusty ground in spring. Nor that the stretch of glade between the old apple trees was the best spot for a salt lick for young deer. And they had decided for themselves that the hillock beside the big oak, sprinkled with corn feed, would attract flocks of autumn geese that honked down from Canada with the first frost.

Everyone in Zenith and around the countryside knew the Carter Caldwells (when Carter Caldwell himself was a boy, and for generations before, the family was known as "those really rich Caldwells"), and present-day Zenith residents could still point out which fields and woodlands remained as part of "the old Caldwell place."

She had been young that fateful spring, just a few weeks past fourteen, and her father had tried to explain to her just why the red flags were there.

The whole program was still in the discussion stages, he said, but the State Highway Commission had selected twenty acres of Caldwell land as part of a new multimillion-dollar bypass system, a proposed six-lane highway to loop around Zenith and make way for the freight trucks and heavy-vehicle traffic going to Baltimore or Philadelphia. There would be town meetings pro and con, her father told her, and the family was getting legal advice from local lawyers, but under the statute of "Right of Eminent Domain," the state of Pennsylvania had the authority to do what it had done — in planting the stakes — at least for now.

"Laws are made by men, and laws must be obeyed by men," her father had said at the dinner table. "But this family isn't through fighting, not by a long shot."

Within days, the highway crew was back at work and new little red flags were set in place, like brilliant, hated flowers, staking claim through meadow, woods, and orchard.

But the other thing, the thing involving the new person, was different. There had been no warning at all.

It was early fall, more than two years later. Henrietta was sixteen and in her third year of high school.

5

Even though he was technically a senior, the young man had missed a lot of school and was assigned to work for needed catch-up credits with a junior geometry class.

The weather was hot and hazy, full of smells of the countryside still touched with summer and vacation freedom, the way September can be in rural Pennsylvania.

Through the half-opened windows of the classroom, the odor of gasoline and warm rubber drifted in from the crowded parking lot. There were four big yellow school buses for crossroads pickups, but anyone at Havendale High with a driver's license preferred his own car. Junior Provanza's new Porsche sat under a small sycamore tree, the turning leaves casting dappled shadows over the bright red paint and the smooth, black upholstery. This was a consolidated county high school and some of the students lived on working farms, but most had parents with homes and a job in the small, nearby town of Zenith, with some commuting to employment in Wilmington or even downtown Philadelphia, thirty-five miles away.

Junior Provanza worked weekends and after school at his father's general store at Millstream Crossroads, and on Saturdays he cut meat for the butcher section. Some of the wealthier students had a different life-style and even rode their own horses to school in good weather, stabling the animals during the day at old Mrs. Curtayne's barns just down the road. The student body was a mixed group. Junior

Provanza strongly felt the status need of his bright new car.

Before the final attendance bell, someone had smeared the inside panes of a rear window with a cut-up apple or pear and now, during class, a half dozen black-and-yellow wasps bobbed and bumped against the glass. The insects were the dominant females, drowsy now, bodies heavy and pendulous, already ready to hive-up for the winter. Yet there was something sensual and demanding in the rhythmic drone, the way the wasps were so persistently drawn to the promise of fruity smells and sweet juices. No one can be sure, however, whether or not an autumn wasp may have one last sting.

But Mr. Engel, the math teacher, was not ready to clear the classroom because of the old wasp trick. He himself had been a student at Havendale High when it was only six classrooms and a cow pasture for a baseball field. And he believed the insects, torpid and slow-flying, were not likely to leave the sticky sweetness of the window panes for an attack. So he settled behind his desk, studied the roll book, and said firmly, "I see we have a new student with us today — Tex Dobson."

"Yes, sir," the new boy in the front row said, his voice low, almost shy. He was tall, so tall that his lean legs in faded jeans and old cowboy boots stuck out into the aisle. The girl several seats behind him was unable to see his face, but the back of his neck was a ruddy brown, crisscrossed with the weather marks of hot suns and strong winds. Big-shoul-dered, hunched over the small desk, he might have been an older man, someone just visiting the class-room, but his words were young, respectful, and carefully courteous.

"I've been called Tex, sir," he said. "And I guess my father might have registered me that way, but now that I'm here, and back in school, I'd like to go by my given name."

"All right. What's that?" Mr. Engel asked.

"I was christened 'Dallas,' " the boy said.

There was a swift, taut silence in the classroom, a void of movement or sound that meant that every-one was about to laugh, if only someone else dared to laugh first.

Mr. Engel was quick to comprehend and said matter-of-factly, "Thank you, Dallas Dobson. And since you're so tall, I'd appreciate it if you would take a desk in the back of the classroom. There's one right behind Henrietta Caldwell, the girl in the blue blouse. I'll speak to you right after class, Dallas, to find out where and on what you need to catch up. I don't think we have a problem."

In a seat across the aisle, Charlotte Amberson twisted around to stare full-face at Henrietta. There was a small, enigmatic smile on her lips, but Hen-rietta could not read her friend's eyes. Ever since early summer, and now right up into the first of the school year, Charlie Amberson had affected huge sunglasses, both by day and by night. She had man-aged to buy herself an extensive collection, and today the dark circles of glass were framed in blue denim, matching her jeans and jacket. Even though the glasses revealed nothing, her soft, curved mouth seemed to be saying, "Well, all right!"

As the person called Dallas Dobson gathered together his books, Retta Caldwell turned her glance away from his big shoulders and the shaggy hairline ragged over the sun-browned neck, and forced herself to look down at the floor. As the young man passed her desk, she noticed the boots again, calf-high with narrow, stacked heels. On the maroon leather uppers there was a little flag of Texas, embossed with metallic color, on the outer ankle. Although they had the dulled sheen of a recent rub-down with saddle soap, the leather was creased and worn and, as Dobson walked quickly to the back of the room, his boots made a slipping, squeaking sound on the polished floor.

For a moment, Retta felt a stab of near dislike toward her best friend, Charlie Amberson, with the opaque eyes and evaluating, sensual smile on her lips. *Charlie, give the guy a chance,* she thought.

The desk chair behind her creaked with Dobson's rangy body weight, and Retta was aware that the new boy must now be staring at her — her straight back, the short red curl of her hair, the narrow collar of her new blouse.

She stifled a sigh, so quickly and completely that it almost brought tears to her eyes. *He's probably got cotton stuffed in those toes,* the girl in the blue blouse thought with a mixture of sadness and warmth. *Or maybe just a bunch of scrunched-up straw from somebody's barn.* His first day in a new school, his first chance to make an impression on the class, and this new person was trying to make it in old, borrowed clothes. No polite "sirs" to Mr. Engel, no extra buffing of the shoes, not even the tarnished Texas stars could change that. This guy was hurting.

Retta Caldwell knew those boots were not really his, that they had once belonged to someone else.

Ordinarily, dinnertime was the best hour of the day at the Caldwells', a time to talk, discuss, or just laugh. They usually dined at seven o'clock, just as the chimes struck on the hall clock, and even though the food might be heated leftovers, the serving dishes sat on old silver trivets. There was a decorative crystal bowl in the center of the table, filled, according to season, with wildflowers or pine cones. Most nights a pair of candles lit the table. Tonight the candles were unlit and a warm fall breeze blew through the opened windows, a wind scented with dry leaves and the faint, ammonia odor of steer manure the yardman had dug in around the asparagus beds. Yet Retta felt a rare and worrisome tension in the beamed dining room, a silence that was deliberate rather than accidental, and she looked sharply at her father and then her mother.

Connie Caldwell was as slim as her daughter, but with dark hair tied back in a ponytail with a string of green yarn. She wore jeans and a green sweater with a pink shirt showing at the neck and cuffs.

"You're very preppy tonight, Mother," Retta said. "You look ready to enroll at Radcliffe."

"Your mother was pretty *and preppy* before that

10

word was born," Carter Caldwell said.

Her mother's answer was unexpectedly short and sharp. "Sweet of you, dear," she said. "But not true. Sometimes looking preppy just means forgetting to put on lipstick, or having to always wear the same old clothes."

"What I meant . . ." Henrietta began, but her mother smiled and passed a plate of beef and mushroom casserole. "Hand this on down to your father. And don't worry about my mood. This hasn't been the best possible day."

The phone in the hallway rang, two short rings to show it was for the Caldwell household, the first party on a three-party line. Henrietta, putting down her fork and turning to her brother, said, "Will you answer that, Two? It has to be Charlie. No one else would be stupid enough to call me during dinnertime."

As her younger brother hurried toward the hallway, Retta said to her father, "That certainly can't count as one of my two calls for tonight. You know how crazy and irresponsible Charlotte can be. . . ."

"It won't count," her father said laconically.

When Henrietta turned sixteen and her brother was nearly eleven, the Caldwell house had become a sudden maelstrom, with the telephone ringing a dozen times a day. So one evening, a few months earlier, the family had a one-sided conference. Carter Caldwell, Senior (Carter Caldwell, Junior, was always called Two) made an announcement at dinner: "From now on, each of you children can receive two incoming calls a day, and you can make four outgoing calls if you like, except, of course, long distance. On charge calls, check with your mother and me. We're not going to have our lives disrupted with all the nonsensical calls you get," he said with finality.

She had laughed aloud, Retta remembered. Her father's face had been so stern, so determined, just like those old pictures in the upstairs hallway when he was a solemn little boy taking horseback riding lessons.

"No need for you to get so fierce about it," she had told him. "Two and I won't have any trouble. We'll just tell everyone our father is a first-class eccentric."

Caldwell had smiled. "We're going to be a much happier family all around if you have more trouble handling *me* than your mother and I have handling you."

Her brother came back to the table. "You were right, Retta. That *was* Charlie. She says you know what she wants to talk about. . . ."

Retta went to the kitchen for the dessert tray: four plates of plain sliced cake ready for a spoonful of wineberries and a pitcher of cream. It was not a family favorite; not that the dessert didn't taste good, but it was economy food and they had it often. Wineberries grew wild along the country lanes in the summertime, brambled bushes weighted down with wine-red fruit. Country folk around Zenith didn't respect the berry much because it was runny when cooked and wouldn't set at all for jellies and jams. But the Caldwell children picked basketfuls every

12

July and August to stock the freezer.

Once, a few years ago, the family-owned news-paper was making higher profits. The Caldwells still had daily household help, and young Two — not even old enough to go to school — had said to Aunt Blue, a respected old black lady who came in to do the cleaning and cooking, that he didn't like wine-berries, they were nothing but second-class rasp-berries, or blackberries without guts. Aunt Blue had gone into a rage and ordered Two to leave her kitchen "which is as much God's temple as any church on earth." But when she heard him crying out on the back doorstep, she went out to hug him and rock him on her knee, saying, "I just get frightened some-times when I hear young people too proud to thank the Good Lord for what He puts on earth every summer."

Her mother's mother had died long before Retta was born, yet it always seemed to her she still had two grandmothers. Grandmama Caldwell was a very real person, a tiny, fine-voiced woman with blue-gray hair, who came to her son's family on twice-yearly visits and whose letters from Florida, thin and spidery scrawls on pale beige notepaper, never failed to enclose two crisp five-dollar bills, one for Retta and one for her brother. Once Henrietta had asked her father why Grandmama Caldwell's money felt so silky, seemed so different, and he had told her with a laugh, "You'll find this hard to believe, but your grandmother washes out those five-dollar bills in her bathroom hand basin and irons them flat before mailing them. And she even sprinkles on a little of her lilac cologne. She told me herself. Even if she can't see them as often as she'd like, she wants everything to be perfect for her grandchildren, the sweet old dear."

It was Aunt Blue who seemed to be the other grandmother. It was she who let the young Caldwells press raisin faces into the cookie dough before she baked it; carved the scariest faces on November pumpkins; and walked Retta and Two through the old herb garden again and again till they both could tell the difference between basil and tarragon, parsley and cilantro, and lemon mint from the finger sprigs of garden mint that went into iced tea. She had taught them to be kind to all three cats and give each one an equal hug at bedtime. She showed them how to count to ten and then start laughing, instead of getting hurt feelings and running sulking to their rooms. She often turned the Bible station on the kitchen radio down to a background murmur and told the children little singsong stories about herself, her own childhood, and her life down in the deep South. "Start out wise," she told them repeatedly. "Learn to take a little bad with the good. I did that, and pretty soon I got good most of the time."

Retta had been aware, even as a young girl, that she loved both old ladies, though for different reasons, but when she thought of grandmothers, it was almost always Aunt Blue who came to life first in her thoughts.

Now the wineberries seemed a symbol. *A little bad with the good,* Retta thought as she spooned the soft, half-frozen berries onto the cake, the juice thin and staining. It seemed to her the Carter Caldwells were having wineberries more and more lately. Almost every night, in fact.

As she backed her way through the swinging doors to the dining room, holding the tray, she heard her father say, "Well, Connie, if Hugo Provanza wants to drop his weekly ad, I appreciate that he came in to tell me about it in person."

His wife's voice was distressed. "But the Provanzas have run that full-page ad in the *Zenith Press* every week since I was a little girl. Did he say why he — "

"Our paper just isn't reaching the right people anymore, Connie. Hugo says he gets a better response on his ad if he just makes it a throwaway to stick in mailboxes. Not everyone subscribes to the *Press* these days, you know."

Caldwell shook his head at his daughter. "Pass me by, Retta. Maybe Two wants an extra dessert. Or I'll have mine later with the eleven o'clock news."

"That's partly the trouble, isn't it?" Two said. "Small-town papers don't matter much anymore, do they? All the big stuff is on TV, anyway."

"Not quite *all* the big stuff, Two. And the shopping malls in Wilmington and Philadelphia are booming." He was answering his son, but seemed to be addressing himself more directly to his wife. "Hugo Provanza told me a bit of news today that I could never get from any TV commentator. He's decided he needs a lawyer from Philadelphia to help him out on this highway thing, someone really smart. We're not the only ones who could be hurt. If that bypass goes through, it could cut the Provanza property in two, with their house on one side of the road and the store on the other. He said it would be better for him if the six-lane highway could go through his buildings, not between them. Then they'd have to pay him for the loss of the house *and* his business, not just some pittance for the land they take. Either way, it's a bad deal for him."

The rest of the evening was serene, almost as peaceful and silent as the dark woods beyond the living room windows. Two made a couple of phone calls and got two back, but they lasted only a few seconds each with conversations that seemed to be no more than, "Hi ya," then a couple of chuckles, and an, "Okay, see you tomorrow."

Retta curled in a corner chair, leafing through a Spanish edition of *Jane Eyre.* It was her favorite book, and the familiar English words seemed to shine out through the Spanish, almost whispering the magic story as she turned the pages. She had decided not to call Charlie back.

Her parents sat in wicker-basket chairs at a round table, playing chess. When the late news came on TV, they stopped playing, their hands still on the chessboard, fingers touching lightly.

Later that night, so late that she wasn't sure what time it was, Retta heard the phone ring in the upstairs hallway outside her bedroom, then the scurry of feet as Two leaped out of bed to answer it.

There was a mumble of voices and Two called out, "Don't worry, Dad. A man asked who it was and when I told him my name, he hung up. Must have been a wrong number."

Her father's voice was low but clear as he called out from behind his closed bedroom door. "All right, Two. Let's say it *was* a wrong number. But if the phone rings again — this time of night — let me answer it."

Retta's senses sharpened as she heard the warning tone in her father's voice. She noticed a fine line of light limned along the narrow windowsill of her bedroom, just under the hem of the red draperies. It could be moonlight, or it could be the first early rays of dawn coming over the horizon. Before Retta could decide, she was asleep again, and as far as she knew, the phone did not ring again.

Chapter
2

All over the United States, towns like Cleveland, Amarillo, and Gary, Indiana, kept getting bigger and bigger with more people and more houses, even though Zenith, Pennsylvania, which was older than any of them, kept getting smaller and smaller. Once, about a hundred and fifty years ago, the same era the Caldwell family founded their newspaper, the *Zenith Press,* the town had its own hotel. Zenith was a railroad passenger stop for travelers en route from Washington and Baltimore to Philadelphia. The Zenith Arms had been a small, perfect hotel with a wide veranda with rocking chairs and gentlemen from the South in white gloves to serve tea or mint juleps while the ladies of the party freshened up.

Without a dining car on the train, passengers always dined on chicken and biscuits at the Zenith Arms before huffing and chugging the last thirty-five miles into Philadelphia.

About ten thousand people lived in and around Zenith then, the in-town merchants in their big clapboard houses along the main streets; the Quakers out on prosperous farms, the fields as precise and neat as homemade quilts. The "gentlemen farms" were for the really rich, with long, green barns, split-rail fences, and hunting mares brought in from Kentucky and Ireland.

Some of old Zenith was still there. The railroad depot had been torn down years ago, and the old hotel was now a retirement home for Sisters of the Order of Mercy. But there was still a post office and a volunteer fire department, the only two buildings that always flew an American flag, regardless of regulations, in both sunshine and rain. Many of the grand old merchants' houses had been divided into apartments, and the only movie house had closed down just as soon as a drive-in opened in Wilmington. But the main street was three blocks long with a drugstore, an appliance emporium, four men's apparel shops, and a few stores to sell almost anything one might need, if you didn't mind limited stock.

About a half dozen shops already had gone out of business, plate-glass windows facing the street boarded over. The gray stone building that housed the *Zenith Press* was as graceful and staunch as ever, but there were failed businesses on either side of it. The main street of Zenith had become a major thoroughfare, bumper-to-bumper on Saturday mostly with shoppers headed for the malls of Wilmington, or even Philadelphia.

"I get so angry sometimes, I could just cry," Retta had said to her mother only last year. "I looked up Zenith in the atlas and it's a little nothing, just a name so small an ant couldn't read it. It's like marrying a dwarf or having a darling baby brother with two heads. Don't those stupid atlas people know we love this town? It's not a fly-speck dot on the map to us."

"Just don't bring the subject up at the dinner table," her mother had said. "Nor the fact that Ye Olde Butterchurn is moving into the Wilmington Mall. Your father knows all about those things. Ads at the newspaper are down about fifty-five percent this year. Even all the local sports coverage, my editorials, and that crazy social stuff Charlotte's mother writes — well, it gets us some new readers and a few phone calls, but the advertising revenues just aren't there like the old days."

"But Poppy always wanted us to be open about what we thought," Retta protested. "Why can't I tell him how I feel about Zenith?"

"Just give him a chance to rearrange his priorities," her mother said. "Caldwells aren't good at being failures. Your father is awfully hard on himself these days. . . ."

Charlotte Amberson (nicknamed "Charlie" because her mother's name was also Charlotte) had been Retta Caldwell's best friend since fourth grade. Charlie liked to tease and often said Retta had an A-average in school only because she got up so early each morning. And Mrs. Amberson remarked sharply one day that "God just gave the lucky little blue-blood a twenty-six-hour day, while the rest of us peasants do our best on twenty-four."

The simple truth was that Henrietta Caldwell loved to get up at dawn. Even on the darkest winter morning, when the weather was so full of wind and blown snow that the upstairs windows coated over, she enjoyed the challenge of a cold floor and a quiet house. It was always Retta who tiptoed down first to plug in the coffee maker, feed the dogs, and turn up the thermostat. Mornings worked for her and she worked well in the mornings. And she liked the extra time to be Henrietta Caldwell, herself and alone.

In past years, after Aunt Blue had retired and lived in a small house about two miles down Tuckpoint Road, and when the weather was right, Retta used the early hours to bicycle over the graveled roads to check on the old lady. She had a key to let herself in.

Aunt Blue, three times married but with no children, insisted on living alone without a dog, a TV set, or even a telephone. "If anything that ain't in my Bible happens out there in the big world," she said once, "I can trust Henrietta to ride over and tell me."

On that last day, Retta would always remember, the old house seemed unusually still. A clock ticked somewhere and Aunt Blue's harmonica was sitting on the newel post of the staircase, an odd place for it to be. But the silence was a special silence.

Aunt Blue had died sometime in the night and Retta found her in bed, hands folded on the chenille bedspread which was turned down as neatly and precisely as if it had been measured with a ruler.

Aunt Blue had been brought up in a convent in Gethsemane, Kentucky, and she loved to tell about those days, while sipping tea in the Caldwell kitchen and massaging her firm, red gums with a snuff stick.

"Our rooms were set up in the old slave cottages behind the main convent," she had told them, "all fancied up with curtains and rag rugs. In early times, young white ladies who wanted to become nuns could bring slave girls as their dowry for entering the order. They didn't need to bring money or family jewels — just a couple of black girls the family owned.

"Retta, when you study in school, you'll find that history don't go back as far as you think. My own great-grandmother was a slave, one of those girls brought in as dowry, and that's how I got to live the orphanage life. When I got bigger, they hired me out to do day work, but I was born and reared behind that convent.

"It's God's way that babies just keep coming, so by the time black folk weren't slaves anymore, there were so many orphans that the girls had to sleep four to a bed. I was always a neat sleeper. That's how the nuns taught me. I was so well trained that in my whole life I never turned over in bed once."

Retta remembered vividly that Aunt Blue had

seemed perplexed and silent for a moment, and then she added, "I'm not talking about *marrying*-turning over, Retta. I'm talking about *sleeping*-turning over." Then she said severely, "You don't have to ask me no questions. You be a good girl and your mother will tell you everything you need to know when the time comes. . . ."

Her real name was Mrs. Paula Saint-Scales, and Retta knew that was the name her mother would use when she wrote the obituary. Only the Caldwells had called the old lady Aunt Blue. It was a nickname born because Mrs. Saint-Scales had a deep and almost religious conviction that there wasn't enough blue in the world.

"The Good Lord must have been partial to blue," she had explained, "or He wouldn't have used it so much for the sky. When it came to food, He got distracted." So Mrs. Saint-Scales preserved at least a quart of dark blue elderberry juice each summer, and used it to color certain foods throughout the year.

"It's a derbyberry anyway," she had explained to Two, with some heat. "How can folks call it an 'elderberry' if they don't have no 'youngerberry'? Makes no sense. At least where I come from, folks know what to *call* things."

It was never potatoes or fish or cauliflower that turned up blue at the Caldwell dinner table, but it might be a pie crust, a pear compote, or a tray of hot blue muffins on the sideboard on a Sunday.

Now Henrietta touched the old lady's folded hands and found them soft but chill. There was peace here, no anger, no protest, no struggling against the end. Pride had stayed with the old woman until the last.

Henrietta felt an instinctive thing she must do. Aunt Blue would want to be free now, really free — girlhood, pig-tailed, Kentucky-blue grass-free.

She opened all the windows in the bedroom so the spring breezes could blow in and out across the bed, ruffling what they wanted, bringing odors of dew and saplings and green things growing. Dawn was just beginning to touch color to the horizon, a glowing pink, pale still but clear. It would be a day of cloudless skies.

It was weeks later, long after the burial in Holly Hill Cemetery, that Retta discovered Aunt Blue's house key. In the strange excitement of that morning, she had zipped the key into the inner compartment of her school purse. And, for reasons she did not quite know, she decided to keep it there.

The compact yellow Volkswagen, with 62,000 miles on the odometer but a new set of tires, had been a semi-surprise on Retta's sixteenth birthday. She had already taken drivers' education at school and for years she'd been allowed to drive the family car over the meadow to the pond for winter skating. Connie Caldwell had lived in Zenith as a girl, not far from a skating rink, and the younger Caldwells had been taught to skate when they were just children. It was usually Retta who drove the station wagon down to the pond on an icy morning with fried-egg sandwiches and a thermos of coffee.

She had passed her driver's test in Coatesville on her first try.

Charlie Amberson had given her a Swift 'N Sweet floral kit for the car as a birthday present, a can of lilac-jasmine spray that made the interior smell like a deodorized women's rest room at Penn Station. Retta stored the can in the glove compartment.

Two had bought her a tiny, female religious figure, garbed in blue, and hung it in the back window of the Volkswagen, insisting it was a replica of the patron saint of bullfighters, the Virgin of Macerena.

"Who knows, *bonita*," he said. "The beautiful Señorita Caldwell might just be lucky enough to pick up some hitchhiking *torero*."

"You've got the wrong *señorita*," Retta said with a laugh. "I don't know how Poppy feels about bull-fighters, but I *do* know how he feels about hitch-hikers. He gave me a big no on that even before he turned over the keys."

It was six months after she got the yellow car and her license, and just the day after she'd seen Dallas Dobson for the first time, that she saw him for the second time. Or thought she did.

With her driver's license had come her first job. Five mornings a week, before school, she drove over to the Armstrong house to pick up the society column, "Chatter by Char," that Charlie's mother wrote for the Caldwell paper. The column, full of local chitchat, horse meets, church suppers, engagements, and weddings, was currently the most popular feature in the paper. Carter Caldwell had hired Charlotte Amberson right after she had left her third husband for the last time. Mrs. Amberson needed the work and turned out to be good at it, gathering most of the news by phone, then delivering the copy herself.

But in the last few months, she had not felt able to drive into Zenith. It wasn't because of the late hours she kept, or even the frequent sips of fine Madeira she poured from the decanter, Mrs. Amberson insisted.

"The belle of the county has lost some zip," she had told Carter Caldwell. "I've developed a phobia. Not *agoraphobia*, mind you, nothing radical like that. I have a *controlled* phobia. It's all enemy territory out there until after three in the afternoon."

So Retta did the daily pickup and delivery every morning between seven and the first eight o'clock class at Havendale High.

This morning, too early for Mrs. Amberson, she was meandering along the country roads to pass time. Retta drove slowly, almost daydreaming, listening to the rhythmic sing of the tires on the gravel, yet keeping her eyes alert to the mists ahead. Typical of Pennsylvania in autumn, an early mist rose from the roadside grass and bushes, a miasmic fog that moved upward and began to evaporate into the growing warmth of the morning, almost as if it left the ground.

She was on a narrow back lane with barely room for two cars to pass. On either side of the road were ditches still thick with the grass of summer and

26

patches of broad-leafed sumac, the dusty leaves barely touched with the rusts of fall.

These roads were familiar to Retta and she didn't need a map to know where she had been or what lay ahead. She knew she was not far from the old Kennelly farm, neglected and in financial trouble for years, ever since the Kennelly sons had been killed in Vietnam and their father had been thrown from a horse and broken his hip and then his heart, or maybe it was in reverse order. Mr. Kennelly had not been able to keep up his barns and horse operations properly, though once he had been famous for his class Arabians. His only stock now was a half dozen old horses of that breed which he kept and fed for sentimental reasons.

At this point, just before the Kennelly farm, the road made two deep curves, almost half of a figure eight. One could see the first curve and then, some distance ahead, the second curve, but there was an obscuring stand of roadside birches halfway in between.

It was there, at those two curves, that she thought she saw him, misted over by the light fog. He seemed to be walking on the edge of the road, ahead and away from her. If it wasn't Dallas Dobson, at least it was someone tall, in boots and a light-colored windbreaker, and there was a long, urgent lope to his stride.

She glanced at the speedometer and then slowed to a crawl, ready to honk the horn and wave, but when she looked up again, the roadside was empty.

Retta rolled down the window and continued to

drive slowly. She was puzzled, even a little upset. She had only wanted to wave. . . . Carefully, she scanned the heavy weeds in the ditches, the dewy grass along the roadside. But there was no one in sight. And no mark that she could see of muddy footprints or bruised and broken bushes where someone might have slipped off the road and hidden in the woods.

Chapter
3

Charlie Amberson, Junior, never came downstairs when her friend stopped by to pick up the newspaper column. She liked to sleep late. The Ambersons lived in a rented two-story country cottage, old and quaint. It was a red-brick structure, wreathed and vined over with decades of Virginia creeper. The creeper was green most of the year, with masses of red leaves coming in late autumn. Then, in the cold winter months, it was just a mass of bare and gnarled old vines with a few household windows peeking through. "It's like living in a damned bird's nest," young Charlotte often complained. "If I ever *do* get pregnant, I'm likely to give birth to a nestful of eggs."

The front door was unlocked as always and, as Retta pushed it open, Mrs. Amberson called out, "Just chase a cat off a chair somewhere and pour yourself some tea. I'm putting the jazz into the Kerns-Hancock wedding. Then you can dash into town and stop the presses."

Retta loved the Amberson house on these early mornings, the rooms as full of clutter and emotional turmoil as the rooms of her own house were filled with peace and caring. Retta knew that Mrs. Amberson often slept on the couch, usually in the same clothes she'd been wearing the previous evening, tossing and restless, switching at daybreak from Madeira to pots of steaming tea. She smoked brown cigarettes, holding the long, narrow cylinder in her teeth as she typed, giving her face a constant look of scorn, almost like a cynical smile.

"I'm gonna give you *heart*, Boss Caldwell," she had told Carter Caldwell when she first asked for the job. "You're from such an old, elegant family, the real elite, inherited money — what's left of it — the biggest house in the county. I don't think you know what *goes on* with everyday people out in sacred readerland. I'm going to find out and put it all down."

The column was bright, witty, and very personal. If church supper refreshments included German potato salad from a favorite grandmother's recipe, that information got into the story. If a bride sewed all six dresses for her bridesmaids, that was news. And the day Charlotte Amberson persuaded the cooks at the annual ox roast for the Po-Mar-Lin Volunteer Fire Company to give her their secret recipe for barbecue sauce, the *Zenith Press* had to print an extra edition to keep up with reader demand.

"I got a hot one today, Retta," Mrs. Amberson said that morning as she typed. "The wedding I'm writing about now — the bride met the groom on the construction site over at the new mushroom farm."

"I don't see anything very romantic about that," Retta said.

"Don't worry, I put all the romance up front." Charlotte Amberson began to read out her copy in a singsong voice. "The bride wore a satin gown made by her great-aunt Jolie Nabors, and her veil was attached to a white orchid headpiece that matched her orchid bouquet. The members of the wedding party wore silver tuxedos, with a single pink rose as boutonnieres for the best man and ushers, and a miniature white orchid for the groom."

Retta sipped her tea and smiled. "You're just making that up as you go along, aren't you?"

"Like heck I am, honey. This is *journalism*, right down to the last rum raisin in the groom's cake. And you know what the kicker is, what makes your old Aunt Char so downright readable?"

"No," Retta said.

"I found out how the lovely bride and her macho bridegroom happened to meet on that construction site. I got it typed in right between the satin ribbons on the pews and the three-tiered wedding cake. It just so happens that she's a professional plasterer, and the groom had been hired on as an assistant lather. She was the boss! Now that's modern, that's *today*."

Mrs. Amberson sighed, snuffed out her cigarette, folded her typed sheets neatly, and slipped them into an envelope. She handed it to Retta. "There you are, cupcake. I wish it were coverage of the United Nations, but at least I'm working up to my talents. And I do get better readership than your mother with her do-gooder editorials."

Retta had heard this strain of teasing jealousy before, so she said simply, "Well, Mother's been doing those editorials for only about three years, since Two and I grew up, and I think she's very good at it."

Mrs. Amberson sighed. "Of course she is. She's a fine writer and I'm just mad that I can't write that way. But she'll never stop that bypass highway from going right through this part of the countryside. And I don't have to read my tarot cards to know that."

"Nothing's definite," Retta said. "The *Zenith Press* just wants its readers to know the law, and to be informed of their options."

"Spoken like a real Caldwell," Mrs. Amberson said. "Boring, but true." And then she stopped. "Pretend I didn't say that, Retta. I'd be a lost soul if your father hadn't hired me, and if you didn't drive my copy into town each day."

"I love to do it," Henrietta said. "It's a kind of training for me and it helps earn my allowance."

Mrs. Amberson lit another cigarette and ran a nervous hand through her hair. "You know I can drive perfectly well, and have for years, but I can't face the big world out there until three o'clock. I can't calm down. I tried to talk the whole thing out with a psychiatrist in West Chester. He wanted to tie it in with religious guilt. I used to be a church-goer, you know. This well-meaning shrink asked me if I thought my 'three o'clock problem' had anything to do with the fact that Christ was crucified two thousand years ago at exactly three o'clock." She laughed without humor. "I told him I didn't operate on Jerusalem time, and he told me to find another doctor. He didn't treat jokers."

Retta was aware that Mrs. Amberson was tense, anxious, stalling for time, trying as always to prolong these moments of conversation that kept her in touch with youth and the outside world, two things she had begun to fear. "Mrs. Amberson," Retta said gently, "we're both on deadline. If I don't get this material into Zenith right away, I'll be late for my eight o'clock class."

"Okay, okay," the older woman said, walking toward the front door. "But by the way, I'd like to know how you think my little Charlotte is getting along these days. I see more of you than I do of her, you know. She's always taking those long walks of hers and hiding up in her room the rest of the time. How's she doing in school? She hardly ever tells me anything. But I can trust you, can't I, Retta? You'd tell me, wouldn't you, if she were into drugs or anything, or if she and some boy were messing around? You'll be honest with me about Charlie, won't you?" She put a rough, restraining hand on

Retta's arm. "If you weren't, I think I'd kick your aristocratic little butt right out the front door of Tara here. . . ."

Henrietta felt a knot of sudden and intense anger in her chest, and her cheeks were hot. "Mrs. Amberson," she said, trying to keep the tears out of her voice, "I simply do not understand you or people like you. You are speaking of someone I love and respect, my very best friend. How can you do this?"

Mrs. Amberson was instantly contrite, her eyes moist and shining. "Oh, Henrietta, where's your compassion? You've got to let a neurotic old shut-in talk like this once in a while. Young Charlotte is all I've got and — "

"And that's an even worse thing to say," Retta cut in. "You can't claim you've 'got' Charlotte, like she's something you *own*. Parents can love children and enjoy them, but they don't *own* them like they're little birds in a cage with a lock. And how about you, Mrs. Amberson? Don't you 'own' yourself? You're supposed to make *yourself* count in life. . . ."

Though most of the morning fog had burned away, Retta warned herself to drive with extra care. Twice in one morning, her emotions had veered off center.

It was almost twenty minutes to eight when she reached the newspaper offices, still shuttered and locked for the night, and slipped the Amberson copy through a slot in the front door. Soon the whole county would know about the silver tuxedos and the rum raisins in the groom's cake, and everything else, she thought grimly.

34

The final eight o'clock bell rang just as Henrietta opened the door of the math classroom. With a quick nod of apology to Mr. Engel, she hurried to her desk. Her thoughts were still far outside the classroom. *What's happening to me?* she thought. *When did life stop being easy to handle? When did so many things cease to be simple and dependable?*

Her pencil dropped from the spine of her notebook and rolled into the aisle, just behind her. As she bent to pick it up, she realized Dallas Dobson was already in his seat. She turned and glanced at him quickly. His face was intent and impersonal, eyes looking straight ahead. But there was no fog in this classroom. She had not imagined it. He *was* wearing a windbreaker, light-colored, not white exactly, but a faded beige.

Both Caldwell students brought parental notes to school the next day, asking to be excused from afternoon classes. Henrietta ate an apple as she drove home and, when she got there, her parents and brother were waiting in the station wagon at the end of the lane. She parked her car at the gate and joined them.

The town meeting was scheduled for one o'clock in a second-floor conference room at the Zenith bank. It was an all-beige room, with beige rugs, beige draperies, and three rows of folding chairs, cushioned in beige. There was a large map propped on an easel stand, a speakers' table with five chairs, and a hand microphone. Behind that a wall of blown-up photographs were pinned side by side across the span of the room.

"It's a pro and con meeting," Mrs. Caldwell had explained on the drive to town, "a place for concerned citizens to speak out. If either of you has anything to say — say it. Otherwise, just sit up tall and look damned mad about the whole thing."

There were about twenty people in the folding chairs, and two men behind the table with the microphone. Since their faces were unfamiliar, Henrietta guessed they would speak for the Zenith bypass and the highway planners in Harrisburg. In the second row of chairs, Retta recognized two librarians, a clerk from the state liquor store, the Zale brothers from the appliance shop, and Mr. Berk who owned Towne Fashions.

Hugo Provanza sat in the front row. Retta recognized him, not from his burly shoulders or bald head, but because he was wearing a Havendale High football jacket with Junior Provanza's number on it. Mr. Provanza had left school in the seventh grade but was a regular rooter at all Havendale sporting events.

Just outside the beige-draped windows, the mounted bank clock ticked loudly, a reverberation like a sharp hiccup running through the tension of the meeting room. At a quarter past one, Carter Caldwell said to the men at the speakers' table, "Gentlemen, I think everyone who plans to attend is now here."

It was a Mr. Burt Myerson who stood up, introduced himself, and said he spoke on behalf of Harrisburg. With a yardstick, he traced the route of the proposed highway on the easeled map, explaining in some detail the current traffic statistics and then the increased number of vehicles that would be attracted by the new bypass.

"What we propose to do," he said, "is to facilitate the passage of traffic on this new interstate highway and lift the burden of transport that is now streaming through and jamming up your town, the town of Zenith."

The older Zale brother raised his hand, like a child in school, and said loudly, "You seem to forget that *some* of the traffic is driving into Zenith to shop there. We *need* those customers."

"I think you will get *more* customers," Mr. Myerson said smoothly, "if your town becomes more *attractive* to shoppers, if we can *lighten* the traffic load now on your narrow main thoroughfare and the side streets."

One of the librarians rose to her feet and addressed both Mr. Myerson and the room in general. "You're not listening to your own words, sir," she said firmly. "And unless we're speaking different languages, your proposed plan will induce customers *to forget* about Zenith and drive to shopping malls in bigger towns. Isn't that what the term 'bypass' means? That the town of Zenith and its inhabitants and merchants will be *passed by*?"

A flutter of applause swept the room. Mrs. Caldwell was taking notes while Carter Caldwell was frowning at the eight-foot panorama of photographs on the wall. Retta and Two were clapping with the others.

For the next forty minutes, there were discussions back and forth between the townspeople and the men from Harrisburg. For every citizen argument against the new highway, Mr. Myerson had an answer, a list of statistics, or a demonstration graph to show economic growth in other towns involved in bypass situations. To Retta, the man seemed falsely cheerful, almost as if he were humoring little children.

At exactly two o'clock, Burt Myerson pushed aside his chair again and walked to the enlarged pictures. "Here," he said, "we have a photographic blowup of the entire farm and residential area outside Zenith that will be affected by construction. If you will compare the route on the map with the photographs, you will see that we have laid out the new highway to spare as many homes, businesses, and farm buildings as possible." He waved his hand to indicate on the photographs where the bypass might go. "I think our planners did very well indeed."

"Your plan says you're not going to *knock down* any of my buildings," Hugo Provanza interrupted, "but you cut me in half. I'll end up with my general store on one side of a six-lane highway and my house on the other."

Carter Caldwell got to his feet without a word and stepped close to the panoramic photographs, tracing carefully over the black and white surface with the index finger of his right hand. Retta noticed that his other hand was behind him, clenched so tightly that the knuckles flinched white.

When he spoke, his voice was deliberately calm and unemotional. "Mr. Myerson," he said, "your planners did so well that they have eliminated our house and outbuildings entirely. Our structures do not show on these photographs, nor are they sketched on your map."

"Oh?" Mr. Myerson said. "The map was drawn *from* the photographs. Just where is your place?"

"Your proposed highway passes south of us, through both fields and meadowlands, and our home is right here." Caldwell put his hand, fingers outspread, directly over a large, dark clump of trees in the photographic blowup.

"I see. That's an oversight, but a correctable one," the man said smoothly. "I'll have an engineer stop by your place to get an idea of mass and measurements. Then we can put you on the map. You see, our team took these aerial photographs at a considerable height and with a telescopic lens. They didn't penetrate your heavy cover of trees."

Retta listened to the man's easy words and felt emotion rush through her till her lips were stiff and numb, as if sucked dry by a sudden fear. They had been secretly spied on, a plane right over their own house, but high, so high that they could neither see nor hear it. When had that tiny silver cross droned through the sky, taking these terrible pictures? What had they all been doing then, so unaware that overhead a powerful camera was determining the fate of their beloved Springhill?

"We might be doing you a favor," Mr. Myerson said, "by thinning out your timber when we build the bypass through your property. You seem to have an oversupply of shade around your house."

"You wouldn't *dare* do that," Two Caldwell said, his voice shocked. "Some of those trees are William Penn oaks, planted more than two hundred years ago. My father's family has always lived there. We love those trees. . . ." Casually, Mrs. Caldwell lifted an arm and put it around the back of her son's chair.

" 'Dare' isn't a word we need in our vocabulary at the highway department," Mr. Myerson said. "Not when we have the law on our side, the statute of 'Right of Eminent Domain.' That law gives the commonwealth the right to decide what's best for the majority of the people." He paused. "Each landowner affected by our plans has a right to hire a lawyer to examine his case. Or he can put his pros and cons on paper for my department. We are still in the discussion stage, hence this meeting. We are still open to suggestions."

"But you just said '*when* we build the bypass through your property,' " Two protested.

"A manner of speaking, sonny," Myerson said, gathering together his sheaf of papers. "Just a manner of speaking. We're still flexible. And the state will compensate all owners for land confiscated at the going rate for real estate, the price to be decided on. We'll try to be fair," he said, looking impassively at the group and then more pointedly at Two. "But remember, we can't pay you for your memories. Or your dreams."

40

Chapter
4

Henrietta Caldwell had always believed a touch of melancholy could add to the pleasure of life, that a temporary background of gray moods could hype the lighter tones, bring out the brightness in everyday things. Yet she could not understand the strange new sadness underlying her thoughts for most of the week, since the morning after her harsh words with Mrs. Amberson. It could have been that incident, she knew. Or it might stem from something else.

But the next day, and the next and the next, there had been no blue cigarette smoke, no offers of sweet tea while Charlotte's mother typed out the last paragraphs of her newspaper copy. No, each morning now, a completed column was left on the front porch, held down against stray winds by a potted aster plant tinted with the purple and red colors of autumn.

Behind the front door, Mrs. Amberson must be sulking, or perhaps she felt sad, too, Retta thought. *Or maybe she's waiting to see if I would be foolish enough to tell Charlotte what she said.*

Now the columns were dropped off at the *Zenith Press* each morning a full half hour ahead of schedule. That gave Retta extra time to follow a different route to school each day as she wished. But for the past few mornings she had, without wondering why, chosen the two-lane country road that curved past the Kennelly property and the big, sagging horse barn.

Fall that year was touched with Indian summer. On each side of the road tall clumps of goldenrod grew four feet tall, the flowering clusters heavy with pollen and dust from the road. Retta was acutely aware of the beauty of these autumn mornings, the isolation of the back roads, the movement and color of the flowers, the tiny rhythmic sting of sound as bits of gravel spun up from the roadway and hit the side of the car. It seemed to her that her senses, her appreciation, her longings had reached a peak of intensity that she had rarely been aware of before.

This morning she drove more slowly than usual, then pulled to the side of the road and brought the car to a stop to watch a giant Monarch butterfly, its wings a mesh of black and orange. It drifted across the road and settled on a wand of goldenrod, the color of its frail wings almost blending into the dusty yellow flower. Retta watched, almost without thought, caught up in the delicate magic of the moment.

Suddenly, with no warning, someone stepped out from a clump of sumac bush and slammed a hand on the hood of the car. The voice was cold, touched with deep anger, as Dallas Dobson said, "All right, Miss Caldwell. I have had just about enough of this. Tell me why you have been following me."

For a moment, she was stunned into silence, then opened the car door and stepped out. She wanted to be standing herself when she talked to this tall, hostile stranger. Though she had seen him every day in school for nearly two weeks, this was the first time they had spoken.

"Following you? *Me* following *you*, Dallas Dobson? This is my road, too, you know. I *live* near here. This is the way I drive to school."

"You don't always come this way," he said. "Monday was the first day I saw you. I ditched you that time."

"Then you *were* walking along the road that morning. There was that fog — " Retta stopped sharply, then said, "And why are *you* keeping track of *me*, may I ask? Why did you duck out of sight when I came around the curve that morning?"

The tall boy took his hand off the hood and jammed it deep in his jeans pocket. "I didn't want you to see me. I don't want people feeling sorry for me," he said.

"Do you *live* here? What are you talking about?"

Dobson shrugged. "I'm not from this neighborhood. Old Mr. Kennelly and his wife live here. Alone.

I hired on to groom and service the six horses. They're old but they're good Arabian stock. I feed them, exercise them a little, and muck out the stables every morning early, seven days a week. The job pays, and on weekends I can ride them if I want to."

"But why are you angry with me? Didn't you want me to see you walking? Are you ashamed just because you don't have a car? Lots of people — "

"We have a car," he said. "A pickup. But I have to leave it for my dad. He's a cripple now, you know."

"How would I ever know that?" she said.

He shrugged again and kicked at the graveled road with his Texas boot. "It's such a big thing in our lives, I just presumed everybody 'round here had heard about the accident.

"Here's how it is," he said, looking straight at her for the first time. "I've been hitching a ride over here mornings, with a milk truck. Then I walk over to the main road to get a hitch to school. I thought you were trying to track me. Something to tell your friends about. I thought you wanted to be sorry for me."

The butterfly lifted itself from the goldenrod and the stalk bounced up gently, sending a dust of pollen onto the ground. They watched as it drifted to the other side of the road and then out of sight.

"As a little kid in Texas, I used to want to catch those things," Dobson said, "but my brother explained that if you touch a butterfly's wings, well, they're so delicate, it can never fly again."

Henrietta looked at her watch. "Your brother's

right, I guess. But we've got other problems. We'll be late for class. Don't argue with me. Just get in. I'm giving you a lift."

Retta took off down the road with a little squeal of gravel. Dobson sat in the passenger seat, his knees touching the dashboard, his head just inches from the sunroof. The girl glanced at him and noticed his hands: big, brown, folded quietly on one knee. He caught her glance, then turned casually to crank down his window.

"That will make it better," he said.

"What do you mean?" she said.

"Fresh air. I've got special permission to shower in the men's locker room. If I'm late, I just skip the first class."

"That isn't what I was thinking at all," she said vehemently. "Lots of people at Havendale smell of horses. It's a good smell. Take the Drexel brothers, for instance. They ride to school every morning if the weather's good. They like to smell like horses. . . ."

Dallas laughed softly. "Gentleman's manure. There's a big difference. They ride it; I shovel it."

He asked to be let off near the rear door to the gym, and when she stopped the car, Retta said, "Look, I can give you a lift any day. If you're at the Kennelly gate, you ride."

He was thoughtful a moment, then said, "Miss Caldwell, I don't want to get you in trouble with your parents. Maybe they wouldn't like you doing favors for Dallas Dobson."

"It's just hitchhikers they worry about," Retta said

quickly. "You're a fellow student, after all. And my parents aren't like that, anyway. You'll see when you meet them sometime."

"Meet them? Thanks, but I don't think I ever will," he said, and set off in a brisk run toward the school building.

"Monday," she called after him. "I mean it, Monday morning. . . ."

But she could not tell whether Dallas Dobson had heard her or not.

That evening, her father called to say he would be held up at the office till seven-thirty. Two ate his dinner on a tray in front of the TV, but Mrs. Caldwell put the salad in the refrigerator and three dinner plates in a low oven. She and Retta waited.

When Carter Caldwell did come home, he and his wife seated themselves at the table while Retta went to the kitchen for salad and warm food.

As she pushed her way through the swinging door, she heard her father say, "We just don't know yet. All the figures aren't in. So far, we're no worse off than we were last month, but no better off, either. It's just too early to tell."

"Retta, go to the cabinet and bring your father a glass of red wine, will you? He's had a hard day."

Retta poured a glass of Bordeaux into an old stemmed goblet and set it on her father's placemat. Then she poured a second goblet for her mother. She looked at both parents, aware of their thoughtful silence, the worried concern on their faces. At that moment she knew they were not so much caring parents as two separate and adult people, preoccupied with their own problems.

Maybe later, she thought. She had meant to tell the family, at dinner, all about meeting Dallas Dobson. Yet either the matter wasn't important *enough* to bring up or it was *too* important. Retta wasn't sure. But she decided that this was not the right moment to mention her arrangement with the new boy at school.

Chapter
5

The first week was uneventful. For three straight days, Retta picked up Dallas Dobson at the end of the Kennelly lane, then dropped him off at the entrance to the school drive so he could sprint back to the showers. It was an association both constrained and polite: a few words each day, a smile of thanks. Nothing more.

On Friday, she put a Willie Nelson medley in the tape deck and listened as she drove to the Kennellys'. Dobson smiled as he got in the car, then picked up the lyrics to "Sunday Mornin' Comin' Down" in a soft, rich tenor, with a distinct Texas twang. He drummed his long, hard fingers against the dashboard, almost as if he were playing background guitar.

Just before he got out of the car at the school gate, he said lightly, "I know you picked Willie Nelson for me, the good-ole-boy stuff. How about I provide the music next week? I've got an early tape of Duke Ellington doing jazz. It's old but still good. . . ."

"I like Ellington," she said, feeling a flush of embarrassment touch her cheeks. "But I wasn't thinking of good ole boys. Willie Nelson is a favorite of *mine*, too."

"A little of each," he said. "We'll balance out. A little of each."

But on Monday he was not at the Kennellys' gate nor in math class, either. Not till Thursday was he there, and Retta guessed by the agitated way he was pacing the gravel lane that he had forgotten about the Ellington tape.

As he swung into the car, he said abruptly, "My father was kind of sick and I had to take his place at work."

"Sick?" she said. "What does the doctor say?"

"Nothing," Dobson said. "It isn't that kind of sickness."

He took a math book out of his jacket pocket and leafed through the pages to the right place. "I've been on the double," he said, "working the Kennelly chores early so I could get to the feed store on time." His voice sounded tense, impatient. "First I lose two years at school after my father's accident. And now

I lose three days out of a single week. I'm not sure I can catch up."

"You could have called me," she said, "to tell me you wouldn't need a lift. I waited each morning."

"Call you?" he said, and his tone was guarded and impersonal. He flipped a page in the math book to a new lesson. "I didn't think that was necessary, or that it was something you'd want me to do."

They drove on in silence. Dobson held the math book in one hand, his eyes narrowed, his lips moving slightly as he concentrated on the equations. His left hand lay in repose on his knee. Suddenly, she noticed a deep, livid scratch reaching from his thumb, over the back of his hand, and up into the sleeve of his jacket.

She heard her own quick, involuntary intake of breath and reached out to touch his hand. "You're hurt," she said. "How did you get a scratch like that?"

He did not take his eyes off the book as he spoke. "A barn cat," he said simply. "I was forking in hay and got too near her hideaway. She's got kittens in there. She jumped out and gave me a warning."

"It's so deep," she said, her fingers still resting lightly on his hand. "It could get infected. . . ."

"I'll clean it in the shower," he said.

"I don't believe in barn cats, even if they do keep the mice down," she said. "It isn't fair to turn a tame cat into a feral one. Couldn't you give it a little milk once in a while? Couldn't you try that?"

He didn't answer, but when she had pulled into the school drive and stopped, he said, "Thanks.

Thanks for picking me up today." He opened the car door. "And let's not worry about that barn cat, Retta. It's between her and me. Some things just don't want to be tamed, you know."

As he jogged up the driveway, Retta saw Junior Provanza hail him and then walk toward him with his twin sister, Parma, and a female cousin she knew was visiting the Provanzas.

Dobson waited till the trio caught up with him and together they walked toward the rear doors of the school.

Retta felt a stab of emotion so unexpected that she had to grip the steering wheel to bring it under control. Besides taking Mr. Engel's math class together and their almost silent morning rides, she never saw Dallas Dobson, did not know where he lived, or what he did with his spare time. She was experiencing something irrational and unwelcome. It was the emotional discomfort of simple jealousy. She did not know he had made other friends.

Fall weather doesn't turn into winter in Pennsylvania until the rainy winds of November pound the last leaves from the trees and blow ice crusts over the morning dews. This year even the rains were late. Bright fall leaves, a fiery red and gold, stayed until almost Thanksgiving. Then, after three days of gray, misting downpour, the winds cleared the trees so completely that bare branches were like black etchings against the sky.

It was a bittersweet time for the Caldwells. Without the autumn flowers and brightly colored leaves to add a mood of carnival to the countryside, the red flags in the route of the new highway stood out brighter than ever, unfaded by winds or rain.

Sometimes Dallas was waiting at the Kennellys' gate five days in a week. Then for two weeks in a row he might be there only Thursday and Friday. On the rides to school, he rarely spoke, frowning over the pages of the math book, drumming his fingers restlessly on the red leather dashboard.

One day he did bring an Ellington tape. He slid down deep in the car seat, both hands cupped behind his head as he listened with closed eyes, humming along softly with the violins in "Blues in C." "It belonged to my brother," was all he said.

Next morning, Retta slipped the cassette into the tape deck just as she pulled away from the offices of the *Zenith Press.* When she sighted him waiting at the Kennelly gate, she rolled down her window and let the sweet, sophisticated music sound out into the cold morning air.

He smiled at her as he got into the car, a quick, grateful smile, almost shy. "I wasn't sure you liked it," he said. "It tells me something about you, Retta. Something I like a lot."

And those were the only words they exchanged that late fall morning.

Since Charlotte Amberson did not drive, the two friends met at the Amberson house when they needed to study together. It was a natural exchange. Charlotte helped Retta out with a half hour of Spanish conversation (the Ambersons had lived in Puerto

Rico, attached to the state department, before the last divorce) and Retta paid off with an hour of intense tutoring in math. It was usually not more than ten in the evening when she turned her car into her own driveway.

It was Charlotte's idea to have Dallas Dobson join them. Mrs. Amberson had silently apologized to Retta for asking her about Charlie by greeting her one morning with a finished column and a light kiss.

"The cowboy's worse off than I am," Charlie had said. "At least I know I hate all forms of math and I don't plan to go to college anyway, unless Mother makes a big fuss. But he's a high-I.Q. type and he's still going to flunk that class if somebody doesn't help him."

Only that morning she had sat in class, apprehensive and oddly ashamed, trying not to listen as Dallas stumbled wildly when called on for an answer. He finally had to give up. When Mr. Engel called on Retta next, she told him deliberately that she hadn't been able to understand that problem, either. Mr. Engel looked puzzled, then put a red check next to CALDWELL in his grades book.

On the first night the three studied together, Mrs. Amberson put her head into the door of the small study. She was bright-eyed and alert, fruity with the smell of Madeira and brown cigarettes. When Charlotte introduced Dobson, the older woman shook his hand and then whispered, as if to herself, "Gad, what a hunk."

"Don't mind my mother," Charlie said when the door closed. "She gets all her witty lines from late movies on TV." But Retta saw her friend's eyes were bright with tears.

It was a Thursday night in late November when Charlie called during the dinner hour and Retta excused herself to take the call.

"It's a message from Billy the Kid," she said crisply. "He'll be waiting in front of the Provanza market around seven-thirty tonight. He can hitch that far. His daddy took the pickup truck to visit a lady, and Billy needs transportation."

"You don't have to talk to me in code," Retta said sharply.

"I wasn't sure if Dallas Dobson is a welcome name at your house," Charlotte said.

"I don't know why you'd say that," Retta said.

"Hey! This is your best friend you're talking to, Miss Caldwell," Charlotte said. "I notice you never invite him over to your house to study."

It was a quarter to ten and the trio still had three pages to review when Dobson closed his book and said, "I think I've learned all I can for one evening."

"But the test's on Monday and you have to work most of the weekend," Retta said.

"Let *me* worry about that," he said. "At least I know more now than I did a month ago."

But at the Ambersons' gate, Dallas Dobson put his hand on the steering wheel, almost as if he wanted to stop the car. Then he said quietly, "It's still early, Retta. Can't we go somewhere? There are things I want to tell you."

Retta felt her heartbeat quicken, a rapid, erratic rhythm, almost as if she were frightened. "The Dairy Queen Drive-In closes at ten," she said lightly. "And except for bars, there's nothing still open in Zenith."

Suddenly, she was acutely aware of something she had forgotten for months. The key was still in her red handbag, now on the backseat. An almost involuntary memory of Aunt Blue's house flashed through her mind: the silence; the privacy; the front room with the long, red couch with lace doilies on the arms; the birch logs and kindling in the fireplace, ready for a match. No one would ever need to know. . . .

She paused and looked at the young man beside her, his face thoughtful in profile, the only sound in the car the warm, even cadence of his breathing.

She ran the tip of her tongue over her dry, cool lips and then willed herself to say, "I can't think of anywhere to go around here this time of night, Dallas. It's all just small-town."

"There are things I've been thinking about that I wanted to tell you," he said again.

"If you don't mind just sitting in the car, we can always park over on the Kennelly road," she said. "There's never any traffic there this time of night."

He nodded and Retta backed carefully into the Ambersons' gravel drive, then pulled forward and made a sharp right. If Mrs. Amberson was watching from an upstairs window — and Retta had the feeling she was — she would know that they were not driving straight home.

She rolled the window halfway down on her side

of the car, and felt the cool night air touch her face. The Kennelly house, with a single light on the second floor, was just around the bend, and she could hear the whisper of night wind in the trees and the almost silent sounds of birds and animals moving in the darkness. The breeze had the damp, green smell of lichen and mosses, touched with the dusty sweetness of goldenrod. Dallas put his arm around the back of her car seat, not touching her, but close enough so she could smell the scent of saddle soap and feel the faint heat from his hand.

"Maybe you don't even want to hear what I have to say," he began. "If you want me to stop, if you want to start the car and drive on home, just say so. I'll understand. Believe me, I'll understand, Retta. I don't want to come on too strong. I don't want to put you under any obligation to hear me out if that's something you'd rather not do. . . ."

He stopped, staring out thoughtfully through the dark windshield, almost as if he were not sure how to go on.

"Please," she said softly. "Please say what you want to say."

He took a deep breath, closed his eyes tightly for a moment, then opened them. She waited, then turned to face him directly. "Please. I mean it. It must be important, what you're thinking about."

"All right," he said abruptly. "It's just this, Henrietta. I think we are going to be more than friends. So there are things you should know about me, things I want to tell you myself."

Chapter
6

She said nothing, waiting, and when he spoke again his voice was calm and under control, as if he had thought about these words a long time.

"I know you are Henrietta Caldwell, and all that goes with that. One day, right after we got here, my father drove his pickup past your house and told me, 'That's where the Caldwells live.'

"I'm Dallas Dobson, a kid out of Texas. I know who my father is. I live with him. But he never married my mother, or my brother's mother, either. Technically, Dallas Dobson is a bastard."

He touched the back of her hair lightly, fingering the softness of the little half-moon curls.

"My brother's mother was a girl from Zenith. I

never knew her. When she got pregnant right out of high school, my father ran away with her to Texas. He did the thing he liked to do best — bumming around the rodeos, taking care of stock for eating money, and picking up prize cash when he could. My father was one hell of a rider before the accident. As a kid, he was a great ice-skater, too. We didn't see any of that in Texas, but he told me about it. Anyway, that first lady left him after about four years, and he kept the little boy. He was my brother. Sam Houston Dobson was what they called him.

"They lived in trailers, ranch bunkhouses, motel rooms, even the back of pickup trucks. Sometimes Sam Houston got to school, sometimes he didn't. But he was one of the best trick riders in the Southwest. Anyone would tell you that."

He laughed. "Once, when Sam Houston was only eighteen, my father took him and me to Hawaii for the start of the rodeo season."

"I'd never think there were rodeos in Hawaii," Retta said.

"There are. Most of the big-timers skip them, but there's good prize money. Sam Houston won a saddle worth nearly five hundred bucks."

"That must have made your father very proud."

Dallas shrugged. "Maybe, but father had hoped the two of them would win more. We had to sell that saddle to fly back to the mainland."

"And you? What about you, Dallas?" Retta asked softly.

"I'm a different case," he said. "My brother was six years older than me. And my mother, the girl that had me, was just a kid, just turned seventeen, my father told me. She'd lied about her age and got a job with a traveling rodeo as a back up clown. They played San Antonio one summer and my father signed up with them for a while. That's when they got to know each other.

"My father told me my mother wore a big red and white clown suit with a yellow wig and turned-up shoes. She painted red circles on her cheeks, he told me, and drew big black eyelashes on her face so she looked crazy, but all beautiful at the same time. If a rider gets tossed or is hurt, it's the clown's job to run into the ring and shout and swing a big cape to lure the steer or the bronc in another direction. They dress and *act* like clowns, but they are more like animal trainers and they have to be quick and brave. A lot depends on them.

"My mother was the best, my father told me. Once he was thrown by a big pinto, and she ran out and grabbed the bridle so my father didn't get stomped to death." His voice was suddenly warm with affection and pride. "You know, because of her build and that baggy clown suit, people didn't even guess she was pregnant. I was out there with her, right into her seventh month."

"But she and your father never got married?"

"No," he said flatly. "My father didn't want to, I'm sure of that, and my mother — well, she was just a kid, you know. She had her baby in a neighborhood clinic down in Waco and planned to give it away to a rich family with no children, but my father wouldn't let her." He was silent for a long beat and then said, "My father wanted me and he got me. We've been together ever since."

"And your brother Sam Houston?"

This time the silence was so deep, so pronounced, that Retta wondered if he had heard her at all. Then he spoke quietly, almost in a hoarse whisper. "This hurts me to talk about, Retta. It's something I've been having trouble with for nearly three years. Sam Houston is dead. He and my father were coming home by motorcycle one night after a big bash at some buddy's ranch. The cycle went off the road and hit a tree. When the highway cops got there, they were both lying on the ground. Sam Houston was dead and my father had his right leg shattered right from the ankle up through the hip. And he was bruised and unconscious because his head hit that tree. It was three days before he could tell anyone what happened."

"What did happen?"

"Well, I can't blame him for it, really, he had enough troubles. My father told the cops that Sam Houston was driving."

"And you don't believe that?"

"Put it this way, Retta. My brother wasn't a drinker and my father was. He's been a womanizer and party man as long as I can remember. It's just the way he is. But he can't force himself to remember or, at least, admit who hit the gas that night. Lately, when he's really drinking, I can tell he wants to tell me something — but just can't. Sam Houston was his favorite. Maybe he doesn't want me to hear the truth.

"After the accident, I just dropped out of school for two years to take care of my dad. He had a lot of pain and nobody but me to help him. I bagged groceries at supermarkets, for a while I had part-time work on a peanut farm, and weekends I hustled any kind of horse job. We were drifters. There was no one to notice whether Dallas Dobson was in school or not. So Havendale High is like a last chance for me."

"But why not in Texas? Why in this part of Pennsylvania?"

Dallas shrugged. "Just as soon as he was well enough to get around on crutches, my father started to say he wanted to go home. He was born in Zenith, you know. His mother and father were kind of old and they're gone now. My father was an only child. His parents rented one of those row houses behind the state liquor store." He laughed abruptly. "If you know that section of town, that tells you something about the Dobson family tree."

As Dallas talked, Henrietta heard every word he said, but she was also listening to the profound silence that surrounded them. It was a night with stars but no moon, and the trees and heavy growth along the roadside were only dim shapes, black on black. The wind sounds were light, rhythmic, and distant, while the inside of the small car seemed to echo with memories of the Ellington music.

Henrietta's thoughts seemed as loud in her mind as spoken words. *How can I be sure this is real? How can I believe that it is truly me sitting in the darkness, listening to a stranger tell me faraway things about himself? It is almost as if I have stopped being Henrietta Caldwell and have become someone else. Except for this person sitting next to me, no one in the entire world knows where I am right now. Not my parents, not Charlotte, not Aunt Blue. . . .*

"I needed to tell you because I never want you to feel sorry for me," Dallas Dobson was saying. "It isn't as if my mother just *gave* me away. My father *is* my father and she knew he wanted me." He paused. "Maybe you'll think this is just another tall story for him to tell me, but I believe it.

"My mother's married now," he went on. "She lives in some little town in Texas, with a good husband and a pair of twin girls. But she wanted me to know who and where she was, my father says. So I can find her anytime I want to. He has her married name and address on a card in his wallet. I just have to ask for it."

"Are you going to?" Retta said. "Is that what you plan to do?"

He shook his head. "I don't think so. I used to dream about it, but not now. Without Sam Houston, and with my father crippled and all, maybe I don't need a mother anymore."

Suddenly his voice lowered, the sentence trailing off almost to a whisper. Retta leaned toward him to catch his words, her cheek almost touching his.

"I only miss my mother sometimes now," he said softly. "Like on holidays, when other people have families. Or when I see a sweater or some kind of necklace in a store and I think how much I'd like to buy it for her. She probably thinks of buying things for me sometimes. Just a young kid, she was. She must wonder about me sometimes, certainly every time my birthday rolls 'round."

"A baby," Retta whispered. "I think she probably thinks of you mostly as a baby, almost like when she saw you last."

"She only kept me with her in the clinic a few hours," he said. "I used to imagine that if she *had* stayed with us, she'd have called me. . . ." He paused.

"Called you what?" Retta said.

His words were barely audible now. ". . . she'd have called me 'Little Cowboy' or something." He took his arm from around Retta's shoulders and rubbed the dark windshield with the back of his hand.

"What's the matter?" Retta asked. "What are you looking at?"

"I don't know," he whispered, then put a finger to his lips. "Quiet a moment," he said, and listened intently. Then he frowned. "What could it be? I hear movement, Henrietta. I've heard it twice now. Don't you hear something? There's someone or something out there."

Retta listened, staring at the black windshield and the black road beyond. When she held her breath so the silence in the car would be complete, she was aware of the quickening beat of her heart. Still she heard nothing.

Carefully Dallas rolled down his window and waited, listening to the dark, leafy stillness of the night. "Turn on your parking lights," he whispered.

The soft lights prodded the nearby darkness, but lit nothing but a stretch of gravel and roadside weeds. "Now your headlights," he said quietly.

She turned the lights to bright. They both gasped at what they saw. First just a pair of eyes, gleaming red in the car lights, and then the outlines of a small, gray fox, standing motionless directly ahead of them in the road.

"He must be sick or hurt," Dallas said. "Otherwise he'd make for cover. I'm going to look at him." He stepped from the car, his movements slow and easy, and walked toward the little fox.

Retta stepped from her side of the car and followed. "He's shivering. He's cold or *something*," she whispered.

Without warning, like a toy collapsing, the fox dropped down to the roadway, hind legs stretched out, small muzzle resting on its front paws. In the headlights, they could make out its coloring: gray and buff with black markings on the ear tips and long tail. The animal was panting, the narrow red tongue coated and dry.

"Young," Dobson said. "No more than a few months. Foxes 'round here kit in springtime. He's too young to fend for himself." He bent down and cautiously touched the black, leathery tip of the fox's nose. "Hot," he said, "like a sick baby."

Putting one big hand on the animal's skull, just behind the ears, he held it immobile while he felt first the hind and then the forelegs for breaks or other injury. "He's got to be sick. Probably wandered off from a den near here. No healthy fox would tolerate humans touching him this way."

"We can't just leave it," Retta said. "He could die here or be hit by a car." Dallas slipped off his windbreaker and put it over the young fox like a blanket. "Let's take him to my house," she said. "My father will know what to do."

The young man lifted the fox carefully with the windbreaker tight around the body to hold the legs firmly trussed. "I don't want him scratching or biting from fright," he said.

The fox looked at them with sharp, vulpine eyes, dimmed a little by fever, and made no attempt to escape.

The car tires spun briefly on the loose gravel as Retta turned the car around, then tractioned into speed as she maneuvered the curves of the country lanes leading to the Caldwell house.

"Home, baby," he said softly to the animal. "Retta's gonna take you home."

When she came downstairs and stepped outside again, he was just where she'd left him, standing by the back door, cradling the fox in his arms like a human infant. The big house was dark except for one upstairs light which shone dimly, laying a precise white rectangle on the cold ground.

"What did your father say?"

Henrietta hesitated. She had rushed upstairs to her parents' room, knocked lightly, then called through the closed door, "Wake up, Poppy. We've got a sick fox outside. What should we do?"

There was no answer. Both parents were as silent

as if they were asleep, yet Retta sensed movement somewhere in the bedroom. "Pops," she whispered again. "A sick fox . . . what shall we do?"

Then she thought she heard the sound of her father's voice, soft, almost muffled. Perhaps he had said, "Tomorrow, Retta." Perhaps he had said something else. She did not know. Gently, she turned the knob and put her shoulder against the door. It did not move. She realized then that her parents' door was locked from the inside.

"What did he say we should do?" he asked again.

"Nothing," Retta said. "I didn't want to wake them."

"All right," Dobson said. "Here's what we'll need: a couple of big bath towels and something like a laundry basket to put him in."

"I can get all that," Retta said.

"And a cup of warm milk — just warm, not hot — about three tablespoons of brandy, and a couple of aspirin."

"Will you come inside and help me?" she asked.

"No," he said quietly. "I'll just wait for you here."

She brought out the basket and towels first, then heated the milk and poured it into a small Gorham pitcher from the silver coffee set. There was a bottle of aspirin in the downstairs bathroom, brandy in the liquor cabinet.

Outside, Dallas sat cross-legged on the ground; the fox, wrapped in a towel, immobile in the crook of his arm. With his free hand, he crumbled two aspirin into the milk and added a splash of brandy, stirring the mixture with his finger.

"Too hot," he said softly. "We'll let it cool for a

minute or two." Retta knelt on the ground beside him, cradling the little silver pitcher in her hands. She was aware of the rhythmic panting of the little fox, so ill, so docile, and yet so pulsing with life.

Dallas shifted the animal until he had it grasped firmly but safely between his knees. Again he tested the milk with a finger, then nodded. With two fingers, he pulled out one side of the fox's muzzle to make a little pouch leading down to the throat. He took the pitcher from Retta with his free hand.

At the first few drops of liquid, the fox struggled inside the towel wrappings, then lay still except for the quick red tongue lapping at the medicine. Dallas talked to the animal as he poured the droplets slowly, patiently, soothing it with the sound of his voice.

In moments, the brandy and the aspirin took effect and the fox was as languid as a sleeping child. Dobson placed it gently in the wicker basket, still in its toweling wrap, and then covered the top with the other big towel, tucking the edges in tight.

"That should do it," he said, and touched Retta's hand in the darkness. "We should know by morning."

"It's so late," she said. "Let me make you a bed on the couch in the library."

"No," he said firmly. "I'll lie right here. It wouldn't be right to sleep in your house unless your parents asked me to."

"But they're not like that," she protested. "I told you that before. . . ."

"See you in the morning," he said.

She did not hurry. She waited until she had brushed

her hair and teeth and slipped into a long-sleeved nightgown before she went into the hallway to turn off the upstairs light. She touched the switch and waited until her eyes were accustomed to the darkness outside.

The night was moonless, lit only by the far light of stars, yet as she looked down she felt she could see him clearly, a lanky figure curved in a half circle around the fox's basket, covered by a towel. There was something private, almost intimate, in that moment. She shivered, though from something other than cold. *I know so much about him now,* she thought. *So much more than just what he tried to tell me.*

Chapter
7

It was not the dawn sunlight that waked her, but the awareness that someone was in her room. She opened her eyes to see her father sitting on the edge of the bed in blue jeans and shirt, with the sleeves of an old cashmere sweater knotted around his neck. A mug of coffee steamed on the night table.

"Poppy, why are you awake so early?"

"I didn't really wake up, Princess. I just didn't seem to get to sleep last night."

"But I knocked and — " She sat up suddenly, with the memory of Dallas and the sick fox. Her eyes turned to the bedroom window overlooking the back lawn.

"He's gone," her father said. "I drove him over to

the vet's about an hour ago. Doc Stewart was on night duty. Then I dropped him at the Kennellys'."

"You saw him? You've met him?"

Her father nodded. "I did. And I just wanted to have a few words with you before the family wakes up."

Retta felt the dryness of panic in her throat. "And the fox? What about our fox?"

"That young vixen has a strep throat," her father said. "Sick as a skunk, or a fox in this case. The vet has her caged. He's going to keep her on antibiotics for a little while. He believes the fox would have died out there if you hadn't found her."

"Last night I tried to get your advice."

"Don't worry," he said. "Young Dobson told me what you did. Warmth, aspirin, food, and a little stimulant. You did the right thing."

Through the dim morning light, Henrietta realized her father's face was grave, subdued, and he seemed to be watching her closely. "Nice lad," he said, "but he was lucky he didn't get bitten. Wild foxes often have rabies, you know."

"He was careful. And, as I said, I tried to ask you what to do."

He took a sip of the hot coffee, then handed the mug to his daughter. "I know you did, Retta. And I should have come out to talk with you, but, well. . . ." He paused and looked at her thoughtfully, somewhat embarrassed, almost too young for the faint wrinkles in the forehead, the touches of gray in his hair. "It was an important night. I'm going to fly out to California today on business. And sometimes it's hard saying good-bye, if only for a day or two. I hope you understand that, Retta."

A rush of deep emotion and affection swept through her as she understood his words.

She sipped the coffee until she felt sure her voice was under control. "Of course, Poppy," she said. "Of course."

"I'm afraid, Retta, that with all the worry about business at the paper and about that damned highway, your mother and I haven't been giving you the time and attention we ought to. I know you're growing up, but I don't want you to grow away from us. Not yet, anyway."

He paused and his next question, though light and casual in tone, brought a quick touch of color to his daughter's cheeks. "How long have you been seeing young Dobson?" he asked.

"I don't really *see* him, not in the way you mean," she said. "We don't date or anything. I just drive him to school each day."

"*Every* day?"

"Yes, when he can make it. He hitchhikes to the Kennellys' where he's a stable boy. I take him from there. They have a pickup truck, but his father needs it to get to work."

"But you were with him last night."

"Yes, I was. We were studying together at Charlotte's. You see, he had to drop out of school for two years and he's way behind. He came to Havendale High to try to catch up."

"He's new in these parts?"

She nodded vigorously. "Yes, he and his father

just moved back here from Texas. His father is Daniel Dobson; he works at the feed store."

"Danny Dobson?"

"Well, I guess so. You mean you know him?"

"Not really. He was a friend of a friend, before he left Zenith." He paused, frowning a little, as if trying to sort out his thoughts. "But isn't Dobson a little old for you? The Danny Dobson I knew had a son. He'd be about twenty-five by now."

"That would be his brother Sam Houston. He was killed in an accident more than three years ago. Dallas is eighteen, going on nineteen. About two years older than I. Maybe he seemed older to you because he's so tall."

"What concerns me, Retta, is that you've driven this young man to school many times, even dozens of times, and yet you never mentioned him to me or your mother."

Retta felt a sting of tears in her eyes as she heard the rebuke in her father's voice. "There is nothing to tell, really," she said. "Absolutely nothing. We go to the same school. We're good friends, that's all."

"About that fox," her father said obliquely. "Doc Stewart says you can pick it up in about three days. Take it back to the spot you found it, and let it loose. If its lair is nearby, it can backtrack home."

He rose and walked to the door. "If I'm still in California, maybe young Dobson can help you. I'm taking you at your word, Henrietta. Just good friends."

He had already stepped into the hallway when she made up her mind and called after him. "Wait a minute, Poppy. I almost forgot to give something to you."

She put her feet on the cold floor without bothering with slippers and went to her closet. Inside, hanging on a hook, was her red school purse. She unzipped the inner compartment and took out something which she handed to her father.

"I know you're executor of Aunt Blue's estate. This is for her house. It's an extra key."

As it turned out, Carter Caldwell was delayed in California, Dallas Dobson was absent from school three days in a row, and Retta had to return the fox to the woods herself. Dr. Stewart had put the animal in a wire cat-carrier. It was completely healed, transformed again into a feisty, wild creature, alert and unafraid, its thick, bushy tail sweeping nervously back and forth, eyes bright and sly as Retta carried the cage to the car.

The weather had turned cold and this morning a deep, penetrating chill froze the muddy backroads into iron ruts and caught the fox's breath in a frosty white cloud just off the end of its nose.

Retta parked her car where it had been parked four nights before and took the cat-cage from the car. The road was deserted. She set the cage on the ground, then blew on her cold fingers to limber them before unsnapping the double-wire door. The fox seemed to hesitate a moment, the tip of its black leather nose inched just a wary step toward freedom. Then it darted toward the woods, leaping the roadside ditch in a single graceful arc that knocked dew-frost from the bushes.

There was the sharp sound of boots on the frozen ground, and Retta turned to see Dobson running toward her from the Kennelly farm, books under his arm, one hand raised in a wave.

"I wanted to be with you," he shouted and then, as he came closer, "I just couldn't help it, Retta. I've been working days at the feed store for my father. He drinks, you know. Not always, but more lately."

"Let's get in the car," she said. "I should have worn gloves."

She turned on the car heater and a waft of warm air touched their faces, smelling, after six months' disuse, of dust, oil, and the sticky scent of rubber. Dallas put his books on the floor and sank low in his seat, his long legs tucked under the dashboard. He tried to warm his hands by rubbing them on the denim of his sharp knees. Retta noticed at once his broken fingernails, and the deep burn, red and crusted, along the back of one hand.

He put his healthy hand over the burn defensively. "I told you I didn't want you to be sorry for me," he said. "I'm just trying to decide what it is I'm responsible for, what my father expects of me, and what I owe him." He paused.

"He drinks when he's blue or angry, and then I can't reason with him. Last night he began shouting that he missed Sam Houston more than any man could be expected to stand. He said he didn't want Sam's things around anymore to remind him that Sam Houston was dead. He said he never wanted me to mention my brother's name again. He shouted those things over and over, like he was trying to convince himself they would work some kind of magic with his feelings. That they'd help him to forget somehow.

"Then he tried to burn Sam's clothes, even his music, and when I pulled the stuff out of the fireplace, well — I got burned, that's all." He rubbed a hand over his forehead savagely, as if to brush away thoughts he didn't want to be there.

"He's sick, I know that, because he's got terrible angers inside his head and he's afraid to face them or try to get rid of them. I have to feel sorry for the man. I know he hurts in his leg and in his heart and his head and everywhere else, for that matter. But I don't seem to know how to help him, that's what's so hard on me. And I think he ought to realize how much I miss Sam Houston, too."

A light snow flurry had begun and soft flakes stuck to the windshield. Retta turned on the wipers, welcoming the sound and rhythmic movement in the tense silence of the car.

"I shouldn't dump on you, Retta," he said, "but I'm not finding any answers. Last night I put my hand in the fire for my brother because I don't want to forget him, or lose things he had touched. It *can't* be right to pretend that that great guy just never *was*. But my father. . . ." He paused and sighed. "I wish my father was like that fox back there — a healthy animal with nothing but a sore throat, something so simple I could make him well and set him free. . . ."

Chapter
8

The state of Pennsylvania sits in a hybrid location, about four states south of chilly Canada, yet above the Mason-Dixon line and the warmer climate of the South. Sometimes the weather stays moderate, spongy ground and soft wind so full of warmth and moisture that yellow forsythia can be duped into blooming at Christmas time. In another year, snows and winds can drift over the fields and highway long before Thanksgiving. Blizzards in that state can blow up as quickly as a squall over water.

This year the first storm came the fourth Tuesday in November, a few drifting flakes in the early morning, with a stiff wind and a thick mist of granular snow by ten o'clock. At Havendale High, the storm coated the north side of trees and blanketed school buses and parked cars, a shifting, drifting cover of white that glistened with sharp, frozen crystals.

By lunch hour, the storm was blowing in full fury, singing winds sounding at every window and driving snow adding to the soft, flaky ground cover in a slick, dangerous layer. The sky was dark and a leaden gray, as devoid of sunlight as if someone had pulled an off-switch. A county snowplow pushed into the school parking lot, backing and filing, until its great metal blade cleared driving paths from the school to the main road.

At the end of the three-o'clock class, the principal's voice sounded over the loudspeaker system. "We're canceling all further classes for the day," he said. "The county highway department has issued a bulletin that we're in for a real blow. All students depending on school buses for transportation go directly to the west parking lot. All students providing self-transportation are advised to go straight home. I repeat: Students with self-transportation are advised to go straight home."

Retta cupped her hand over her mouth and nose to keep out the knife-sharp cold as she ran for her parked car. Already the cars looked alike, humped and white with snow, but she recognized the Volkswagen at once. Dallas Dobson was standing beside it, hands in his pockets, stomping his feet sharply on the hard-packed snow.

"One more favor, Retta," he said quickly. "I need a lift to the Kennellys'. I tried to call but the lines must be down. I've got to spend the night there.

Those Arabians are on a feeding schedule, six tonight and six in the morning. They'd get colic or kick their stalls into splinters if they missed a meal. The old man could get out to the barns tonight, maybe, but with this storm, I know he can't make it in the morning."

"Quick then," she said. The windshield wipers cleared little arcs of vision on the snow-crusted glass. Retta put the car in reverse and caught her breath as the rear wheels spun without traction on the slick snow. She tried again with greater speed, and in moments the car was turned toward the exit gate, following a school bus that was tailgating Junior Provanza's red Porsche, roofed and dappled now with hard snow.

The plow-cleared main highway was easy, but turning into the tertiary road that led to the Kennellys' was like entering a different world, ominous and silent. No one had traveled this lane in several hours and the snow was unmarked by tires. Eddies of snow swirled over the surface and it was difficult to know where the sides of the road ended and the ditches began.

Retta proceeded with caution, holding the steering wheel firmly, hoping to feel the security of tires cutting through the snow and down to the hard, graveled surface. But the car seemed to wallow and shift in the deepening drifts.

A half mile in, Dallas peered through the windshield and said, "Let me off here, Retta. I'll walk in and you go back."

He touched her cheek lightly with his cold fingers and got out of the car. But the smooth surface of the snow was deceiving. He sank deep over his boot tops and went floundering forward, buffeted by the wind and struggling like a man in deep water.

She turned down her window a crack and shouted into the wind. "Dallas, you'll never make it. We'll have to get back to the main road and wait for the snowplows. I'll try backing out."

She put the car in reverse and looked through the rear window, but could see nothing through the falling snow. The wheels spun, kicking up snow and bits of gravel, but the car settled into a rut and would not move. She gunned the motor but heard Dobson shout, "No more! You're just digging yourself in!"

He worked in silence for a few minutes and she saw what he intended to do. With his gloveless hands, he tore at the snow-wet wineberry bushes and gathered up armloads of weathered goldenrod, pulling the brittle plants up by the roots. He laid the bundled material behind the rear wheels and then plodded up to the driver's side of the car. "Move over," he said. "Let me try."

Slowly, carefully, he tried to urge the car backward, hoping the tires would find traction on the bushes and branches. The wheels spun, gripped, then spun again. "We need one more booster," he said, and went back into the snow. The field at the side of the road was fenced with a split-rail barrier, long weathered timbers of locust trees laid one on top of the other in a tongue-and-groove structure.

With a powerful wrench, Dallas loosened the top rail and carried it back to the road, jamming it tightly under the two rear wheels.

This time the tires caught on the solid wood and began to inch backward. "All right, Retta," he said quietly. "I'm going to try to follow our tire tracks back to the main road." He switched on the headlights and the beams shot yellow shafts through the whorls of snow. "We don't want to hit anyone coming *or* going," he said. "You be my eyes out front, and I'll try to watch the back."

Leaning hard on the horn, he began to inch the car backwards. The shrill, insistent sound of the horn seemed to be picked up by the wind and echo around them in all directions. The minutes seemed like hours, and the winding lane an endless blur of drifts and danger. At last the main road showed in the rearview mirror, and the rear wheels of the car hit solid macadam.

There were no other cars in sight and the broad, cleared strokes made by the snowplow had already begun to catch shifting drifts of snow. "We can worry about the horses later," Dallas Dobson said. "I'm getting you home."

From the first moment inside her own house, Retta sensed that something wasn't right, but she could not say what it was.

Her mother met them as they came in the front door, stamping the snow off their feet on the mat. With extended hand, she said, "You must be Dallas Dobson," even before Retta could speak. Their Irish setter, Gypsy, sniffed the young man's boots and wagged her feathered tail. "See, the dog likes you already. Come in, come in." Mrs. Caldwell smiled again. "And now that you're here, you must spend the night. I insist on it. We're all just country folks in weather like this."

When Dobson looked doubtful, she put a hand on his arm. "My husband phoned to say he's sleeping at the office because Highway 111 is completely blocked. You just phone home and tell whomever is there that you're staying with the Caldwells."

"No one at home is going to worry about me," he said, "but I had planned to hike back to the Kennellys'. I can't reach them by phone. Mr. Kennelly can get out for tonight's feed, but I've got to be there tomorrow. I take care of their Arabians, you see."

"Don't you worry, young man," Mrs. Caldwell said. "If the storm is so bad that we can't get my car out by daybreak, I'll lend you my husband's cross-country skis."

When Dallas Dobson suggested he try to dig out the walks and snowbanks that were drifting around the closed doors of the garage, Mrs. Caldwell's answer was strangely personal and condescending. "Don't feel you have to work for your supper. You're perfectly welcome in this house, Dallas."

Dobson said simply, "We get snow in Texas sometimes. It's best to dig out before it gets the best of you."

Retta stayed in her room most of the late afternoon. Her mother had turned on a rock station on the kitchen radio and the steady beat filtered up through the old house, making it difficult to concentrate. Retta sat on the window seat and played Spanish language tapes on her cassette deck. It pleased her to drown out the music from the kitchen with the precise, accented voice of someone outside the family. From the window, she could see Dobson clearing the walks, working rapidly, rhythmically, throwing shovels of snow in great arcs on either side of the paths. He had taken off his windbreaker and hung it on the branch of a small apple tree. Even in the cold, his denim shirt clung to him, and Retta could see the dark stain of perspiration between his shoulder blades. From somewhere inside the house, someone turned on the yard lights.

There was a tap on her door and Two said, "Mother asks you to go tell your boyfriend that dinner is ready. He can wash up in my room. He's going to sleep there, too."

The kitchen was empty when Retta went downstairs, but she noticed at once the elaborate preparations for dinner; a chicken and cashew nut casserole from her mother's "emergency shelf" in the freezer had been heated in the oven. There was a tossed green salad and a silver basket of fresh cornmeal muffins, as small as pigeon eggs.

Retta pushed open the door to the dining room and gave an involuntary gasp of surprise. The table had been set with their best Lenox china and crystal. On the sideboard stood a tray with fluted glasses of raspberries and small cups for after-dinner coffee. In the center of the table was a china pot of flowering begonias. Tall, pink tapers burned brightly in Grand-mama Caldwell's silver candlesticks. Retta tried to stifle a feeling of confusion and concern, emotions so intense that her cheeks felt aflame.

Her thoughts were churning. *What was the fuss all about?* she wondered. *Would Dallas, just a Texas cowhand, really — he told you that right away — would he feel awkward and out of place with all that silver and candlelight?* There seemed no direct clue, no guidelines to what was happening. Her mother was always a good hostess. It was like Mrs. Caldwell to prepare an interesting dinner for a guest, but this was too much like a party, too much like showing off. What *was* it all about? It couldn't all be just for Dallas and the three Caldwells, Retta thought. It was like her mother was play-acting, trying to impress someone else, almost as if another guest were expected to join them at dinner. *Why?*

In the kitchen, Retta snapped off the blaring radio, then called to Dallas from the back door, grateful for cold wind on her face. He removed his jacket from the apple tree, then carefully tamped snow off the shovel before propping it near the back door. Someone, Retta saw, had already located her father's cross-country skis and leaned them against the door.

But there was no chance to run upstairs and ask her mother questions in private. And since she didn't quite understand her own roiling emotions, her almost violently protective feelings toward Dallas and his pride, Retta couldn't decide just what those questions ought to be.

Mrs. Caldwell came through the swinging door of the kitchen wearing a long plaid hostess skirt and a low-necked red sweater. Small pearl earrings matched a double string of pearls, and with every movement she wafted the odor of spicy cologne.

"Ah, you two," she said lightly. "Five minutes till dinner. Retta, perhaps you'd like to freshen up, and you can show your friend to Two's quarters. He'll be bunking there tonight."

When she got to her own room, Two, standing at the bathroom sink, called through the half-open door. "Your boyfriend is gonna use my space. I'll be through here right away."

A few moments later, he stepped out for inspection, his face shining, blond hair plastered down with water. "Do I look okay?"

"You look as good as you can," she said sharply, not trying to mask her emotion and anger. "Why is she *doing* this to me, Two? To me *and* to Dallas?"

"Doing what?"

"You know as well as I do. Best china, raspberries . . . even candles."

"We always have candles in the dining room," he said. "You know that."

"But we don't always *light* them," she said, "as you darn well know."

"I don't know what you're mad at *me* for," Two said, hurt and defensive.

"It's just by *chance* that he's here at all. It's freaky weather. He didn't *plan* it this way. Why can't she just be natural? Can't she realize he's just a boy, an ordinary person?"

"Gee, Retta," he said. "Keep your voice down. Why don't you just come out and say you love the guy?"

She stared at her brother in disbelief and when she spoke her tone was low, almost savage. "Why, you irresponsible little freak! Get out of here this minute! And don't ever come into my room again without permission. Not *ever!*"

When he left, she stood at the bathroom sink splashing cold water on her face until she could no longer feel the tears, hot and unwanted on her cheeks. *Why did I do that?* she thought sadly. *Two, of all people. But why did he say that about love? What is happening to me?*

When she at last went downstairs, the others were already seated at the candle-lit table, and there was a plate of chicken casserole at her place.

Dallas rose as Retta entered the room, and moved to pull out her chair. She seated herself and he pushed the chair back into place, lightly touching the back of her neck with his fingers, still stiff and chilled from the snow. When he seated himself again, Retta looked across the table at him and saw him smile, not a laughing, open smile, but just a quick movement of the lips and a flash of warmth in the eyes. For a moment she felt tears again in her own eyes.

He knows I've been crying, she thought. *He knows but he doesn't know why; yet, whatever it is, he wants to make it right. Of course he's a Texas cowhand, but he's my Texas cowhand. He's thinking about me. He doesn't care about the candles and the silver and the little fluted glasses on the side-board. Dallas Dobson cares about how I feel, he cares about me.*

Connie Caldwell passed her daughter the silver basket of muffins, but Retta shook her head, then forced herself to concentrate on the bright, flickering flame of the candles, demanding her emotions to subside, her cheeks to cool. Splintered thoughts ran through her mind like quicksilver: He touched me, he smiled. There is a table between us, there are other people here, but he and I are completely together in this room. . . .

Her thoughts were so intense, so singing with conviction in her brain, that she did not hear her mother speak. Connie Caldwell had asked, "Not hungry, Retta? You're not eating a thing."

Chapter
9

The sun was muted in a clouded gray sky, and
Retta had to check her bedside clock to see if
morning had come. It was a few minutes after seven.
She had overslept.

She hurried to the window overlooking the front
drive to see if he had left, but the roadway was
drifted over, as smooth as frozen cream. She saw a
crisscross of wild bird tracks and the light, patterned
trail of a woods rabbit, but no mark of tires or skis.

She reached for her robe. I must wake him, she
thought. He must get to the horses. A moment like
this had never happened before and she was almost
weak with anticipation and excitement. *I can touch*

his shoulder, she thought. *I can watch him open his eyes.*

But the extra bed in Two's room was empty and made up, a blue blanket neatly folded at the foot. Her brother was still asleep, arms curled under his head. Stepping softly, Retta went to a window and pulled up the shade on a dormer overlooking the rear of the house and the sloping meadow. The answer was there. He was gone. A pair of ski tracks traced a curving path over the crusted snow, disappearing off beyond the big farm pond.

How clever, she thought, with a touch of sadness. He's taking a shortcut to the Kennellys'. How country-smart, how ingenious to know the right thing to do. But she suddenly felt lonely and small and left out. He had done what he had to do. He hadn't needed her help after all.

A light wind sprang up, sending little whorls of white across the ground. Even as she watched, her forehead pressed against the cold windowpane, Retta saw snow blow into the narrow ski ruts, almost wiping from sight any trace of his passage.

By Monday all the main roads had been plowed open, but Dallas Dobson was not at school. On Tuesday, his desk was empty again. On the third morning, he hurried in just as the last bell rang. When Mr. Engel stood at the blackboard, diagramming a problem, Dallas passed her a scrawled note which read: *Sorry, sorry. Snowed in with the horses. Provanza is my transport. He's got his father's four-wheeler and chains.*

She nodded her head and felt the sudden warmth as he leaned forward and touched his fingers to the back of her neck.

Mr. Engel asked to see Dobson after class and, though she waited for him outside the classroom, he did not come and she had to hurry to make Señora Escudero's class.

By noontime a winter sun broke through the gray clouds. Pale light glittered off the massive drifts left by snowplows, and sent rivulets of water streaming across the parking lot. The snowman someone had built on the school's west lawn turned soft and wet. First it lost its black coal eyes and then its broom.

Alone in her room that evening, Retta took the note from the pages of her math book and smoothed it out under the light of a reading lamp. There were only a dozen or so words on the paper and they told her no more at that moment than they had in the classroom this morning. But she read the note again and again, then shut her eyes and ran her fingers over and over the thick, blunt handwriting, as if she were trying to extract new meaning from the words through a kind of emotional braille.

Sometime during the night, the hall phone rang and waked Retta from troubled dreams. She heard her father, who had come home, answer, say a few quick words, and then the house was quiet again, but she could not go back to sleep. With a blanket around her shoulders, she sat in the curve of the window seat, staring out into the darkness. The night was filled with liquid noises as snow melted into the roof gutters, and icicles on the eaves shortened by every drip. The big fir trees had dropped their load of wet snow and now stood black and stark along the drive. It was going. As quickly as the storm had come, it began to melt away.

During lunch hour, the principal's voice came over the loudspeaker system to remind the student body that there would be a countywide teachers' meeting in West Chester that afternoon, and all students were requested to be off campus by two o'clock.

Even before she went out to her yellow car, Retta knew that Dallas would be waiting for her. "We both have time today," he said simply. "I'd like you to see how *I* live. *We* live, I should say."

"Do you want to drive?" she asked, and he nodded.

The car followed the main road for about three miles and then Dobson turned toward backcountry, passing Provanza's market, and then down onto a gravel and dirt road that traveled away from the fenced and well-groomed farms and estates and through a grubby settlement with sleeper vans, rusting mobile homes, and a few rundown clapboard houses in an area called Little Tennessee. Here clothes fluttered from a wire line behind every residence, and in front of most there was a thin, fierce watchdog, tugging and barking at the end of a short chain.

Beyond Little Tennessee were a few makeshift country places with chickens in the front yard and relics of broken-down cars and farm machinery in the back. Here the flat fields were stubbled with rotting pumpkins and snow-wet cornstalks, and even the grazing land was poor, rough with stones and hummocks and scattered with cow dung.

Finally, Dallas made a sharp right and smiled at her without joy. "We're over on Snuff Mill Road," he said. In this area, Zenith River ran fast, full now from melting snows, still turning the old waterwheel at the snuff mill, a red-brick shambles of a building a century old, perched at the edge of the stream. Beyond the mill was a long, single street with narrow, brick houses on both sides. Most of the structures were in ruin but eight had been brought back to use, windowpanes in place, roofs and front porches in good repair.

Dallas pulled up in front of the last house. A rough drive curved round to a backyard shed. The house and the street seemed to be deserted. There were no children at play, no wandering pets, no movement or sound anywhere except the creak of the waterwheel and the frothing rush of the old mill stream.

Dallas unlocked the front door and held it open for Retta. Inside, he took her short red coat and hung it on a coatrack made of moose antlers. "Here's where I live," he said, gesturing with a sweep of his hand.

It was a small room with a rag rug in the middle of the floor, some rodeo posters tacked to the walls, a table and chairs, and one long, worn couch in cracked, brown leather. There were andirons in the fireplace but no sign of logs or kindling, not even a sprinkling of ashes. It had been swept clean. The windows, without curtains, had green shades pulled so low now that the room was almost dark.

"The kitchen is behind that door. Upstairs there are two bedrooms and a bath," Dallas Dobson said. "One room's a kind of storage space, and my father sleeps in the other one."

He pointed to the corner table and then the couch. "I study over there and I sleep here," he said. "I cook and I keep things clean."

The couch sagged with years and wear, a nest of worn leather and broken springs, with a plaid horse-blanket folded neatly at one end. And there was one fancy lavender pillow with an embroidered cover of pansies trimmed in lace.

Retta could feel Dallas looking at her, searching her face, gauging her reactions to what she saw. She had a strong urge to stand close to him, touch his young, serious face, and whisper, "Please believe me. It's all right. It doesn't matter. . . ."

Instead, she managed to say, "It's very nice."

He shrugged and moved toward her and his voice was close and husky. "I've lived in worse places," he said.

Suddenly, from overhead, there was a heavy but muted movement, the creak of bed springs, the sound of boots on the floor. Dallas winced visibly and clenched his hands. They stood as they were, close together, and neither spoke as they heard the sound of rubber-tipped crutches moving across the bedroom, over to the top of the stairs. Slowly, moving as if each step were painful, they saw first the crutches, then the cowboy boots of Danny Dobson as he moved cautiously down the flight of uncarpeted stairs.

Retta stared as if mesmerized until the man was standing directly in front of her, his weight balanced heavily on the padded crutches supporting him under each arm.

Retta felt she had never seen a better-looking man, lean and broad-shouldered, with thick, fair hair and eyes that were blue and steady as azure marbles. Danny Dobson stared at her almost impersonally, letting his gaze check out her face, her unsteady smile, and then the contours of her body. He was frankly appraising and sardonic in his judgment of the young woman standing before him.

He swayed a little on the crutches, then shivered as if his knees gave him pain. When he smiled at her, Retta caught the sharp, rancid smell of liquor and realized the man had been drinking, but his voice was cold and scathing as he spoke. "I guess you two didn't figure I'd be home this time of day, right?"

Dallas shrugged and said simply, "It's your home as well as mine," and then, "This is Henrietta Caldwell. Retta, my father, Daniel Dobson."

Dobson moved forward a step on his crutches and held out his hand. Retta took it and found it hard and smooth and surprisingly cool, not matching the anger in the man's eyes.

"Caldwell," he said, still holding her hand. "You look it. The same airs. A Caldwell through and through. . . . Just what I might have expected."

"That's it, Father," Dallas said sharply. "You've said enough."

Daniel Dobson dropped the girl's hand and wheeled around sharply on his crutches, putting one hand on the mantelpiece for support, staring down at the cold, empty fireplace, his shoulders heaved with emotion, almost a dry sobbing, as he struggled to bring himself under control.

Then he turned and spoke to his son. "They drove me home early because my legs hurt and because I got a little drunk on the job. Maybe you can pick up the truck down at the feed store." He tried to smile at them both but his eyes were opaque and without warmth. He punched his son lightly on the arm. "Come on. Don't be tough on the old man, kid. You know how I get sometimes. . . ."

Outside, Dallas rolled down the car window on the driver's side and drove the next five miles at top speed, without speaking, to the feed store where his father worked. A battered pickup truck was parked at one side of a weighing shed.

When he got out of the car, Retta slid behind the wheel and set the shift for reverse, but Dallas leaned on the open window, as if willing her to stay. He stared at her thoughtfully for several moments. His eyes were not steel-blue like his father's, but a deep gray-green with flecks of brown, and his young face was infinitely sad as he reached in to put his big hand on Retta's as it rested on the steering wheel. He held it so tightly that her bones hurt and she could feel the pulse of blood in the veins, so full and steady that she did not know if it came from his heartbeat or her own.

"No matter what you think, Retta," he said at last, "I still love him. And he's part of whatever I am."

"I know that," she said. "You don't have to tell me. But. . . ." She paused. "I think you're also afraid of him."

"No, no," he said with sharp conviction. "It's the other way around. He's afraid of *me*. He's crippled, he doesn't have Sam Houston anymore. And he's afraid I might leave him some day."

"And you never will?" she asked.

"I don't know," he said. He took his hand from hers and jammed it deep in his jeans pocket. "That's something I can't tell you."

On the Friday after Thanksgiving, Mr. Engel opened his classroom and gave Dallas Dobson a private test. Dobson passed junior geometry with a B-plus, and was immediately assigned to a senior group studying basic trigonometry.

Retta still drove him to school most mornings, but the daily meetings in math class and the study sessions at the Ambersons' were over.

Chapter
10

Carter Caldwell made two more trips to California, one in the last week of December. He promised his family he would be home for Christmas, and Retta thought it was her father's car early on Christmas Eve as a pair of headlights turned in the drive and slashed through the darkness. But it was Dallas Dobson in a pickup truck.

He knocked at the back door, carrying a Jerusalem cherry plant, the dark leaves glossy as green leather, the plump, round fruit a bright red-orange. It had begun to snow and when Retta opened the door and stepped outside, she saw a few feathery flakes had settled on his hair and made a white fringe of his eyelashes. *How lovely and how sad,* she thought. *I now know how he will look as a very old man.*

"What a nice gift, Dallas," she was able to say warmly. Then, "But I'm embarrassed. I have nothing for you. I didn't know we were going to do this."

"I just wanted something for *you*," he said as she took the plant. "It isn't much, I know."

"It's *everything*," she said impetuously. "We'll use it for a centerpiece tomorrow. And you *will* come for Christmas dinner. I know my parents will say yes."

"I can't do that," he said. "I'm cooking at my house. My father won the turkey raffle at the feed store and I'm fixing it. He's invited some lady he knows."

"You can cook a turkey?" she said with surprise.

He nodded. "A turkey, the dressing, some sweet potatoes, and cranberries. I bought those canned." Retta found herself smiling, almost without meaning to. "And I've just about decided I'm going to try to make pumpkin pie."

She knew her smile might turn to laughter, so she held the Christmas plant in one arm and embraced him with the other. She held him tight, her face pressed against the smooth, cold fabric of his windbreaker, laughter almost smothered. "I'm not laughing *at* you," she said in a choking voice. "I'm laughing *with* you. A pumpkin pie. . . ."

He was silent, not moving, and she looked up quickly, afraid she might have hurt his feelings. But he was smiling at her, and kissed her mouth until the laughter died away.

A few moments later, she brought the Christmas plant into the dining room. Her mother turned from setting the table and said, "What was so funny out there, Retta? I heard all that noise."

"There's no way to explain, Mother," she said. "Dallas Dobson just said he could bake a pumpkin pie."

It had long been a tradition at Havendale High School, since it was founded more than eight decades ago, to hold the senior prom early in the second semester. In the old days, male students from working farm families were released from school on May first so they could help with the plowing and planting and get the meadows ready for summer pasturing. So the prom was always held in the school gym on the first Friday night after Valentine's Day.

"It's the fifteenth," Dallas said to her one morning on the way to school. "I've got enough credits now to qualify as a senior. I'd like you to go with me. We can double-date with Junior Provanza and Charlotte Amberson. He told me he's going to ask her."

Retta decided on silence about Charlotte. Just last evening, late, when Mrs. Amberson was sleeping, Charlie had called her to tell her that Junior Provanza had called about the prom and her mother insisted she turn him down. "It's not just Junior," Charlie had said. "And not just because he's a butcher, but that doesn't help either. My mother will never think *anyone* is good enough for me."

"I've wanted to ask you out other times," Dobson continued, "but I just can't. I've been saving money, you see. One of the times when I thought my father was off drinking somewhere, well, he told me that he'd really gone into Philadelphia that day to see a bone specialist. His legs *can* be fixed, Retta. He told me that. But the operation is expensive. He has no insurance and the feed store won't help out because the accident happened before he came to work for them." He put his hand slightly on her shoulder, then tightened his grip until she winced. "Think what it could mean," he said, "for a man like that to *walk* without crutches again." He paused. "My father doesn't know it, but I've been saving money for that operation."

"We could go halves on expenses for the dance," she said. "I get paid, you know, for delivering that society column each morning."

"No," he said quickly. "I'm only going to have one prom in my lifetime, and I want the whole thing. I want to buy the tickets, I want you to tell me what color you're wearing, and let me pick the corsage. I want to pick you up at your house for once. I want to do everything I'm supposed to do."

"Then I'll tell you about my dress later," she said. "I'll try to find something in Zenith."

"I know you have almost a month," her mother said later that afternoon, "but why not drive with us to Philadelphia on Saturday? Carter feels we're getting nowhere with the people in Harrisburg. He wants to consult with an experienced lawyer, Luis Berger, in Philadelphia. Someone who's an expert on the 'Right of Eminent Domain.' We'll drop you at Bonwit's and pick you up after our appointment."

Retta spent two hours at the big store, examining the collection of formal wear, and she tried on a dozen before narrowing her choice down to two: a full-length, strapless dress of soft red organza; and a full-skirted gown with cap sleeves and a rounded neckline, the whole thing made up of rows and rows of pale blue and green lace.

When she put on the red dress for the second time, the saleslady had said, "We'll have the seamstress loosen it a little under the arms. You're quite busty, young lady. Otherwise, it's perfect."

When her parents arrived in front of Bonwit's to pick her up, Retta asked her father if he could drive around the block a few times while her mother helped her to decide.

The saleslady held out both dresses on hangers, moving them a little to show their lines and flow. Mrs. Caldwell cocked her head and was silent for some time. Then she said, "It really all depends on you, Retta. What is your aura these days? Would you say you're more blue-green? Or are you in a red phase of your personality?"

Retta felt a spasm of frustration. "Mother," she said impatiently. "Mother, I wanted your advice, not some pop psychology. I'm all mixed up. How do I know what my *aura* is? Don't say anything more. Let me do it by myself."

Retta closed her eyes and turned around three times, then reached out toward the two party dresses. As her fingers closed on the light, soft fabric, she knew she would be wearing red.

100

* * *

The senior decorating committee had been sworn to secrecy, so the transformation of the gym was a surprise. It was decorated as a surrealist nightclub with black and white streamers, dozens of clusters of matching balloons, and chairs with small tables, alternately clothed in black and white. The lights were covered with silver cellophane so the whole room had a misty, moonlit quality.

Dallas had picked two white gardenias on a red ribbon as a corsage, and Retta tied them on her wrist. For himself, he had rented a deep blue tuxedo with a white ruffled shirt, and with his hair long to the collar, his manner grave and subdued, Retta thought he looked like some handsome courtier out of the Middle Ages. He was much taller than she (and wearing those old, shined-up Texas boots with stacked heels) and when they danced, he held her close, her face almost buried in the froth of white ruffles. He was a confident dancer only to slow music, but she did not mind sitting out every other set.

Halfway through the evening, Junior Provanza came into the gym, guiding his twin sister, Parma, his date for the evening. Parma often liked to tell school friends that her mother had explained to her that she had been born first, the dominant twin, and that was why she was bulkier and at least a head taller than her brother. Her prom dress was of deep blue velvet, off-the-shoulder, and Parma had selected elbow-length white kid gloves to wear with it. Her dark hair was groomed into a thick, bell-like page boy that curled just under the chin line. Like most of the girls, her eye makeup was heavy, and deep red lipstick set off the unhappy pout of her lips.

"Momma says I gotta go with Junior," she had explained to Henrietta a few days earlier. "The guy I like is in the Army, and Junior's got some love problem. He won't talk about it, but he's just *sick* over someone.

"I'm gonna borrow an outfit from my cousin, kind of early-Grace-Kelly stuff. It just doesn't seem right to buy a formal just to dance with your brother."

The two Provanzas stood together at the edge of the dance floor, both sullen and self-conscious, till Retta whispered to Dallas, "Let's dance over and switch partners a few times. I mean, it's the senior prom for them, too."

Dallas and Retta exchanged dances with the twins three times before several other couples sensed what was going on and asked the Provanzas to exchange dances also.

The decorating committee had covered the big gym clock with black and white streamers, so time seemed to float by, unmarked, with no way to check the hours. Between dances, Dallas managed to hold Retta's hand, lightly, warmly, and he kept his fingers on her wrist, a small, intimate gesture, even when Mr. Engel and his wife had joined them at a black and white table.

Without watching the hands or hearing the tick of a clock, Retta was aware of the swift passage of time, the excitement, the fresh wonder that brushed over the whole evening for her. Dancing, sitting at

102

the tables, she felt calm and poised, yet moved with an almost giddy happiness.

What if I kept a diary? she thought to herself as she and Dallas moved through a smooth, almost liquid, dance number, his shirtfront soft and clean as clover against her cheek. *What would I write in it about tonight? I don't know, I just don't know for sure,* an inner voice whispered back to her. *I think I would leave the pages blank. I would put down nothing at all, just leave the pages untouched for years and years until I could remember everything with clarity and depth, and then search my mind for the right words, the forever-words to put my feelings on paper. I am still Henrietta Caldwell, but tonight I just want to feel, not think or speak. Or ask myself any questions.*

To signal the last dance, to let the prom crowd know the evening was almost over, Mr. Engel stood at the control panel and turned the decorated gym lights down low, low, and lower until the big room was dimmed into an artificial twilight.

As they moved together to the music, Dallas bent down to whisper, "Henrietta, is it like what you wanted it to be?"

She squeezed his hand in an affirmative answer, and he tightened his arm on her shoulders, moved and exhilarated by her gentle, wordless "Yes."

Yet, as he drove her home, Dallas fell silent. He steered with one hand on the wheel, the other resting lightly on Retta's knee. His touch was so warm, so personal, that it stirred a deep longing through her whole body. Yet, she sensed he had become withdrawn, thoughtful, even moody. As she looked at his still profile, she felt alone, puzzled, left-out. She knew he was thinking now of something besides the girl in the red dress who sat next to him in the pickup truck.

When they walked up the flagstone path toward the house, both were aware of movement, the sound of someone pacing about on the side terrace.

Carter Caldwell did not hear them approach. He was alone on an open flagstone porch that had been cleared of redwood furniture for the winter months. His back was to them as he stood next to a low stone wall, a brandy glass in one hand. It was a night of clear moonlight and he seemed to be staring through the big trees, down the corridor of light and shadows, watching the moonlight form a shimmering path on the water of the farm pond. There was something so unexpected, so puzzling about her father, in solitude, looking off into the darkness, that Retta lowered her voice to a whisper when she said, "Poppy?"

Caldwell turned quickly, a half smile on his face, like a man wakened from a dream. "Gad, you two! I didn't expect to see you till all hours. . . ."

"It's almost two o'clock," Retta said. "And Dallas gets to work by six in the morning."

"I just couldn't get to sleep," her father said. He lifted his glass. "I decided on a stiff brandy and some time to myself." He gestured toward the woods and moonlit pond. "I never get tired of looking at that view."

The three of them stood together for a moment,

silenced by their individual thoughts and the beauty of the night. It was her father who spoke first, jarring the moment of magic that had joined them together. Strangely, he spoke almost the same words that Dallas had uttered just a couple of hours ago.

"Well, Dobson," he said. "This prom . . . was it what you hoped it would be?"

Dallas was thoughtful and then said, "This has nothing to do with Retta, remember. She was the prettiest girl there. I wanted her to be happy, but. . . ." He seemed at a loss for words, then he continued, "I don't know what I expected, but I do know it wasn't there. Tomorrow I'll show up at the Kennellys' and I'll do that the next day and the next. And I'll still be a dozen credits short of being a real senior. Nothing's changed. The prom wasn't really *anything*, except to be with Retta. It was just the same people but in fancier clothes. And it was still the school gym, even with some balloons floating around. I thought I would feel *different*. Maybe there's something wrong with me."

Her father's tone was serious, thoughtful. "I think I understand what you mean. For some people, it's never the right time for proms, Dallas. Maybe you're one of them. Maybe you're already too much a man for these things."

"Maybe I'm too old, or maybe I wasn't young long enough," Dallas said. "Whatever my feelings were tonight, they caught me by surprise. At least some of them."

He leaned forward in the moon-touched darkness and kissed Retta — a light, swift kiss on her hair.

"Good-night, and I love you," he whispered. "I love you a lot."

Moments later, she heard the pickup truck pull out the front gate, and the night was so still that she began to wonder if he had spoken at all. Or if those were just words she wanted to hear.

"I'm going to bed now, Poppy," she said. "But I have to ask you something. Why were you waiting up for me, tonight of all nights? Are you worried — about Dallas and me?"

"No, no, it's not that at all," he said. "I don't want you to think that." He took a sip of brandy and then a deep breath. "Retta, your mother wanted to tell both you and Two tomorrow. But I think you should know now. I'm standing here looking out at this magnificent land and a solitude that won't be ours much longer. Mr. Berger called from Philadelphia today. We lost our last appeal to the highway department. They agreed to pay us the minimum worth for our land in a lump sum, but the Zenith bypass is going to come through."

She was torn between searing anger and an acute sense of helplessness. Anger seemed the more stable emotion.

"Why us?" she said bitterly. "Why now? We are all so happy here. Caldwells have always been here. The old cave where Two and I played, the daffodils we planted at the pond, those fir trees that Grandmama Caldwell put along the drive every year since you were a boy. It's not fair. It can't happen. I can't *stand it* if a highway ruins our lives."

"We *have* to stand it, Henrietta," her father said.

"And I believe we will. Not because we're Caldwells and have strong backbones, but because it's the law. The state has decided that this highway is 'for the good of the people,' and that just proves we're only people, after all. Caldwells can get hurt, too. There's nothing more that your mother and I, or a high-priced lawyer, can do."

Henrietta ran from the terrace and up to her room without turning on a light. Moonlight lay in squares on the floor and she threw herself facedown on the bed, not caring about the new red dress or the fragile flowers on her wrist. She buried her face in the pillow but her eyes were dry, sobs mute. She tried to make her mind as blank as an empty page. She did not want to know or analyze the thoughts that might be there. With so much joy and so much sorrow in one evening, it seemed safer to experience no emotion at all.

Chapter
11

With the beginning of March, several things happened that marred the mood and routine of the Caldwell household. Carter Caldwell flew to California twice in two weeks. The phone number at which he could be reached was scrawled on a pad next to the upstairs phone: Whenever he called home, his wife took the phone into their bedroom, snaking the cord under the door and shutting it tight.

One Saturday morning, a middle-aged man in a business suit came to call and walked through the whole house, room by room, with Mrs. Caldwell. He stayed a long time.

Next Saturday, the same man came again with

two other men and they went through the same careful inspection. "Just business, dear," her mother had said brusquely. "Keep your brother out of our way and I'll explain everything when and if the time comes."

And then there were the strange phone calls, usually late at night. Twice Retta answered, and at her first hello, the calling party hung up.

But it was on St. Patrick's Day, the seventeenth of March, that the first menacing gargantuan highway construction machinery showed up first on the main road and then on the Caldwell property itself. Retta knew she would remember that date forever, not only for the machines, but because Junior Provanza had made everyone laugh at lunchtime by wearing a green felt bowler and matching necktie. And he told Retta similar road equipment had appeared that morning near his father's store.

When she drove home later that day, she saw that the barbed-wire fencing on one side of the meadow had been clipped open. And in another area, a whole stretch of rails from the split-rail fence had been removed and dumped in the roadside ditches.

Day by day, the destruction increased. All the machinery was painted yellow, the bulldozers, trucks, cranes, and power saws. They moved at speed along fence lines, and then turned to bite deeper into the acreage, knocking down trees, clearing away boulders, and scooping up the earth to make an access road. From dawn till near dark, the air sang with the whine of electric saws. Many of the Caldwell trees were so big that they had to be cut down, sawed up, and hauled away before a bulldozer could get through.

To Retta, the huge yellow machines were like things alive, demented dinosaurs that roared and ate the earth closer and closer to the house. Whole stands of trees — birch, oak, wild fruit trees — were snapped off and bulldozed into huge piles, branches interlacing; splayed, twisted roots stretching, turned up to the air. Everywhere was the smell of wet soil and the sick-sweet smell of dripping winter sap.

"Can't we do something?" she asked her mother desperately one day. "Can't we at least cut down our own trees for logs or timber? Must we let everything just be destroyed this way?"

"No, we cannot claim the trees," she said, her face pale and taut. "Your father and I wanted to do that but the answer was no. That land has been condemned. Nothing on it belongs to us anymore."

Retta began to study more and more at school, staying as late as possible, or stopping at the Ambersons', or even driving around the bleak countryside, far from her home, until the yellow machines came to rest for the night. She felt more at peace if she did not have to hear them, even though she knew they were parked out there, somewhere in the dusk. Sometimes Dallas rode around with her until it was time to work at the Kennellys'. They rarely spoke, but he kept his arm around the back of her seat, fingers smoothing her hair or gently touching her cheek, as lightly as a man soothing a kitten.

110

One late afternoon, Retta took the country lane that passed Little Tennessee, then looped back around the north end of the Caldwell land. The sight was ugly and defeating. Over the past few days, the power saw and big bulldozers had taken down the graceful rim of dogwood and tulip trees that had protected the farm pond and hidden it from sight. It was easily seen from the main road now. It stood raw and naked, its banks bare, the water a turgid snow-gray, with chunks of ice still floating on the surface.

Near them a bulldozer roared along an access road, then disappeared from sight. Dallas said, "Damned cowboys. They don't even know how to drive those things."

And then there was another sound, faint, shrill, and human. It was Dallas Dobson who heard it. "Stop the car," he shouted. "Stop here, Retta!"

She turned off the motor as Dallas leaped from the car, stepped high over a tangle of cut barbed-wire fencing, and raced toward the pond. "We're coming," he shouted.

It was then she saw a little boy, not more than six or seven, standing on the bank, shouting and waving his arms. On the pond nearby floated the old paddleboat, the little pleasure craft she and Two had played with for years. Someone had untied the rope that held it to the pier. Lying on the ground, knocked down by the bulldozer, was a warning sign her brother had made in woodcraft class. Spattered with mud now, the sign still read clearly: NO SWIMMING, NO FISHING, NO BOATING, NO *NOTHING*.

The young boy was close to hysteria. He pointed

at the water and sobbed, "My little brother's in there."

The big yellow bulldozer, making a return trip, sighted the figures on the bank. Dallas shouted at the driver, "Get the paramedics! There's trouble here!"

As the driver reached for his two-way radio, Dallas stood motionless for a few seconds, scanning the surface of the gray water, touched into ripples by a breeze and rocking slightly with small, jagged sheets of ice.

Then he pulled off his boots and jacket and dived in quickly, jackknifing through the surface and arrowing toward the muddy bottom. For long moments, Retta could not see him at all. Then he surfaced, sucking in for breath, and dived again.

"Run," Retta said to the young boy. "Tell your daddy to come here."

"My daddy's at work," he said.

"Get your momma, then." She pushed him from behind. "Run! Get somebody!"

The boy ran off toward the direction of Little Tennessee. Dallas surfaced and dived again, so rapidly that she could not see his face or read his eyes. Could he ever find anyone in those murky waters — and in time? Retta was not wearing a watch, but her heartbeats pounded out the seconds and the minutes.

The construction worker came running toward the pond. "I got through," he said. "The paramedics are coming from Zenith."

Water, cold, dark, splashing, closed over Dobson as he dived and surfaced again and again. Then, after an eternity of tension, he surfaced holding a small boy in his arms, a child no more than four years old, limp and inert as a cloth doll.

The highway worker helped to pull Dobson and the unconscious boy onto the bank, saying over and over again, "Help's comin', man. Help's comin'."

Dobson bent over the limp body, clamping his mouth over the little boy's. He sucked in deeply and spat out the pond water that came into his own mouth. Then he laid the child facedown on the bank, head tilted downward, cheek resting on a folded arm, the small, blue-lipped mouth pried open. He knelt over the boy and began a rhythmic pressure on his ribs, trying to press water from the lungs and keep the heart beating. The child's eyes were closed but with each powerful push on his rib cage, a thin trickle of pond water spilled from his lips.

A woman who looked not much older than Retta came running over the muddy field to the pond. She surveyed the scene, her eyes bright with tears, and then said to Retta, "I'm his mama. It's in the Lord's hands. Fall on your knees and pray with me."

The two young women knelt side by side on the damp ground, lips moving with silent pleas. The boy's mother had her eyes shut tight, face tilted toward the sky, and her grip on Retta's hand burned like fire, the sharp, digging nails drawing an ooze of blood.

The construction worker was bending over Dallas, talking in a low, urgent voice, but Dobson never changed his pressure and rhythm. Suddenly, the little boy vomited violently and uttered a single cry of panic.

113

His mother ran to her son, but Retta stayed on her knees. "We need you, God," she said. "Let him stay alive. Let him be a grown-up boy. All of us want that. God, I'm trying to trust You. . . . Dallas trusts You. . . ."

The thin, urgent wail of a siren snaked through the air and grew louder as it reached the Caldwells' gate. Then the paramedics in their red van made a sharp turn into the meadow, speeded down the lane between the apple trees, and pulled up to the spot where Dallas held the little boy, limp but with his eyes open, holding fast to his mother's hand.

The night darkness seemed to press against the walls of the house, making an opaque mirror of the big front windows, dancing now with the reflection from the fireplace.

Mrs. Caldwell had driven into Zenith with Jimmy-John (the boy had recovered enough to whisper his name to Dallas at the pond) and his mother in the paramedic ambulance. Retta called her father at the newspaper office and explained what had happened. He had driven over to the hospital to meet his wife.

Dallas sat in front of the fireplace, his long arms and legs protruding from one of Carter Caldwell's jogging suits. In the room off the kitchen, the clothes drier still turned, drying out his pond-soaked clothes. His wet boots stood in front of the fireplace, steaming a little in the heat.

"Mrs. Jessup is so grateful to you, Dallas," Retta's mother said.

114

"We have a lot to be grateful for," Carter Caldwell said. "No way of knowing for sure how long that little tad had been in the water. But the doctors say there is no brain damage. Jimmy-John was sitting up in bed drinking orange juice when we left. All his responses are normal. He'd have been talking his head off if he weren't so shy. The doctor's going to keep him in the hospital a couple of days for observation anyway. He *did* get a lot of cold water in his lungs."

"That poor lady," Mrs. Caldwell said. "Now all she's got to worry about is paying hospital and doctor bills. Her husband is just a part-time picker in a mushroom house."

"But I *told* you," Henrietta said. "The state and the highway department have to take responsibility for *everything*: doctor, hospital bills, and maybe some talks with a good psychologist so that Jimmy-John doesn't go through life with drowning nightmares. Maybe other damages for pain and suffering. That highway worker told Dallas he had asked his boss to replace that fencing and put our warning sign back up. He knew the highway builders had made that pond an 'attractive nuisance,' and that's against the law."

"Do you have the man's name?" Caldwell asked Dobson. The young man nodded. "And what exactly did he say?"

Dallas was silent a moment, then said, "Let me think about it. I'm not quite sure."

"But you told me everything!" Henrietta said. "All you've got to do now is go into town tomorrow and give Squire DeLepino a deposition. Tell him just what you told me. He'll take it from there."

Retta knew she was pressing, that her voice was high and tense, but she had not been able to calm down since the shocking moment when she heard the plea, "My little brother's in there."

"It isn't often that we get a story right on our own property. We'll take a picture of you tomorrow, Dallas, for the front page. Our readers will want to know what a hero looks like."

Dobson seemed uneasy. He passed the back of his hand over his forehead as if he had a fever or felt faint. Mr. Caldwell took over with concerned authority. "We should not underestimate the trauma of what you two young people went through this afternoon. Retta, if you take a hot bath and get into bed, I'm sure your mother will bring you a dinner tray. Dallas, you just wrap yourself in a blanket and we'll get your clothes tomorrow. Right now, I'd like to drive you home."

"But *I* wanted to do that," Retta said.

Dallas shook his head, his face troubled. "Let your father do it, will you?" he said. "And Mrs. Caldwell, could you skip that part in your article with my name in it, especially the hero part? And the picture?"

"We're not on deadline," she answered. "Let's talk about it tomorrow. Are you sure you're well enough to go home?"

He shrugged. "Maybe I swallowed more pond water than I thought. I feel all cold inside."

Chapter 12

News of the rescue spread fast through the community. Before breakfast, the phone had begun to ring. Her mother was talking to Mrs. Amberson when Retta waved good-bye and left for school.

She might have been forewarned but she wasn't. She sighted Dallas waiting for her long before she reached the Kennelly gate. He carried no schoolbooks and his shoulders were hunched, both hands jammed deep into his jeans pockets. As she drew up at the side of the road, he signaled her to roll down her window.

"I want to tell you straight off," he said. "I'm not going to Squire DeLepino or anyone else to give a deposition about what happened yesterday. And I'm not going to have my picture taken for your paper. It's over and done with. My father doesn't want me to get involved."

"*Get* involved? You *are* involved. You know something that can help someone else."

"It could go hard for him down at the feed store, my father says, if word got round that the Dobsons are troublemakers. He could get fired. We're not exactly wired in this community, you know."

"But it's the *right* thing to do, Dallas."

"My father doesn't think so and I won't go against what he says. He's always been square with me."

"I just don't understand."

"All men aren't created equal, my father said that last night. All men aren't born Caldwells. . . ."

"Will you stop thinking the Caldwells are something special," she said, a new heat in her voice. "It's Dallas Dobson's turn to stand up and be counted."

He looked at her evenly, his eyes cold and steady. "Maybe I'm just not ready for that," he said.

They stared at each other for some moments, stunned at the depth and danger of their anger. Then he said, "I guess you want me to find another way to get to school from now on."

"I didn't say that," she protested.

"Not in words," he said bitterly. "Not in words, but I can read your face, Miss Caldwell. But remember this. He could have given me away when I was just a kid. But he didn't do that, did he?"

He struck the side of the car suddenly, with the flat of his hand, a hard, fast blow, like a cowboy goading a bronco. The sound echoed through the

118

quiet morning woods as sharp as a rifle shot.

Retta gunned the motor and took off alone. Gravel as loud as the sting of hailstones hit the sides and underbelly of the little car as she sped away.

It wasn't that they refused to speak to each other. They just avoided being in the same places at the same time. At lunchtime, Retta was aware he sat at a table in a far corner, bringing his lunch in a brown bag rather than risk meeting her in the cafeteria line. Several times she had sighted him studying in the library, his head resting deep in the cup of his two hands, the palms blanking out his vision on both sides, like a horse with blinders. And Junior Provanza was picking him up at the Kennellys' each morning. Junior's twin sister, Parma, had told her that, putting her arm around Retta's shoulders and whispering, "It's better that you broke up, I think. He's almost nineteen and that's too old for you. And besides. . . ." Retta had moved quickly away and into a classroom.

Evenings were no better. She checked out some Spanish language tapes from the library and played them in her room night after night, eager to hear a human voice, to let it drive away the melancholia that kept splintering her thoughts. The silence of the telephone was maddening, loud as a phantom shriek, echoing through her imagination like a kind of demon. He had never called her at home, she rationalized, and certainly he wouldn't do it now.

Carter Caldwell made a fifth trip to California, and one afternoon, when she called her mother at the newspaper to get permission to spend the night at the Ambersons', she was told Mrs. Caldwell had an appointment at the bank and wouldn't be available until the close of business.

Retta left a note and drove over to Charlie's. She was embarrassed and aware that Mrs. Amberson was treating her differently, soft-voiced and solicitous, offering Retta tea and ginger cookies as if she were some kind of invalid.

Even lying in the twin bed in Charlotte's room, lights out, the radio turned low to a rock station in Coatesville, it was hard to sleep. At midnight, Charlotte said softly, "Don't mind me, Retta. Go ahead. Cry if you want to."

"I don't need to cry," she said sharply. "I have nothing to cry about."

"Sure you do," Charlotte said. "I don't even have a boyfriend and I find something to cry about at least twice a week. A sad song, hurting a sweet nerd like Junior Provanza, my future — we've all got something to cry about."

By midspring the days had stretched longer, so long that the Caldwell family could see the highway damage all around them until the sun faded around seven in the evening. The land stripped of ground cover, the mounds of uprooted and bulldozed trees, the thirty-foot gully behind the house that would soon be a six-lane highway; even the huge yellow road machines were visible from every window, standing silent for the night, like dangerous, lethal insects, caught in a brooding torpor.

"April is the cruelest month. . . ." Those words from the famous poet, T.S. Eliot, ran through Retta's thoughts as she sat at the dinner table one evening. Her father was home again, his face tanned by the California sun, but his eyes were sad; two little lines had etched themselves at the corner of his mouth.

He wants to tell us something, she thought, *something he knows we don't want to hear. This is the way we do things, the Caldwell family. We use the dinner table for our forum, to plan and talk and ask and explain. Careful, civilized, loving each other.* Her heartbreak over Dallas was deep, so pervasive, that she believed she could not be hurt further by anything her father had to say. But she was.

"All right," her father said as her mother passed dessert, plates of fruit and cheese. "It's time we talked. Your mother and I have made some mighty big decisions. We had to. But we still want to hear what you two have to say."

Neither Retta nor her brother moved or spoke.

"This family is going to make a big move. The *Zenith Press* has been losing money, too much money. But we've managed to sell the building and presses to a printing firm. The profits weren't much, but we're lucky to get what we did. And we have arranged to sell this house to a hotel conglomerate."

"Yes," their mother said. "Those men you've seen looking over the house — they've decided to buy it, and what land the highway department left for us, to make into a country motel, the kind of place city folk might like to come for a weekend. They also agreed to buy much of our furniture, a few good antiques, and some other pieces which fit in here and wouldn't be right for where we're going."

"A motel?" Two said in disbelief. "A *Caldwell motel*?"

"Not Caldwell anymore," his father said briskly. "It will be called The Red Fox Inn. The promoters will start with our six bedrooms and three baths, then build a unit for thirty more rooms, extending from the rear of the house. I've seen their plans, and they are going to make a first-class establishment. They expect to enlarge the kitchen, too, and put small tables in this room as a country restaurant."

"*My room,*" Retta said in a low voice. "You mean strangers will sleep upstairs in *my* room?"

Her father nodded. "The buyers liked that room especially, the size, the double views. There is some talk about making it into a country bridal suite."

"But where will *we* be?" Retta asked.

"We will be starting out fresh," her father answered. "The Caldwell family has enough assets to build a small plant and start a new newspaper, plus purchase a good ranch-type house in Thirty-Nine Palms, California. Your mother and I would like to make the move by the middle of May. Before the highway is completed here, and before the summer heat sets in out there. I'll go on out ahead."

"Carter," his wife said gently. "You've forgotten one very important thing." She turned to Retta. "Both you and Two have grown up here on Springhill, but you, Retta, especially, are at an age when old friends are deeply important to you." She paused. "If you *want*, you can stay on here till June, then come back to Havendale High for your senior year. You can graduate with your class and friends. Mrs. Amberson has agreed to have you stay with Charlie and her, just like one of the family. We'd pay room and board, of course, and we'd be generous. Without her job at the *Zenith Press*, the Ambersons will need the money. Would you like that, do you think?"

Retta could think of nothing to say. She was aware of her own silence, then the silence of her parents, waiting for her response. But instead of answering her mother's fateful query, she asked her father a new question.

"Why do they call the town Thirty-Nine Palms? Are there exactly thirty-nine palm trees there?"

He laughed. "Maybe not yet, but there will be. It's a completely new desert development. Kind of an instant city about twenty miles from Palm Springs. Ranch houses, lots of swimming pools, a country club, and three new golf courses. Our newspaper will be the voice of the community from the very beginning. We're taking our talents and skills where the money is, Retta."

Retta knew she had been stalling for time, trying to collect her thoughts and emotions. Her next words were so grave, so portentous that she had to force herself to speak. It was like closing a heavy, brass-bound door, something so strong, so final that she would never be able to open it again.

"You're wrong about my choosing to stay here with friends," she said. "Maybe before, but not now. I want to stay part of this family. . . ."

Later that evening, restless and unable to sleep, Two brought up a couple of soft drinks from the kitchen, then sat at the foot of his sister's bed to whisper in the dark.

"You're coming with us for *sure*?" he said.

She nodded. "But I simply cannot understand what's happening. A full continent away! How can they *do* this to us?"

Her brother was thoughtful, a small, wiry figure hunched up in the darkness. "I think I understand why we must leave, Retta," Two said at last. "It's what Carter needs, mostly. He loves this place so much, and he's loved it *so long* . . . well . . . he can't stand being nearby, can he, Retta?"

Mrs. Caldwell began preparing for the move to the West Coast with her usual efficiency. She bought sheets of colored stick-on dots from a Zenith stationery store and explained her color coding to the family. Blue dots for all the furniture and housewares that were included in the sale of Springhill. Red dots for the give-aways or "maybes," articles that would probably go to a Coatesville auctioneer for resale. And yellow dots for all the "musts," the things the Caldwells loved the most — furniture and family heirlooms — that must make the trip to California.

Local movers came to start packing, and each day, after school, there were fewer books on the shelves, kitchen cupboards were stripped down to a minimum of articles for daily use, and the Gorham silver coffee service was gone from the dining room sideboard.

One afternoon, Retta overheard her mother say quietly to her brother, "Please believe me, Two. I know how hard it is on you and your sister. But those yellow dots you've stuck on *so many* things . . . you've got to thin out your 'musts.' The house in California isn't that big. And we'll be living differently out there."

Chapter
13

After the first of May, decisions and plans became realities. Carter Caldwell closed down the office of the *Zenith Press* and cleared out his big desk in the library at home. He left for Thirty-Nine Palms the next weekend.

In the woods and machine-racked fields around the Caldwell property, activity was stepped up. Now the great yellow machines were visible from the main roads, the side roads, and every window in the house. The great muddy trough directly behind the house was deepening. For Retta, the swift and noisy yellow machines were more than ever like a swarm of demented, uncontrollable hornets, backing and filling in giant clouds of dust, ceasing their erratic destruction only when night fell.

One of the prime chores of the highway workers now was to sort out, amass, and pile up the great jungle of felled timber behind the house. Trees were dragged and pushed and bulldozed over the earth to be heaped into towering piles until there were finally eight massive stacks of trees, thousands in each pile. And around these pyres the bulldozers buzzed and circled, making broad, deep slashes in the earth to act as firebreaks.

"Firebreaks!" Retta asked her mother in disbelief. "They're not going to *burn* those beautiful trees!"

"That's the way they plan to do it. Those trees don't belong to us anymore," her mother said wearily. "But we'll be on our way to the new house before then, Retta."

The following week, two giant moving vans backed up to the Caldwells' front door and began loading the items marked with yellow dots. The air was rancid with the smell of their diesel engines and the big, tripletread tires ripped ribbons of sod out of the front lawn. *T.S. Eliot was wrong,* Retta thought sadly. *April is not the cruelest month. May is worse — much, much worse.*

The moving vans were scheduled to make the cross-country trip in five days, and on the fourth day, Mrs. Caldwell flew out to help set up the new house. Two moved in with friends, since his twin beds had been shipped out, but Retta opted to stay at Springhill alone.

"All right," her mother had agreed with reluctance. "The dogs don't go to the vets for their fly-out trip till next week. They'll keep you company. But I don't want you brooding, Retta. You can keep busy and help me a lot by sorting out the last three trunks of papers and records in the attic. Everything that might be important to the family — birth records, school report cards, anything of that sort — put aside for me. And the rest, including nearly twenty years of those Christmas cards I've saved, just throw them away."

Rainstorms had threatened the area all day, with clouds dark and gray-green as old bruises, and flashes of lightning that ripped open the sky like bright, jagged zippers. At school, Retta tried to concentrate on work, ignoring the heavy overcast that darkened the classrooms, and the damp, raw smell of impending rain. Yet by four o'clock there was a sudden rift in the heavy clouds that showed blue skies. At sunset, the sky was a delicate pink, touched lightly with wisps of white clouds. The storm seemed to have passed.

At nightfall, Retta brought a tuna sandwich and a cup of tea up to the attic with her. She was sorting through the second trunk, half lost in the memories of first grade drawings and children's valentines, when she was aware of someone pounding on the back door, three floors below.

She ran down the stairs and knew, from the sight of his bright yellow hard hat, that the caller at the door was a highway worker.

The man was big and stocky, hair gray under the trim of his hard hat. His voice was careful, almost apologetic, when he said, "I've been authorized to inform you and your family, Miss, that there's been a change in our schedule. You were informed sometime ago that the surplus trees wouldn't be set afire for another ten days. But Official Weather says we've got some wet days ahead. We're going to have enough trouble incinerating green wood. We don't want it wet, too."

"What are you trying to tell me?" she said.

"Well, the total burn-up on those surplus trees can take as long as three or four days. But we want to get started. We've got orders to light up tonight."

Retta closed all the shutters in the house, then made a fresh cup of tea and went back to the attic. Over her head, a single high-watt light bulb swayed on a long cord, sending shifting shadows over the old trunks and the sorted piles of paper.

She no longer knew what time it was, how long she worked alone in the attic when something in the second trunk caught her attention, not because it was conspicuous — but because it wasn't. Her fingers touched several sheets of paper, held together with a rusted paper clip, tucked in the side pocket of the otherwise empty trunk.

As she carefully unfolded the dry, brittle sheets, flecks of paper dropped on her jeans, as light and fragile as flower petals. There was no date, so it wasn't part of a diary. It had no title, so it wasn't a class assignment. There was no salutation or signature so it wasn't a letter. Whatever it was was written in a rambling, loose style, as if someone were talking on paper. The handwriting was not completely familiar. It was somewhat like her mother's but smaller and lighter, with erasures and cross-outs as if the writer did not know quite what to say.

Retta glanced at the first few sentences and then put up her hand to stop the light bulb from swaying. Her tea was cold but she sipped it anyway, glad for the acrid tannic coolness on her dry lips.

Now don't get me wrong, were the first words Retta read. Then:

> *I want you to understand from the beginning that I'm not really dumb. I know what a girl should do and what she shouldn't. I get around. I read. And I have two older sisters. So you see, I know what the score is. It's important that you understand that.*

The next half dozen sentences had been blacked out, so Retta turned the page.

> *You see, it was funny how I met him. It was a winter night like any other winter night. But the way the moon tinseled the twigs and silver-plated the snowdrifts, I just couldn't stay inside. The skating rink isn't far from our house — you can make it in five minutes — so I went skating. But first I borrowed my sister's lipstick and then brushed my hair hard, so hard it clung to my hand and stood up around my head in a hazy halo.*

> *My skates were hanging by the back door all nice and shiny, for I'd just gotten them*

for Christmas, and they smelled so queer —
just like fresh smoked ham. My dog walked
with me as far as the corner. She's a red
chow, very polite and well-mannered, and
she kept pretending it was me she liked,
when all the time I knew it was the ham
smell. She panted along beside me, and
her hot breath made a frosty little balloon
balancing on the end of her nose. The night
was breathlessly quiet, and the stars winked
down like a million flirting eyes. It was all
so lovely.

It was all so lovely I ran most of the
way. I had to cut across someone's back
garden to get to the rink, and last summer's grass stuck through the ice, brown
and discouraged. Not many people came
through this way, and the crusted snow
broke through the hollows between corn
stubbles frozen hard in the ground. I was
out of breath when I got to the shanty —
out of breath with running and with the
loveliness of the night.

When I started to skate, it was snowing
a little, quick, eager little soaplike flakes
that melted as soon as they touched my
hand. I waited a moment. You know, to
start to skate at a crowded rink is like
jumping on a moving merry-go-round. The
skaters go skimming around in a colored
blur, like gaudy painted horses, and the

shrill musical jabber re-echoes in the night from a hundred human calliopes. Once in, I went all right.

And then he came. All of a sudden his arm was around my waist so warm and tight, and he said very casually, "Mind if I skate with you?" Then he took my other hand.

That's all there was to it. Just that, and then we were skating. It wasn't as if I had never skated with a boy before. Don't be silly. I told you before I get around. But this boy was different. He was tall, very tall, and at least three years older than I. And he could skate like a professional, almost as if he'd been born to skate with me.

At first I can't remember what we talked about; I can't even remember if we talked at all. We just skated and skated and then we began to laugh at something, and soon we were laughing at nothing at all. It was all so lovely.

Later, we sat on the snowbank at the edge of the rink and just watched. It was cold at first, but pretty soon I felt warm all over. He threw a handful of snow at me, and it fell in a little white shower on my hair. He leaned over to brush it off. I held my breath. The night stood still.

Then he sat up straight and said, "We'd better start home." Not, "Shall I take you home?" or "Do you live far?" but, "We'd better start home." See, that's how I know he wanted to take me home. Not because he had to, but because he wanted to.

It began to snow harder as we walked. Big, quiet flakes that clung to twiggy bushes and snuggled in little drifts against the tree trunks. The night was an etching in black and white. It was all so lovely, I was sorry I lived only a few blocks away. He talked softly as we walked, as if every little word were a secret. He said he thought we should go out again sometime, then something about how nice I looked with snow in my hair, and — finally — had I ever seen the moon so close? A misted moon was following us as we walked, ducking playfully behind a chimney every time I turned to look at it. And then we were home.

The porch light was on and we stood there a moment by the front steps, as the snow turned pinkish in the glow of the colored light and a few feathery flakes settled on his hair. He had been carrying my skates and he put them over my shoulder and said, "Good-night now. I'll call you." . . . "I'll call you," he said.

I went inside then, and in a moment he was gone. I watched him from my window as he went down the street. He was whistling softly, and I waited until the sound faded away so I couldn't tell if it was he

133

or my heart whistling out there in the night.
And then he was gone, completely gone.
I shivered. Everything was quiet.

The last two pages were blurred, almost as if they had gotten damp in the trunk, or someone had cried. From outside, Retta heard a series of distinct but muffled sounds, like the bursting of distant balloons or the cottoned puff of explosions.

She laid the last handwritten pages on the floor, and used her finger to trace them word for word, forcing meaning from the smudged pages.

And that was two months ago, the writing said, *two months ago last Thursday. Tonight is Tuesday, and my homework's done, and I darned some socks that didn't really need it, and I worked a crossword puzzle, and I listened to the radio, and now I'm just sitting. I'm just sitting because I can't think of anything else to do. I can't think of anything — anything but snowflakes and ice skates and yellow moons and that Thursday night. The telephone is sitting on the corner table with its old black face turned to the wall, so I can't see its leer. I don't even jump when it rings anymore. My heart still prays, but my mind just laughs. Outside the night is so still — so still I think I'll go crazy — and the white snow's all dirtied and smoked into grayness, and the wind is blowing the arc light so it throws weird, waving shadows from*

the trees onto the lawn — like thin starved
arms begging for I don't know what.

There was a sudden increase of light in the attic, as if a surge of energy had gone through the light bulb. Retta looked up but the bulb was just as it had been before, no brighter, no less.

The last lines of the page were written in a hasty scrawl, as if the effort to put the words down had become too sad for the writer to bear. They read:

And so I'm just sitting here, and I'm not feeling anything. I'm not even sad, be-cause all of a sudden I know. All of a sudden I know. I can sit here forever, and laugh and laugh while the tears run salty in the corners of my mouth. For all of a sudden I know. I know what the stars knew all the time; he'll never, never call — never.

Retta sat motionless, wondering what it was she had read, and who was speaking out with such heartbreak, almost like herself, from those old pages.

Then she became aware of intense heat and a light film of sweat on her forehead. Something had happened, something had changed. A spasm of panic clutched her throat. She folded the pages together, put them in her jeans pocket, and ran to an attic window. A loose shutter moved under her fingers and she pushed it outward into the night.

Behind the bulldozed firebreaks and stretching over hundreds of yards were eight huge bonfires, so alive with licking, biting flames that they seemed to have a life of their own, like demons, malevolent and tortured.

From the intensity of the blazes, Retta judged that the wood had been doused with flammable liquid before lighting. That would account for the small, muffled explosions she had heard as each mound was lit and burst into flames. Already slender limbs had begun to buckle with heat and fall back into the fire. Bunches of flaming leaves burst off the branches and sailed into the night sky. It was as if everything she had known all her life was going up in an inferno.

As she ran downstairs and toward the fires, she knew she was crying because her eyes stung with tears, but it was anger, not sorrow, that was her deepest emotion.

She hurried down one of the plowed-up auxiliary roads until she was in a direct line with the conflagrations, facing one of the blazing heaps of brush and timber. Then she stopped short, feeling the heat scorch her cheeks and turn tears dry and sandy on her eyeballs. The trees seemed like living things to her, writhing and collapsing in the flames, and the fire was noisy, both crackling and sucking, as it consumed the timber. The acrid smoke smelled of whatever kind of tree was burning — wild apple, cherry, spruce, or king maple — and the air was sweet and pungent with the smell of scalding sap.

She was so consumed with anguish and horror at what was happening that she did not hear a car nor the footsteps of Dallas Dobson until he seized her by both shoulders and forced her to move back from the flames. She fought him with fury, pounding at his chest, kicking against his hard cowboy boots, crying in soft, breathy sobs like an exhausted child. She knew she was hysterical, almost out of control, but it seemed that nothing could stop her pain.

He held her tight, trying to pinion her arms with one of his own, using his free hand to smooth her hair and touch her cheek with his fingertips. "Charlie called me. Provanza called her. The fires are lit on their land, too." And then his voice was low, no more than a whisper, a little singsong of love and comfort. "I couldn't let you be alone, baby," he said again and again. "I couldn't be away from you."

He turned with her in his arms so his body was between her and the flames. Her emotions were so taut, so raw, that she did not completely register the change from anger and hysteria to the new passion that gripped her. She moved closer to him, touching his face, feeling that she could never kiss him enough. As she reached up, he put his big hands at her waist to support her, and she seemed to sway on the tips of her toes, barely touching the earth.

Without speaking, in a mutual motion as fluid as if they were one body, they sank to the ground, never losing their embrace, never breaking their kiss. Retta believed with all her soul that she was ready for what now seemed inevitable.

It was Dallas Dobson who broke the spell. He sat up suddenly and put his head in his hands, like a man in despair. For moments he was silent, and then, as she sat up beside him, he took her hand and kissed the palm, as if he were laying some golden promise within her grasp. But his voice was taut with bewilderment and emotional pain.

"Retta," he said, "trust me. This is all wrong for us. It *can't* be this way. I *can't* be a spoiler like my father. . . ."

If they spoke after that, she couldn't remember, but she felt her thoughts, her breathing, become more calm, more rational. They sat apart, not touching, but neither made a move to go back to the house. They turned to look at each other at the same time and she tried to smile. In the blaze of the firelight, she saw him as through a screen of red, every feature distinct but enlivened with brilliance. In his eyes she could see a tiny, quivering reflection of the flames and knew he must see the same fires as he looked at her.

Chapter
14

The two days that followed had the fragmented, painful quality of a nightmare. Powerful things were happening to Retta and her life. She knew this was true but could not trust herself to believe it. The dogs, badly frightened by the fires, stayed close to the house, whimpering and panting. Retta set out a pan of water for them before leaving for school each morning.

Other farms with condemned lands had had their trees set to burn. For miles around, the air was flecked with bits of charred ash and the thin trail of smoke curved all the way from the outskirts of Zenith and off into the distance where the proposed highways snaked toward Baltimore.

At school on the last day, Retta checked her locker for forgotten library books, got a month's refund on her parking slot, and turned in her current texts. During that final lunch hour, Mr. Engel led her classmates in a farewell cheer that ended, "Retta! Retta! Rah! Rah! Retta!"

Dallas Dobson sought her out between classes, just to walk a few steps together, and sat at her table at lunchtime, looking at her, watching her face.

"No way? You're sure there's no way you could stay?" he asked the last day.

She shook her head. "Mother got back from California yesterday. Our plane tickets are for tomorrow." Then she answered his question before he spoke it. "Leaving is hard enough, Dallas. I don't want you at the airport. Please."

Yet it was more than her own immediate feelings that bothered Retta. The strange bit of writing, so akin to her own fears, burned in her mind. She put the pages in an envelope and set them on the fireplace mantel in the front hall.

There was no longer food in the refrigerator, and since Two was going to the airport with friends, Retta and her mother had dinner in the front hall, perched on packing barrels, with hero sandwiches Mrs. Caldwell had bought at Provanza's.

In the early evening, the phone rang constantly from family friends wanting to say a last good-bye. Charlie Amberson called three times, the last to ask if Retta would fly back from California to be maid of honor if Charlie got married, or even had a date for that matter. Maryanna Nairn, a nearby neighbor, stopped by with a dozen daffodil bulbs dug up from her own garden. "When they bloom in California, remember us," she said, then ran to her station wagon in tears.

It was nearly midnight before Retta could find the quiet moment she needed to question her mother. At last she turned from a packing barrel and said, "We can't do anything more tonight, except this, Mother."

Retta went to the mantelpiece and picked up the envelope with the tattered pages.

"I want you to tell me what it means." She slipped the pages out of the envelope and handed them to her mother.

Connie Caldwell drew in her breath sharply and took the fragile pages carefully, as if they might be hot to the touch. She sank down on the edge of a packing crate. "From where, Henrietta?" she said. "I haven't seen these pages for years."

"In a trunk in the attic. I found them just before . . . just before the fires were lit."

Connie Caldwell and Retta studied each other for a moment, and then Mrs. Caldwell said, "I hope you will try to be understanding. These pages are about something that happened to me a long time ago."

"But it's not a diary, it's not a story. What is it?"

"It was a report to a doctor."

"Were you ill?"

"Yes, but in a very special way. What happened in those pages happened to me. I tried to put it down just as I remembered it, just as I felt it."

Mrs. Caldwell put a hand over her eyes, then shook her head, as if she had found a thought there she couldn't tolerate. She looked squarely at her daughter. "Remember, I was Connie Jagerfeld then, just a small-town sixteen-year-old, living with her family in Zenith. It just happened. I went skating one night, met a boy who almost changed my life. I can't say I simply fell in love. It was more than that. I was infatuated, I was obsessed. I could think of nothing else. My own feelings got beyond me.

"As those pages tell you, I waited more than two months for a phone call. It was too much for me. In those days, one couldn't easily discuss problems with parents. Or my older sisters, for that matter. Anyway, I just didn't have the words. I couldn't sleep. I couldn't eat. And suddenly I began to cry, alone, in school, in crowds, for no reason I could put my finger on. I was melancholy, deeply, deeply depressed."

"Are you sure you want to tell me this?" Retta asked.

"Perhaps I should have told you before," her mother said. "But at sixteen, I didn't know where to turn, so I made an appointment with our family doctor, old Doctor Felix. I went secretly, after school. I tried to explain to him that I was sick because I was in love. Good, kind, dear man — he thought I meant I was pregnant."

"And were you?" Retta said.

Her mother smiled a little and shrugged. "One evening together. . . . Except when the boy and I were skating together, we didn't even hold

142

hands. . . . When I told Dr. Felix that, he said to me, 'Maybe it would help if you wrote it all down. Tell me in your own words what happened, how you feel. Then maybe I can help you.' "

"And that's what's on those pages?"

"Yes," her mother said. "I cried so hard that sometimes I couldn't see the paper, but I got it all down."

"And?"

"I brought my thoughts to Dr. Felix the next week. I sat in his big chair, watching him as he read, but I couldn't tell from his face what he thought.

"When he finished, he returned the pages to me and said, 'This will be between you and me, Connie. Your broken heart, I don't have any medicine to cure that. Maybe you can help yourself. My diagnosis is that you're a damned good writer. Make that talent work for you.' "

Her mother laughed lightly. "You know most of the rest. I forced myself to apply for a job on the school newspaper. I wrote girls' sports news for two years, then I was promoted to editorial. The editor of the paper finally asked me for a date. And that's how I got to know Carter Caldwell."

"And the other person, the boy you wrote about. Did he ever call you?"

"Back then, do you mean?"

"Back then."

"Yes, he did. About four months after that night at the skating rink. Gossip moves fast in a small town. I almost guessed what he wanted. The girl he'd been dating — they'd had a falling-out that night at the skating rink — was pregnant and wanted him to go away with her, leave town. He said that if I'd date him, if I'd pretend I was his girl all along, he could claim he wasn't the father. I told him I would never do that."

"And?"

"He and the girl left town. It was over as far as I was concerned. I heard they had gone somewhere down South."

For Retta, the small pieces of coincidence and fate were locking themselves together, piece by piece, into an almost complete picture. It was more than just Dallas and she. She remembered now the concern, the questions her father had asked her the morning after they had found the little fox together. And her mother's behavior that first night when Dallas stayed for dinner. The bright eyes, the pearls, the music, the candlelight.

"And that person from long ago," Retta said, trying to conceal the tremor in her voice. "You know where he is *now*, don't you, Mother? And he *did* call you again. . . ."

"Yes, to both questions. He called me some months ago and said he wanted to see me. He asked me to meet him in Zenith." Mrs. Caldwell began to pace the brick-floored foyer, short, quick steps that telegraphed her inner agitations. "I told him I would never do that."

"And he kept calling?"

"I'm not sure, but I think so. Remember those late-night calls we've been getting? Someone either says 'wrong number' or just hangs up? I think that's who's calling. That would be his way."

"And, Mother, that night of the big snowstorm, when Dallas had dinner and stayed the night with us. . . . Am I right about this? Your party clothes, the special dinner, the way you acted . . . that wasn't just for Dallas, was it?"

"He was a guest in our house. I wanted him to see us at our best. I wanted your friend to like me. . . ."

"But it wasn't *all* for him alone, was it? You wanted him to tell *someone else.*"

"That could be true, Retta. Some hurts are very deep. I suppose — in my secret heart — I may have wanted him to tell someone else about that evening."

Retta paused to be sure her voice was under control. Then she said, "The boy you loved so much — that was Danny Dobson, wasn't it?"

Mrs. Caldwell nodded. "It was Danny Dobson."

"And you didn't think I should be told about it?"

"Retta, please. Remember I said I hoped you'd be understanding. . . ." Her mother took a deep breath, then continued. "I didn't know that Danny Dobson had another son after Sam Houston. For weeks I didn't even know you *knew* someone named Dobson. I didn't hear of it until your father told me, after the night the two of you found the fox.

"But I'd noticed changes, your daydreaming, your new quietness, the look in your eyes after you'd been studying over at Charlie's. Then I learned there was a new Dobson in our lives. I realized what you must be feeling. I believed I owed you silence, a chance to make up your own mind. And I needed time

145

myself to think about Connie Caldwell, to be sure my own scars were healed."

Retta got to her feet and put out her hand to stop her parent's pacing. For the first time, she realized she was taller than her mother.

"Please," she said softly. "I *do* want to understand. But I need the absolute truth. Why are we doing all this? Mother, have we changed our lives because a highway came through our farm — or are we moving to California because Danny Dobson is back?"

Her mother's words were suddenly strong and sure. "Listen to me, Henrietta, and believe me. I am going to California because the man I love is there. In everyone's past, there is *some* pain. Mine was deep. Maybe I hung onto it too long. But I know myself. I married the man I love, deeply and truly. I haven't lived a lie these past twenty years."

The only phone still connected was in the upper hall, and when it rang, Retta Caldwell said, "That must be for you, Mother. No one would call me this late at night."

Mrs. Caldwell frowned, looked puzzled, then waited till the phone had rung three times before going up the stairs. Retta heard a few muffled words, then her mother's voice. "It's for you, Henrietta. Danny Dobson's son wants to talk to you."

As Retta picked up the phone, she heard a bedroom door down the hall close softly and realized with a heartbeat of gratitude that her mother was granting her privacy.

Dallas's voice was deep and resonant. "I'm calling

from the phone booth outside Provanza's market," he said. "The damndest thing has happened." A pause. "Are you there, Retta?"

"Yes, yes. What is it you want to tell me?"

"I was thinking about you so much, I just couldn't stay home. So I've been driving around for hours in the pickup. Finally I went home and turned in the drive without lights because I didn't want to wake my father. Then I went into the front room and I hadn't switched a lamp on yet. I was just standing there, thinking. Then I heard a noise upstairs that I couldn't figure out."

"What was it?"

"I had to find out, so I went out the back door and climbed onto the porch roof. I never made a sound, Retta. I crawled over to my father's bedroom window and looked in. I guess he thought I wasn't home yet. I nearly fell off the roof. He had a drink in his hand and his crutches were over on the bed. He was talking to himself and *walking back and forth.* Not even a limp. That man can walk, Retta! Can you hear me, my father can *walk.*"

"He can *walk?* Without crutches? The pain, the limping, they weren't *real?* All this time he's just been *pretending?*"

"The important thing, Retta, is that man can *walk.*"

"But he's lied to you. Over and over again, he's lied to you, Dallas. Don't you see that? He bullied you, made you pity him. He didn't give you a real chance, did he? And you're not *angry?*"

"Right now I'm too stunned to be angry. I'm confused. He must have been afraid to level with me.

147

After Sam Houston, he must have been afraid I'd leave him, too. I don't think it matters too much why he lied to *me*, Retta. But how could a man do that to *himself?*"

Retta realized her breathing had become fast and shallow, touched with panic. She ran the tip of her tongue lightly over her dry lips before trying to speak. "What does this all mean, Dallas?"

"To us or to him?"

She paused. "To him, I guess."

"I'm not sure, Retta. I've got to think. But I didn't want you leaving for California without knowing what I know. . . ."

At ten o'clock the next morning, the plane left from Philadelphia airport enroute to Los Angeles, with a connecting flight to Palm Springs. Mrs. Caldwell had asked for three window seats so each of them could say his own farewell to the sprawling mass of Philadelphia and the green fields and thick woods of Pennsylvania.

As the plane climbed for altitude, Retta looked down, her forehead pressed against the small oval of the plane's window. Directly beneath her she could see the big-city mixture of glass-cube architecture and placid older streets lined with the red brick of Colonial architecture. The plane was still low enough to cast a ground shadow over the parks and the broad, blue ribbon of the Delaware River.

The big airship arced west, passing in moments over the farmlands and winding country roads immediately outside Zenith. Retta peered down in-

148

tently, trying to find landmarks, but at the plane's altitude, cars disappeared, woods became brushlands, and roads and fences faded from view. The route of the new highway was clear. She saw the raw, stripped earth and the bonfires that sent up sharp beacons of light, like mirror reflections, and a smudge of fire-cloud that followed the long, curved route of the bypass like a thin, gray boa of smoke.

Retta closed her eyes. There was no use hoping, no use straining. She could distinguish nothing below, fence or field, that had, for nearly seventeen years, marked off the place she'd called home.

Chapter
15

There were eight other recently finished houses on the street called Desert Lily. The Caldwells' was the last one, on a corner lot, a sprawling new adobe house with a low front wall and sliding glass doors on all three bedrooms, leading out to a pink cement patio that matched the decking around the pool.

Everything was new, from the jacuzzi whirlpool in the master bathroom to the trash compactor in the kitchen that bagged and crushed household garbage with jaws of steel. Except for three transplanted palm trees, tall and graceful, the back garden was not landscaped, but Mrs. Caldwell had made a bright, clay-pot garden at one end of the pool with summer zinnias and white-flowered periwinkle that bloomed and flourished in the desert heat.

At night the family gathered for dinner around a glass-topped table on the patio. Mrs. Caldwell tried such recipes as snow crab with lobster sauce, avocado stuffed with chicken, shrimp with Japanese vegetables, and a bean curd called "tofu."

The sun seemed to glare down from the sky from six in the morning until nearly eight at night, when the stars came out, brilliant in the clear desert atmosphere.

Unlike the countryside, neighbors here were close. From their garden, the Caldwells could not only see the lights of neighboring houses but they could often hear the murmur of voices. After one "California dinner" of barbecued beef with alfalfa sprouts and pita bread, Two said in a loud whisper, "Mother, isn't there such a thing as a *potato* in this state?"

Thirty-Nine Palms was ringed on three sides by high, stark mountains, monoliths of granite as dry and formidable as the desert floor. They made a dramatic background to the brilliant green of golf courses, the blue sparkle of one pool per house, and the graceful groupings of palm trees. There were masses of planted flowers everywhere, attracting green and purple hummingbirds, darting and sucking nectar, looking like flying blossoms themselves.

For the first two weeks, Retta wore sunglasses, even inside the house, and kept her bedroom draperies drawn. "Could it be possible that California could be too beautiful?" she asked her mother. "Couldn't it rain just a *little*?"

151

Her yellow car had arrived and sat baking in the desert sun. A Pennsylvania student transferring to Stanford had driven it west. The sight of it brought Retta close to tears.

Her brother was embarrassed at having made two "bicycle friends" the first day, two young teenagers who lived a block away. They took him first to the just-opened, air-conditioned mall with thirty shops, plus fountains, and gardens under glass. And they also showed him how to hike the faint desert trails that led to small oases, and even how to find the hidden waterfalls not far from Palm Springs.

One afternoon, Retta herself made a solo trip to the mall, but felt like an alien under the lofty sky-lights, with the moving ribbons of escalators and the huge, indoor potted trees. Everyone her age seemed to be wearing cut-off jeans with tank tops and sandals, bodies sunburned to an even caramel, with sun-bleached hair and eyes blocked out by huge sunglasses. No one had the kind of face she longed for: strong, weather-beaten, and with green-brown eyes that wanted to see and be seen.

There had been no phone call from Dallas Dobson.

One night on the terrace, Two whispered to her, "Why don't you call *him*, Retta? We all know how much you're hurting."

"I can't," she said simply. "It wouldn't be the same."

As each blue-sky day and starlit night passed, Retta felt more remote from the joy and security of the familiar Pennsylvania life. Whatever it was, she hadn't been able to hold it. It had eluded her.

One night in bed, she turned her thoughts into prayers and said ruefully, "Listen to me, God. This is a multiple-choice question. Are You going to break my heart till I can't stand it anymore? Are You going to help me to forget him? Or are You going to let him find me again?"

Somehow she had not thought of a letter. Her brother signed for it and brought it to the luncheon table on the terrace. "For you, Retta," he said. "Air Express. That means it cost him almost ten dollars and he had to drive into Zenith to mail it."

It also means, she thought as she took the envelope, *that less then twenty-four hours ago, Dallas Dobson stood in the post office in Zenith. And this letter was in his hands.*

In the solitude of her room, Retta pulled the draperies just a little, enough to send a shaft of light across the letter. It was short, just two pages, written in strong, black letters, as if the writer were hunched at a table, pressing the urgency of his words onto the page.

Dear Henrietta:

I did three things since I saw you. And I want you to know. First, I went to Squire DeLepino and gave him a deposition on what happened down at the pond that day. I gave him the name of the hard-hat and the license number on the bulldozer. Squire says the man won't be hard to locate. And with my sworn statement, and whatever else he can get, the Jessups have a good case.

Second, I talked with my father. I told him I knew he could walk if he wanted to, and I told him how I found out. He was angry at first, then scared. I know he wanted to shout or punch me across the room — or go out and buy a bottle, but he didn't. He let me talk and then he talked. We talked like people, like friends. I told him that wherever I was, I'd still be with him because I love him. I told him how much it meant to me that he kept me, that he never put me out to be someone else's son.

Today is the first day he went to work without crutches. He promised me he's going to try to get his act together and I believe him, Retta. He has to, in fact, because I made it clear I was leaving him for three months, crutches or not.

And the third thing, and I need your help on this, Retta. I got a copy of Arabian Horse Times from Mrs. Curtayne. I knew she'd subscribe. There was an ad in the classifieds. A ranch between Palm Springs and Indio is looking for summer help. I called the number and talked to a Mr. Bradley at Rancho Arabian. He *and his wife own the place. I told them what I know about horse care and how much I wanted the job. But they didn't want to hire me over the phone. So I told them about you. Can you drive out to Rancho Arabian and pin down the work for me? I hope you will do that. The ranch is listed in the phone book.*

I'll have to be back here to finish up and graduate in the fall, but if I get the job, we can have almost three months together. I could leave here next Tuesday, and when we circle over the desert, I dream I'll see that little yellow car coming to meet me. I have the money for air fare, you know. My father won't need that operation.

If I'm saying too little, Retta, it's because there is so much to say. We need this time together, don't we? And it's right that I come where you are.

If the Rancho Arabian folk don't want to hire me, I'll have to face that. And if you won't want me to come, I'll have to face that, too. But I'll never believe it. You have my phone number.

> *(I'll say it when I see you —)*
> *Your friend,*
> *Dallas Dobson*

They could see her at four o'clock, the Bradleys said on the phone, and told her how to proceed to Bob Hope Drive, make a right turn off to Ramon, and then make a left turn when she got to Desert Moon Road. Drive all the way out, first on blacktop, then dirt. Make a right where the dirt road ends and go through the double gates. That's where the Rancho Arabian acreage begins, and the only house and barns one can see are ours.

Both Bradleys were waiting for her in the cool, rambling ranch house. She was aware of big leather couches, bright paintings, cowhide rugs, and the soft hum of air-conditioning. The Bradleys were a young couple, in their midthirties, and almost look-alikes with blond, cropped hair, jeans, and range boots. Both were so tanned that their eyes looked blue-painted in their faces.

Retta followed and listened as they showed her first the apartment for the new horse man — a small, neat two rooms and bath, just off the main house. Then they walked over sandy gravel paths to the outdoor pens, split-railed squares with corner bubblers of fresh running water in each and a shady overhead protection of sheeted, corrugated iron for the horses. A huge tom turkey with dusty feathers and scarlet wattles followed them everywhere, squawking and scolding.

"We call him Doctor Vet," Mrs. Bradley said with a laugh. "He looks out for the Arabians almost as carefully as we do."

"We would want your boyfriend to remember that horses need special attention in sun country," Mr.

156

Bradley said. "These Arabians are highly sensitive to sunburn. They can get in just as much trouble as human beings."

"Oh, I'm sure he knows something of that from Texas," Retta said quickly. "He's been around horses since he was a little boy." She was impressed with the Bradleys' attractive and efficient operation. She wanted them to feel she truly represented Dallas Dobson. She wanted them to trust her. Therefore she tried to make the tour of the ranch without her sunglasses, so she could look at the Bradleys in a direct and straightforward manner, but the temperature was in the high nineties and the bright glint of sunlight off the sand and shale were too much for her.

On the fence of each outdoor stall was a placard stating exactly how many pounds of hay and pellet supplements were to be given to each horse. "We want someone as dependable as a time clock. These horses are on a rigid schedule. We haul their feed to them twice a day, exactly at six A.M. and six P.M. We don't want any colic or barn fever. Do you think your friend is trustworthy?"

Retta told them about the snowstorm, the Kennellys' old Arabians, and the back-country skiing. "In all the time I've known him," she said, "he never missed a day at work. Sometimes he even worked two jobs."

Inside the long, cool barn were a dozen top-breed Arabians, ranging in color from a dun brown to a light gray, almost silver in the dim light of the stalls. As the Bradleys' footsteps sounded out on the concrete floor, each horse in turn put its head over the half door, whinnying and stomping, waiting to be caressed and talked to. Only one mare got the voice treatment without hands-on attention. Because she was allergic to the bite of a certain desert gnat, the horse was stalled behind tight, heavy screening and only taken out to air in the cool of the evening. Another Arabian wore a headdress of beaded strings to flick away flies that caused infections to its sensitive eyes and ears. The headdress swung and rattled every time the horse moved its head. Two of the younger horses had playthings in their stalls, big wooden apples, painted red, hanging from the roof by a rope.

"The young ones can get so bored cooped up in this hot weather without something to play with," Mrs. Bradley said. "We expect your boyfriend is genuinely fond of horses. These highly bred animals need a lot of attention. They seem to know they're valuable."

Retta told them a little about Dallas's background with rodeos in Texas, how much he had learned from his father. "I think he not only loves horses, he respects them. He thinks they are splendid animals."

"What's most important to us," Mr. Bradley said, "is someone not only with knowledge and barn skills, but one who has that extra something, a person who can look at a horse, touch it, and say with confidence, 'That animal is in good health.' My wife and I travel a lot in our business, and we want someone with enough savvy and common sense to recognize trouble when he sees it, and call the vet."

Retta tried, as courteously and frankly as possible, to answer all the questions they asked, and to fill in what she thought they should know about Dallas Dobson.

At the end of the tour of barn and equipment buildings, they walked to the big outdoor exercise ring. It was empty now, baking in the late afternoon sun. "Whomever we hire is going to spend a lot of time in this ring," Mr. Bradley said sternly. "And we'll expect him to adapt to our desert hours. Now, he *will* have use of our pickup truck. He won't be bound and tied to this place. But we expect long hours and we want a horseman who can adapt."

"Please tell me what you mean," Retta said.

"In this summer heat, we can't exercise the horses in the daytime. It's too much for them. Your friend Dobson will have to work out a schedule for our approval. The horses can be exercised *only* before six in the morning and *after* nine o'clock at night. You'll notice this ring has special incandescent blue lighting. That's so the horses won't see shadows to stumble over, even their own. I'd expect Dobson to keep on the job, no matter how late, till each horse has its daily workout."

Mrs. Bradley looked at Retta, a question in her eyes, and when Retta said nothing, the woman said, "But I don't see why you couldn't help him. Or just be with him while he works the horses. Maybe he's like an Arabian himself. Maybe he likes company."

Retta looked around at the ring with its white

wooden fences, screened-in viewing porch, the big lights, and the coiled lunge-lines for exercising. "You have an elegant operation here," she said. "Anyone would be proud to fit in."

"And one last thing we'd better discuss," Mr. Bradley said. "It's of prime importance. We have a fourteen-year-old son, Burton. He's in school right now, but he's beginning to be an expert horseman and we want him to continue that way. And we want him to learn everything possible about Arabians and the operation of this ranch. We'd expect Dobson to answer questions, give orders when necessary, and make use of the talents of a lively fourteen-year-old. Do you think he has the patience for that?"

"I'm sure of it," Retta said with enthusiasm. "He would like it very much, I think. He had a brother himself, you see, an older brother who — " She stopped, surprised at the catch in her voice. "What I mean to say is, he liked his older brother so much, I'm sure he'd remember how Sam Houston treated him."

Mrs. Bradley put her arm around Retta's shoulder, then turned to her husband. "That settles it, darling, don't you think? Dallas Dobson is the right man for the job."

Mr. Bradley put out his big hand to Retta and said, "Let's shake on it, Miss Caldwell. Tell your boyfriend we'll expect him next week."

"And if we like him half as much as you do, my dear," Mrs. Bradley said, "we've got a gem."

* * *

Retta put a glass of ice water beside the phone and watched the clock. She had decided to dial the number at the exact moment of six.

After her interview with the Bradleys, she had come home to tell her mother that Dallas had the job. Then she showered, changed into fresh jeans and shirt, and touched cologne to her hair. It was almost as if she were going to see him in person, and she could not quiet the rapid beat of her heart or the turmoil in her thoughts. Dallas had the job. He had the right to know that as soon as possible. The sound of his voice and how she reacted to that voice would be her lodestar, the key to the important words she wanted to say next.

In far-off Pennsylvania, the Dobson phone rang four times, and then a fifth before a man answered it.

"My son's not here, Miss Caldwell," Danny Dobson said evenly. "He's still over at Squire De-Lepino's. Left here about an hour ago. The Jessup case. But you know all about that."

"Yes, I do," she said.

"Well, they rounded up that highway worker to make his own statement," Dobson said. "And to validate what Dallas already had to say."

"Then can you do this for me, please, Mr. Dobson?" she asked. "Take down this number to be sure he has it. Tell him to call me tonight. I'll wait up till I hear from him."

"Can't you give me the message?"

"No, I'd rather talk to him directly." She gave Danny Dobson the California phone number and waited for a response. Then, into the silence, she said, "Are you sure you have the number correctly? Are you sure you'll give him my message tonight?"

Danny Dobson's tone was sardonic, even amused, but she sensed the hurt in his voice. "Don't worry, Miss Caldwell. Even a broken-down cowboy's got some sense of honor."

Carter Caldwell had stayed in Thirty-Nine Palms to have dinner with his new advertising manager, and his family ate a nearly silent meal on the patio. They were all caught up with the tension of waiting, the acute sense of seconds ticking by.

Night in this part of the desert came abruptly, when the sun slipped behind the looming mountains and snuffed out the day. Tonight it left brilliant streaks of red and pink, edged with a spreading gray at the horizon.

By eight o'clock the table had been cleared and the Caldwell house was quiet. Retta sat with her mother and brother in the dusk, looking out over the desert garden. New fruit trees had been planted and the miniature limes gave off their sharp, juice-green odor in the cool of the evening. There was a half moon, pale as a night moth, and its thin light gilded the three palm trees and imprinted their slender shadows like an etching on the surface of the swimming pool.

It was after eight o'clock, which meant it was after eleven in Pennsylvania, and still Dallas Dobson had not called.

"He *will* call, Retta, I know it," her mother said quietly. "This is different."

From off in the distant night, somewhere at the foot of the mountains, came a high, eerie yapping, the sound of a wild coyote pack on the prowl. The loneliness, the feral abandon in their call, made Retta shiver. She folded her arms around herself in a kind of hug, hoping to draw confidence from the warmth of her own body.

"My friends tell me there used to be hundreds of coyotes round here," her brother said. "With all the building, they've had to find new feeding grounds nearer the mountains." He peered at his mother and sister through the darkness. "My friends say that water is the big problem. Sometimes they come down in the night, dozens of them, and drink out of swimming pools."

Retta said nothing, absorbed in her own thoughts. Her brother turned to her and said, "Coyotes mate for life. Did you know that, Retta?"

"Oh, Two," she said helplessly. "I know you're trying to be helpful, but you're just making things worse.

"And you, Mother," she said, "you're no help *at all*. Just saying over and over again that he is going to call doesn't make it *happen*. What do you really and truly think about his coming here? I know what *I* think — but can't you tell me your thoughts? Can't you be of some help? What am I starting here? I don't even know how this thing is going to *end*. . . ."

"No one ever does, Retta," her mother said. "Love — even a chance at a little happiness — it's always a gamble. It's all up to you and Dallas. No one else, absolutely no one else can — " Her mother stopped, listening.

Then they all heard it. Inside the house a phone had begun to ring.

MAUREEN DALY was a high school student when she launched a brilliant writing career with "Fifteen," a story for which she won third prize in the Scholastic Writing Awards Competition. She was still a teenager when she published her first short story, "Sixteen." When she wrote *Seventeenth Summer,* her landmark young adult novel that went on to be a bestseller, Maureen Daly was not yet twenty.

About *Acts of Love,* Ms. Daly says: "I was inspired by the deepest joys of my daughter, Megan. And by that summer in the small Pennsylvania town when she defied the building of a highway and fell in love with a young man who cared deeply about the things she cared about."

A novelist, journalist, and screenwriter, Maureen Daly has traveled extensively. She has written several works of nonfiction for adults and is the author of a collection of short stories for teenagers. Ms. Daly lives and writes in Palm Desert, California.

point™
Pass the word!

Order these NEW titles chosen with you in mind!

BANKING ON DEATH
was originally published by
The Macmillan Company.

Books by Emma Lathen

Accounting for Murder*
Ashes to Ashes*
Banking on Death*
Come to Dust
Death Shall Overcome*
The Longer the Thread*
Murder Against the Grain*
Murder Makes the Wheels Go 'Round
Murder to Go*
Pick Up Sticks*
A Place for Murder*
A Stitch in Time*
Sweet and Low*

*Published by POCKET BOOKS

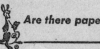

Banking on Death

Emma Lathen

PUBLISHED BY POCKET BOOKS NEW YORK

BANKING ON DEATH

Macmillan edition published 1961

POCKET BOOK edition published October, 1975

L

This POCKET BOOK edition includes every word contained
in the original, higher-priced edition. It is printed from
brand-new plates made from completely reset, clear, easy-to-
read type. POCKET BOOK editions are published by POCKET
BOOKS, a division of Simon & Schuster, Inc., 630 Fifth
Avenue, New York, N.Y. 10020. Trademarks registered
in the United States and other countries.

Standard Book Number: 671-80108-2.

Library of Congress Catalog Card Number: 61-14708.

Front cover illustration by John Melo.

Printed in the U.S.A.

Contents

1: PRINCIPALS AND INTEREST

Wall Street is the world's money market. Hundreds of millions of dollars can change hands over luncheon; the fate of a factory in Belgium, or a mine in Michigan can be sealed when a banker dictates a letter. Two young physicists from California can raise money to expand a backyard tool shop into a missile-producing giant, British investors can buy a plantation in the Mississippi Delta, little old ladies in Paris can sell Imperial Russian Bonds—on Wall Street.

All of this buying and selling—of stocks and bonds, of francs and drachmas, of wheat and cocoa—requires the skilled activity of thousands of specialists: traders, brokers, lawyers, analysts, underwriters, insurance men, mutual fund men, floor men—and messenger boys, bankers, typists, statisticians, file clerks, editors, salesmen, wire men, tipsters, Dow theorists, consultants.

It also requires talk.

Outside, gray December clouds promised snow and hapless pedestrians scurried along, collars upturned against the sharp wind. But high above the street, modern heating effectively sealed the conference room against the weather; there was only the lingering pungency of cigar and cigarette smoke.

"That was a good meeting," Walter Bowman said, as he shoveled papers into a bulging brief case. "Short and sweet. I'll be glad when we've sold that twenty thousand shares of Cooper-Pipe, John."

The Sloan Guaranty Trust, although occupying a substantial site on Exchange Place, is, in fact, the heart of Wall Street. The third largest bank in the world, it is far too important to concern itself with, say, Christmas Savings Clubs; you go to an uptown branch for that. The Sloan invests, underwrites, finances.

Twice each month, the Investment Committee of the Trust Department meets to review these important operations. Senior trust officers and members of the Research Department convene in a glass-encased conference room on the fortieth floor for, with luck, a short round of self-congratulation, or occasionally, for a long session of disagreement and—because bankers are human—recrimination.

Today's session had been brief; there had been unusual unanimity of opinion. Whatever the reason—it might have been a sluggish stock market, or it might have been midwinter lethargy—it left the two men still sitting at the conference table in good spirits. Walter Bowman, chief of the research staff, because he had been able to persuade the committee to adopt his recommendations, and John Putnam Thatcher, senior vice-president and director of the trust department, because he loathed all meetings.

The elevator eased itself to a cushioned halt at the sixth floor; Thatcher waited for the doors to open on the trust department, and for the play to begin. It was standard operating procedure for the floor receptionist to buzz the entire department when the tower elevator passed on its upward journey to collect him. Thatcher knew this and was grateful for a system which protected him from public knowledge of his juniors' lack of assiduity. He savored the atmosphere of hectic activity which greeted him as he passed through the typists' pool with appreciation. Each desk was occupied, each head bent over its keyboard, and each machine beat out a crisp staccato. In the file department, drawers were rolled briskly open and shut, clerks stared intently at odd pieces of paper and messenger boys moved down the aisles radiating a sense of purpose. The noise level dropped sharply on the other side of the double doors which separate the clerical force from the staff. Such division into haves and have-nots was the result of "functional creativity" practiced by the architect when the Sloan was last remodeled; it had been hailed with acclaim by *Architectural Forum*—and with relief by a filing staff periodically subject to raids upon the archives by officials too impatient to wait for the workings of normal channels. This arrangement, explained the architect, would enable trust officers to work in noiseless serenity and maintain the calm control so desirable in bankers. To Thatcher, the sepulchral silence that now enveloped his division was a perpetual irritant, evoking visions of furtive movements and whispered conferences.

There was, however, nothing whispered about the angry voices which suddenly came to him as he turned to enter his own suite of offices.

"Young woman," growled a deep voice that was totally unfamiliar to him, "I have already explained to you that this is a matter of some importance and . . ."

"Please, Mr. Snyder," said Thatcher's secretary in tones of genteel anger, "unless you have an appointment, I am afraid . . ."

"It's Schneider, if you don't mind. Schneider, S-C-H- . . ."

Thatcher advanced into the room and surveyed the disputants. Miss Corsa, usually lymphatically calm, stood defiantly behind her desk, prepared to defend it against assault. She was looking wildly at a heavy-set man in his middle fifties now brick-red with indignation. She greeted Thatcher with an exaggerated sigh of relief.

"Oh, Mr. Thatcher, I'm so sorry. I've been trying to explain to Mr. Snyder . . ."

"Yes, I heard you," said Thatcher, turning courteously to his uninvited visitor. "Mr. Schneider, is it?"

While he was unprepared to countenance brawls in his office, he was curious about anyone who could ruffle Miss Corsa. Schneider, now that his choleric flush had subsided, seemed ordinary enough.

"Yes, it's Arthur Schneider. I've been trying to explain to your secretary that I'm in New York for only a day or two before going on to Chicago. Now I realize that you have many demands on your time—don't we all?—but I'm inclined to agree with Grace that the simplest thing to do is for you and me to sit down together and thrash this thing out—I think it will save time for all of us in the end."

Thatcher bowed to the inevitable. Clearly it would be quicker to placate the man than to get rid of him, although who "Grace" was and what "this thing" was remained obscure. Accordingly he turned to Miss Corsa and in a brisk voice asked, "Am I free for the next half hour?"

Miss Corsa, who valued routine, was not pleased with his capitulation but the request—which was actually a code that Thatcher had taught her with some difficulty—soothed her. She sat down and consulted an appointment book. Turning quickly to the pages she needed, she ran a pencil down a list.

"You have an appointment with Mr. Withers at three, Mr. Thatcher," she said without looking up.

Both Thatcher and Schneider were spared the necessity of checking their watches; Miss Corsa coldly turned a small desk clock to face them before she withdrew to her dictation book. It was two thirty-five.

"Perhaps we can at least outline the situation in the little time we have," Thatcher said. "Won't you come in, Mr. Schneider?" Standing aside to let Schneider precede him into the office, he wondered if the name of the president of the Sloan Guaranty Trust would operate as powerfully on Arthur Schneider as it did on most of his visitors.

Schneider marched triumphantly into the office, dropped his overcoat in one of the shabby, comfortable armchairs which Thatcher had retained in the face of spirited resistance by the Sloan's interior decorators, settled in another, and launched into his narrative before Thatcher could sit down.

"You'll have guessed that this is about the Schneider Trust," he said expansively. "Now that Hilda is dying, the matter of finding Robert has become critical. We can scarcely be expected to sit around indefinitely, waiting for him to give some sign of life. Quite apart from the annoyance, we have no assurance that he's alive at all or that we ever will hear from him. I'm sure that you appreciate our position."

"Certainly," lied Thatcher as he circled his desk: the Sloan handled more than twenty thousand trusts, a fact Arthur Schneider might be pardoned for not knowing. On the other hand, the Schneiders seemed to be a very disorderly tribe; they were either dying, missing entirely from the scene or raising Cain in bank offices. He wondered if Schneider would drop any clues as to the nature of his problem.

"Frankly, we are none too satisfied with the way that young man of yours is conducting the search. He seems to have no conception of the urgency of the situation or the amount of money involved. Now that Hilda is so near the end, Grace—and of course Martin and I—think that it would be ridiculous to allow further delays to confuse what is, God knows, a confused enough situation."

"Exactly," murmured Thatcher absently. His attention had been riveted by the reference to a "young man" of his. Which of his underlings had been unfortunate enough to have to cope with Arthur and the somewhat sinister, if unknown, Grace? If it were really a young man, then this was one of the small trusts—the so-called nuisance accounts—on which beginners at the Sloan were allowed to cut their eye teeth. They were legacies of another age; today the Sloan accepted no trust under a million dollars. But, remembering Schneider's treatment of Miss Corsa, Thatcher realized that he might be using the word "young" as an abusive rather than a descriptive epithet, in which case the trust involved might be very substantial. The course of wisdom was to confine himself to noncommittal remarks until he had more information. Fortunately Arthur Schneider seemed to require very little prompting from his colocutor. He was once again in full flight.

". . . and I have been trying to impress on Nicolls that unless he can get results in the very near future—that is to say, before Hilda dies—then it would be nonsense to hold up distribution of the estate until we can determine Robert Schneider's whereabouts. God knows the whole thing has been muddled enough already!" Schneider paused, apparently for breath, while Thatcher concentrated on the one familiar name that had come his way. Kenneth Nicolls was the trust officer. A small estate then, but giving plenty of trouble. They always did, he reflected. Arthur's basic complaint, however, seemed directed against his relatives and not against Nicolls. Poor Hilda's only offense seemed to be in the manner of her dying, unlike that fellow in *Macbeth*. Robert must be the real difficulty.

"Of course, the Sloan doesn't handle many missing heir problems these days. Life has become too much a matter of files and records for that," he essayed tentatively.

"It's typical of Robert," retorted Arthur bitterly. "I wouldn't put it past him to do this deliberately. After all, he's still a young man and we know that he came out of the Second World War all right. I ask you, is it reasonable that a man should drop out of sight completely when he knows he's coming into a hundred thousand dollars?"

"Certainly not," said Thatcher, his banker's instincts revolted at the suggestion.

"You can see how it makes everything most irregular." Schneider was quick to sense sympathy. He was now settling down to say what he had come for. "Of course, I do see that as trustees you must exercise every reasonable precaution, and I assure you that I have explained this in great detail to Grace. It wasn't easy"—he frowned in retrospect—"but she now realizes the nature of your responsibilities. Naturally I sympathize with her problems. We could all use some more money, and I think we have found a way to satisfy everybody. In any event I have promised her that I would put the facts clearly before you."

"Very wise," said Thatcher judiciously, wondering if the foregoing conversation represented a fulfillment of that promise. He hoped that Grace was Arthur's wife. So much nattering from any other woman would really be intolerable, but Schneider's general posture was not that of the henpecked husband. "You said, I think, that any further delay in the distribution of the trust could be avoided. What did you have in mind?"

Schneider hitched himself forward in his chair and lowered his voice impressively. "A partial distribution— yes, a partial distribution. Now don't say that you can't," he went on, stabbing his pipe in Thatcher's direction, "before you see the justice of this. It may take years to locate Robert. After all, when Hilda dies, the money legally belongs to us. All we want is to have what is ours. It's outrageous that we should be kept kicking our heels until Robert shows up. Which he will," he concluded sourly.

Thatcher discovered that he had been laboring under a misconception which was scarcely surprising under the circumstances. Apparently all the Schneiders were joint heirs to one trust fund, and Robert's absence was raising the devil with the administration and disposition of the trust. This kind of mess should never have been left to young Nicolls, who was probably sweating blood. Or even worse, making rash promises which would compromise the bank's freedom of action.

He made a mental note to have a talk with Charlie Trinkam about the degree of supervision that was right and proper for the junior staff. On the other hand, unlimited exposure to the Schneiders might turn Nicolls into a better and a tougher trust officer.

"What did you plan to do with Robert's share?" he inquired.

"Naturally that would be held in trust for him by the bank," replied Arthur with dignity.

There was now no doubt in Thatcher's mind but that the Schneiders were important to the life of whatever town they infested. Himself born and bred in Sunapee, New Hampshire, he recognized the leading family syndrome if anybody did. But premature distribution of trusts was also a matter about which he knew a great deal.

"You understand Mr. Schneider, that we are generally very reluctant to . . ."

"Certainly, certainly," Schneider interrupted, "we realize that this presents a great many problems for the bank, and we are prepared to assist in every way." His grievances again threatened to deflect him. He tapped his foot impatiently. "This is a sort of penalty for those of us who have stayed at home and taken care of the family business while Robert wanders to God knows where without giving any sign of life. Nor is there any reason for this kind of behavior." He warmed to his subject: "Completely unreasonable. We may have been unsympathetic to some of his more outrageous activities. . . . However, that's neither here nor there. I have already pointed out to Grace that we must cooperate to the hilt. We're ready to do everything we can to help you find him. Not that that's much, I'm afraid. He's been gone over fifteen years, you know."

"Indeed, I didn't realize that it was so long," said Thatcher with perfect truth.

This remark appeared to gratify Schneider. "Yes, it's been over fifteen years. You should know that we've discussed this with our attorneys and we want to be perfectly reasonable—about posting bonds and that sort of thing—and I daresay that you're just as anxious as we are to have the trust closed out and off your hands."

Thatcher was instantly alerted by the mention of attorneys. Was this a delicate hint that the Schneiders were preparing to go to court for an order directing a partial distribution? He contemplated his visitor, then relaxed.

There was nothing delicate about Arthur Schneider, and if a court order were in the air it would be an attorney sitting across the desk. He decided to ignore the remark; instead he put a question that had been bothering him for some time.

"And what has Nicolls said to this suggestion?"

"Good heavens! I haven't spoken to him about this. I knew he would need your approval for whatever he recommended. So it seemed much simpler to come straight to you and make sure you have a clear view of the situation."

Thatcher was genuinely amused by this view of executive authority at the Sloan and by the vision it conjured up of every single person with whom his subordinates came into contact lined up in his waiting room. But he was more pleased that Nicolls had not been required to make any hasty promises or harsh refusals. It took, Thatcher had concluded, five to ten years for a trust officer to learn the art of the gentle let-down. The period depended on the individual's endowment of natural deceit. He himself had been an uncommonly quick learner, and now put his talent to practice.

"I am, of course, delighted that you came," he replied cordially. "I can say, quite honestly, that I had no idea of a partial distribution of the trust. That is, in the event of its becoming due for distribution." He felt that it would be unseemly to refer to Hilda by her first name and had no idea what her last name was. He skirted further reference to her. "However I can assure you that your proposal will receive every consideration."

Schneider's heavy-jawed face lit with a contented smile. "That's all I ask," he began, but his congratulations to Thatcher and the Sloan on their sagacity were cut short. Miss Corsa walked into the office.

"Mr. Withers at three, Mr. Thatcher," she announced while looking over Schneider's head.

"Of course. Thank you Miss Corsa. Mr. Schneider, I am afraid that . . ."

"No, no, no apologies. Absolutely right. Withers is your president, isn't he? Can't keep him waiting." Schneider laughed with practiced joviality—Thatcher could see him in conference with Brad Withers talking about your "young man" Thatcher—and rose to grasp Thatcher's hand across the desk. As he gathered his coat and hat, he continued in satisfied tones. "All I wanted was the assurance that you would give this serious attention." Feeling for his pipe, he looked around the office, then commandingly at Thatcher. "I think you'll come to see that a partial distribution of the estate is the only answer."

After another round of farewells before Miss Corsa's desk, to which Miss Corsa remained completely indifferent, he was able to speed Schneider's departure with promises that the Sloan would be in contact.

Thatcher watched his visitor stride down the hall and disappear around the corner. Not quite the country cousin if he recognized Withers. The unquestioning self-confidence, not to say arrogance, of a man who hires and fires.

"Miss Corsa, do we know who this Schneider is?"

Miss Corsa produced a business card. If invited she could obviously contribute a few strictures of her own. The card read:

Schneider Manufacturing Company
Felts and Industrial Textiles
100 Central Street
Framingham, Massachusetts
Arthur Schneider, President

"New England," muttered Thatcher. "I thought so." He flicked the card with a forefinger, then added, "Will you try to get young Nicolls in here today or tomorrow, Miss Corsa? Apparently he's the one who can explain all of this to us. Tell him I'll want a memo about the Schneider Trust." If nothing else, Thatcher thought, he could protect members of his staff from the kind of hectoring of which Schneider was capable. No member of the Sloan had to tolerate bullying—at least, not for a nuisance account.

He dismissed the Schneiders from his mind, as he stood in front of Miss Corsa's desk. "Let's see. I wanted to put through a call to Everhardt tomorrow. Will you remind me, Miss Corsa? And I'll want to talk with Walter Bowman later in the day. I think that's all I had on my mind."

Miss Corsa noted the requests in her book and then, as Thatcher prepared to return to his own office, permitted herself the ghost of a prim smile.

"You won't forget your appointment, at three-thirty?"

"Appointment—with whom?"

"Mr. Withers."

"Good God!"

2: PAYMENT DEFERRED

Normally Thatcher planned an early departure from the bank after a meeting of the Investment Committee, so that he could devote a long evening in his apartment to his own review of the Sloan's investments. But this afternoon Brad Withers had detained him with an enthusiastic description of how the Sloan's "corporate image" could be improved by an expanded program of public relations. It was therefore almost six o'clock when Thatcher returned to his desk, to find its otherwise virginal surface embellished by a note from Miss Corsa indicating that he had an appointment with Kenneth Nicolls at eleven o'clock the next morning and by a memorandum from Nicolls himself. As he picked it up, Thatcher reflected that the familiar yellow papers represented a rush job; Nicolls had obviously been galvanized by the imminence of his first direct contact with the august head of the trust department. He settled down to read.

SLOAN GUARANTY TRUST COMPANY
Trust Department
(INTER-OFFICE MEMORANDUM—NOT TO BE USED
OUTSIDE OF THE TRUST DEPARTMENT)

To: John Thatcher (cc C. Trinkam)
FROM: K. B. Nicolls
SUBJECT: Schneider Trust

DATE: Dec. 10
FILE NO.: 137-42-11
CODE NO.: 67-(N)

1. *Creation of Trust*

The Schneider Trust was established on April 19, 1932, by Klaus Arthur Schneider for the benefit of his grandchildren. The original trust *res* consisted of certain securities chosen by the grantor and having a market value at that time of approximately ten thousand dollars. The Sloan Guaranty Trust was appointed trustee in the original trust document with full powers for the reinvestment of the trust funds in accordance with the laws of New York State governing the investment of capital by fiduciaries.

2. Terms of the Trust

The terms of the trust do not permit distribution of income. All income is to be reinvested and added to the principal. Upon the death of the last surviving child of Klaus Arthur Schneider, the entire trust corpus is to be distributed to his grandchildren (or to their issue in the case of death). The grandchildren do not share equally but take *per stirpes:*—that is, equal segments of the trust follow the line of each child and the grandchildren take as representatives of their parent rather than as individuals.

Thatcher grunted his dissatisfaction. He resented Nicolls' painstaking definition of *per stirpes*. In his opinion, his subordinates should leave that sort of gobbledygook to the law department and say what they mean in plain English. Or have the tact to assume that twenty-five years in the trust business had left him with a working knowledge of the basic vocabulary. He continued reading:

3. Investment of Trust Funds

The approximate value of the trust, if liquidated last week, would have been three hundred thousand dollars. A complete schedule of current investments is being prepared. The original investments of the settlor were extremely satisfactory (including blocks of IBM and RCA acquired in 1932) and no substantial reinvestment was undertaken until after World War II. Large purchases of Polaroid and Minnesota Mining and Manufacturing were made at that time and contributed to the impressive rate of growth of the corpus.

"My God!" Thatcher muttered, " 'The impressive rate of growth of the corpus!' "

4. Schneider Family

Klaus Arthur Schneider died in 1933 and was survived by all of his three children. The elder son, Arthur Schneider, senior, died in 1942 leaving one son, Arthur Schneider, junior, and one daughter, Grace Schneider Walworth. The younger son, Carl Schneider, died in 1936 leaving one son, C. Robert Schneider. The only daughter, Mrs. Hilda Schneider Henderson, survives; she is seventy years old, and has one son, Martin E. Henderson.

In addition to the trust, which in 1932 formed a very insignificant portion of Klaus Schneider's assets, the grantor left a family business to his three children. Voting stock in Schneider Manufacturing Company was left to his two sons, and non-voting stock was left to his daughter. A year after the grantor's death, Carl Schneider sold his interest to his brother Arthur Schneider, senior. The president of the Schneider Manufacturing Company is now Arthur Schneider, junior, and Martin Henderson is Vice-President in charge of Sales and Distribution.

5. *Distribution of the Trust*

The trust becomes due for distribution upon the death of Hilda Henderson, last surviving child of Klaus Schneider. Formal notification was received by the Sloan Guaranty Trust, on October 25, of this year, that Mrs. Henderson had suffered a stroke from which recovery is extremely improbable. Her physicians at Lenox Hill Hospital anticipate death within six months at most.

The children of Arthur Schneider, senior, and Hilda Henderson have all been in contact with the Sloan Guaranty Trust. They have been unable to supply any information as to the whereabouts of Robert Schneider, son of Carl Schneider, and to date efforts of the Sloan to locate him have been unsuccessful.

Thatcher glanced over the last page again. "The children of Arthur Schneider, senior, and Hilda Henderson have all been in contact with the Sloan Guaranty Trust." The "all" confirmed his fears that the Sloan was involved with far too many Schneiders; and he was still in the dark as to the rash promises that Arthur Schneider (presumably junior) had extorted from Nicolls.

He swept the memorandum together and pushed it into his brief case. Not quite what he wanted, but to do young Nicolls justice, he had pulled the information together quickly enough, considering that he had no idea why it was wanted. And presumably he would outgrow his enjoyment of technical jargon.

Nevertheless, thought Thatcher, as he closed his office door and started down the corridor where cleaning women were already busy with their evening rounds, he was not much further along than he had been when Arthur Schneider left his office.

Most of the doors he passed stood open on dark and vacant offices. Five o'clock was the nominal closing time at the Sloan Guaranty Trust, and at five o'clock secretaries and file clerks firmly saluted their superiors and the trust department was left to those who had to stay. Frequently Thatcher encountered Charlie Trinkam or Everett Gabler, while Walter Bowman's staff was legendary for its devotion to duty afterhours. He was amused to note, however, that in the December preholiday bustle, it was only around the corner, where junior officers were domiciled that there were still signs of life. Brad Withers might contemplate with pleasure a corporate image of a Sloan staffed with gravely dedicated toilers who strained every sinew for the public weal but Thatcher knew the facts of life; only the junior staff was ostentatiously chained to duty.

The frosted glass panel which bore the name "Kenneth B. Nicolls" was lighted, and sounds of activity came from within. On an impulse, Thatcher tapped briskly.

"Come in," Kenneth Nicolls called without interrupting his tie-knotting. "I'm not lending you any more ties, Joe, until you bring back that green one you borrowed last month," he continued as he finished his critical self-examination in the small mirror hung on the closet door, straightened to his full six feet, and turned to survey his visitor.

"My God!"

"Not quite," John Thatcher said. It was painfully apparent that Nicolls was not kept afterhours by the exigencies of duties at the Sloan.

Instead of a soberly attired young banker, mature of judgment and devoted to duty—what he had hitherto been presented with—Thatcher beheld an embarrassed young man whose blond hair contrasted painfully with a red face, clearly in a dilemma about his exposed shirttails.

"Do you have a minute to spare, Nicolls?" he asked him.

"Certainly, sir," the younger man said hastily. He would be late meeting Joyce, but nothing could be done about that. From pure nervousness he made an ineffective pass at smoothing his hair.

"It won't take long, I trust," said Thatcher without sarcasm. "I'd just like to hear some more about the Schneider Trust that you handle." He looked severely at Nicolls, who shifted awkwardly, then continued, "I've had an incomprehensible interview with Arthur Schneider that I hope you can explain. And why don't you sit down?"

The question of tucking his shirt in was settled, Nicolls thought confusedly as he obeyed Thatcher's injunction. His own immediate superior, Charlie Trinkam, was a jovial type whose camaraderie had always contrasted with Thatcher's somewhat aloof manner. And Thatcher seemed more forbidding than usual as he sat in front of Nicolls' desk looking with patent disapproval at the Modigliani-adorned wall.

Trying to hide his growing apprehension, Nicolls circled the desk, pulled out a drawer and rapidly made a mental review of his handling of the account. No junior bank officer relishes the thought of dissatisfied clients complaining to his superiors.

But Thatcher's irritation was directed toward himself, not Nicolls. He had stopped at his subordinate's cubicle without thinking, and he disapproved of impulses which by-passed the normal institutional routes of communication. It was one thing to interview young Nicolls in the morning after he had had an opportunity to consult with Charlie Trinkam; it was another to catch him off guard, half-dressed, and without benefit of briefing. But Nicolls seemed to have pulled himself together, so perhaps no harm was done.

"Good Lord," said Nicolls pulling folders out of his desk, "has he been bothering you too?"

"He has," replied Thatcher grimly, "and I want to know why."

"We can't locate one of the heirs to this trust, and he's furious at the possibility of a delay in distribution."

"Better start at the beginning. I don't really understand why Klaus Schneider should have set up such a small trust if he was a man of substance."

Nicolls nodded as he sorted some papers. "Yes, it really was a sort of gamble. The old man had collected some insurance in 1932. He was a shrewd businessman and decided to take a flier in the market, buying when prices were at rock bottom and tying it up for a substantial length of time." Nicolls warmed to his subject, "Of course, he didn't foresee the war, but he did very well. He picked up some RCA at the middle of the depression . . ."

Thatcher broke into what was clearly going to be an enthusiastic description of market behavior since 1932:

"And you're sure there was no desire to skip the children."

"Oh, no, sir," Nicolls replied. "The Company—Schneider Manufacturing Company—was really the bulk of his very substantial fortune. He'd started it in 1875 or 1880 and it was very prosperous—they started out with textiles, then branched out into industrial cloth." Thatcher must have looked blank, because Nicolls added, "Things like felt linings for paper machines, and musical instruments. It's all very specially made, you know. Well, in any event, the business was left outright to the old man's children. . . . No, this trust was no more than a little gamble."

"All right, Nicolls," Thatcher said mildly, "I'll bow to your superior wisdom. Now we have three hundred thousand dollars. . . ."

Nicolls took the sentence to indicate interest in the portfolio; he again broke in. "Yes, sir, at least three hundred thousand dollars. In fact I have hopes of a trifle more if it's distributed in the near future."

Thatcher noticed the satisfaction; all trust officers became zealots, he thought, with amusement. "And you've been handling the investments?" he asked.

"For the last year and a half, sir," Nicolls said enthusiastically. He rubbed his jaw in a somewhat sheepish gesture. "It was my first independent account."

"I'm sure you've done excellently by these people. Better than they deserve. But what I want to find out about is this missing heir business. Now we have the old man—did you say his name was Klaus?—setting up a trust for his grandchildren. Right?"

Nicolls nodded, and Thatcher continued, "And there are four grandchildren who do not share equally. Now they are—"

"Robert Schneider and Martin Henderson, who get one hundred thousand dollars each because they are only children. And Arthur Schneider and his sister, who get fifty thousand dollars apiece. Of course, if Robert Schneider turns out to be dead, and has no heirs, then Martin would get one hundred and fifty thousand dollars, and the others would take seventy-five thousand each."

"Yes," said Thatcher. "Then it's clear enough why the others want the question of Robert settled. How did this all come up? You said the bank had been notified of Hilda's condition. Who told us? Arthur Schneider?"

"No, sir. Martin Henderson, Hilda's only child, wrote me at the suggestion of the family lawyer. So I wrote back asking him for the addresses of the other heirs. Well, a few days later, he called me up and asked me to lunch. At the Pavillon," he said, dwelling with obvious pleasure on the recollection.

"Do you mean that Martin Henderson lives in New York?"

Nicolls looked surprised. "Yes, sir, he handles the sales office for Schneider Manufacturing in New York . . ."

"Good God!" Thatcher exclaimed wrathfully, "if Martin Henderson lives in the city, and Martin Henderson gets a double slice of the trust, and it's his mother who is dying, why in the name of all that's holy is it that insufferable ass, Arthur Schneider, who erupted in my office as the spokesman for this whole pack?"

Nicolls couldn't help grinning. "I suspect he likes to look on himself as the head of the family. Then, of course, he is the president of Schneider's, and far more important in that area. . . ."

"Well, never mind," Thatcher said. "Tell me about your lunch. At the Pavillon, I think you said."

Nicolls nodded. "We talked about the trust, and it turned out that he really wanted to know why it was necessary to find Robert Schneider. None of the family had realized that all the heirs would have to be found before the trust could be distributed; I think that he was also surprised at the amount involved. When I told him that it was a question of several hundred thousand dollars, the fat was in the fire."

It appeared that Martin Henderson had communicated with Arthur Schneider, who lived near the Schneider Manufacturing Company in Framingham, Massachusetts. And Arthur Schneider had communicated with his sister Grace Walworth, who lived in Washington.

"I thought I had explained everything carefully," Nicolls said ruefully, "but the next thing I knew, I was getting telephone calls from Mrs. Rowland Walworth." He made an expressive gesture.

"She said . . ." prompted Thatcher.

"Well, it's hard to say. She was furious that she should

have to wait to find Robert; she was furious that we hadn't found Robert. And that was about all I could make out."

"What did you say?" Thatcher asked with genuine sympathy. Not everybody can deal with hysterical women.

"To tell you the truth, sir, I just made soothing noises. I didn't say much—just sort of sympathized with her. Mr. Trinkam said that I should put everything in writing. He suggested that I write to all three of the heirs, outlining what I had already told Martin Henderson." He dug into the folder on the desk and handed Thatcher a paper. "Here's a copy of the letter I sent."

As Thatcher read the letter, Kenneth leaned back, and nervously lit another cigarette. What was this all about? Thatcher, in turn, read the letter with an inward sigh of relief, and handed it back.

"It seems sensible and straightforward, Nicolls. Did it placate Mrs. Walworth?"

"I'm not sure. That was the last I heard from her. Directly, that is."

"What is she doing in Washington, by the way."

"Army wife," Nicolls said, meaningfully. "Her husband's a colonel. They've lived all over, and settled down in Washington about ten years ago."

"Any children?"

"Two step-children," Nicolls replied. "I really don't know what she thought about the letter, because I have a feeling that the men in the family shut her up. The next thing that I knew, I got a letter from Arthur Schneider saying that he wanted to talk to me, and suggesting that I consult Martin Henderson about a convenient appointment for the three of us."

"When was this?" Thatcher asked.

"Last month. We met at Mr. Henderson's apartment. It's on Waverly Place," Nicolls added, somewhat defiantly.

"Naturally," Thatcher said. "Before you tell me about this meeting, let me ask you another question. What have we done about instituting a search for this Robert Schneider? I don't like to think that we are going to let the heir to such a substantial amount just disappear. And are you completely convinced that the family really doesn't know where he is?"

Nicolls drummed idly on the desk, while he considered

the possibility of interrupting this conference to call Joyce and warn her that he was going to be very late. Thatcher's obscure amusement at the Pavillon and Waverly Place, however, left him strongly disinclined to hazard a conversation with a presumably irate young woman in his presence. And, he thought, he could scarcely ask him to leave the office. Resigning himself to an evening of apology and expiation, he addressed himself to the question that Thatcher had asked.

"It's extremely complicated. I gather that Robert Schneider's father, Carl, fought bitterly with his brother Arthur; in fact, they had to part company, and Arthur Schneider bought his brother out. Shortly after that, Carl killed himself. That means, you see, that since he was a boy, Robert Schneider has had nothing to do with this branch of the family. It seems reasonable to believe them when they say they don't know what's become of him."

Thatcher inclined his head. "We'll suspend judgment on that. Have we instituted any sort of inquiries?"

Nicolls looked slightly shamefaced. "Only the most routine sort of search," he said. "Robert was expelled from Dartmouth in 1939 and hasn't kept up with any formal alumni activities. He never asked for a transcript of his college record, so presumably he never went to another college and didn't use his educational background when he went job-hunting. I wrote to the men who roomed with him for three years, and they had all lost touch with him."

Thatcher nodded. "Did they expel him during his senior year? It must have been something serious. If they've kept them that long, the colleges usually try to get them through."

"Martin didn't know the exact reason. Robert had left Framingham by that time, and was living with his aunt in Fitchburg. The rumor was that he had gotten some girl into trouble. He had a reputation for being a wild kid."

"Do we lose sight of him at this point?"

"Not completely," Nicolls replied. "He enlisted in the army, and was stationed at several points in the United States before being sent to England and North Africa. Camps at Texas, California, Ohio. And I've checked with army records in Galveston, Los Angeles and Cleveland. He never applied for a veteran's bonus in these states.

24

But," Nicolls added with feeling, "a hell of a lot of other Robert Schneiders did, and it's taken quite a lot of time to check them all out."

Thatcher smiled. "No Army Reserve connections, I take it."

Nicolls shook his head. "An honorable discharge in 'forty-five, and only too glad to get out of the army. Who can blame him?"

The two veterans—one of Korea, the other of the AEF—nodded knowledgeably. Thatcher thought aloud for a moment; "And he didn't go back to Fitchburg."

"His aunt had died while he was in the service and she was his only real tie there."

"Would he have any money?"

"Whatever he saved in the service," said Nicolls who had found no difficulty in spending every cent of his army pay. "His father lost his shirt in the depression experimenting on new methods and machinery before he ultimately committed suicide. The aunt left Robert about ten thousand dollars' worth of securities. While he was in the army he arranged to have them held for him at the Irving Trust Company. When he was discharged in New York, he picked up the stocks and bonds."

Thatcher interrupted; "But if he's still holding them, you might be able to get him through a stockholder list . . ."

"No, sir, I've tried that. They were mostly railroad preferreds and New England textile firms. He used his brain and sold out."

Thatcher again knitted his brows. "The telephone book," he suggested. "If he was demobilized in New York, and held things at the Irving Trust, perhaps he was thinking . . ."

"There are five columns of Schneiders in the Manhattan directory alone. I have talked with every one of them. They all live in Yorkville, speak with thick German accents and have never heard of our man. The same thing holds for the Bronx, Brooklyn, Queens, Staten Island, Nassau and Westchester." Nicolls' voice held a note of gentle triumph.

"Well, well, you mustn't be disheartened," Thatcher said bracingly; his august position spared him this sort of chore, thank God. "If we can't get him from that angle, we'll have to try another. What about organizations? Was he an Elk—or a birdwatcher?"

"The trouble is that he disappeared at the wrong age for us to trace that sort of thing. He hadn't really started an adult life or created any settled habits before he left for the army. He left Framingham when he was seventeen; people just remember a sulky kid with no identifiable characteristics. And a general search is going to be a very expensive proposition."

Thatcher nodded approvingly. "Yes, and possibly time-consuming." He thought for a moment, then added, "Now when this remarkable Arthur Schneider was ranting in my office this afternoon, he did mention his hopes for a partial distribution when Hilda Henderson dies. I'm interested in hearing what you said to him."

Nicolls permitted himself a frank shrug. "Well, you've met him, sir. We met in Martin Henderson's apartment, and the fact of the matter was that he did most of the talking."

"I can understand that," Thatcher said, with feeling.

"He wanted to be sure that we really did have to find Robert before any money was distributed. . . ."

"And you said that it was necessary, I trust."

"Yes, Mr. Thatcher. I had already had a long talk about it with Mr. Trinkam, so that we were quite clear."

"You didn't bring up a partial distribution?"

"Certainly not."

"Good," Thatcher said heartily.

Nicolls frowned in recollection, then, a shade uneasily said, "I think that I remember Arthur Schneider's saying that something would have to be done."

"What did you say to that?"

"Nothing," Nicolls said.

"Excellent," Thatcher said. "The best thing a banker can do is cultivate silence. . . ." He looked at his watch. "Good Lord, I've kept you from your evening far too long. I'll be going," he said as he rose, "but I think that we'd better step up our inquiries about Robert. Have you done anything about our bank connections."

Nicolls, puzzled by Thatcher's obvious satisfaction in what appeared to be a totally confusing situation, also rose. Unconscious now, of his exposed shirttails he said, "I've checked all the banks in all of the areas where

Robert was stationed, with no results. But I haven't made any attempt to circularize banks and credit agencies on a national basis, and I've kept our advertisements local. It's a question of how much we can . . ."

"If worst comes to worst, I want to trace every Schneider in the country," Thatcher said heartily. He turned to go saying, "I think that your idea about veteran's bonuses is the right one, you know. It restricts us to the right age group, at any rate. You might push a check on all the states that you haven't already tried."

"Yes, sir," Nicolls replied.

"You've done very well in a difficult situation, Nicolls."

"Thank you, sir," Nicolls said fervently—to an empty office.

Thatcher had gone. Nicolls sat down, expelling a breath of relief.

"Yes, the boss is always a burden, isn't he?" a grave voice remarked. Thatcher had reappeared in the doorway. "Just out of curiosity, do you have any idea of how big the Schneider Manufacturing Company is?"

"About five million gross," Nicolls said mechanically.

Thatcher appeared to do some calculating. "And if we don't find Robert, his $100,000 is split up among the other heirs?"

"Right," said Kenneth.

"Splendid! We want to find him then. The Schneiders don't need the money, and I am not altogether sure that they deserve any windfalls. Good evening."

3: RESEARCH AND DEVELOPMENT

In the end, finding Robert Schneider cost no more than the price of lunch at the Harvard Club two weeks after Arthur Schneider's descent on the Sloan Guaranty Trust.

John Thatcher invariably dined there on the day before the Christmas holiday, usually with Tom Robichaux, whom he had first met forty years earlier, in Harvard Yard. Robichaux had subsequently surprised his friends and relations by becoming an astute and competent investment banker when an unusually high mortality rate among his more sedate cousins propelled him from a promising career as a playboy into the family firm. Now, looking like a somewhat disreputable British colonel, he was the only Robichaux of his generation at Robichaux and Devane. John Thatcher and the Sloan had been doing business with him for years.

Neither sentiment nor business prompted Thatcher and Robichaux to eat a protracted lunch at the Harvard Club each December twenty-fourth. They were merely avoiding the dislocations that the preparation of inevitable Christmas festivities at their respective institutions entailed. And, if possible, parts of the festivities themselves; Robichaux because he preferred to conduct a strenuous social life in more appropriate surroundings, Thatcher because he found office parties embarrassing and somehow pathetic.

"Among other things," said Robichaux, gesturing for a refill of their drinks, "I don't approve of drinking in the office."

"Agreed," said Thatcher.

"Especially eggnog out of cartons with good whisky poured into it. Waste of liquor."

"Yes."

"And then last year—no, it was two years ago, I guess—my secretary threw her arms around me and kissed me. For God's sake! Made it harder than hell to go back to work on Monday. She burst into tears and apologized."

John Thatcher toasted him in silence: Tom, he thought, showed surprising diffidence for a man who had been through two spectacular divorces, and an even more spectacular alienation-of-affections suit.

"I know what you're thinking, John, and let me tell you that that's a different thing entirely," Robichaux said with mild indignation.

"I know it must be," Thatcher replied. "Come on, Tom, finish up. I think they have a table ready for us."

In the dining room, both men applied themselves to the menu in serious silence; only after soup, roast beef, baked potato—"For God's sake, no sour cream!"—and salad had been ordered could Tom Robichaux, who took food and drink seriously, be expected to turn his attention to conversation. This consisted, invariably, of a series of vigorous descriptions of the various inconveniences to which he had been subject since their last meeting. Thatcher, who knew how well he enjoyed life, listened to the catalogue of grievance: the airlines had cravenly allowed themselves to be cowed by a snowstorm, which reached blizzard proportions, two weeks earlier and disrupted Tom's complicated plans for a business trip to Detroit; Dorothy Robichaux, a statuesque blonde some thirty years her husband's junior, was demanding and apparently getting an extraordinarily expensive pearl necklace. One of Robichaux and Devane's security analysts was leaving the firm.

"I tell you, John," he said, pushing away the soup plate, "I don't know what these boys think they're doing. Blaine wanted twenty-five thousand a year."

"Where's he going?" Thatcher asked idly.

"To Brewer and Collings." Robichaux inspected the beef, nodded approval to the hovering waiter, then added, "and if they're giving him more than seventeen-five, I'll eat it."

Tom's lament, Thatcher knew, required no reply from him; beyond grunting encouragingly occasionally, he confined himself to eating. He felt for his companion the tolerant affection that forty years induces; amused by his picaresque private life, he knew that Tom's monologues were occasionally salted with shrewd and useful observations about business. At the moment, however, he was embarked upon a familiar refrain:

". . . and the way business has been for the last year, I tell you I can't sleep nights. Not a damned thing worth anything. I'm paying some of the fanciest salaries on the street, and nobody comes up with a thing." He put knife and fork down, and peered accusingly across the table at Thatcher.

"And you know that I'm right. When was the last time we did anything for you people at the Sloan?"

"I don't know," Thatcher answered. "It must have been . . ."

"I'll tell you," interrupted Robichaux. "Last February. You took part of the Wilkinson Steel offering."

"Been doing research on the Sloan before you came to lunch, have you?" Thatcher said provocatively.

With his fork halfway to his mouth, Robichaux was

moved to expostulate; "Now you know better than that, Putt!"

His earnestness, coupled with the now rarely-used schoolboy nickname made Thatcher laugh aloud; Robichaux interpreted this as lingering skepticism to be dispelled by a show of frankness. "I don't deny that we'd like more of your business, but that's just the point I'm making. I'd like more of a lot of people's business."

"Who wouldn't, Tom? Now that you've got all your complaints out of your system, do you feel better?"

Robichaux forked his salad, and replied in a good-humored voice, "You know, Putt, someday I am going to knock your block off. You're too damn superior."

"And too virtuous, you usually add," Thatcher interpolated. "Since you couldn't lay a glove on me thirty years ago, I don't know why you should think that you can do it now."

Robichaux looked at him appraisingly. "We're both in pretty good shape, aren't we?"

The judicial tone again made Thatcher laugh; "For men of our age, Tom."

"Our age, hell!" Robichaux said. "Listen, seriously we have turned up a special situation that you people may be interested in." He leaned back, and watched the busboy clear away the empty plates with a critical eye.

"Coffee? And apple pie? That'll be two," he told the waiter. "And cheese with that pie. Now what was I saying?" he asked Thatcher innocently.

"Something about a situation we'd be interested in," Thatcher prompted. "Come on, Tom, start selling me."

"We're underwriting a small new issue sometime next month. Buffalo Industrial Products. They've doubled their earnings in one year, and they're going to do even better in the next few years. I'm doing you a favor even offering you any."

"Electronics?" Thatcher asked.

"You know that's just what I said when Ed Fitzgerald turned this up for us. No, they're not an electronics firm. You'll think that I've gone crazy. They produce, among other things, textiles. Ah, here's the coffee." He smiled blandly at his old friend.

Thatcher eyed him. "Tom, I know you too well to think that you're trying to sell textiles. . . . No, wait a minute."

He stopped. As the waiter put coffee and pie before him, he recalled young Nicolls' description of the Schneider Manufacturing Company. "Are they in industrial textiles, Tom? In felt?"

"Damn it," Robichaux exploded, "how did you know that?" The waiter, startled by his outburst, stood apprehensively over him. "Put that down, man. Now, John, how much do you know about all of this?"

Thatcher stirred his coffee; "I've got my sources, Tom," he said gravely. "Go on, tell me about it. No, it was just a guess. I really don't know a thing about them, never heard the name before in my life."

Robichaux looked at him with suspicion. "You'd better not. Well, they're going public at about twenty dollars a share and I think they'll get to sixty dollars in a year." He glanced at his companion; there was no doubt that Thatcher was interested in this. Robichaux continued. "They produce a full line of machinery and parts and equipment for the paper and pulp industry. Their most important product is this felt, which is used on the Fourdrinier paper machine. A sort of belt. Now as I understand it, these felts wear out in a week or two, and have to be replaced, so the felt belts are one of the biggest items of their sales. That's why I called them a textile firm."

Thatcher sipped his coffee. "What accounts for the sudden spurt in their growth?"

Robichaux launched into a pet speech; "Well, you know what's been happening to pulp and paper firms. Why, Minnesota Pulp alone has doubled its capacity in five years, and is spending fifty million in the next three years to put in eight more mills. This new chemical hardwood pulp process really cuts their cost. Then, of course, new packaging and new uses for paper keep . . ."

Thatcher interrupted. "Yes, I know, but what about these supply firms? I thought that the industry was pretty well stabilized."

"Well, that's just it," Robichaux said. "They're not only stabilized, they're stuck in the mud. Just the other day the Canajoharie Felt Company was sold to Collets and Singer. The Canadian outfit you know. All these small firms have been plodding along, doing things the same old way, for God knows how many years."

"And this—what was it? Buffalo Industrial Products? It's a paper firm?" Thatcher asked.

"That's the thing," Robichaux replied, "this bunch is getting ready to really move with the paper industry. They've introduced the first real improvement into this felt business in years. You know that each of these belts had to be individually fitted to the machine? Well, out at B.I.P. they've just worked out a way to standardize them, and install them every time they wear out without a lot of special people coming in. Fitzgerald says that if it works out it will cut some firm's costs by as much as 10 per cent."

He stopped for a moment and Thatcher waited for him to make inroads on his pie. He was curious enough about the felt business to alarm Robichaux slightly, he realized. Robichaux resumed his explanation, choosing his words with obvious care.

"Now this is getting them some big contracts by itself but Ed says that the real money will come from a process they're developing that is going to make it possible to replace the felt with a sort of synthetic or wire—I don't understand these things—so that the replacing wouldn't have to be undertaken so frequently. Doing a lot of research and all of that sort of thing. Apparently it isn't just the cost, you see, but the nuisance of having to refit every few weeks. The boys in the paper industry are really very excited about this."

"Custom fitting the felt does seem a little out of date," Thatcher remarked. "Tell me, what do you know about the Schneider Manufacturing Company? They produce felts, don't they?"

Robichaux frowned in concentration. "Schneider Manufacturing—oh, yes, of course; they're up in Massachusetts. One of the old-line producers of the felts. What is all this interest in felts?"

Thatcher beckoned the waiter for another cup of coffee; "Well, it really arises out of quite another matter."

"All right; if you are really interested in Buffalo Industrial Products, I'll send you the red herring that we got up on it. As long as you don't have any special axe to grind."

"Tom, you're getting too suspicious. If Buffalo Industrial is as good as you say, I think you can count us in. I'll have to talk to Bowman. But I would like to see that preliminary prospectus." He sat thoughtfully for a while, then roused himself to find Robichaux still watching him with a question in his eyes. "Let's take our brandy inside, shall we?"

In the library, they encountered friends, so that it was three o'clock by the time Thatcher and Robichaux left the Harvard Club. An early appointment for dinner guaranteed Thatcher against prolonged participation in the Sloan Christmas party, so that it was not the need for escape that prompted him to suggest accompanying Tom back to his office to collect the prospectus on Buffalo Industrial.

Scrambling into the taxi, Robichaux settled himself comfortably then said, "We can send it over this afternoon."

Answering the unspoken inquiry, Thatcher said, "I'm just trying to get away from the office."

"I don't believe you," Robichaux declared bluntly.

"You know, I don't believe myself; I think I am getting nosier the older I get."

"I wish you would stop harping on age," Robichaux said with a spasm of genuine irritation. Thatcher sat lost in his own thoughts.

The trip downtown was impeded by crowds of package-laden pedestrians. When they were finally deposited at Four Broadway, Thatcher roused himself to notice that Robichaux and Devane had not found it necessary to surround the investment banking business with glass and chromium; it remained oaken and decently dark. It was the way an office should be, he thought, as he followed Robichaux into the third-floor waiting room, except for the sounds of strained revelry that drifted out of the inner offices.

"They're standing around looking guilty," Robichaux grumbled, as he returned from his room. "Damnedest thing. Here's the prospectus, Putt. Let us know as soon as you can if you want part of it."

"Thanks, Tom. I think you should count us in. Have a good holiday. My best to ... ah, Dorothy. Spending a quiet holiday at home, are you?"

Since Robichaux's home was a baronial Long Island estate with drafty halls, stables, and a large staff, the question might have been interpreted by a more perceptive intelligence as ironic, but Robichaux was unruffled.

"Yes. Just a quiet few days. Drop in any time, for drinks."

Saying that he would try, which neither man believed for a minute, Thatcher made his farewells, and walked down the hall to the elevator. He knew that at this moment Tom was bruskly interrupting the Christmas celebrations of—what was his name?—Fitzgerald—to catechize him about the Buffalo Industrial Products Corporation and its possible interest to the Sloan. Constant vigilance is the price of profitable banking. His interest would make Robichaux wonder. Not unnaturally. It made him wonder, himself.

He stood for a moment by Bowling Green savoring the last light of a clean clear day. The snow, somewhat dirty now, still banked the streets and bustling crowds formed bright colored patterns in their last minute flurries of shopping. As he walked along he felt a mild satisfaction with winter in New York.

It was dissipated soon enough. At his office, he found the sixth floor of the Sloan Guaranty Trust *en fête*. The inevitable crepe paper, incongruously Victorian, was draped over angular fixtures. Although the Christmas party was not scheduled to start until four o'clock, there were secretarial whispers and gigglings. The trust officers were standing around in small chatty groups; Charlie Trinkam was apparently telling one of his famous stories. Even Everett Gabler, looking ministerial as ever, had abandoned his work. John Putnam Thatcher strode through the waiting room and down the corridor, nodded curtly to Miss Corsa, then shut himself in his office. *That* would give them something to chat about.

Pulling out the prospectus that Robichaux and Devane had prepared, he read that the Buffalo Industrial Products Corporation would, after securing approval from the Securities and Exchange Commission, offer to the public 100,000 shares of common stock, par five dollars, the offering to be underwritten by Robichaux and Devane, the Erie Company, Waymark-Simms and others. The capital would be used to finance extensive expansion of facilities, including the building of a new factory; capitalization accounts indicated that this was indeed the first step toward stable expansion. There was, he noted, no debt.

Thatcher put the prospectus down and leaned back. A

small company, starting from even smaller beginnings, just about to move into the big leagues. Now what was there? ... he snapped his fingers with sudden enlightenment. He knew what had been nagging at the back of his mind. Turning rapidly through the prospectus he found a list of Directors and Officers: Stanislas V. Michaels, President; Elroy C. Novak, Vice-President; Carl Robert Schneider, Vice-President; Jean M. Novak, Treasurer.

Thatcher expelled a satisfied sigh. Carl Robert Schneider. In a firm producing felt for paper machines.

"Mr. Thatcher," said Miss Corsa, who had opened the door and now stood disapprovingly in the doorway, "they want to know if you care to come and help mix the punch."

"I would be delighted to, Miss Corsa, provided that you will drink some," Thatcher replied mendaciously.

"Oh, I couldn't," she said before she fled down the hall to announce his coming. Christmas parties were greater ordeals for Rose Theresa Corsa than for John Putnam Thatcher. He was merely fastidious; she was well brought up. But Thatcher was in high good humor as he followed her down the hall. The only problem, he thought, as he greeted his staff nervously assembled around the improvised bar, was how to explain to young Nicolls that he had unearthed the missing heir.

Telling him that it was a hunch would be setting a very bad example for junior members of the staff.

4: BANK HOLIDAY

Every seven years Christmas falls on a Wednesday, and the world of employer-employee relations is shaken to its foundations. Every right-minded employee knows that one day is insufficient for a complete and proper celebration of Christmas. Every right-minded employer knows that a five-day weekend is an unthinkable violation of the entire concept of the working week. And so one day off is given; but the employer knows that he has been mean, and the employee knows that he has been victimized. A little friction is inevitable and even the personnel of so august an institution as the Sloan Guaranty Trust found their holiday unusually erratic and turbulent.

For example, Rose Theresa Corsa was forced to sandwich into thirty hours an incredible number of activities. She participated in an office party, every detail of which had to be recounted to two younger sisters; she attended midnight Mass; she rendered prodigious culinary assistance to her mother; she sat down with a large group of relatives to a high holiday feast which stubbornly combined all the elements of classical Neapolitan cookery with those of a traditional American Christmas Day dinner; and she reviewed the day's events with her closest friend, Maria Angelus. The result of this hilarious round of activity was that she failed to prepare her wardrobe for the following day and arrived at her office one hour late for the first time in four years.

For Charlie Trinkam, Christmas had been even more harrowing. The associate chief of the Trust Department was preparing to surrender his long-cherished status as perpetual bachelor and man about town. He accompanied his young and lovely affianced, a recent graduate of Wellesley, into the wilds of Westchester for formal presentation to her family. Misled by a disjointed and enthusiastic phone call from their daughter, her parents were expecting a stripling recently emerged from Princeton. Upon being presented with a contemporary they exhibited symptoms of alarm which, Charlie realized, even his talents would require more than twenty-four hours to allay. And he had been right. After a day of painful civilities, he left a sobered fiancée, entrained for Grand Central and spent the night wondering whether he would enjoy a lifetime of being mistaken for his wife's father. By the time he arrived at the Sloan Guaranty Trust on December 26, he was ripe for murder and savagely demanding the instant attendance of his hapless juniors to review all troublesome portfolios.

At least one of them, Kenneth Nicolls was in no condition to placate an irate superior. The one-day holiday had caused him to forego his usual trip to San Francisco for a family reunion. Instead he had joined a group of Harvard classmates similarly isolated from far-flung homes. Their day, starting sedately enough at St. John the Divine's, proceeded to a comprehensive tour of those spots in New York City with which every young banker, lawyer and advertising man should be familiar. On the morning of December 26 he awoke with a knifing pain centered over his right eyebrow and a sense of impending doom.

Even John Thatcher had not escaped unscathed from the festive season. While impartially fond of his three children, he had markedly variant reactions to the families with which they had allied themselves. Inevitably the set of in-laws he liked least was centered within easy reach of the city. He had successfully avoided the demands of a family Thanksgiving, momentarily forgetting that the shortened December holiday season would make a trip to one of his more distant children impracticable. He was left fair game for the delights of Christmas in Connecticut.

He incautiously opened his visit with an inquiry about his daughter's health and Laura, nearing the end of her fourth pregnancy replied in detail, leaving her father with the gloomy conviction that her conversation over the last ten years had become largely obstetrical. Her husband, Ben Carlson, a pleasant and normally tactful young doctor, compounded his father-in-law's irritation by cornering him in the game room and gently suggesting that he curtail his daily bout of tennis in the forthcoming season. Thatcher was convinced that the seeds of this remark had been germinated on a steaming August day when he had roundly trounced his son-in-law in three sets of homeric length and was prepared to discuss the point; instead he had to endure a heavily saccharine reading of the *Christmas Carol* by Ben's father. Tradition asserted that the children enjoyed this yearly feature enormously. As nearly as Thatcher could see, his eldest grandchild, an intelligent boy of eight, looked as if he would dearly love an anesthetizing slug of Scotch to carry him through the ordeal. What was denied to Timothy was not denied to him. He retreated to the dining room to mix himself a drink, only to be cornered by Mrs. Carlson, who wanted to discuss both her investments and the approach of her latest grandchild. Outraged at the idea of discussing his daughter's Fallopian tubes with anybody, he escaped only to fall prey to a long and ill-informed analysis of the international situation by Cardwell Carlson, a professor of classics at Columbia. Release eventually came only with the early morning train to New York, which he rode with the dissatisfaction of any urbanite at being compelled to travel an hour and a half to reach the city. His cup of grievance overflowed when Miss Corsa's absence made it impossible for him to deal with his mail. Quelling the impulse to start ringing up hospitals, he reminded himself that it was the day after Christmas and, just because she never had been late, it was unreasonable to suppose that she couldn't be if she set her mind to it. Thatcher sat and waited, counting the things he couldn't do until she arrived. He succeeded in working himself up into a very satisfying bad temper by the time Miss Corsa burst in.

"That's all right, Miss Corsa," he snapped, breaking into her flow of apologies, "but please get Nicolls in here as fast as you can." His tone implied that the affairs of the Sloan Guaranty Trust had reached a crisis during her unscheduled absence, which only the immediate production of Ken Nicolls could resolve. Rose Corsa still in her overcoat flew to the telephone, distressed and guilty but gratified that her presence was indispensable.

Ken Nicolls, fresh from a grueling interview with Charlie Trinkam, was in his office wondering if the events of the previous evening had caused permanent injury to his right eyeball. He received the summons from Thatcher with a grimace of pain; he staggered to his feet and prepared to do his duty. He abandoned all hope of presenting to the world the picture of a rising young trust officer; his goal now was to appear conscious.

"Good morning, Nicolls," said Thatcher, in a brisk businesslike voice, "I think that you'd better try Buffalo Industrial Products for your Schneider." He had decided not to tender any explanation with this information. Simple omniscience would be his line.

"Sir?" said Nicolls weakly, wondering what in the world Thatcher was talking about.

"Schneider. Robert Schneider. You are a bank officer in charge of the Schneider Trust and engaged in a search for Robert Schneider. There is one at Buffalo Industrial Products. See if he's the right man," he added tartly.

"Where is it?"

"What?" Thatcher looked at Nicolls with exasperation, then in dawning comprehension.

"Buffalo Industrial Products is, curiously enough, located in Buffalo, New York," he said acidly. "Go and call them up, and," he concluded on a slightly more human note, "you'd better get yourself a Bromo Seltzer first."

Nicolls removed himself from Thatcher's office in confusion, and decided to dispatch Sheldon, the office boy, to the corner drugstore. He did not feel equal to asking the employees' dining room for assistance and, besides, he strongly doubted whether the Sloan Guaranty Trust recognized the need for stocking hang-over remedies. In this, he did the Sloan an injustice.

It was just as well that he secured maximum fortification before putting through his call. The long-distance operator treated him with a severity which indicated that, as far as the Bell Telephone Company was concerned, December 25th was just another working day. If they could maintain their standards of efficiency, then other people could too. There was a strong implication that Nicolls wasn't really trying to be helpful. It was with a sense of relief that, after alarming clicks and buzzes, he was finally connected with Buffalo.

"Good morning. Buffalo Industrial Products. Can I help you?"

"Good morning. I would like to speak with Mr. Robert Schneider."

"Mr. Schneider?" said the voice suspiciously. "Who's calling please?"

"This is Mr. Nicolls of the Sloan Guaranty Trust in New York."

"I'm sorry, Mr. Nicolls, but you can't talk with Mr. Schneider."

"Well, if he's out, would you have him return my call as soon as he comes in," said Nicolls patiently.

"I think that you'd better talk with Mr. Michaels," said the voice in some confusion.

"About what?" said Nicolls in greater confusion, but the only answer was a series of clicks, followed by a man's voice saying simply that this was not Mr. Michaels' office, this was the shipping department. There were more clicks, then a dead silence for a short interval.

"Hello," boomed a confident male voice. that made Ken wince, "I understand that you want Robert Schneider."

"Yes," said Nicolls with irritation, "I represent the Sloan Guaranty and I must speak with Mr. Schneider. The matter is urgent."

"I don't give a damn how urgent it is," replied the voice triumphantly, "you're going to have a hell of a time doing it. He was murdered two weeks ago!"

Two hours later Nicolls was reporting the results of his morning's work to Thatcher. There was no doubt that it was the right Robert Schneider. His Social Security and military records in Buffalo listed him as born in Framingham, Massachusetts, in 1918. He had come to Buffalo Industrial five years earlier from Rochester where he had worked for Eastman Kodak. On the night of December 13th, he had been murdered in his apartment where he had been found several days later. The police were searching for clues. Nothing conclusive had come to light yet, according to Michaels.

"Did it sound as if they were just building up their case, or is it a genuine mystery?" asked Thatcher who had listened to the story with what Ken regarded as bloodless calm.

"Apparently the police haven't gotten anywhere. Michaels, of course, warned me that he just knows what he reads in the papers," he replied.

"Well, what about children? The trust is divided between grandchildren and their issue, isn't it?"

"Good God, I never even thought about children. But Michaels said that he was living alone."

"That does not preclude the possibility of children, you know. Get busy and find out if there are any. The trouble is that you've let this murder go to your head. Remember, it's your job to get the trust distributed, even if the heirs are vaporized one after the other. You mustn't let a little sensationalism throw you off the track." With this fatherly lecture, Thatcher sent a chastened Nicolls back to work and tried to return to his own. But, even senior vice-presidents are not totally immune to a little sensationalism. Having fished the mysterious Robert Schneider up from the murk, he was slightly annoyed that the man should turn around and die still as much a mystery as

40

ever. He gazed absently out of the window: Tom Robichaux must have someone around his office who had gone out to Buffalo to talk to the company before Robichaux and Devane had agreed to the underwriting. Probably that someone had met Robert Schneider. He reached for the telephone.

At five o'clock that afternoon Thatcher hugged the wall of the Stock Exchange as he forced his way along Wall Street against the tidal wave of humanity that was racing for the subway. He was always surprised and a little dismayed by the number of white-collar workers in the financial district. This was the only hour of the day when you saw the real order of magnitude involved. He inched along to the eastern end of the street and entered the Antlers. A stocky smooth-faced man of about forty rose immediately from a booth and held out his hand.

"I'm Ed Fitzgerald, Mr. Thatcher. Tom Robichaux told me that I could give you some information about Buffalo Industrial Products."

"Very kind of you to come, Fitzgerald." The two men shook hands and Thatcher told the waiter to bring them martinis. While they waited for their drinks, they took covert stock of each other. Fitzgerald was obviously watchful, and Thatcher cursed Robichaux who clearly had instilled his subordinate with the fear that the Sloan might be trying to pull a fast one. He spent five minutes allaying these fears as best he could before going on to ask Fitzgerald what he knew about the people at Buffalo Industrial.

"I spent about a week there before we decided to bring out the issue. The management's quite small, you know—really consists of Michaels, Schneider and Novak."

"And what's Schneider like?"

"Well," said Fitzgerald looking infinitely suspicious, "Schneider is the real production hot shot. Michaels started the firm and ran it in a small way. Then, he took in his son-in-law, Roy Novak, who takes care of the financial details and the selling. Novak's a good man in his own field, but he doesn't touch the production end of things. They hired Schneider five years ago and he's come up a long way since. Is that the kind of thing you wanted to know?" Thatcher watched the waiter put the drinks down and nodded in silence. Fitzgerald sipped his martini, and continued to look dubious. "Well," he proceeded, "Schneider talked Michaels into putting a little money into some experiments and ultimately developed this new process of theirs for the mass production of felts. They used to be hand-fitted every eight days or so. He's got a lot of bright ideas for technical break-throughs and he teamed up with Novak to persuade Michaels into going public. It's obviously the right thing for them to do now that they've reached their present size and can look forward to an immense expansion."

"Michaels didn't like the idea?"

"No, Michaels—who's a stubborn ox of a Pole—has run the show single-handed for a long time and he obviously isn't crazy about going public. But he's not unreasonable and he realizes that it's the best thing to do in the long run. Novak handles him very well and Michaels' daughter had helped to persuade him into agreeing."

"Isn't Schneider much good at handling Michaels?"

"Well, I would guess that getting people to do things isn't Schneider's strong point. He's pretty cocky and too apt to talk to Michaels—or anyone else for that matter—as if they can't see the nose in front of their face. But," Fitzgerald added hastily, "there's no danger of losing Schneider. Michaels knows his defects all to well by now and has learned to live with them. He's put up with him for five years because his ideas pay off and he'll go on putting up with him. Besides, Schneider owns 10 per cent of the business now."

Reflecting that there were other ways of losing Schneider than through firing him, Thatcher asked Fitzgerald what Schneider was like personally.

"Personally?" Fitzgerald looked puzzled. "Well, just the same I'd imagine. Maybe a little pushy. Are you thinking of employee relations? Schneider doesn't have much to do with the men personally. They've got a first-rate foreman who doesn't seem to mind Schneider. Mostly I suppose, because he looks as if he could take Schneider apart with one hand and wouldn't mind doing it."

"Well, really," Thatcher said cautiously, "I meant what was Schneider like in his personal life. Did you see him at all away from the plant when you were there? Do you know if he was married, for instance?"

Fitzgerald now looked thoroughly mystified. It had

probably not occurred to him to wonder if Schneider had a personal life. But, consulting his conscience and deciding that Robichaux and Devane could have no objection to his placing at Thatcher's disposal his meager store of facts in this area, he obligingly marshaled his thoughts.

"I don't know too much about that, of course. I got the impression that people out there didn't like him too much . . ."

"Did you?" Thatcher interrupted.

Fitzgerald, who had obviously not considered this before, paused before he answered. "Well, no, I guess not. Of course I didn't see much of him . . . but he's a sort of loudmouth. Know the type?"

Thatcher agreed that he did. Fitzgerald scratched his jaw reflectively. He had been asked to bring back information about many companies, but nobody had ever asked if he liked the personnel. "I know that Novak tried to get him to join a local golf club once so he'd meet some of the finance people around Buffalo. He didn't want to and Novak gave up when he came to know him better. Probably decided it was just as well if people didn't meet Schneider. I did the town with him one night when I was up there. He's a pretty heavy drinker, but he stayed sober enough to talk shop all evening. He didn't say anything about being married and he didn't act married. By and large, I'd guess, he's one of the world's natural workers. Is that the kind of thing you wanted to know?"

"Yes," said Thatcher, "that's what I wanted to know. He doesn't sound very attractive. Did you get the impression that he expects to come into money?"

Fitzgerald had decided to humor Thatcher; he weighed the question. "What kind of money? He expects to get to the top in Buffalo Industrial and step into Stan Michaels' shoes, I should say. With the way that company is going, that may easily amount to seventy-five or eighty thousand a year in a little while. In fact," he added leaning across the table and waxing enthusiastic, "with this new process that they're planning, they can easily look forward to capturing 60 to 80 per cent of the market in industrial felts. Now, if you take into consideration normal industrial expansion in the next years, this would produce a yearly gross of about—"

But Thatcher had not come out for this drink in order

to listen to yet another monologue on the subject of the felt industry and its future. The remedy was in his hands. Reaching for the check and his coat, he benignly let fall his bombshell.

"I'm afraid they may have to do a little recalculating, if all this depends on Schneider. He was murdered two weeks ago. You may want to do a little recalculating too. Thanks for having this drink with me. I've enjoyed our talk, and you've given me a lot of information."

Feeling rather pleased with his exit line he left Fitzgerald looking totally bemused. A good deal later Thatcher was to realize that this was his first serious mistake in the case.

5: WITHHOLDING STATEMENT

"Send Nicolls in, will you, Miss Corsa?" John Thatcher said the following morning. Early sunlight still dappled his office, but he was confident that Kenneth Nicolls, like Miss Corsa, would be assiduously at work, having arrived with grim punctuality. Miss Corsa in fact, had been at her desk, faintly reproving, when he arrived a half-hour earlier, at eight-thirty.

"Ah, there you are, Nicolls. I hope you are feeling better today. Sit down."

Ken, a good deal less limp than he had been the day before, decided that no response was called for. He waited uneasily, while Thatcher cast a benevolent eye on him, then said, "Well, have you thought about our next step?"

"Our next step, sir?" Ken echoed.

"Hasn't it occurred to you, Nicolls," Thatcher said with some asperity "that the murder of the heir to $100,000 imposes some obligations upon the trustees."

"Frankly, I am at a loss as to what we do," Kenneth replied.

"So it seems. You young men are chained to your desks buying and selling. Acting as a trust officer is a far more

44

demanding profession than that," Thatcher said severely. "And interesting."

Kenneth Nicolls was stung with the injustice of this. For two years at the Sloan, he thought with indignation, all he had been asked to do was to sit at his desk, buying and selling. It was not an unreasonable inference that this was what a trust officer did.

Thatcher, however, had not waited for a reply to his remarks, but was continuing: ". . . so that this Schneider who has been murdered was the heir to $100,000. Obviously this is a matter of some interest if the Buffalo authorities are in difficulties about finding a motive for his murder. It's our duty to communicate this fact with them. Although, of course, they may already know it."

With lightning rapidity, Kenneth Nicolls discarded his vision of himself as a rising young executive in a citadel of conservative respectability. To hell with it, he thought, as, metaphorically speaking, he blinked his eyes, and shook his head.

"I think we can assume," he heard himself saying in a tone of voice he had never before allowed himself to use with his superiors, "that the Buffalo people don't know anything at all about the trust. I've been assuming that Robert Schneider himself had more or less forgotten about it; he didn't realize the sum involved and we certainly haven't turned up any signs of interest on his part while we were searching for him."

Unaware that he had been midwife to a spiritual rebirth, Thatcher nodded his agreement. "I think that's a safe assumption to work on," he said as he rang for Miss Corsa. "At any rate, we certainly should get in touch with the police ... Miss Corsa, I want you to drop whatever you're doing right now and put through a call. To the Buffalo Police." He exchanged a mildly conspiratorial look with the young man sitting opposite him, but Miss Corsa did not rise to the bait. She acknowledged his request by nodding in silence.

"And," he added, "we want to talk to the officer in charge of the investigation of the murder of Robert Schneider. Tell him we have some important information for him."

A fleeting look of satisfaction crossed Miss Corsa's face. "Oh, is he dead?" she asked.

Thatcher raised his eyebrows, "Yes, he's been killed ... oh, no, Miss Corsa. Not your Schneider. His cousin."

Miss Corsa, losing interest, withdrew.

Thatcher swiveled around to Nicolls. The boy, he thought was beginning to look a little more alive. "Now Nicolls," he said crisply, "for the moment I want you to hand over your other accounts to Charlie Trinkam. He'll have to reassign them. You will concentrate on this Schneider trust. There are some questions that we are going to want answered in the fairly near future." He thought for a moment then inquired, "How is Mrs. Henderson, by the way?"

"Sinking rapidly," Kenneth answered.

"But still afloat," Thatcher said. "Why do the Schneiders bring out the worst in all of us? At any rate, you haven't been bothered by the rest of them lately, have you?"

"No," said Kenneth. He amended the statement, "At any rate, not yet. We sent out a letter to all of them saying that we were studying the possibility of a partial distribution just about a week before Christmas."

"Well, we have better news for them now," Thatcher said. "I take it we can look upon the death of this man as good news for them. That is, if there are no children."

Kenneth looked at him with interest. "You really do think there are children, don't you?" he commented.

Thatcher turned to study the pattern of shadows that the sun left behind as it rose. "Just extrapolation," he said with a brief smile. "Everybody seems to have children these days."

You old fraud, thought Nicolls. But he listened attentively, as Thatcher outlined what he had learned about Robert Schneider from Fitzgerald. " ... a moderately disagreeable, but not an uncommon type. It's remotely possible that he did lie low out of malice."

Kenneth rubbed his chin dubiously, but whatever comments he had intended to offer were interrupted when the telephone rang.

Thatcher answered. "Yes, Miss Corsa. Good. What did you say the name ... Captain Self? Well, put him on, if you will? ... Good morning, Captain Self. This is John Thatcher, Sloan Guaranty Trust."

A brief crackling. Then, "Yes ... if our facts are right

. . . yes, if it is, then your man is the Robert Schneider for whom we've been searching."

Again the line crackled. Kenneth began to feel the awkwardness common to third persons to a telephone conversation, when Thatcher waved him to the extension in the corner. As he picked up the phone the crackling turned into a deep, calm voice asking, " . . . can you tell?"

"Our Robert Schneider," Thatcher said, "was born in Framingham, Massachusetts, in . . ." he looked to Nicolls. "Nineteen eighteen," said Nicolls. "My associate, Mr. Nicolls," Thatcher explained to Self. "His father was Carl Schneider and his mother was . . ."

"No, that fits," said the voice of Self without any audible excitement. "Stan Michaels called us up last night. Said you'd called. Told us you were looking for him." He stopped talking and the line buzzed faintly; then he added, "What did you want him for?"

"He was the heir—or rather one of the heirs—of a trust that we administer," Thatcher said carefully. "We are going to be distributing the trust in the fairly near future."

Again there was silence on the line. Captain Self was not a man to plunge into conversation, thought Nicolls. "How much did he stand to get?" Self asked.

"One hundred thousand dollars," Thatcher replied, matching his brevity.

Self apparently whistled, because the telephone emitted a sibillant squeak.

"What kind of trust is this?"

As Thatcher explained the trust, Self remained silent. Then, in a completely detached voice, he asked for the names and addresses of the other heirs.

Replying that Mr. Nicolls could supply these, Thatcher listened with amusement as Ken spelled the names and addresses, while Self said nothing.

"Is there anything you can tell us about the circumstances of Schneider's death?" he asked the laconic policeman.

"Not much. He got hit on the head, but the body wasn't discovered until two or three days later."

"Do you have any idea of who . . . or any suspects?" Thatcher asked.

"Plenty of them," Self said shortly. "Trouble is, that

47

weekend was one of our big snowstorms. Having a hell of a time checking on who was where. Everything was pretty much disrupted. Now," he said, clearly checking a list, "now we'll have to run a routine check on Arthur Schneider, Grace Walworth, and Martin Henderson." He sounded resigned.

"What we were wondering about here," Thatcher said, conscious of Nicolls eyeing him, "was something about Schneider. We've lost track of what he's been doing since 1945."

"What did you want to know?" Self asked.

"Marriage and children," Thatcher said concisely. "You see, any children of his would stand to inherit their father's share of the money."

Again there was silence on the line. Then Self's voice, more detached and calm than ever: "Schneider had a wife and two children. Two boys, seven and nine." "Good Lord!" said Nicolls distinctly, but Self continued. "They lived apart: separated but not divorced. Mrs. Schneider has the boys."

"Do you happen to have the address available, Captain Self? We'll have to get in touch with her."

"Mrs. Kathryn Schneider lives at 204 Sycamore Street, Batavia," Self said promptly and without expression. He paused. Then, apparently feeling that he should be more forthcoming he added, "She's a schoolteacher."

As it became apparent that Self was going to volunteer nothing more, Thatcher thanked him for the information and assured him of further contact, rang off, and said to Nicolls, "A man of few words, but sensible, don't you think?"

"Do you take it that he becomes even more terse when it comes to the wife?"

Thatcher was thoughtful as he replied, "Yes, but I was interested in those suspects. He sounded sincere, didn't he?"

"Of course he may just have meant that there were a lot of people who didn't like Schneider."

"I wish," Thatcher said, "we could find somebody who did like him. It would restore my faith in human nature. Family, business associates . . ."

"And an estranged wife," interrupted Nicolls.

"Yes indeed. Do you see what this means?" Thatcher

asked, looking with narrowed eyes at Nicolls, "It means," he said, without giving the younger man a chance to reply, "it means that the bank is now trustee for two minors whose mother is possibly a murderess."

There was a moment of silence in the office, broken only by the distant chatter of Miss Corsa's typewriter. Kenneth, startled by Thatcher's seriousness, was suddenly uneasy.

"And," Thatcher added authoritatively, "this means we have a mandate, an absolute duty to inquire into the whole affair. Those boys are a responsibility of the Sloan."

"Inquire into a murder?" Kenneth said, frankly incredulous.

With no visible sign of distaste, Thatcher answered, "Certainly. Now let's get down to business. I expect that the police will contact the Schneiders quite rapidly. Certainly over this weekend. Self sounds like a competent man." This represented, Kenneth knew, an accolade. Somewhat bemused, he watched Thatcher open a drawer, then look up to add, "I think that you had better take a trip and look into the whole thing."

"To Buffalo?" Kenneth asked.

"Certainly not. To Framingham," Thatcher said briefly. "I'll talk to Martin Henderson myself. Let's see, today's Friday. . . ."

Nicolls watched Thatcher make a few notes on a desk pad, then ring for Miss Corsa. Apparently he was dismissed. Well, he thought, the new Nicolls takes over.

"Mr. Thatcher, I'm going to have to know a little more of what you have in mind. What do you think I am going to do in Framingham?"

John Thatcher looked mildly surprised. "Well, presumably the police will have told Arthur Schneider about his cousin's death. They probably won't do more than some formal checking. You can tell him about the children. And watch his reactions."

"Do you mean to tell me," Kenneth persisted, "that you suspect Arthur Schneider, or for that matter Martin Henderson or Mrs. Walworth, of having anything to do with a murder." He paused. "In Buffalo?"

Thatcher permitted himself a wintry smile. "I don't suspect anyone, or anything. That's a police job. All I know is that when one of the heirs of a Sloan trust is killed, leaving two small children for whom we are responsible, then we keep our eyes very wide open." Kenneth found nothing to say; Thatcher looked at him for a long moment. "Nicolls, when you have been in the banking business for as long as I have, you will learn that money has a very strange and powerful effect on human behavior. We just want to be absolutely sure that ... oh, yes, Miss Corsa. Now, I've written down the details. We're interested in the murder of one Robert Schneider. It took place ... let's see, Friday ..." Consulting the desk calendar, he checked a date, "Good heavens, Friday the thirteenth. I want to see the coverage in the Buffalo press." Miss Corsa, Nicolls noted as he took his leave, showed no surprise.

Two hours later, Nicolls emerged from a conference with Charlie Trinkam—a somewhat trying conference, at that, as Trinkam was not pleased by the extra work involved in shifting accounts.

And, thought Nicolls, he seemed somewhat short-tempered, these days. Turning to his office, he encountered Sheldon, the adenoidal but good-natured sixteen-year-old, whose last name no one in the office had ever known. As office messenger boy, he functioned officially as mover of calculating machines, ledgers and similar items from desk to desk and office to office. Unofficially he was liaison between the sixth floor of the Sloan Guaranty Trust and the corner drugstore.

He was lounging against a wall, his face contorted by the effort of unaccustomed thought.

"What's up, Shelly?"

"Gee whiz, Mr. Nicolls," said the boy despairingly, "where am I supposed to get old Buffalo papers? She tells me to get two weeks' worth, but she doesn't tell me where to get them." "She" was unmistakable, thought Kenneth, pulling out a cigarette. Smoking in the halls, while not strictly prohibited, was a luxury he had hitherto denied himself. I'm getting to feel at home here, he thought. Lighting the cigarette, he pondered Sheldon's problem while the boy watched him hopefully. No ideas.

"Why don't you steal them from the Public Library?" Nicolls suggested jokingly.

Sheldon was momentarily blank with admiration, and

then, as his fertile imagination explored the possibilities, positively gleeful.

"Thanks, Mr. Nicolls," he cried as he loped down the hall.

"Good God, Shelly, it was a joke!" Nicolls shouted. But when impelled to move, Sheldon moved. He was gone.

And, mused Nicolls, if being a competent successful trust officer at the Sloan Guaranty Trust entailed murder investigations, there was no reason to assume that it did not also entail responsibility for raids on the New York Public Library. Not in the job description, of course, but . . .

6: PROGRESS REPORT

Having unleashed the havoc of a police investigation in at least three cities and assigned his subordinates to a number of difficult if not impossible tasks, Thatcher availed himself of the prerogatives of the executive and temporarily put the whole affair out of his mind. His round of activities ultimately led him to the Research Department where he found Walter Bowman almost submerged in reports, clippings, notes, graphs and ribbons of figures, all bearing on the rumored merger of a small razor blade company with a huge electronics firm. "Electric shavers, Walter?" said Thatcher assuming his customary role of devil's advocate. He then voiced considerable skepticism about the possibility of a merger and, alternatively, the possibility of long-term profit for the Sloan if a merger did take place. Bowman brandished his information like a weapon and the resultant duel, conducted with gravely courteous logic by Thatcher and violent enthusiasm by Bowman, lasted a full hour before Thatcher conceded that there was after all, a great deal to be said for Walter's position. They then proceeded to lunch where Bowman refueled himself with a double order of steak and potatoes and told a number of ribald stories about a well known market letter writer.

When Thatcher returned to his office in the afternoon he was surprised to find a triumphant office boy depositing on his desk two large folios, clearly marked "Property of the New York Public Library."

"I got them, Mr. Thatcher," Sheldon said with simple pride.

"Good work, Sheldon," Thatcher said gravely to the boy.

Miss Corsa, who had just spent ten minutes ineffectually trying to show Sheldon the enormity of his crime, succeeded in controlling her sense of outrage only until the door closed behind him.

"But, Mr. Thatcher," she said in a scandalized voice, "we can't steal from the public library!" Miss Corsa had been well brought up by the New York public school system; she had been taught that a violation of library property ranked somewhere above treason in the roster of capital crimes, and that one *always* washed one's hands before touching a book. While the distance of the Sloan ladies' room had necessitated some compromise on the second point, she was not yet prepared to cede one inch in defense of the first.

"Not stealing," murmured Thatcher soothingly, "merely borrowing. After all, that's the function of a library. I confess this is not precisely what I had in mind, but I refuse to dishearten a promising young man. Sheldon has a great career ahead of him." He saw that Miss Corsa was prepared to protest again and hurriedly continued, "And, in order to further that career and preserve the decencies, Miss Corsa, I want you to return these papers later today without in any way revealing the culpability of either Sheldon or the Sloan."

Dismissing Miss Corsa with a magisterial wave of the hand, Thatcher grinned maliciously and settled down for a good gloat. Sheldon had made off with complete files of the *Buffalo Courier-Express* and the *Buffalo Evening News* from December 7th to the present. Flipping to the issue for Friday, December 13th, he started to scan the headlines. After two false starts (one juvenile street killing and one hit-and-run) and one conscienceless departure from duty to read what the citizens of East Aurora were saying about the proposed location of a shopping center in their midst ("I will fight this amendment of the zoning ordinance to the last ditch. I did not become alderman to

52

preside over the dissolution of our fair community. We are not another bedroom suburb."), Thatcher found himself wishing that the Buffalo press could bring itself to introduce a little order into its make-up. By the time he had gone through every section of the issue for Sunday, December 15th (the Buffalo Bisons did very well that Saturday), he was wondering what dark forces were at work to suppress any mention of the murder. But the afternoon paper for Monday, December 16th, came through with a two-inch notice on the first page. The body of C. Robert Schneider had been found late Monday morning in his apartment. Death had occurred some time before the discovery. Police were investigating. That was all; apparently the *Buffalo News* had caught the alarm just before going to press. Opening the *Courier* for Tuesday morning Thatcher sighed with satisfaction. There were articles, pictures, and a promise of diagrams within.

INDUSTRIALIST
FOUND SLAIN

Buffalo, N.Y., December 17—C. Robert Schneider, prominent Buffalo industrialist, was found murdered late yesterday morning in his apartment at Delaware Avenue and Edward Street in the heart of downtown Buffalo. An investigation is being carried out by Buffalo Metropolitan Police under the command of Detective Captain Peter J. Self. An autopsy has been performed by Erie County Coroner William R. O'Donald, who announced that death occurred late Friday night or early Saturday morning. Mr. Schneider was Vice-President of Buffalo Industrial Products, Inc., which maintains offices at South Lake Street in Lackawanna.

Stanislas V. Michaels, President of Buffalo Industrial Products, became alarmed when Mr. Schneider failed to arrive for an important conference on Monday morning. He telephoned Theodore K. Baracawicz, superintendent of the Edward Street Apartments, to institute an investigation. Mr. Baracawicz entered the apartment and found Mr. Schneider's body. Mr. Schneider, fully clothed, was lying on the floor of his study with his head battered in. A blood-stained marble book end was lying nearby. Police authorities say that repeated blows were struck with a heavy object in a violent and determined assault. A macabre note was struck by the presence of a large Christmas wreath on the desk in the study.

Mr. Schneider was last seen in his office on Friday. He left for the day at seven o'clock in the evening after checking certain plans with Paul F. Reardon, plant foreman. Mr. Reardon, who helped the dead man dig his snow-bound car out of the plant parking lot, said that he appeared to be in cheerful spirits.

SCHNEIDER LOVE
NEST UNBARED

Buffalo, N.Y., December 17—A search of the apartment of murder victim, C. Robert Schneider, revealed signs of habitual occupancy by a woman. Mr. Schneider was unmarried.

Searchers reported the presence of feminine underclothes and nightgowns in the bedroom of Robert Schneider's apartment. A woman's toilet articles were found in the bathroom, which also contained a pale green silk negligee.

The discovery of two bottles of champagne in a cooler in the kitchen of Mr. Schneider's apartment and the preparation of platters containing paté de foie and assorted cheeses has given rise to speculations that Mr. Schneider may have been planning to entertain his paramour on the night during which he was killed.

Police have traced the purchase of the champagne to the Old English Liquor Store at 236 Main Street. Mr. Schneider is reported to have visited the store at approximately eight o'clock that evening. The salesman, Henry P. Miller, says that the victim chatted about the hazardous driving conditions caused by the blizzard then in progress and remarked that he hoped his little party would not be called off because of snow.

MYSTERY WOMAN
SEEN WITH WREATH

Buffalo, N.Y., December 17—The police have just announced that they may have witnesses to the actual arrival of the woman whom Robert Schneider planned to entertain on the night of his murder. Mr. and Mrs. Richard V. Daniels and Dr. Donald Curtis have stated that, while they were standing on Delaware Avenue at eleven thirty on Friday evening, they saw an unescorted woman turn into Edward Street in the direction of the side entrance to Mr. Schneider's apartment house. The three witnesses had just emerged from the annual Christmas party at the Buffalo Club and were attempting to locate a taxi in the blizzard. Due to the driving snow they were unable to observe the woman closely, but they report that the woman was wearing a fur coat and carrying a large Christmas wreath. A wreath was found next to the body of Robert Schneider. Mr. and Mrs. Daniels and Dr. Curtis will be taken to view the murder wreath this afternoon in an attempt to secure positive identification. Mr. Daniels is Vice-President of Lakeshore Realty, Inc., and Dr. Curtis is Chief of Surgery at Buffalo City Hospital. Mrs. Daniels is the former Miss Jean Manning of Dunkirk.

SNOWSTORM
HAMPERS POLICE

Buffalo, N.Y., December 17—The blizzard which dumped eighteen inches of snow on Western New York last Friday and Saturday has added to the difficulties of investigators in the Schneider case.

Police are checking the movements of all known associates of the dead man on the night of the murder as well as the presence of any strangers in the vicinity of the Edward Street Apartments. But gale winds and reduced visibility left most bus and taxicab drivers too busy to think about the identity of their passengers. Furthermore, sources close to the police report that many of Mr. Schneider's friends and co-workers have stated that they were two or three hours late on the fatal night due to drifts on the highways and the closing of the Lake Shore Road by State Police.

Most stores on Delaware Avenue closed early Friday afternoon in order to permit employees to leave before roads became impassable. Detective Captain Peter J. Self, who is in charge of the investigation, reports great difficulty in locating any witnesses in the area. A door to door interrogation of residents and shopkeepers along Delaware Avenue in the quarter mile separating Edward Street and the Hotel Statler is now in progress.

The next news item was accompanied by a photograph of a room containing several defiant-looking policemen pointing to a sinister chalk outline on the floor and an arrow hovering mysteriously in the air and pointing in the same general direction.

POLICE SEEK
MYSTERY CLUE

Buffalo, N.Y., December 17—Police investigating the mysterious death of C. Robert Schneider have expressed concern over the disappearance of an unknown object from the dead man's apartment on the night of the murder.

Pools of blood forming on the floor of the study near the victim's body (see pictures at left) may provide a clue as to the identity of his assailant. By the time police arrived on the scene of the crime on Monday the blood had coagulated, and the impression of an object measuring two and three-quarter inches by one and a half inches was clearly visible (see arrow). Police reason that the object must have been removed after the tragedy, presumably by the murderer.

A laboratory analysis of the blood particles has revealed traces of paper fibers. Speculation has arisen that the object may have been a small box such as jewelers provide. Merchants in the greater Buffalo area are being circularized to check their records in the hope that a recent sale to Robert Schneider may conceal a clue to the identity of his murderer. Anyone having information as to the nature of this object should communicate directly with Captain Self at police headquarters, by calling MOhawk 3000.

SCHNEIDER'S CO-WORKERS MYSTIFIED

Lackawanna, December 17—The men at the main plant of Buffalo Industrial Products at 1130 South Lake Street expressed sorrow and anger today at the bludgeon slaying of Vice-President C. Robert Schneider.

Stanislas V. Michaels, president of the company, spoke highly of the dead man's devotion and integrity. "We all admired Bob's zeal and dedication," said Michaels. "This is a great loss to us. We will give the police all the information and assistance in our power."

The men on the line were equally saddened. "Mr. Schneider was more than a boss; he was a friend," said Frederick Zukowski, head of Local 432 of the American Federation of Labor. "We shall miss him a great deal. His murderer must be discovered."

All the workers at Buffalo Industrial Products expressed astonishment at the slaying and were unable to suggest any motive.

Mr. Schneider came to Buffalo Industrial Products five years ago as Production Engineer. He had been previously employed by Eastman Kodak in Rochester, New York. He rose rapidly, becoming Production Manager in 1954 and Vice-President in 1956. His generosity and sympathy were recognized by all, and there is sorrow today in Lackawanna where C. Robert Schneider is mourned by his many friends.

Breathing a sigh of relief, Thatcher closed the issue for December 17th and gave thanks for *The New York Times* which restricts itself to stately analyses of the situation in West Berlin and Federal Reserve credit policy. On the other hand he had gotten a lot of unlikely information about Robert Schneider who had definitely ceased to figure in Thatcher's thoughts as a sulky seventeen-year-old. And any man who managed to surround his murder with champagne and silk negligees could not be the industrious drone that Fitzgerald had described. Robert Schneider not only found time for at least some extracurricular activities, but, what's more, he was determined to invest them with some aura of cosmopolitanism. Come to think of it, Thatcher reflected as he turned pages, there had been that business at Dartmouth. He should have realized that Fitzgerald couldn't be relied on to recognize anything outside of a market analysis.

Thatcher idly flipped over to the first page of the December 18th issue. Probably the Buffalo newspapers had exhausted their supply of facts and would content themselves with a rehash and portentous hints about police progress. But, no, by Tuesday morning the *Buffalo Courier* had discovered the existence of Schneider's marriage. Kathryn Schneider, looking pale and harassed, figured prominently as "Murder Victim's Estranged Wife." If the papers could be believed, Mrs. Schneider, in her determination to disown the now famous green negligee found in her husband's bathroom, had unwisely allowed herself to be drawn into general comment on her marital situation. Thatcher shook his head disapprovingly. This was no time for a prudent woman to be expressing dissatisfaction with the deceased, no matter how temperate or justified her criticism. Indeed, he mused, taking in the steadily ominous overtone of the article, it was clear that the Buffalo journalistic world was putting its money on the wife and probably typing up descriptions of her tearful entrance into custody, just in case.

Thereafter, the newspapers contented themselves with keeping the story warm so that at the first hint of an arrest and subsequent trial, it could be rekindled into flame. But the eruption of a paving contract scandal on December 20th relegated the Schneider case to the inner pages and the first page became reserved for tantalizing statements about "imminent disclosures concerning the

57

complicity of City Hall" and "alleged accusations aimed at figures close to the City Council."

Having had more than enough of the Buffalo press, Thatcher buzzed his intercom impatiently. Miss Corsa entered warily, her eyes averted from his desk.

"All right, Miss Corsa, I'm done with all this. They can go back now."

"Very well, Mr. Thatcher," she said half-heartedly, "shall I take them?"

"What?" Thatcher's attention was caught. He grinned. "I don't think you have the necessary criminal talents. Have Sheldon do it; he'll probably talk them into paying him a reward."

Miss Corsa picked up the folios and made for the door with alacrity.

"Oh, and would you bring your book in after you've seen Sheldon?"

Thatcher leaned back in his chair and started to compose a letter in his mind. When Miss Corsa reentered, she slipped into the side chair, settled her book on her knee and coughed formally. It was a familiar signal for them both. Without thinking, Thatcher automatically began to dictate.

Dear Mrs. Schneider:

The Sloan Guaranty Trust Company of New York, in behalf of which I am writing, was appointed trustee of certain funds by the grandfather of your late husband, C. Robert Schneider, in 1932. Principal and interest are to accumulate until the death of the settlor's last surviving child at which time distribution is to be effected to his grandchildren or to their issue. If, at the time of the termination of the trust, any of the distributees are minors, the Sloan Guaranty Trust is charged with certain duties until such distributees shall have achieved majority.

The settlor's last surviving child, Hilda Schneider Henderson, aged seventy, suffered a cerebral hemorrhage last October, and I am informed by her physicians that no hope of recovery can be entertained. It therefore appears probable that distribution of the trust will occur before your two sons have reached twenty-one years of age, and it will be necessary to institute the proper legal proceedings necessary to establish guardianship for your children.

If you will forward to me the name and address of your legal counsel, I shall be happy to supply him with copies of the relevant trust documents and inform him of the affidavits necessary to establish the identity of your two sons.

It will perhaps be of some service to you in planning the disposition of your husband's estate to know that in the event of a distribution within the next few months, the market value of the share of the trust evolving on each of your sons will be approximately fifty thousand dollars. Only interest will be available during minority.

If I can supply any further information or assistance, please do not hesitate to communicate with me.

Sincerely yours,

John P. Thatcher
Senior Vice-President

"Please have that typed up immediately and send it air mail, Miss Corsa," he said crisply. It would have been difficult for anyone to realize from his tone that he was motivated by considerations of common charity for that harassed and slightly stupid woman in Buffalo. It was Thatcher's experience that there are very few predicaments in life which do not seem rosier when a hundred thousand dollars has suddenly been added to the family bankbook. Furthermore, he reasoned astutely, the letter should put her in the hands of a lawyer, where she clearly ought to be. Any right-minded attorney who got his hands on Kathryn Schneider now was not going to content himself with dealing with her trust problems.

7: GOOD WILL

In the end, it was not until Monday that Kenneth Nicolls arrived in Boston prepared to "watch reactions." At three-fifteen in the afternoon he sat in the lobby of the Sheraton Plaza waiting, with no enthusiasm, for Arthur Schneider to appear. The Sloan's Travel Department had been courteous and efficient in providing transport to Logan airport: Arthur Schneider, on the other hand, was first unreachable, then brusk and impatient when asked for an interview at what he described as "disgracefully short notice." Ken looked at his watch. It was Schneider who had suggested a meeting at the Sheraton Plaza and dismissed Kenneth's offer to present himself in Framingham. Not really the ideal place to conduct what Ken foresaw as an awkward interview.

He examined the dimly lit lobby. Lobbies in Boston, it was apparent, attracted a different group than did lobbies in New York. Directly across from him, a red-faced man in an ancient brown suit was impatiently tapping his foot; next to him, two grandmotherly women in identical flower-decorated black straw hats sat with folded hands. A slim red-haired girl with a beaver jacket thrown over her shoulders was rummaging in her bag in the corner, while behind Kenneth four salesmen with bulging folders were arguing about somebody named Max.

But no Arthur Schneider. Ken rose and strolled over to the cigar counter. Behind the potted palms sat a young man in a blue blazer and rumpled gray slacks; from his expression of resignation Ken guessed that he was awaiting the descent of a relative, probably female. Two secretaries, with extremely high heels and extremely long cigarettes were perched on the sofa, casting haughty little glances of appraisal around them.

But Arthur Schneider had not arrived. Ken resumed his seat and prepared to wait. The two elderly women, apparently at some agreed upon signal, rose and walked in complete silence to the Trinity Place exit. As they left, the revolving doors debouched a haggard young woman dragging a four-year-old boy after her; she sank into the nearest vacant chair, expelled a noisy sigh and watched her son crawl along the floor with lackluster eyes.

The man in the brown suit was eyeing the entrance with increasing restlessness, muttering something to himself from time to time. The redhead sat quietly in the corner. Kenneth glanced at her. Very good legs. She raised an interrogative eyebrow as she intercepted his appraisal, and he returned to his watch: three-thirty. Still no Arthur Schneider. Frowning slightly, he tried to recall their conversation. Schneider had barked something about having to come into Boston. Probably business. Still, if he had been detained he could very well call the Sheraton.

"You're not by any chance Mr. Nicolls, are you?"

Kenneth looked up, then rose quickly; it was the redhead. When he admitted his identity, she laughed.

"How ridiculous! We've both been sitting here like bumps on a log. Oh," she said as she noted his puzzlement, "I'm Jane Schneider."

As he shook hands with her Kenneth concluded that wherever she got her looks, it was certainly not from her father. A small straight nose, creamy skin and deep blue eyes he had missed in his original appraisal. He approved, and was moderately surprised to hear that she in her turn had been appraising him.

". . . don't look like a banker. Not that I really know many bankers, but you do expect a paunch." She looked at him critically, "And you're not even bald."

Kenneth smiled somewhat foolishly. "Are you waiting for your father too, Miss Schneider?"

"Well that proves that Daddy is right, doesn't it?" she demanded of the world at large, apparently oblivious of the inhabitants of the lobby who were watching the encounter with interest. "He says I have a disorderly mind. I should have started by explaining that he asked me to pick you up," she said with a little rush of words, "and drive you out to Framingham." She tucked an arm through his, smiled up at him, and drew him along as she chattered. The secretaries looked indignant.

Kenneth replied that he could think of nothing more pleasant than being driven to Framingham, but that he certainly didn't want to inconvenience anybody.

She interrupted his disclaimer, "Oh, it's no trouble at all," she said propelling him through the exit. She proceeded briskly toward a bright yellow Thunderbird double-parked near the entrance. "Here we are," she said as she settled herself behind the wheel and waited for him to circle the car. Ken felt that he was being swept along by a torrent but he arranged himself in the seat obediently. Sweeping around in an illegal U-turn, she accelerated with a roar toward Commonwealth Avenue.

"I hope you're not nervous with women drivers," she remarked as she cut smartly in front of a large truck.

"Never," Kenneth said stoutly.

"Good. Of course I particularly wanted to be in on all of this. Daddy was simply furious when he left."

As Kenneth could think of nothing to say, he remained

silent. She turned to look speculatively at him: "Don't you want to know why he couldn't meet you?"

Repressing a shout of warning at a red light which she was certainly going to ignore, Kenneth said that he was very curious indeed. Then he put out an arm to prevent himself from being hurled through the windshield.

"The police," Jane Schneider said with relish, as she braked. "My poor respectable father is being grilled by the cops."

"Oh now," Kenneth protested, "they're just making a routine check . . . Good God, watch out! . . . Sorry."

"Frightened?" Jane Schneider said demurely. Kenneth took a long look at her. Enchanting to look at, yes, but nuts. A true Schneider.

"Do you always drive like this?" he inquired mildly as they sped along.

"Always. What do you mean, making a routine check? Do you know why the Boston police called my father and requested an interview?" she asked, then added, "Urgently."

"I think it is probably to tell him that his cousin Robert is dead."

"Is that why you came up? For another urgent interview." Her infectious laughter bubbled to the surface. "We've had nothing but requests for urgent interviews today." Of course she didn't know it was murder, Ken thought, but Jane Schneider was either remarkably indifferent to the death of a relative or, and this was more likely, Robert Schneider was no more than a name to her.

"I came up," Kenneth said cautiously, "to talk to him about a number of matters concerned with the trust. I take it you know about the . . . the difficulties we have been having." He looked, with spurious interest, at the scenery of the Worcester Turnpike: car repairs, funeral homes, hamburger stands.

"I see that you're at least as careful as a banker, even if you don't look like one," the girl said accusingly. "You've met my father, haven't you?"

Kenneth admitted that he had.

"Well," she continued in a reasonable tone as they sped along, "then you must know that I have heard all about the trust. And almost nothing else."

As Kenneth digested this, she added in an affectionate

tone of voice, "He is a fuss-budget, isn't he? No, you don't have to answer that. Do you know this part of the country at all?"

And, to his relief, the conversation turned to New England as they drove erratically on.

Jane Schneider looked very much like the girls Kenneth had squired around New York, a little prettier than most, but not basically unlike them. She had, it appeared, recently graduated from Mount Holyoke, and Kenneth had known other recent graduates of Mount Holyoke. But, he thought, there was something different about her, something ... he grabbed the door as they took a sudden sharp turn, and sped down a side road. A traffic cop shook his fist menacingly at the Thunderbird, and Jane waved back cheerfully.

"He's given me seven tickets," she confided to Kenneth. "He hates to do it. Every time he writes one out, he explains that he got his first job at Schneider's. That's it, by the way."

Kenneth, who had been mesmerized by her driving, looked out with real interest at the building past which they were speeding. Across the railroad tracks a sign proclaimed "Schneider Manufacturing Company" above a four-story building that looked as if it would cover a city block.

"I had no idea it was so big," he commented. The wings of the building reached forward to the tracks with the right wing obviously housing the offices; a somewhat modern entrance, painted white, had been installed, and through the high narrow windows fluorescent lights gleamed whitely in contrast to the gathering darkness outside. The other wing cast no brightness on the snow; the windows were blackened with age. Altogether a somewhat forbidding place, Ken thought. Probably built later than the earliest textile mills somewhere toward the end of the last century, but with their austere, forbidding façade. Behind the factory, stone walls enclosed a frozen river.

"It's the biggest employer in Framingham," Jane said absently. Kenneth laughed, and after a moment she joined him. "Yes, I see you recognize the source of the quote, don't you." She had become involved in a maze of side

63

streets; the factory and its industrial neighbors were left behind and they drove on into a residential section.

"I'm trying to avoid Framingham center. It's a madhouse at this time of night," she explained. "I'm not trying to kidnap you."

Gallantly Kenneth was prepared to deny any objections to being kidnaped by Jane Schneider when he was thrown backward by a jack-rabbit start from a stop sign. No use trying to be flirtatious, he thought. Not when you're risking your neck.

They drove on in silence through the rapidly darkening countryside. Soon they had left street lights far behind them; they were almost in the open country when Jane pulled into a driveway that Kenneth had not seen, and with a screech of brakes stopped in front of a substantial red brick house and jumped from the car.

"Home," she announced slamming the car door behind her. Clambering out of the car after her, Kenneth looked at the house; solid New England Colonial with good simple lines. There seemed to be a meadow to one side, and tall, snow-laden pines behind what must have originally been stables stretching out from the house. On the snow piled deep along the stone fence and the driveway, fingers of light from the house brought muted brilliant reflections. To a Californian, it looked like a Christmas card.

In the welcoming warmth of the hallway, he found himself being introduced to Mrs. Schneider and said as much to her before he remembered himself and apologized for intruding upon her.

"Certainly not, Mr. Nicolls," she said pleasantly. "We like the house at this time of year too, and we're the ones who have put you to a good deal of trouble. Besides subjecting you to my daughter's driving. You'll need tea, or something stronger to revive you."

Jane was hanging her coat in a closet, and turned back to take Ken's coat. "Isn't Daddy home yet?" she asked.

"No," Mrs. Schneider replied, leading the way into a living room dominated by an enormous fireplace in which several logs of a size undreamed of in New York apartments were burning merrily. "I think that he expected to be home a little earlier." She waved Kenneth into an easy chair on one side of the fire. "Now, what can we offer you?" she asked. Kenneth decided that an intruder, indeed a spy, could not abuse the hospitality proffered by taking strong drink; he decided on what seemed to be a prudent compromise.

"Sherry, please." Jane, he noticed, had cast a skeptical look at him, giving him the disconcerting impression that she knew sherry was not one of his favorites.

He listened to Mrs. Schneider's easy flow of apologies for her husband's absence. Here was the solution to Jane Schneider's good looks. Mrs. Schneider was a slightly dimmed version of her daughter, with hair a reddish-brown instead of copper, and a slightly thicker waist. But excellent legs, Kenneth noticed, seem to remain excellent. He was about to initiate suitable small talk when he was forestalled.

"Mr. Nicolls says that Robert Schneider is dead, Mother, and that the police are just notifying Daddy," Jane said as she carried her own glass over to the fireplace and joined them.

Mrs. Schneider put her drink down. "Good heavens!" she said in a shocked tone. "Dead?" Kenneth kicked himself for a tactless fool; Schneider's death might be a casual conversation piece for him and for Jane, but the disclosure should have been made more gently to a woman who had, after all, known Robert Schneider.

With a glance at his face, Mrs. Schneider shook her head. "No, Mr. Nicolls, it's not a great shock." She sipped her drink pensively, "But it is always something of a surprise when someone you know is dead." The flames sent flickering shadows through the room.

"I didn't know that you ever knew him, Mother," Jane said, in a matter-of-fact voice.

Mrs. Schneider frowned as she searched her memory. "Well, of course he was just a boy when I first married. Then after ... after his father's death I didn't see him at all, of course. I think that the last time I saw him was at his Aunt Marie's funeral, just after the war."

Kenneth had never felt less adroit. He knew that Mrs. Schneider's guarded reference had been to the fight between her husband and his uncle. And to Carl's suicide.

"Oh Mother, Mr. Nicolls must know all our family skeletons by now," Jane said, who also noticed her mother's carefulness. "And we certainly are a family with plenty of them."

Mrs. Schneider roused herself from a revery. "Jane, you really are impossible. Of course, Mr. Nicolls, I forgot you must know about all of this. And for heaven's sake, Jane, let's turn some more lights on in here." As Jane rose to snap on the corner lamps, Kenneth mumbled something to admit that he did know about the family situation, but Mrs. Schneider continued her recollections. "It must have been in 1945. I went up to him, at the funeral, to say hello. He seemed very unhappy . . . oh, here's Buddy."

A red-haired boy of about fourteen had erupted into the room and stood, in exaggerated surprise, at the sight of a stranger. "Mr. Nicolls," his mother said, "my son, Arthur, Junior. . . ."

It was after six o'clock when Arthur Schneider finally arrived to disrupt what had been an unusually pleasant afternoon. Kenneth liked both Mrs. Schneider and Jane. Even Buddy, a replica of his father, was a nice lad. The family was unexpected and a little unconventional but warmly friendly. It would force some revision of his picture of Arthur Schneider, Kenneth thought. Surely this family would not tolerate the pompous ass that Schneider had seemed to be. A slamming of the front door told him that he would have a chance to see.

Mrs. Schneider went to the hallway to greet her husband. Jane winked at Kenneth, and mouthed, "Watch this." Kenneth stood up in some apprehension.

A glance at Arthur Schneider, as he stomped into the room, was enough to show that he was thoroughly out of temper. His face was flushed, perhaps with cold, but his lips were tightly compressed. Nevertheless, he ruffled his son's hair, kissed his wife on the cheek, and greeted Nicolls, before he sank heavily into a chair and accepted a sherry from Jane with a somewhat absent, "Thanks, Kitten." His domestic obligations fulfilled, he looked about him, and said, "Well, I suppose you all know about Robert." He shot an accusing look at Kenneth, who nodded.

"Mr. Nicolls says that he has died," Mrs. Schneider began in a soothing voice.

"Oh Mr. Nicolls does, does he? Does he say that he has been murdered? And that these pinheaded numbskulls had the effrontery to ask what I was doing on the night he was murdered?"

"Arthur!" gasped his wife. "Murdered!"

"I always knew that he'd come to a bad end," Arthur continued, "but this . . ." The enormity of being murdered overwhelmed him.

For a moment nobody said anything. Then Mrs. Schneider, apparently feeling that this conversation was unsuitable for young ears, shooed the protesting Buddy to his room.

"Gee, Dad, do you have an alibi?" he cried from the hall.

"To your room, young man!" his mother said firmly.

"Well, Daddy, did you?" Jane said.

Arthur Schneider frowned at his daughter. "Now listen here, young lady. . . ."

But Jane could interrupt her father with impunity. She continued in a reasonable tone. "There's no use pretending that I care anything at all about this man that I've never even seen. But I do care about you. So, do you have an alibi?"

"Josephine, I don't know what we're . . ." began Arthur. He broke off, took a sip of sherry, then said, "Yes, my girl, I do have an alibi. And you're as bad as the police." The Schneiders, Kenneth decided, had either forgotten his existence or decided to admit him to the family. John Thatcher would approve, but he felt very much out of place. Both Mrs. Schneider and Jane were clearly determined to hear the whole story.

"Arthur, when was this murder?"

Arthur indicated to his daughter that his glass could be refilled. "It was apparently the weekend I was coming back from Chicago. . . ."

"Arthur!"

"Daddy, not really!"

"And," Arthur continued, "I told them that if the Mayflower in Washington wasn't a good enough guarantee that I wasn't murdering this miserable . . ." again his feelings got the better of him and he waved his hand in a mute, but perfectly comprehensible expression of exasperation.

"You see, Arthur," Mrs. Schneider said with a smile. "All's well that ends well."

"It's all right for you to say that, Mother," Jane said returning with some sherry which she handed to her father. "You two were perfectly comfortable in Framingham and Washington. I was the one who suffered." Her mother laughed, then turned to explain to Kenneth what had apparently become a family joke.

"My husband was flying home from Chicago that weekend. Let me see it was . . ."

"Friday the thirteenth," he prompted. She looked at him for a moment, then went on. "Yes, Friday the thirteenth. Well, of course there was a terrible snowstorm so they had to reroute Arthur's plane to Washington, where he very sensibly checked in at the Mayflower, and had a good night's sleep before coming in the next day."

Arthur shifted impatiently, but did not interrupt. "I, on the other hand," Jane said, taking up the narrative, "went to meet my father at Logan Airport, despite the snow."

"I shudder to think what your driving must have been like," her mother commented.

Ignoring the interruption, Jane continued. "The plane was due at nine-thirty. At ten they announced that it would be delayed. I sat and waited. Meanwhile the snow was still falling."

"And I was getting frantic," Mrs. Schneider added.

"At twelve o'clock I called Mother to tell her that the airline still said the plane was coming in."

"I do hope, Mr. Nicolls, you sympathize with me. My husband flying, my son with the Outing Club, my daughter at Logan on the worst night of the year."

He grinned at her exaggerated tones, and Jane strolled behind her father and massaged his shoulder gently, in a gesture of affection. He grunted, clearly in a better mood. "It was snowing very heavily," Mrs. Schneider said, "and the end result was that Jane called at two to tell me that there was still a possibility that the plane might be coming in, and I told her that her father was in Washington."

"Yes," said Jane, "by this time it was impossible to drive out of Logan, so I had to spend the night there. No coffee, no bar, nothing."

"You'd think they'd know about things like that, wouldn't you?" Kenneth commented. "The trick is to get to somebody who does know. Never ask at the ticket counter."

"Never call and ask if a plane is going to be on time," Mrs. Schneider said. "They always lie."

"It's all that glamour," Jane announced. "They spend so much time in their snappy uniforms, and in those glamorous planes and offices that they don't pay any attention to simple efficiency."

"I don't know what I paid for at college," Arthur Schneider broke in, "I admit mistakes do happen, but this nonsense about glamour . . ."

"No, Daddy, you can't deny it. How could anybody lose a plane . . . not to speak of your luggage . . . if they were trying to do anything but look pretty."

"You must admit, Arthur," his wife said, "that you were quite wild when you discovered that, on top of everything else, they lost your overnight bag."

Arthur stood up. "Well, mistakes do happen." He forestalled an answer from his daughter, and apparently feeling that small talk had gone on long enough, turned to Kenneth. "Well, now that I've complained about everything, we had better get down to business. Mrs. Schneider and I would be delighted if you'd stay to dinner but let's see if we can get a little peace in my study and get our conference out of the way first."

"I think that's unfair," Jane cried. Her father merely said, "Off with you now," and, leading the way to the study, said to Nicolls in a confidential tone of voice, "Women don't understand a thing about business. You wouldn't think so, would you, but my daughter studied economics at college. Ha!" He was obviously proud of his family. Kenneth said the appropriate things and followed him into a small book-lined room.

"Didn't want to say so before," Arthur said, "but I guess this means that Robert's share of the trust will be split among the rest of us. I can't really complain about going in to those damn fools at the police. Twenty-five thousand isn't bad for one day's work."

They had not told him about the children, Kenneth realized with a sinking heart. Jane and Mrs. Schneider had their work cut out for them at dinner, he thought, as he drew a deep breath.

"Well, Mr. Schneider, not exactly. . . ."

8: JOINT AND SEVERAL LIABILITIES

The oblique and respectful inquiries initiated by the Sloan Guaranty Trust were, of course, by no means the only investigations into the death of Robert Schneider. At just about the same time that Kenneth was diffidently discussing the trust with Arthur Schneider, Captain Peter Self of the Buffalo Metropolitan Police was asking questions at Buffalo Industrial Products. And he was neither oblique, respectful nor diffident.

"Naw, Schneider didn't bother me," Paul Reardon, the line foreman at B.I.P., was saying to him. "You had to know how to take him. He was like a horse with blinders on. He was on his way up with his bright ideas and the hell with anyone who got in his way."

"That can't have made it easy working for him," Self commented.

"So? A lot of guys are like that, only Schneider didn't bother with any sugar coating. I could handle him."

"Yes," agreed Self quietly, "everyone says you could. I'm not worrying about that. I'm trying to find out what kind of guy couldn't handle him."

"Besides," added the foreman with a confident grin, "I've got an alibi. I walked two blocks home through the snow half an hour before Schneider ever got to that liquor store. And I've got four people to prove that I stayed there all night. It's the first time anything good has ever come of living with my in-laws. Italians, you know," he explained gloomily, "they like the idea."

Self did indeed know. He had personally checked the Reardon-Manetti household ten days ago and he remembered vividly his encounter with an excited mother-in-law who refused to let her imperfect control of English interfere with her volubility. He had wondered then how the cheerful Reardon managed to fit in with that pack of passionate, doe-eyed Latins.

"Forget about your family troubles. Tell me about Schneider."

"It's like I told you. He didn't have trouble with the line. Even when he was Production Engineer and was around the men more. He was the boss. He gave orders; we took them. He wasn't around enough to be more than a pest. Nobody liked him, but that's all. It's the brass he had trouble with."

"I know about that. Tell me more. Did he play the races? Was he a lush?"

"Naw. He went over to Fort Erie a couple times in the season maybe if he didn't have anything to do, but he never put down any bets around here. And he drank, but nothing to write home about."

"And women? What do you know about that?"

"I know what I read in the newspapers. He had a green nightgown in his washroom. So, he was normal. We never thought he was a pansy. Why all the fuss?" said Reardon, with his first show of truculence.

Self smoothly moved on to ask about Schneider's last conversation in the parking lot, before he had driven home to be murdered. The single spat of irritation had told Self all he wanted to know. All the rest was a smoke screen. He already had a file an inch thick on Robert Schneider's personal habits in and out of the plant. For that matter he also had a file on Reardon's activities as bookmaker for the plant. But that wasn't what held his interest now as he droned on about Schneider's last leave-taking. So Reardon knew all about Schneider's mystery woman. Self had wanted to know if it was common knowledge. If Reardon knew, then what were the chances that Michaels knew? Did Novak know and, most important, did Kathryn Schneider know? She might not be in touch with the gossip around the plant, but certainly the other two would. He would have to be very cautious with Stan Michaels. But, nevertheless, he very deliberately made his way to the front office and in a flat uncompromising voice told Michaels, "We'll have to have another talk. . . ." And he asked his questions with no hint of apology until he got what he wanted, Stan Michaels' breaking point.

The room seemed very quiet after Michaels' outburst. They eyed each other wearily—two large, bull-necked men of middle years who were strangely different; Stan Michaels, whose arms flailed over his desk as he exploded into protestations and threats, and Self, sitting immobile and contained, as he quietly alternated interrogation and appeasement.

"Take it easy, Stan. We're not looking for a fall guy."

"All right, all right. So I didn't get along with Schneider. Who did? Is that any reason why I should kill him. I didn't even have any insurance on him."

"People don't kill just to make money. Sometimes they kill so they won't lose it."

"Lose it!" A sweeping arm imperiled the desk lamp. "In another ten years Schneider would have made a millionaire out of me. He already nearly got us the biggest contract of our lives. You're talking through your hat."

"What about these rumors that he was trying to force you out?"

"In a pig's eye! Look, Roy Novak and Jeannie and me hold 90 per cent of this business. Even after we go public, I'll still have control. If there was any forcing, it would have been me who did it. But I put up with him because he was a money-maker and I would have gone on putting up with him. I'm just telling you this so you'll know I wouldn't have had to kill him if I wanted to get rid of him."

"If he was so important and so valuable, wasn't he dissatisfied with just 10 per cent?"

"Sure. He was always dissatisfied, just on general principles. I was letting him buy more bit by bit. But in his own quiet way, he was a big spender. He didn't have much spare cash ever. I would have been dead and gone for twenty years before Schneider owned 40 per cent of the business."

"Well, he may not have been great on saving, but he was due to come into a hundred thousand dollars of cold cash. He should have been able to do some bargaining with that."

"What!" Michaels assumed the posture of a man belted in the midriff. It looked very phony, thought Self, but then all of Stan's gestures were larger than life.

"Yes, rich relatives in New York."

"So what?" grunted Michaels, recovering his belligerency. "A big roll still didn't make him kingpin around here.

I'm getting sick of this. This is the fifth time you've been here. And you're not the only one. I've got everybody on my neck. The underwriters are raising Cain, Roy Novak's away seeing about some licenses just when I could use him here, and we need a 30 per cent jump in production if we're going to be able to nail down this new contract. And you want me to spend all my time telling you where I spent the night of December 13th! Well, I've told you. Right here. I couldn't get that damn Pontiac started on the ice, the radio said the roads were closed, so I said the hell with it and sacked out on the couch. Now beat it and let me get some work done."

"O.K., Stan, let's not make a federal case out of this. You say you spent the night here. But all we know is that you were here the next morning when Reardon showed up, and he says you looked as if you were on the couch all night. Your clothes were rumpled and you needed a shave. That doesn't mean that you couldn't have gone down town and come back here before morning when you found out you couldn't make it out to your place in Hamburg."

"O.K., I don't have an alibi. Nobody in Buffalo has an alibi for that night."

"I know it," said Self. "That blizzard was a godsend for whoever pulled this job. Everybody either got home four hours late, or they tried to get home and couldn't so they showed up at a relative's house around midnight or they took a bus and the driver can't remember because he was too busy skidding on ice, or they put in a call to the AAA which couldn't get to them for three hours, or they slept in their office without any witnesses. Paul Reardon's the only man in Erie County who has an alibi and he has in-law trouble instead."

"Well, if you've got all that to worry about, Pete, take a load off your mind and forget about me. I didn't have any reason to kill him."

"All right, so he couldn't push you out. What about Novak? He must have counted on coming into the business some day ever since he married your daughter. After all, they say he was the bright young man around here until Schneider came. Roy wouldn't like that much."

"Nuts. Roy got along with Bob Schneider a lot better than I did. Besides Roy's never been on the production end, just the financial end—even before Schneider came. You know, Roy started off as an accountant."

"Then what about his stake in the business? Was he still going to step into your shoes?" pressed Self.

"Sure, sure. Jeannie will inherit my holdings and she and Roy will have control. Schneider couldn't do any more after my death than before," Michaels was now visibly sweating, but he summoned up a weak grin. "Besides, you're worried about me murdering Schneider, not Schneider murdering me. Remember?"

"Actually, it was Novak I was asking about," said Self quietly. He paused and then continued, "But we can wipe that out now anyway, Stan. We've checked up on him. He was in Montreal just the way he should have been and sitting in on a poker game that didn't break up till late at night."

Self affected not to notice the heavy sigh of relief which Michaels tried to restrain too late. So Stan not only knew all about it, but he was quite certain that Novak had known too. Had the two men discussed it? Self thought not. It was not a subject on which Michaels could be expected to be forthcoming, and Novak was notorious for his tact; as are most young accountants who marry the boss's daughter. The only thing to do at the moment was to try another tack.

"Did Schneider ever take things home from the plant?"

"Sure he did—papers, drawings, sometimes a trade journal if it had an article he wanted to read."

"I don't mean that sort of thing. Something that would go into a small box."

Michaels, in sheer gratitude at having left behind the whole question of Novak, was even trying to be helpful.

"In a box? You mean a piece of equipment? Why should he do that? He didn't have a shop, and he wasn't much with his hands anyway. None of them are nowadays."

"You know what I mean. It was in the *Courier*. Somebody took something from his apartment after he was murdered. There was a mark in the blood—about two and three-quarters inches by one and a half. It was made from some kind of cardboard."

"What makes you think it was a box? Maybe it was some kind of a ticket."

"Yes," agreed Self patiently, "it could be anything like that. What I want to know is whether he could have taken any small object from the plant that would be important to anyone else."

"Look, Pete, we don't make guided missiles; we make felt. Nobody's going to pull a blackjack to steal a screw from one of our machines. They're just plain ordinary screws."

Self was inclined to share this view and, as both men were now speaking in the robot monotones of complete exhaustion, he brought the interview to a speedy close and took his leave.

It was significant that he had not once broached the topic of Schneider's relations with women.

Stan Michaels' entrance into Reardon's glassed-off cubby hole was elaborately casual.

"I'm sorry I didn't get in earlier, Paul," he began, "I want to clear the weekend schedule with you."

"I've made one out if you want to take a look at it." Reardon passed a scrawled piece of paper across to Michaels who didn't bother to pick it up. He had hitched himself up on a corner of the desk and was morosely staring at his swinging shoe.

"That damned cop has been back again," he said irritably. "How can we get anything done if he's underfoot all the time?"

"It's a pain in the neck. He was down here too this morning. The men don't pay much attention to him any more."

"Like hell they don't. Production's been off ever since he started nosing around. It gets them jittery to have him digging up every fight anyone ever had with Schneider."

Both men looked through the glass wall toward the production line in token homage to this statement. Neither was under any illusion that they were talking about Self's effect on the workers—a remarkably phlegmatic group of Slavs who looked about as jittery as a bunch of tractors.

"Yeah," agreed Reardon, dourly wondering what was coming.

"And if that isn't bad enough, he's started yapping about Schneider's private life. Who did he see after hours, how did he spend his time, where did his money go? This is a factory, not a confessional."

Oh hell, thought Reardon. So that's what's burning him. I thought he didn't know. I suppose you can't expect him to see that the little tart isn't worth all this. She's looking for trouble, and she'll find it one way or another.

". . . and I don't see how we can be expected to know about that sort of thing." Michaels was now frankly avoiding Reardon's eyes, and his voice had ended on a note of outright interrogation.

"Well, we told him we don't know anything," slowly replied the foreman, trying to warn Michaels, reassure him, and maintain formal ignorance all in one breath.

Michaels turned around and the two men looked at each other. Complete communication was achieved without one more word spoken.

"Thanks, Paul. The schedule's fine. I won't have to make any changes." Michaels hoisted himself off the desk and blundered out the door, leaving Reardon relieved and thankful that he had been spared any open discussion.

Stan was not nearly so satisfied with the results of their talk. His fury at being forced to beg silence from his foreman was submerged by alarm. Reardon's quick comprehension made it all too clear that he was dealing with common knowledge. Sooner or later Self would pick up the trail. He hurried back to his office and dialed his daughter's number. He found himself counting the rings until she answered. On the eighth, there was a click.

"Jeannie?"

"Oh, Poppa, why do you keep calling? I just got the baby to sleep."

"Listen, honey, Pete Self has been around again."

"Well, what difference does that make to me? I barely knew Bob Schneider."

"Jeannie, you've got to be careful. Pete's asking about everything."

But Stan Michaels was not as adept as Reardon at tactful, unspoken communication; he struggled to express his concern.

"The police are checking up on Roy—asking about how he and Schneider got along."

"Well, they haven't been to me," his daughter shrilled

defiantly, "Why should they? It wasn't Roy who was always at Bob's throat."

Michaels was now sickened with anxiety by his daughter's defensive hostility. Ordinarily she was more inclined to sullen silence than to ringing hysteria.

"Honey, they're bound to find out," he pleaded. "We've got to think up a story."

"Leave me alone. What are you after? I don't know what you're talking about."

"Jeannie—"

"No! I've got to hang up, Poppa. The baby's crying." The telephone clicked finally as his daughter broke the connection. He started to redial then put the phone down. "Oh, Jeannie," he muttered. And held his head in his hands.

After she slammed the receiver Jeannie Novak lit a cigarette with jerky movements and began to pace up and down the cluttered living room, her housedress sweeping the floor as her high-heeled mules clicked back and forth.

Poppa was making things much worse. Self was bound to notice how alarmed he was. And once Self started to think in that direction, he wouldn't have any trouble finding out more. Why had she let Bob take her into Buffalo to the Chez Amis where they must have been seen? They should have gone over to Canada the way they always did. But Bob was so pigheaded; he had to have his own way and he hadn't felt like driving. He was a bastard. They all were. They didn't care what happened to her. And she was sure that Reardon had seen them in the parking lot out at the plant. Reardon would talk; he didn't like her. Why, oh why, had she been so bitchy to his wife? Probably it was Reardon who had told Roy.

But it had all been worth it. Bob had made it exciting. Being seen in town had just been a part of all that. Poppa didn't know how bad it was or he wouldn't ever think she could get out of it with some kind of story. Why didn't he take her side anyway? He shouldn't believe that kind of talk about his own daughter. Unless . . . she stopped her pacing. Sometimes he stopped in town for a drink after work. Maybe he had seen her and Bob himself. It was all too probable.

She ground out her cigarette viciously, just as the doorbell rang. For a moment she stood arrested, then automat-

ically she started to twitch her skirts into order and feel
for a comb in her pocket. The bell pealed again. She
picked up the ash tray with its overflowing mass of butts
and hid it behind the wedding photograph on the piano.

She knew who it was before she opened the door. Self
and Jeannie Novak regarded each other silently for a
moment.

"So, you're back again," she said sulkily. "Well, I suppose you might as well come in."

9: DISSENTING SHAREHOLDERS

And while Kenneth Nicolls in Framingham was somewhat
tentatively trying to assess Arthur Schneider's response to
his cousin's murder and Peter Self in Buffalo was grimly
investigating everyone who had ever known the late Robert Schneider, John Thatcher was dismissing a taxicab on
the south side of Washington Square so that he could walk
through the park to Martin Henderson's apartment on
Waverly Place. The snow, which had long since disappeared from Wall Street, was here a clean, crisp white,
shining in the sunlight. The charm of the late afternoon
scene had attracted a good many strollers and the play-
ground was doing a land-office business. His path would
take him past a large snowman he noted with pleasure.
How rarely city children had an opportunity for this kind
of activity. But, as he drew nearer he saw that the statue
had improbable but unmistakable female characteristics.
Clearly not the work of snowsuited toddlers frolicking
merrily in the snow but of some New York University
students with fevered imaginations. A stroller approaching
from the opposite direction paused momentarily by his
side.

"Personally," said the stranger austerely, "I prefer the
old-fashioned variety." And with a courteous inclination of
his head, he passed on.

Thatcher wasted no more time looking for Grandma
Moses vignettes but pressed on to his destination, an

old-fashioned but well preserved brownstone fronting on the park. He mounted the stoop, scanned the bell plates, and then noticed the sign which directed him to the basement for "M. Henderson." Descending into the areaway, he found the correct bell and took time to note that the basement apartment tenant, having his private entrance, would presumably be able to enter and leave the building unnoticed by the other residents.

His ring was almost immediately answered by a tall, broad-shouldered man who greeted him heartily.

"Come in, come in! You must be John Thatcher from the Sloan. I just got back from the office." His smile was startlingly white against a sun tan which had been carefully preserved in the midst of a New York winter.

"Very kind of you to rush back on my account. I'm sorry to inconvenience you."

"Not at all. Delighted I could make it," Martin rejoined, ushering Thatcher down a long narrow corridor and into a room at the back of the house with the air of one ringing up the curtain.

And it was a room that lent itself to dramatic gestures. The original wood moldings and pilasters had been allowed to remain, but they had been painted the same stark white as the walls. The rear wall had been replaced by a wall of glass opening onto a pocket handkerchief garden which was dominated by a slender black marble nymph rising from a small pool. The glass was framed by opulent draperies of a clear, vivid blue silk, and a severely linear divan balanced several deep but narrow easy chairs, all upholstered in a dark, earth brown. The blues and browns were joined together over the modernized mantel in a John Marin watercolor of the Maine seacoast.

Thatcher experienced a certain reluctant admiration. He, too, preferred the old-fashioned type of snowman, but this room was a success. It was aggressively masculine, defiantly modern, and totally artful, but it fulfilled its intended function; it forced you to look at its owner with a new interest. He became a man to be reckoned with. It was not surprising that young Nicolls had been impressed, and Thatcher no longer wondered why Henderson preferred, with some insistence, to receive his callers at his home, rather than his office. If Arthur Schneider had anything to do with the décor of the New York offices of

Schneider Manufacturing they would not provide nearly so interesting a backdrop for a worldly bachelor.

"Scotch or bourbon?" While Thatcher had been examining the room, Martin had opened a deceptively simple teak chest to reveal a fairly comprehensive bar. Restraining the impulse to ask for something esoteric in the hopes of puncturing his host's performance, Thatcher accepted a Scotch and water.

The two men settled down with their drinks and Thatcher played for time with a few noncommittal remarks about his relation to Nicolls and the Schneider Trust. He preferred, if possible, to let the other man assume the burden of opening the discussion about the death of Robert Schneider and its influence on the trust distribution. Long experience had taught him that, in this way, the conversation could naturally be developed into an interrogation of the position of his vis-à-vis. And nothing is more congenial to a banker than the wholesale dissection of somebody else's point of view. But Martin did not seem to suffer from his cousin's compulsion to rush into speech. He responded amiably but uninformatively to Thatcher's ploys for some minutes before finally leaning forward and making his opening gambit.

"I suppose," he said shrewdly, "that it was the Sloan that set the police on me."

"Have they been to you?" replied Thatcher blandly. "We had to communicate with them on the question of proving identification, and they seemed interested in the details of the trust."

"They were," said Henderson dryly. "In fact they now regard the Schneider family as prime suspects."

"Surely not. The man I spoke with indicated that Buffalo was teeming with potential suspects."

"If Bob Schneider lived there for any length of time, I expect it is. He had a genius for strewing the landscape with enemies, if he stayed the same as when we knew him."

"I imagine this is just a routine check so that they can cross you off and concentrate on the local scene. What did they ask about?"

"They asked about alibis, and they're certainly not crossing me off on the basis of mine," said Martin sourly.

"Oh?" Thatcher maintained an air of elaborate unconcern which should have fooled no one, but Henderson was now displaying another Schneider characteristic: he was far too wrapped up in his own grievances to worry about audience reaction.

"Yes, apparently it happened on the night of that big storm we had. I left the office about two o'clock to go to the trade show at the Coliseum. When I came out about five, it was sleeting and snowing and, naturally, there wasn't a taxi in sight. There was nothing much doing at the office so I hopped into the subway and came down here. I had a ticket to the hockey game at the Garden, but it was so bad out that I decided to cook dinner myself and spend the evening here with a book."

Henderson finished this explanation with a comprehensive wave toward the bookcases. Following this gesture, Thatcher noted with distaste that the available literature seemed to consist of the works of Henry Miller and an opened copy of *Lolita*. He decided to give the man the benefit of the doubt and suppose that the evening might have been spent with the pile of stock market reports and tipster sheets which were visible on the desk in the corner.

"Well, well, you're probably worrying about nothing, and they'll find their man in Buffalo within the next few days."

"Yes, or the whole thing will fizzle out. But, just the same, it's pretty annoying to think that, if I'd gone to the Garden and talked to whoever sat next to me, I'd have an ironclad alibi."

"On the contrary, you wouldn't know his name and you'd be spending all your time trying to remember some identifying characteristic. Much less trouble this way."

"Well, anyway," said Martin, recalling his duties as a host, "you didn't come here to talk about alibis and you're not really interested in my troubles. Sorry to bother you with all this."

"Not at all," said Thatcher cordially. "But I'm afraid that you won't find the information I have for you much of an improvement. It seems that your cousin, Robert Schneider, left children—two boys."

"Well, what difference does that make?"

"His share of the trust passes to them."

"You mean, I still only get a hundred thousand?"

"That is the case."

Martin fell into a brooding silence in the course of which he rose and automatically freshened their drinks. Thatcher watched him in some sympathy. In the course of his life it had been necessary for him to deliver unwelcome financial news many times, and he knew that no one, regardless of their income or their bank account, likes to be told that they aren't going to get fifty thousand dollars they had been counting as their own.

"Dammit," said Martin, "it isn't that I need the money, but I had relied on being able to buy a substantial slice of stock in the firm. A hundred and fifty thousand plus whatever I could get for Mother's preferred would have put me in a position to exert a lot of influence, particularly if I could talk some sense into Grace."

"Ah, yes, your mother," said Thatcher wryly, "I should already have offered you my sympathy. This must be a very trying time for you."

"Of course," said Martin examining his cuff links with no visible sign of grief. "We have all reconciled ourselves to the fact that the end will be a release for her." He was completely preoccupied with this sudden drop in his expectations. "I'll be frank with you—"

Thatcher automatically braced himself for a wave of evasion and deceit.

"The business is not doing as well as it should. Mind you, there's absolutely nothing wrong fundamentally. Our intrinsic worth is exactly the same. But it won't be for long if we keep on this way. We've already lost several old contracts and unless something happens we're going to lose more. This is a research-minded economy. There are lots of new firms with bright young men and we have to keep up. I keep trying to point out to Arthur that we simply have to put more money into research and development. But Arthur—"

Martin broke off self-consciously from what clearly would have been a comprehensive indictment of his cousin.

"But then you've met Arthur and you know what I'm talking about. He's set in his ways and being up there in Framingham doesn't help him to get any perspective. He has absolutely no idea of what New York firms are doing today. He seems to think that advertising should be restricted to consumer products. He flatly rejected my publicity budget for next year. I got him down here to have a talk with Jim Benton over at Donner and Berk—they did a study of sales consciousness on the part of some of the smaller industrial firms and the boys there let me have a look at the results. But did it do any good? No! What was good enough for—"

At this interesting point, the bell rang and Martin broke off on the brink of a second attack on Arthur. He excused himself and left for the door. Thatcher realized that the addition of a third person to this interview pretty effectively ended any hope of further revelations. He idly listened to the sounds emanating from the entrance foyer as he rehearsed a few quick exit lines. Martin seemed to be defending himself against a series of shrilly pitched rapid-fire questions from his latest guest. Presently he returned, accompanied by a tall, middle-aged woman who was jerking off her gloves. Thatcher felt a great wave of content as he rose. Surely it must be—? It was. Now the problem was how to delay a departure which was clearly the courteous and correct movement on his part.

"This is John Thatcher of the Sloan, Grace. You remember, he talked with Arthur. This is my cousin, Mrs. Walworth."

Grace Walworth made a perfunctory acknowledgment of the introduction and continued her complaints without pausing for breath.

"I see that I have to come up here to get anything done. There is no use talking to you or Arthur by phone. The only thing it accomplishes is that I become a police suspect!"

Martin grinned maliciously. It was apparent that pouring oil on troubled waters formed no part of his immediate intentions.

"But, you should speak to Mr. Thatcher about that, Grace. He's the man who set the police on us. I myself have already sustained a grilling at the hands of the cops today." He paused long enough for Grace to suck in one long outraged breath and swing her mink coat to one side, presumably to have a clear field of attack, before firing his second shot.

"What's more, he brings even worse news. Robert had children."

"Well," said Grace, impatient of irrelevancies. "Surely,

no one can expect us to support them. There must be a mother or something of that sort."

"No, you don't follow me, my dear," continued Martin in tones of immense satisfaction, "Robert's share of the trust goes to his sons. You don't get the extra twenty-five thousand you've been talking about continuously for the last two days."

"What!" For a moment Grace was blessedly speechless. "Well, that is the limit." She paused to dwell on the late Robert's treachery. "There must be some mistake. They're not grandchildren."

"They don't have to be. Grandfather prepared against all eventualities," replied Martin in more sober tones. Now that the first rapture of discomfiting Grace was over, he was prepared to join in the lamentation and wailing.

Meanwhile Grace, forgetting her original grievance with Thatcher, ignored his existence completely and turned to Martin for solace.

"Something has to be done. It's all very well for you. No doubt Hilda is leaving a very substantial sum for you and you don't have many expenses anyway—not justifiable ones at any rate," she added tartly, throwing a bitter and rather envious glance about the room. Clearly she knew to the penny exactly how much had gone into the remodeling and decorating of Martin's apartment. "But I have to keep up Rowland's position. And it doesn't help things to have him throwing away huge sums on those children of his. Why setting up Philip in his own office has cost us—"

"How is Rowland, by the way?" interrupted Martin in a practiced maneuver to stem the tide of complaints about the cost of maintaining her step-children.

"Fine," said Grace, briskly dismissing her husband's well-being. "But the point is, that I have been absolutely depending on this money and something has to be done."

"You realize, Grace," said Martin smoothly, "that my mother is still alive."

"We all realize," replied Grace coldly, "that the end will be a merciful release for her. And there's no point in your beating about the bush this way, Martin. You've been counting on the money just as much as we have."

"Yes," acknowledged Martin, "it's a blow."

"Well, there's no doubt about what has to be done. Now is the time when Arthur will simply have to raise the

84

dividends. It's simply ridiculous the level to which he's been holding me during the past five years. It's all very well for him. He's taking an immense salary out of the profits and can afford to take a high and mighty tone about retaining earnings in order to increase capital. You don't see him cutting his salary in order to increase anything."

Martin, who had abandoned all signs of playfulness as soon as the conversation turned to money—indeed this seemed to be a characteristic of the Schneiders, who approached the subject with an almost devotional respect—was obviously in some sympathy with his cousin.

"I know how you feel, Grace, but the fact is, unless things improve, there's very little chance of Arthur doing anything except forcing us to take a cut in dividends."

"A cut?" Grace was outraged. "That's out of the question. He can't be allowed to get away with it. If he's such a paragon of business efficiency, why has the firm gone steadily downhill since he took over. I won't stand for it. I tell you, Martin, that if he has anything like that in mind, it's time for a change." She deliberated for a few moments. "You know, Martin, if you could get your hands on enough stock and we voted together—"

Thatcher had been watching Martin play his fish with a good deal of appreciation. He realized that the bait must have been dropped some time ago, and that Martin's patience—and it must have required a good deal of patience to deal with a subject as unfocusable as Grace—was finally paying off. But it seemed that he was not destined to be a spectator at the catch itself. Martin had clearly decided that the interview would proceed more smoothly in Thatcher's absence.

"Very true, Grace, but I'm afraid that all this must be quite boring for Mr. Thatcher and we've already allowed our affairs to take up too much of his time." Martin directed a significant look at Thatcher, who realized that he had no option. "You mustn't let me interrupt your discussion. I really must be going now, but it's been extremely pleasant to have the opportunity to meet you and discuss the trust. I'm sure you'll keep me informed of developments and we shall be seeing each other in the future." He took a punctilious leave of Grace, who seemed surprised to find him still on the premises and allowed Martin to escort him to the door. His host was suavely charming, urged him to drop in for a drink whenever he was in the neighborhood, and saw him out to the doorstep with evident relief.

But Martin returned to the living room to discover that the interlude had been sufficient for the changeable Grace to become immersed in a different problem. And her anxiety was sufficient to convince him that yet another opportunity had slipped by. She was far too worried about her immediate concerns to permit the intrusion of any alien subject matter.

"Martin, I told the police that I was home alone all that night. What will happen?"

"What do you mean? Was there someone else there?"

"No, no, you don't understand."

"What in the world are you talking about, Grace?"

"How did I know that anybody knew? It wasn't until after I talked with the police that I found out that someone had called. That revolting Alice Parker dropped by at midnight to try to borrow some ice. Claims she saw a light, rang the doorbell, and didn't get any answer."

"Who the hell is Alice Parker?"

"She's the woman who lives next door—a prying, interfering gossip. It seems they were having a party. Is it reasonable to expect people to drop by at midnight?"

"Have the police talked to her?"

"I don't know, and it's driving me mad. Are they likely to check with the neighbors?"

"Depends on how seriously they're considering you. You'll just have to explain, that's all."

"And have it get out? Never!"

"I suppose it was—"

"Yes," said Grace slowly, "it was."

10: LONG-TERM LIABILITY

Peter Self had become a Captain in the Buffalo Police Force and Acting Head of its Detective Division for a variety of complicated reasons, not unconnected with his wife's uncle's role as President of the Buffalo Polish-American Democratic Club. But twenty years on the force had left their mark; he had seen bodies with knives in their backs, bodies with ugly gashes in the throat; he had seen sixteen-year-old girls who had been fished out of Lake Erie; he had seen old women who had been beaten with hammers; he had watched stolidly while pathologists pointed to fragments spread on a table and identified missing wives and lost children; he had seen bodies like that of Robert Schneider, grotesquely protesting as they lay in crusted brownish spots more like leaks from an automobile engine than human blood.

He remained what he had always been—unimaginative, competent and essentially unemotional, but he developed a strong dislike for malefactors, including murderers. Corrective treatment instead of prison for a seventeen-year-old thief hurt him like a blow; opponents of capital punishment he loathed.

Twenty years of seeing victims does not encourage a man to take an enlightened view of the treatment of offenders, so it is fortunate that Peter Self was responsible only for the apprehension of criminals. In this, because he was a patient, careful man who wiped his feet before he entered his home, and emptied the pockets of his jackets before he hung them up, he became remarkably successful. His method was simple and uncomplicated: impervious to demands from City Hall or the *Buffalo Courier* he went over the ground again and again.

So, after he finished talking to Jeannie Novak, he methodically drove onto the Thruway and when he pulled his sedan off it an hour later, he did not have to drive into downtown Batavia to inquire about 204 Sycamore Street. He drove the five miles to Sycamore Street and pulled up before a shabby white house, parked, opened the gate and walked up the path to the porch. But as he waited for someone to answer the bell he looked around him again; the Christmas wreath still hanging on the door did not suggest holiday cheer. It was a depressing house with peeling paint and sagging porch, in a depressing neighborhood. A sled stood leaning against the garage.

Kathryn Schneider opened the door. "Come in, Captain Self," she said. After he had inspected his shoes for snow, he followed her into the small living room. The Christmas tree still stood in the corner, and under it a variety of boxes. Pine needles had begun to litter the rug, Self noted, because the tree had been placed in the kind of holder that does not hold water.

"Won't you sit down," Kathryn Schneider asked as she pointed to the couch, and herself sat in the straight-backed chair opposite. Sunlight still lit one corner of the room, and the bold colors of the furniture accentuated the woman's pallor. She was painfully thin with unbecomingly short hair. She wore little make-up, and her somewhat shiny skin gave her the look that Self tended to associate with widows. But she was not wearing mourning for her husband. Her gray skirt and white blouse, neat and somewhat prim, were probably her "teaching clothes" a concession to his presence. She was, Self knew, thirty-four.

"I suppose you think I was lying to you about the money," she burst out as he sat down. "I suppose you can't be expected to believe that I just heard about it today." She pulled a letter from her pocket and handed it to him angrily.

Self read: "Dear Mrs. Schneider, The Sloan Guaranty Trust. . . ." He glanced at John Thatcher's signature, then said, "Yes, I heard from Mr. Thatcher on Friday." He returned to the letter, reading carefully. His lips moved slightly.

Kathryn Schneider watched him in an agony of barely controlled tension; she pulled off her horn-rimmed glasses, rubbed her eyes despairingly, then, finding the silence intolerable, said, "I've sent the boys to my sister in Utica. I suppose that's all right, isn't it? I couldn't bear to have them around here—with the police and reporters coming and going."

Self handed her the letter. "We may have to talk to them again, but we can let that go for a while. At least that," he pointed to the letter she was putting in her pocket, "that makes things a little better. For the future I mean."

The woman shrugged. "I suppose so," she said hopelessly. "I'm just about out of my mind. Yesterday I would have been so happy to know about the money. I spent the day worrying about the School Board. I haven't heard from them . . ."

In the hallway a telephone shrilled, and Kathryn Schneider got hurriedly to her feet. "Excuse me."

Captain Self made no pretense of not listening to the call. "Yes . . . oh, yes Mrs. Poulos . . . No, fine thank you . . . Yes. Well, I appreciate that but I sent the boys to Ellen. Yes, Fred came down last night . . . I thought it would be better . . . Well, not right now, I'm afraid . . . Thank you for calling."

Self stood as she reentered the room.

"One of my neighbors," she explained wearily. "They mean to be kind but they're curious." She looked at him for a moment, then said, "And now I've got another motive, haven't I. You won't believe that I didn't know about the money . . ."

Self listened without emotion as she broke off again, then said, "Now Mrs. Schneider, you're an educated woman. You know I have to ask questions and go over a lot of stories. Including the story about the money. It doesn't mean that I think you had more of a motive than anybody else, or that I suspect you. And if you didn't kill your husband," he stilled a protest and continued, "if you didn't kill your husband, nothing is going to make us think you did." He studied her. "And the sooner we do find out who did kill him, the better things will be for you."

Kathryn Schneider bowed her head as if in silent prayer for a moment, then looked up at him with the ghost of a smile. "I'm sorry, Captain. I'm overwrought, I guess. I'll try to control myself."

"Good," said Self.

"Let me get us some coffee," she said. Self assented, and she busied herself in the kitchen for a few moments, then returned with two cups. Sitting down again, she said, "All right, fire away." Self stirred his coffee thoughtfully; for the first time, he had seen a reasonably attractive woman in Kathryn Schneider behind the fatigue and fright.

"Well, let's start with the money," he said. "You say you didn't know that your husband was due to inherit $100,000. That fits in with what they told me about trying to find him. It's possible that he didn't know about it. Now, what did you know about his family back in Massachusetts."

"Nothing," she replied. "I've already told you that I

married Bob in California when he was just out of the army. He didn't say much about his family—just that his mother and father were dead and that he had lived with an Aunt. Aunt Marie, I think. He didn't mention any other family—I always assumed that he didn't have any."

Self nodded; he had heard this before. "Now when you came back from California. That was just after you were married, was it?"

"Yes. In 1948."

"Now, was there any special reason for coming back?"

"Well, Bob wasn't satisfied with his work with Berndorf Aircraft. He came back to take a job in Rochester, with Eastman."

"Your family is from New York, isn't it?" Self said. He knew that Kathryn Schneider was from Utica, and that a large family still lived there.

"Look," she said persuasively, "can't I make you understand? It wouldn't matter where I came from. Bob just came home one night and announced that we were moving; I was happy to be coming back so that I could see my folks once in a while but that wouldn't make any difference to Bob. We could just as easily have gone to Africa. I think he had forgotten about my family." There was an edge to her voice.

"And he never mentioned his hopes—about coming into money?"

"He never mentioned anything," Kathryn Schneider snapped. She rose and went over to the window; without turning, she continued, "Captain Self, there's no way to make a normal human being understand about my husband. He was crazy. Not just selfish in the normal sense. He didn't think of anything but himself and his work." She whirled and put her hands out before her, as if trying to make a recalcitrant student understand something. "Look," she said heatedly, "do you have any children?"

"Two," Self said, wondering what was coming next.

"Then think about this. After Allen was born, Bob would come home—this is when we were living in Rochester—eat dinner without a word, then go into the living room and work on some papers. He never went to see his son." She frowned at him, in an effort to make him understand. "He didn't even ask about him. His son."

Against his will Self was reminded of the first six

months after young Peter came. It was fifteen years ago, but he would not soon forget ... Kathryn Schneider had the trick of the good teacher, of making the experience reasonable to the student, he thought wryly. She had gone quickly on " ... didn't notice. He wasn't home. He didn't care. About his wife, about his son, about anything." Her voice rose, and she stopped to get control of herself, then continued carefully, "I knew that my marriage was a terrible mistake very early, but I thought that when Allen came ..." She shrugged her shoulders. Sitting down again she faced him and said earnestly, "I couldn't go on. When I knew that I was going to have another baby, I just walked out. Bob never saw Donny. Never once. He never even asked about either of his sons." Self glanced at her tightly grasped hands.

"Why didn't you get a divorce?"

"I am a Catholic, Captain," she replied.

"How did he take it?" Self asked.

Kathryn Schneider leaned back with a weary sigh. "How would I know? I went home to my sister and had my baby. My brother-in-law got a lawyer and we got an agreement that Bob was to contribute to the boys' support. I was feeling pretty terrible."

Self asked, "How did you find out that he moved to Buffalo?"

Again the telephone interrupted them. Kathryn Schneider answered it. "Hello ... Oh yes Ellen ... Yes ... fine. I'm talking to Captain Self now ... yes ... Hello, Allen, are you being a good boy with Aunt Ellen? ..." Captain Self listened to Kathryn Schneider. What reserves of strength she must have in order to summon that bright gay voice for her sons. It was the first time he had ever heard her laugh, he thought, as he looked around the little room; it was a small house for two growing boys, but it showed signs of care; he picked up the two coffee cups and went into the kitchen. Mrs. Schneider was still talking to her sons. Her voice had just the right tone of affectionate amusement; he put the cups in the sink, and looked around. The linoleum was worn and old, but the kitchen had been painted a bright yellow, and blue-and-white curtains hung jauntily at the windows. He returned to the living room just as Mrs. Schneider, a little flushed, came in. The smile she had used for her children was still on her face.

"The boys," she explained. "They wanted to tell me that they are going to go to the farm to see their grandmother." Self made a mental note to find out more about the boys, and about Kathryn Schneider's family, but he said only, "Well there won't be too much more to go over. I was just wondering how you found out about your husband's coming to Buffalo." The question acted on Kathryn Schneider like a cloud obscuring the sun; her smile faded, and the tight worn expression reappeared.

"It was money," she said. "I got a job here in Batavia as soon as I was able. I borrowed money from Fred and Ellen and stayed here with the children for six months, but then I had to take a job. It wasn't easy."

"Yes," Self said in a prompting voice.

"Well, one way and another, I made do. But Bob was very irregular with his payments and Fred—my brother-in-law—kept trying to get him to be more regular. Finally, about two years after I left, Fred found out that he had moved to Buffalo. He called me, to tell me, and I thought that I would go in to talk to him about it."

"When was that?" Self asked.

"It must have been about five years ago," Kathryn Schneider answered. She continued without further prompting, "I should have known better; he just said 'Hello, Kathryn' as if I had never been anything more than a casual acquaintance. I think he had forgotten me. And his two children."

"Did you get him to promise anything?" Self asked.

"Nobody could," she retorted. "I think I must have seen him—perhaps five or six times since then. We always had a fight; I just couldn't stand it—the way he didn't care."

"And he didn't say a word about being a part owner of Buffalo Industrial?"

She laughed shortly. "Nothing. I didn't know anything. I haven't had a cent from him for two years. I just gave up. Don't you see?"

Self thought he did, but he said nothing. She punched the side of her chair with a sort of suppressed rage. "He would have let his sons starve. How can people like that live?"

"Well, he didn't," Self replied somewhat drily. "Now the

problem is this killing. I have to try to place people. We can't place you."

She looked steadily at him. "There's nothing more that I can say, Captain. I was home grading papers all night; doing some ironing, perhaps. The boys were asleep. No matter how many times you ask me, I can't tell you any more than that. Just grading papers. Working to support my sons . . ." Her voice broke.

Your sons whom you carefully sent to Utica, Self thought. Aloud he said in a flat tone, "But, you see, you could have driven to Buffalo and back . . ."

"In that blizzard?" she interrupted, with a sort of desperate sarcasm.

"With chains," he said.

"Oh, Captain! Go out and look at the car. I don't even dare drive it to school on bad days." She pulled at her handkerchief angrily. "Please believe me. I admit that I hated him, God forgive me, I hated him for the way he treated me and his sons. But I didn't kill him." She looked at his impassive face, and added, "I wouldn't kill my boys' father."

"I hope not," Self said as he stood. "I guess that's all for—oh, can you think of anything small—about two by three inches, that your husband had that was valuable?"

She looked at him hopelessly. "I've seen my husband twice in the last two years, Captain."

He nodded, and together they walked the few steps to the door, the good hostess ushering out the welcome guest. As she opened the door, Self glanced at the wreath; her eyes followed his, then she closed her eyes as if the light hurt them.

In the same emotionless voice he used to ask questions Self said, as he looked at her, "You'd better try to get some rest, Mrs. Schneider."

"Thank you, Captain," she replied. Shutting the door behind him, she leaned against it and expelled a long sigh. Get some rest. For what?

She straightened up, went to the living room; automatically she plumped the cushions of the sofa where Self had been sitting. Looking around for the cups, she frowned slightly, then went to the kitchen where she found them neatly stacked in the sink. She stared at them with a kind of fascinated horror. Captain Self put my cups and saucers in my sink, she thought. Captain Self will put me into a prison. She turned abruptly and went into the living room where she sat down on the sofa and stared unseeingly ahead.

The telephone rang. She sat like a woman in a trance. Her mind was racing feverishly. What could she do? Had it been a mistake to send the boys away? The phone rang again, then with a note of exasperation, stopped suddenly.

Kathryn Schneider forced herself to think about the murder of her husband. Motive: obvious, she thought. Opportunity? There was no way to convince Captain Self that she could not have driven the old wreck in the garage forty miles to Buffalo and back: verdict? thought Kathryn Schneider, verdict—guilty. She gave a sudden sob, and fumbled in her pocket for a handkerchief. She brought out, instead, John Thatcher's letter. She read it once again.

I should do something about this, she thought. Legal counsel; she remembered with distaste the noisy little man whom Fred had gotten for her when she was in trouble with Bob. The thought of going to him with her troubles was intolerable. She drew a deep breath and made a decision. Walking to the hallway, she picked up the phone and waited for the operator. "I want long distance, please. Long distance? I want to talk to Mr. John Thatcher at the Sloan Guaranty Trust in New York City ... No, only John Thatcher."

11: GUARDIANS AND CONSERVATORS

Not until he was disposing of his coffee and sweet rolls (all that American Airlines provided passengers foolhardy enough to take Tuesday's early morning flight from Boston to New York) did it occur with some force to Kenneth Nicolls that his superiors might reasonably inquire why a short interview with Arthur Schneider should have necessitated an overnight absence.

Until that moment he had been very pleased with himself. He felt he had exercised considerable social adroitness in side-stepping Mrs. Schneider's dinner invitation and in cutting Jane neatly out of her family circle. The evening had been an unqualified success, in spite of his initial qualms at letting Jane plan their activities. Four years of student life in Cambridge had left him with a deep and abiding suspicion of all genteel New England country restaurants. But Jane had swept him briskly off to a steak house called—appropriately enough—"Ken's" on the Worcester Turnpike where they were regaled with impeccable clam chowder, magnificent steaks done exactly to order, a crisp salad, and a flaky pecan pie. The management successfully resisted the temptation to intrude butterscotch rolls or sherbet-topped fruit salads into this menu, and Jane handled her meal in a workmanlike manner which suggested a complete lack of interest in diets.

By that time Ken had been experiencing a powerful reluctance to end the evening, and his tentative suggestion that they drive into Boston and find a quiet bar in which to while away the time until the last plane was very gratifyingly received. Over a moderate quantity of coffee and brandy, he and Jane explored their social, literary, musical, and athletic pleasures and prejudices so effectively that the last plane to New York had come and gone long before they were aware of it. And to cap it all, when Ken insisted that a meeting in the near future would be eminently desirable, Jane helpfully discovered that a shopping expedition to New York within the next few days had been on her agenda for some time. When they finally parted, equally pleased with each other, Ken returned to the Statler to pass the few remaining hours of the night in a state of euphoria which even the absence of a toothbrush could not dispel.

But now, in the cold light of dawn, it seemed all too probable that the proper course of action for an ambitious young trust officer would have included an early return to New York, the dictation of a comprehensive report to the stenographer on evening duty, and punctual attendance at his desk the following morning. Ken groaned inwardly and speculated on the chances of an unobtrusive entrance into his office suggesting his presence there for some hours. These hopes were doomed.

Having paused briefly for a shave at the barbershop in

La Guardia, he taxied at a snail's pace through interminable traffic jams to the East River Drive where a sudden burst of speed left no time to continue his examination of the state of his shirt and tie. The financial district, crowded as always, inserted another fifteen minutes delay into his schedule, and he was eventually deposited at the door of the Sloan at ten minutes after ten. A rapid survey of the foyer promised him a clear field; but at the elevator nemesis pounced. The operator delayed closing the doors for an additional passenger, and Charlie Trinkam, Homburg tipped at a jaunty angle, stepped in to share the solitude of the late morning elevator with Nicolls. And, thought Ken gloomily, Trinkam could be relied on to have noticed his defection of the previous evening. He steeled himself for a heavily ironic inquiry as to his new working hours, and was therefore pleasantly surprised to receive nothing worse than a comradely buffet on the shoulder.

"Well, well, assuming seniority already, my boy?"

Ken mumbled something noncommittal and thankfully made his escape on the trust floor. But the incident had left its mark. After all, he had been at the Sloan for three years and was beginning to receive independent accounts. It was absurd to assume the airs of a delinquent office boy just because he chose to spend his evening in Boston rather than in New York. Happily Ken could not be expected to realize that Charlie Trinkam, after a night spent proving conclusively that he was a man in the robust plenitude of his powers to the immense satisfaction of himself and his fiancée, would have observed a mass bacchanalia in the trust department with indulgent tolerance.

Nicolls, now carrying himself with a certain reserved dignity, abandoned all thoughts of a surreptitious entry. Marching boldly up to his secretary's desk, he wished her good morning in tones suitable for the formal convening of a summit conference and asked her to bring in her book for dictation as soon as possible.

He had barely begun his report of the interview with Arthur Schneider when Miss Corsa rang through to say that Mr. Thatcher was free and would like an immediate verbal report on his doings. Rendering thanks that his taxi had not been delayed another ten minutes, Nicolls pulled his thoughts together and made his way down the hall.

"Good morning, Nicolls," Thatcher greeted him. "Come in and sit down. I thought we might review our activities. While you've been in Boston, I've seen Martin and had the unexpected pleasure of meeting Grace. It's just as well—I was beginning to think of her as a figment of the imagination."

"Good morning, sir. What is she like in the flesh? As bad as her letters and phone calls?"

"Worse," said Thatcher cheerfully. "In fact, she's so aggressively ill-mannered that I'm inclined to think she's very seriously worried about something. Nerves all shot and incapable of noticing anything outside her immediate range of preoccupation."

"I'm glad I wasn't there."

"Now I enjoyed the interview enormously. Martin is a clever man. Very forthright about his lack of alibi and his interest in an extra fifty thousand dollars. Incidentally, he has no alibi from early Friday afternoon right through the night. As far as time goes, he could easily have gone to Buffalo, committed the murder, and returned to New York."

"Oh, really," protested Ken, "you're not seriously considering Martin as a murderer."

"I admit it's difficult to think of him bashing somebody's skull in—seems a more subtle type—but I find him very interesting. What did you think of his apartment?"

"Superb!" said Ken unhesitatingly.

"Yes, I thought so too. But I meant, what did you think of it financially. If that's his scale of living generally, he's spending a great deal more than his income. That decoration job didn't cost a penny under thirty thousand dollars."

Ken was staggered. Ever since seeing Martin's apartment, he had been fired with enthusiasm for a little remodeling operation of his own. In his idle moments, he had vaguely contemplated substituting a modern fireplace for his own Victorian monstrosity, putting in a storage wall (complete with a small bar) and enlarging the windows. Hastily scuttling this program, he decided to talk to his landlord about a new paint job and let it go at that. It did not occur to him to question Thatcher's estimate. If there was one thing that the vice-president of the Sloan knew about, it was how much things cost.

"Furthermore," continued Thatcher, unaware that he had just sealed the fate of a small apartment in Yorktown, "Martin seems to be a persistent reader of stock market newsletters. We might make a few tactful inquiries at the brokerage houses to see if he's been plunging. I would say that he's a man with very substantial financial ambitions, and I doubt if he expects to realize them through Schneider Manufacturing Company, even though he would obviously like to own enough stock to counterbalance Arthur's control. There's another motive, by the way."

Overwhelmed by this picture of a Martin, hard pressed on every side by the need for money, Nicolls asked about Grace.

"Now there is a woman who makes no bones about her desire for money. Up to her ears in debt, I would say. She's probably been spending twice the family income all her life and when the merry-go-round crashes to a halt, she blames the world for treating her badly. Totally self-centered and totally convinced that she has a God-given right to everything she wants."

"You remember that Robert Schneider's head was smashed in," said Kenneth firmly. His employer was clearly indulging himself with a little romancing and should be brought down to earth. "You can't see Mrs. Walworth packing a blackjack around in her stocking."

Thatcher seemed mildly surprised at this objection. Indeed, Ken thought, Thatcher seemed to regard these sober, middle-class clients of the bank as capable of any crime or violence.

"Not a blackjack, no," Thatcher replied judiciously, "but Robert Schneider was killed with a book end from his desk. I can see Grace, in a fit of irritation, swatting him as she might swat a fly. In fact, when you come to think about it, she seems to have a penchant for transmuting her irritation into action. If she had discovered Robert's existence in Buffalo—and I'm still not convinced that the Schneiders were entirely straightforward with us about their knowledge of Robert's whereabouts—it would be quite characteristic of her to board the first conveyance and rush up to Buffalo for a personal showdown. She seems to spend her life rushing between New York and Boston, and Washington."

"Yes, when you put it like that, it's not entirely improbable. And she certainly seems much more of a possibility than Martin. Does she have any alibi at all?"

"I'm not sure. Martin, you see, wanted to discuss a possible sale of stock by Grace to himself and he didn't want to do it in my presence. He hustled me off in the most charming manner possible before I could introduce the subject of Grace's alibi. She was worried about Arthur's cutting her dividends. But from the way she spoke about her police interview—and, by the way, there is a scene I regret having missed—it seems certain that she has a very inconclusive alibi at best. To do her justice, her supreme bad manners probably stem from the fact that she is half-insane with worry over something. It may just be money, but it might be murder!"

While Ken was absorbing this possibility, the intercom buzzed and Thatcher picked up his phone to listen to Miss Corsa.

"Ah," he beamed with satisfaction, "you'd better get on the extension again, Nicolls. It's Robert Schneider's wife calling from Batavia."

Nicolls wheeled his chair to the side table and wondered how high in the Sloan you had to rise before becoming a speaking partner in these long-distance conversations with Buffalo. Obediently he prepared to listen, as a woman's voice, high-pitched with tension and imperfectly controlled breathing came to his ears.

"Mr. Thatcher? This is Kathryn Schneider in Batavia. Robert Schneider was my husband. You wrote me a letter about a trust fund."

"Yes, of course, Mrs. Schneider," said Thatcher soothingly, "I remember perfectly. Your sons will now be distributees of the trust. And I want to express my . . . ah . . . sympathy for these difficulties you are having."

"Yes, thank you," she said uncertainly. "That is—I wanted to ask you about the money. I mean, exactly how will it be handled?"

"There will be no distribution until the death of your husband's aunt. However, she has suffered a stroke and her physicians do not expect her to . . ."

"No, no. I understand about that. You told me in your letter. That was the first I knew about this trust. Bob never told me about it. How could I know?" She was now frankly on the brim of full-fledged hysteria.

"Of course, Mrs. Schneider," Thatcher broke in soothingly, "just tell me what can I explain to you about the trust"

"Something may happen to me. I might not be able to take care of my sons. What if they have no parents? You said they would have to wait until they're twenty-one."

"Not at all. In any event, they will have the interest while they are minors and, if more is necessary for their maintenance and education, the bank will approve an advance on some of the principal."

"But will the bank take care of them? I'm suspected of murdering my husband."

"The bank will naturally look after your sons' financial interests, and if you wish more personal supervision, that too can be arranged. I'm sure you're upsetting yourself needlessly, Mrs. Schneider. We can go into this in detail if ... er ... any grounds for your fears arise. It's not something you want to rush into ..."

"You don't understand. I may be arrested any minute. The police think I did it. They've been here again. There isn't anyone else with a motive for murdering Bob."

"Now that is not at all the case. There are a good many other suspects," said Thatcher firmly, and his firmness seemed to have a beneficial influence on Kathryn Schneider, who took a deep breath and steadied her voice before continuing.

"Well, I don't know. Maybe there are. Captain Self didn't actually say there weren't. But I can't go on this way. I have to know that something can be arranged for Allen and Donny."

"Naturally. And I will prepare some purely tentative arrangements which you can study and approve. Then you will have peace of mind on that score. I daresay that we'll never need this, but at least you will know that it's there and that's the important thing at the moment. You should try to get some rest, Mrs. Schneider, and remember that the police are investigating a good many other people right now. You only see one side of their activities."

"Yes," she said dubiously but more calmly, "and you'll let me hear from you?"

"Certainly. I will be in touch with you in the very near

future. Don't worry about your sons any more." And with a few more generally soothing remarks, Thatcher rang off.

"She certainly has the wind up," remarked Nicolls, cradling his receiver, "and she does have a good motive—the money from the trust for her children and probably part of that business in Buffalo plus whatever spare cash Robert Schneider had. She sounds like the hysterical type too—might do something foolish on the spur of the moment."

"Very few women can face sudden widowhood, suspicion of murder and the probability of immediate arrest with any degree of equanimity," said Thatcher drily.

"Well, that may be," said Nicolls stubbornly, "but you can't get around her motive. Most murders are committed for financial reasons."

"Then what about the Schneiders?" countered Thatcher.

"That's different," protested Kenneth, conscious of a strong desire to have the murderer far away and uninvolved with Jane's family. Even the arrest of Grace could create all sorts of unpleasant repercussions in Framingham. "People like that don't murder for twenty-five thousand dollars. It doesn't mean that much to them."

"Don't be too sure," said Thatcher darkly.

"At any rate, they're clear up in Framingham. I got the whole story of the evening from them. Arthur was on a Chicago-Boston flight which was rerouted to Washington because of the blizzard. He stayed at the Mayflower, and called his wife from there after he got in. Caused quite an upheaval. His daughter, Jane, drove into the airport early in the evening to meet him and spent the night there. They never did tell her that his plane had been rerouted. She finally called home in the small hours of the morning and her mother told her that her father was in Washington. I think it's disgraceful," said Kenneth with revealing heat, "that the airlines should let a young girl like that stay around all night when they must have known quite early that the plane she was meeting wouldn't come in. A little consideration or even common decency . . ."

"Ah, ha," said Thatcher in some mischief, "then Arthur's daughter has no alibi. She says she spent the night at the airport but can she prove it? Plenty of time for her to fly to Buffalo and swat Robert."

Kenneth was aghast. He was flooded by an alarm

hitherto reserved for threats to his own interests and quite oblivious to Thatcher's open amusement.

"But the airport was closed," he protested. "That's why they rerouted Arthur's plane. How could she fly to Buffalo?"

"Well," said Thatcher with heavy reasonableness, "they don't usually close airports for twelve hours at a stretch. Usually it's an on-again off-again business. Besides she wouldn't have stayed there all night, if there had been no activity at all. She would have realized that the airport was closed if there had been no arrivals and departures all night. The airport must have been closed when Arthur's plane would have landed, but reopened after that; so," he concluded triumphantly, "she has no alibi."

"She called her mother," said Kenneth desperately.

"Ah, mothers. . . . They always cover for their children."

Nicolls eyed his employer with suspicion. Clearly his leg was being pulled and he refused to rise to this new bait.

"There is a good deal in what you say, sir," he replied repressively.

"Of course, all the heirs are worth a good deal of further inquiry," said Thatcher fair-mindedly. "I want a full-scale investigation into Martin's finances and I want to know what Grace is hiding. We might contact our Washington representative and see if he knows anything about her credit standing. Although I could probably make a good guess at it right now. But she may be in even more hot water than I think."

Kenneth realized that Thatcher was no longer being deliberately provocative. He was now deadly earnest.

"But we can't really suspect people like that."

"On the contrary, my boy," said Thatcher taking a lofty tone, "in our capacity as trustee for two small boys left fatherless by this murder, we can suspect anyone. And," he added, coming down to earth with a malicious grin, "I experience no difficulty at all in doing precisely the same thing in my private capacity."

12: JOINT ACCOUNT

Only a firm belief that blood is thicker than water explained why Arthur Schneider found himself irritably pacing up and down at South Station the following Thursday. He knew from experience that his sister Grace was not likely to be a pleasant or cooperative house guest: on the contrary, she would criticize his children, nag about the business and generally make his life hell. It was small comfort to him that his wife could endure Grace's thrusts with unruffled placidity: if Josephine only remarked—as she had every right to—"After all, she's *your* sister," Arthur could explain exactly why it was only right and proper that he maintain cordial relations with Grace, but since Josephine never once reproached him with this, he was denied the opportunity to explain the full extent of his virtue.

He walked impatiently around the car on display. South Station looked like a big, cheap market. It was another grievance. Grace, for some obscure reason, could not trust herself to get off the train at the Route 128 station. She had interrupted his careful instructions and peremptorily directed that he be at South Station to meet her. Forty miles of driving in traffic, thought Arthur. Just like Grace.

Something of his feelings must have been reflected in his expression when, a few minutes later, he made his way through the crowd clustered at Exit 16. Grace, transferring her fur coat to him, gave him a perfunctory kiss on the cheek, then said, in clear ringing tones, "Good Lord, Arthur! What are you scowling at already?"

Three sailors watched them with anticipation. Arthur repressed a sharp retort and said, "Good to see you Grace. How are Rowland and the children?"

The sailors looked disappointed as Grace fell in beside him and they walked to Atlantic Avenue. By the time they reached the car, Arthur had found out that Rowland was still in the Canal Zone—Colonel Walworth was a great man for overseas assignments and a bad man for promotions, Martin had once observed—that Philip was just getting into practice after having borrowed seven thousand dollars from his father, and that Naomi was to go to Europe for a year's study of what Grace called The Voice.

"I didn't know she sang," said Arthur incautiously. Grace settled herself in the car, took off her hat and examined herself critically in a hand mirror before replying. "She has a very nice voice," she said firmly. "Of course she needs more training. The man she's with now was at the San Carlo Opera and he says that a year in Italy would make all the difference. Of course, she'll want to make her debut there."

"Why can't she come up to the New England Conservatory?"

"Really, Arthur," Grace cried in an affected voice, "I don't know what's the matter with you. Naomi is certainly not going to bury herself in Boston!"

Nothing was more calculated to enrage Arthur than his sister's insistence upon a level of sophistication so exalted that anything connected with New England was suspect. Particularly since it was, and always had been, New England money that had paid for the deficits that occurred when a colonel's wife wanted to live on a grand scale.

"It's going to cost you a good deal of money," he was stung into commenting.

"That's exactly what I'm here for," Grace said, triumphantly. "Arthur, I've been telling you all along that you don't understand how enormous my expenses are, with the children and everything. You have no idea. Now if Naomi had a simple background—like Jane—the New England Conservatory might do. But after all, she's been to school all over Europe and it does make a difference in what she expects."

The night before, Jane Schneider, normally the most helpful of daughters, had refused to postpone her extended weekend in New York even though it would entail a departure the morning after her aunt's arrival. One evening was enough she had said, pointing out that it was too much to ask that she sit around for four days to listen to Aunt Grace compare her unfavorably to Naomi. "You see, Daddy, she has a real problem on her hands."

Arthur was forced to admit Jane was right. Naomi was a foxy-faced blonde with a tendency to weight. Their cousin Philip the children referred to as "The Beetle." As for his brother-in-law, Arthur Schneider had always considered him mentally deficient. He glanced at Grace who was nervously stubbing out a half-smoked cigarette. Eye shadow and powder could not cover the deep shadows under her eyes; her fingers might be covered with rings, but they plucked incessantly at the gloves she held in her hands. She looked every one of her fifty years, despite what he suspected was an extremely expensive attempt at camouflage. "Yes," he said untruthfully but conciliatingly, "I can see that it would be the right thing to do for her." He was about to inquire about Naomi's voice, but Grace was not to be put off.

"That's why I have simply had to try, and try again to get some sense out of you and Martin," she said accusingly. "I really don't think you've been very sympathetic to my needs."

"Now Grace . . ."

"Don't 'now Grace' me, Arthur. You know as well as I do that when I was trying to get some action from the Bank about the trust both of you simply avoided me. And now when I want to talk—very seriously, mind you—about the business, you have been trying to avoid me."

Despite his good intentions, Arthur felt his temper rise.

"Absolute nonsense," he snapped.

"Absolute nonsense, hell!" Grace cut in, "I've been ringing your office every day this week and that miserable little creature keeps telling me that you're busy in Boston. What were you doing in Boston, I'd like to know?"

"I tried twice to call you back . . ."

". . . if you're running around Boston doing God knows what, and Martin is sitting on his fanny in New York, trying to look like a Man of Distinction it's no wonder that we can't raise the dividends. And I intend to see that something is done about it."

Arthur honked his horn savagely at a truck that was blocking his way.

"And don't lose your temper, Arthur," Grace said patronizingly. "Try to be reasonable about the whole thing for a change. Now that this miserable trust business has developed—and I'm just sick about it, I'm sure that if we had done something earlier all this could have been avoided—at any rate, now that it develops that we're getting the fifty thousand and no more, you and Martin and I are simply going to have to do something about raising the dividends. Martin agrees with me."

"Well, if you and Martin can figure out just how we're going to be raising our dividends while our earnings are going down, and we still have to pay the bank over a million dollars," Arthur snarled, "I for one would be grateful. Damn grateful."

"Martin said that if we did more research . . ." Grace began.

Arthur again exploded. "My God! Grace, don't you understand English? How the hell is spending money on research going to bring our earnings up?" he shouted. "And where are you going to get the money to do more research. Can't you see that it means putting money in, not taking it out. And we don't have it."

"Well, why not?" Grace said, using a tone of voice suited to recalcitrant children.

"I'll tell you why," Arthur said savagely. "It's your precious Martin. If he could keep our sales where they were five years ago—not increase them, mind you, but keep them level—we could keep our gross up. *And* do some development work." He glared ahead.

Grace gave her brother a long, hard look. Martin Henderson was part of the world in which she had chosen to live: non-New England, non-Framingham. But despite a perpetual contempt and fury with him, she knew that she could trust Arthur as she could not trust Martin. Or, she admitted to herself, Rowland.

"Are you serious, Arthur?" she said in a steely voice.

"Don't know why they can't plow these streets," he muttered as he pulled into the single lane left by the piles of snow on Boylston Street. "What did you say? . . . Yes, of course, I'm serious. I only wish I weren't. I only wish that we could get rid of Martin."

"I thought he was doing a good job. I mean," Grace said authoritatively if incoherently, "the New York office, and everything."

"I've explained this to you time and time again, and I'll explain it now: from 1945 to 1952, anybody who wasn't deaf, dumb and blind could have sold felt. That," he said with heavy sarcasm, "that was when you let Martin talk you into backing him up when he insisted on moving the Distribution Branch to New York. It added $160,000 a year to your costs. Since 1952 things have been getting a good deal tighter, *and* our New York office costs us $200,000 a year." He bit off his words, paused, then added, "And it isn't worth a damn."

"You're not exaggerating, are you, Arthur? To impress me?" Grace said narrowing her eyes.

"Good God, Grace, sometimes I wonder how your mind works. No, I am not exaggerating. The paper industry is growing by leaps and bounds, and Martin not only hasn't got us any new customers, he's letting us lose our old ones. Wisconsin Paper and Novelty."

Grace listened with unaccustomed intentness, as he went on in a grim voice.

"You won't know, but they've been Schneider customers since 1905. And we're in some danger of losing their contracts. I went out to talk to them a few weeks ago. I just hope it wasn't too late." He concentrated on his driving, then said, "Do you realize that that fool never went to Beloit to talk to them. That he dealt with them when Bill Carlson came to New York—by taking him to fancy restaurants, but that he just couldn't be bothered to go to Wisconsin."

"Of course, I've never really liked Martin," Grace said thoughtfully.

Arthur glowered at a hapless pedestrian who had strayed into the street in front of the car.

"What difference does it make if you like him or not? We're stuck with him. And when Hilda goes, we'll be more stuck than ever."

"He gets only non-voting stock, doesn't he?" Grace asked.

"Thank God for that," Arthur said. "But he's head of our sales division, and we won't be able to get him out unless we buy him out. Which we can't. And I am telling you once for all, I am very seriously worried about the way our sales are going."

Brother and sister relapsed into silence after the speech: Arthur, irate with himself for having been prodded, as he always was by Grace, into losing his temper; Grace deep in thought. The five years that separated them in age did not emphasize the difference between them so much as did subtler distinctions. Grace was unmistakably clothed, and very smartly, in New York; Arthur Schneider in Boston. But as they sat in silence in the car, the family similarity emerged. Both compressed their lips as they thought; both had the trick of raising the lower lid of the eye when they were worried. And they were both worried.

As they waited for the light in front of the John Hancock Building to turn to green, Grace looked at Arthur, then broke the silence. "We could really have used that money from Robert's share of the trust, couldn't we?"

Arthur shrugged his shoulders, and laughed shortly. "Every little bit helps, of course, but in terms of the business it wouldn't have made any real difference. We really need to get a couple of big contracts, then everything will be all right."

Grace pulled her bag open, and rummaged for a cigarette. "It really is remarkable how bad our luck is," she said bitterly. "On top of everything else, to have this miserable Robert turn up with a wife and children." Arthur remained silent, and she continued in a dissatisfied tone of voice. "Of course I really don't remember all the fuss, but I do remember him as a boy. There was some trouble up at Dartmouth wasn't there?"

"He was expelled for something or other," Arthur said.

"Martin said it was for getting a girl in trouble."

"Martin would," Arthur replied.

Grace looked disapprovingly at Copley Square as they inched through it and commented. "Let's see, that was after Carl shot himself, wasn't it?"

"Yes," said Arthur abruptly. Neither he, nor his late father liked to be reminded that Carl Schneider had committed suicide. Grace, for some reason or other, seemed to enjoy harping on it. She probably discussed it at cocktail parties, Arthur thought. As for himself, he acquitted himself and his father of any guilt; they bought out his uncle Carl when it became obvious that working with him would be impossible. His subsequent suicide had nothing to do with the business. But, he did not like to contemplate the kind of nervous instability that led to suicide in one's own uncle. But Grace seemed to find it exciting. She was rambling on.

". . . in one family. People don't just disappear."

"What are you talking about?"

"Robert, of course," she said, her voice slightly sharpened with macabre relish. "And the murder. The police didn't know anything about him, or what he had been doing. It really makes you wonder. I mean about what kind of life he had been leading. After all, he was our own cousin."

Grace, Arthur remembered irritably as he stopped at the light in front of the Public Library, always enjoyed the dramatic. He glanced over at her; even her eyes brightened somewhat as she went on.

"I think it is really disgraceful that we don't know anything about what he did. I don't even know where he worked."

"What difference does it make?"

"Really, Arthur! Your own cousin murdered and you aren't human enough to admit that you are interested in him." Her voice rising in excitement grated on his ears.

"I don't see that having my own cousin murdered is a thing that I want to talk about or think about . . ."

"Really you are the limit. Positively Victorian. I think it's perfectly fascinating. His father kills himself, this one is murdered. It's like one of those plays about a cursed family."

"I don't go to plays about families with curses."

Grace laughed shrilly, then said, "Seriously, Arthur, I am dying with curiosity to find out more about . . . oh I have an idea. Why don't you park for a minute?"

"What?" he said, as he accelerated.

"No, no," she cried, "park the car! And we can go into the Library and read the Buffalo papers. They must tell all about him. About the wife, and I think there was another woman . . . oh Arthur!"

"You are a ghoul, Grace," Arthur snapped. "We certainly will not go into the library to read about the murder of our cousin." He was genuinely upset.

A flush still on her normally pale cheeks, Grace frowned slightly, then turned to give her brother a long, thoughtful look.

"Now what?" he said.

"I'm thinking, Arthur," she said slowly. "Just thinking."

13: WATERING THE STOCK

When Jane called Kenneth at his office Friday morning to report that she was having a field day at Bonwit Teller's and looked forward to seeing him that evening, it had seemed simple enough to arrange a meeting after work at the Algonquin. By five-thirty that afternoon nothing seemed simple any longer. Only three hours earlier, Charlie Trinkam had rung through to remind Kenneth that a finalizing letter must go out in the mail that evening for the executors of the Betz estate. Virtuously conscious of a completed first draft of that letter reposing in his files, Kenneth had calmly reassured Trinkam and promised to see to the mailing himself. A quick glance at the draft, however, convinced him that one of the tax tables required some minor revisions. Two hours later Kenneth delivered to his Miss Todd a mass of rumpled and heavily interlined typescript with urgent injunctions for speed and neatness.

He should have added accuracy to his list of requirements. At five-fifteen he erupted from his office and shook the second page of his seven-page letter accusingly at Miss Todd. Wearily she removed the cover from the typewriter which she had optimistically bedded down for the night.

"But what did I do? I can't see if you shake it like that, Mr. Nicolls."

"You left out a paragraph—a whole paragraph!"

"Well, I'm terribly sorry, but I was trying to do it quickly for you. Give it to me, and I'll do it over."

"It's on the second page," groaned Kenneth. "You'll have to do the last six pages."

Miss Todd wasted no more time on idle chatter but squared away to her typewriter, attacking the keyboard with savage ferocity. Kenneth removed himself to his office and started pacing its confined limits in an agony of impatience, unconsciously giving a splendid imitation of the expectant father who has lost control over the creation of his offspring. With heroic self-restraint he quelled the impulse to hover impatiently at Miss Todd's shoulder, knowing that nothing was more certain to lower her already unpredictable standard of performance. The savage tom-tom of her activity was proceeding at an incredible tempo when it came to an abrupt halt; Ken winced visibly at the sound of sheets being ripped violently from the carriage and dropped into the wastebasket. In rapid succession he considered and rejected the possibilities of: (1) urging Miss Todd to accomplish her task at a less tempestuous and disastrous pace, (2) paging Jane at Bonwit Teller's, (3) leaving banking for a less nerve-wracking profession and (4) committing suicide.

Finally he forcibly removed his mind from further contemplation of his present plight and fixed it instead on a detailed reconstruction of Jane's appearance. This had a remarkably tranquilizing effect on his agitation. He had limned out the delicate bonework of her jaw and cheekbones and was lost in satisfaction at the curious identity her face retained in his memory when he awoke to the realization that a justifiably annoyed Miss Todd was addressing him for the second time.

"Mr. Nicolls, it's all done."

"What?—oh, yes, Miss Todd."

"If you wouldn't mind checking it"—this with heavy sarcasm—"so I could go. I have a dinner date."

"So do I," replied Nicolls, hastily scooping up the letter. "Why don't you get ready to go, while I look this over, so you won't waste any time."

Miss Todd clicked off to the ladies' room, not prepared to waste any more time on the inscrutable behavior of bankers in general and Mr. Nicolls in particular. That could wait until the incident was served up to her fiancée in much detail over the dessert.

Nicolls discovered, much to his surprise, that she had presented him with a flawless product. He signed the letter with a flourish, initialed the file copies before tossing them in his basket, and prepared for his own departure. He was emerging from his office when Miss Todd returned and looked profoundly relieved upon learning that they were through for the night. He thanked her, she offered to mail the letter for him and they hastened to the elevator together in perfect amity. In the taxi a few minutes later

Kenneth realized that it was the first time that he had allowed himself to appear to Miss Todd in any light other than that of the weighty and impersonal man of affairs. It must be spring, he thought idly, as he looked out at the leaden January sky. Then he forgot about Miss Todd as his thoughts pressed ahead of his taxi to his destination.

At the Algonquin he hurried across the sidewalk only to find Jane entering the foyer directly on his heels. They broke into parallel apologies.

"I'm so sorry. I couldn't get a taxi at my hotel . . ."

". . . Last-minute rush. I was held up at the office . . ."

"I had to walk to Fifth Avenue . . ."

". . . then the letter had to be retyped . . ."

". . . so afraid you'd be waiting . . ."

They broke into laughter and moved toward one of the corner settees in the lounge. Ken felt a pleasant glow of warmth and a momentary shock of surprise as he helped Jane slip out of her coat. His remembrance of Jane was so vivid, that he had automatically expected her to be wearing the same blue wool dress she had worn in Boston. But she had, reasonably enough, dignified their first night together in New York with a more urban ensemble. Her black silk dress was deceptively simple, relieved only by a knotted gold pin high on her shoulder—and the clean sweep of her radiant golden-red hair. But best of all, she looked happy to be with him.

The waiter interrupted their silent satisfaction with each other and, by the time he brought their martinis, they had found a conversational footing. Jane had never been to the Algonquin before and was charmed with its substitution of comfortable chairs and couches and convenient tables for the usual bar and booth arrangement. They slipped easily into a discussion of Ken's life in New York— his job, his apartment, his favorite places to eat. He was about to point out that this last subject had some bearing on their further plans for the evening, when two men rose from some corner chairs across the room. One man snatched up a brief case and plunged hastily toward the exit. The other was standing, collecting his belongings in a leisurely fashion—it was John Thatcher. As Kenneth had just amused Jane with a spirited and disrespectful word description of his superior, including Thatcher's paralyzing effect on erring and not-so-erring subordinates, he pointed him out. The next moment he cursed himself for the impulse. The movement had caught Thatcher's attention, and when his path inevitably brought him close to Ken's table, Jane whispered, "Oh, I would like to meet him."

Thatcher was now at hand, pausing courteously to acknowledge Ken's presence; Ken rose to perform introductions, and then, in frozen horror, heard his own voice treacherously inviting Thatcher to join them. Jane beamed welcomingly and added her own persuasions.

"Do join us if you have time, Mr. Thatcher. I've heard a great deal about you."

Ken had time for one vast, convulsive shudder, but mercifully Thatcher looked elsewhere for Jane's source of information. He had years of experience with the wives of his subordinates and was adept at overlooking extracurricular remarks.

"And how is your father?" said Thatcher blandly as he seated himself. "I regret that I couldn't get up to Framingham myself the other day."

"Such a shame you couldn't come up with Ken," said Jane, who was clearly unwilling to subtract Nicolls from the expedition, even in retrospect. Ken grinned at this version of Thatcher's role in life and relaxed suddenly in a spurt of devil-may-care abandon to listen to Jane's determined pursuit of Thatcher.

"Daddy is fine, but, of course, he's terribly worried about this whole affair. He's so busy, you know, but he has to spend a great deal of his time soothing Aunt Grace and Martin. Actually that's why I'm in New York. Because Aunt Grace is with us now and she's always so difficult."

"I have met Mrs. Walworth," said Thatcher gravely.

"I know," rejoined Jane. And suddenly they smiled at each other.

"It's so unfair. I don't understand why Martin and Aunt Grace won't leave the management of the business to Daddy, when he's so much better at it than they are."

The two men received this dictum in respectful silence.

"Particularly now," Jane continued. "The murder doesn't really matter for Aunt Grace. I believe she actually enjoys the theatrical side of it, although she complains about being questioned by the police and being an official suspect, she still gets some compensation out of it by being in the limelight. It doesn't seem to occur to her that a cousin of hers whom she knew for twenty years has actually been killed." Her voice trailed off uncertainly. She was genuinely troubled by Grace's lack of feeling and shocked by it. Ken realized in a sudden wave of affection that no daughter of Josephine Schneider was likely to view the brutal extinction of another human being as a matter to be passed over lightly or as a suitable subject for self-dramatization.

"There are people like that," said Thatcher gently. "They don't really absorb emotionally what has happened to other persons. They see only the reflections of the event in their own day-to-day lives. The rest has no meaning to them."

"Yes," said Jane, obscurely comforted, "but Daddy isn't like that. To him it all has meaning. Oh, I know he seems a little pompous and fussy. But his own life is orderly and dignified and he wants everyone's to be that way. He lives his life by a high set of standards and he's used to being well regarded. It's a terrible shock for him to have Robert murdered and his own sister and cousin questioned about their alibis."

"Of course it is, and it does him credit. While I realize that it's small comfort at this point, think how much better it is that he has an alibi for himself and only has to worry about Martin and Mrs. Walworth."

"But you should hear Aunt Grace on the subject," said Jane wryly. "She claims that if Daddy had had the consideration to spend the night at her house in Georgetown instead of at the Mayflower, she wouldn't be in this fix. But you can imagine what she would have said at the time if he had come barging out to her house with no advance warning."

"That's right." Thatcher was all innocence. "There was some confusion regarding your family that night, wasn't there, and your father ended up in Washington while you waited for him."

Why, the old so-and-so! thought Ken in alarmed admiration. So that's what he's up to. He thinks he's going to cross-examine her about her alibi and all in the most social manner possible. Well, not on my drink, he isn't. He's amused himself enough already with that one.

"Yes, it was a flight that will go down in the Schneider

family history. Tell him about your father's troubles, Jane," interrupted Kenneth, firmly directing the conversation away from Jane's activities at Logan.

"Everything went wrong right from the start. Poor Daddy was in a fret for days," said Jane in the gleeful tone appropriate to the recital of complex and comic family misadventures. "He hates to be away from home and always rushes back as soon as his business is done. True to form, he came rushing into Chicago two minutes before a plane for Boston was departing and he bundled himself on to it. Then, an hour and a half from Boston, they ran into our big snowstorm, and the plane was rerouted to Washington. He spent the night at the Mayflower, and ended up taking the train to Boston the next morning. Meanwhile, I spent the night—"

"Wasn't there some trouble about his baggage?" asked Kenneth, alert for any digression toward Jane's alibi. Thatcher smiled benignly at him.

"Of course. That was the final straw. The airlines had lost one of his bags in the last-minute rush at Chicago. Daddy was simply livid. Why, he wouldn't even let his secretary go into town to file a tracer for his bag. He said she'd be fobbed off with some subordinate. So he went in himself to give the manager a piece of his mind. Daddy," proclaimed Jane innocently, "says that it saves time to always see the man in charge."

"I know," said Thatcher simply, forbearing to remark that he himself had been a victim of this principle and had little, if any, sympathy with such conduct. Presumably the man in charge at the airlines, just like the man in charge at the Sloan, had better things to do with his time than placate an irate Arthur Schneider. Well, with any luck, the Sloan at least would soon be relieved of the necessity for further dealings with the man.

"But he got his baggage eventually?" prompted Kenneth, laboring under a grim determination to keep the conversation safely anecdotal:

"Oh, yes, about two weeks later they called up and said they had finally found it. But I think that it's inexcusable that it should have taken that long. Anyway they shouldn't have lost it in the first place."

"Well, well," said Thatcher tolerantly, reaching for his coat while Ken looked on with relief, "I'm afraid I may have kept you from going on to your dinner. It's been a great pleasure meeting you, Miss Schneider, and I trust that you'll convey my regards to your father and tell him that I look forward to seeing him when he next comes to New York. Good night, Nicolls."

"Good night, sir," said Kenneth with simple satisfaction.

"But he's not an ogre at all," said Jane. "Why, I think he's an old dear."

"Well, you may think he's an old dear, but thank God we kept him off the subject of alibis."

"What alibis?" said Jane blankly.

"Now, I know it seems absurd to you, but Martin and your Aunt Grace aren't in the clear by a long shot." There seemed small point in informing Jane that one of Thatcher's amusements was pinpricking her own alibi.

"Martin and Aunt Grace!" sputtered Jane. "But that's outrageous. Why they couldn't kill anybody. It's comic to even think of Aunt Grace doing anything like that. She feels aggrieved if she has to open a door for herself."

"Remember that you know them. The police don't know them and, for that matter, neither does Thatcher. And you have to admit that there's a certain offhand, callous quality about the way they both view this murder that doesn't leave people thinking they wouldn't hurt a fly."

"But that's just the way they talk. Oh, I admit that they're both selfish when it comes to their own convenience, but most people know the difference between that and the ability to commit a murder," Jane now protested.

"I agree, but I still think that it would be a good idea if you didn't speak too freely about their activities on the night of the murder in front of Thatcher. He's in direct communication with the police in Buffalo."

Jane's blue eyes widened at this. It clearly did not fit in with her idea of a dear, sweet, old banker. Just as well she doesn't think of me as connected with the police too, thought Kenneth, as he realized how very much he did not want her to march out of his life.

"But I don't know anything about their activities on the night of the murder," replied Jane reasonably. "After all, Aunt Grace was in Washington and Martin was in New York."

"Let's hope they were," said Kenneth a little grimly.

It was not until some time later when they were taxiing up to the Viennese Lantern, that Jane reverted to the subject.

"You know, Ken, I'm not so sure that it is absurd to think of Martin's murdering somebody for money."

14: PROFIT AND LOSS
STATEMENT

Every weekend, no matter how fine, is followed by a Monday. Kenneth drew his one-hundredth star, then stared glumly at the pad on his desk. Doodling was going to solve none of his problems. He resolutely put thoughts of Jane Schneider—and a perfect Saturday and Sunday— out of his mind, and pulled the memo pad toward him: two items John Thatcher wanted him to check were carefully noted, "Martin and stock," and "Logan." Unfortunately they were the same two jottings that had set off this spate of gloomy inactivity.

Ken was feeling his role distasteful, a reaction that disturbed him. Was this the by-product of age—a developing stodginess and sobriety that looked upon anything out of the ordinary as unsavory? Ken was no fool; he knew that one of the reasons that John Thatcher was a Vice-President of the Sloan while Everett Gabler remained a trust officer was that Thatcher had never developed the pompousness that was a Gabler characteristic— a pompousness that viewed with alarm, urged caution, suggested prolonged consideration, and generally made decisive activity impossible. Ken profoundly hoped that he wasn't turning into an Everett Gabler.

But he was rapidly finding John Thatcher's detached interest in the murder of Robert Schneider less and less amusing. Within the last few days he had come within an inch of indignant exclamations: "Stop it! You don't draw your princely salary to play cops and robbers. The Sloan shouldn't be involved in this kind of thing."

Which was very much the sort of thing that Everett

Gabler, in a more measured, reproachful way, was likely to say. Kenneth drew four more stars. "Be honest," he admonished himself. "You don't give a damn about the Sloan's dignity. You just don't like this spying and probing into Jane's family."

But since he had resolutely been trying to put Jane Schneider out of his thoughts for the better part of twelve hours, this merely added to his impatience. He flicked the pencil across the room; action, no matter how distasteful, was what he was being paid for. He picked up the phone.

On his fourth call, he struck gold. Arnie Berman, at Waymark-Sims admitted that Martin Henderson was a customer, and cordially invited Ken to come over and have a good long talk about him.

"Check one," Ken thought as he put his coat on: "But two?"

He stood for a moment, turning his hat in his hands, then went out to his secretary's desk.

"Miss Todd," he said with a frown, "will you have time to do a little job for me this morning?"

"Certainly, Mr. Nicolls," she said automatically, without looking up from her typewriter.

"I want you to call the airlines and find out about how long Logan Airport in Boston was closed on Friday the thirteenth."

"Closed?" she asked.

Ken patiently explained what he realized was a somewhat obscure request: "There was a bad snowstorm that night and flights were grounded in and out of Logan. I want to know about what time flights started operating."

She stared at him in frank surprise, then made a note, and said, "You mean you want to know what planes started flying. That is, where they were going and all that."

"Yes," he said, trying to think of some reasonable explanation for his interest.

"My brother is a repair man for Northwest Airlines. I'll call him and ask what's the best way to find all this out." To Claire Todd, most of the requests beyond simple typing that she had encountered at the Sloan verged on the bizarre; this was no odder. Ken stared for a moment, then started down the hall, when she added, "Is it all right if I have to call Boston?"

"O.K."

The second chore done—and not with his own hands. This did not remove responsibility, but it served to modify it somewhat. Nevertheless, Ken profoundly hoped that Jane Schneider never found out that he had checked her alibi. He also hoped that Logan Airport had been closed tighter than a drum all through the cursed night of Friday the thirteenth.

He realized that he had not been successful in keeping Jane Schneider from interrupting his work, and on the trip down in the elevator concentrated on not thinking about her to such an extent that he made his mind a perfect blank.

". . . high-hatting your old friends," he heard someone saying as the metal doors glided open at the main floor. Turning, he saw John Calderone disappearing toward the Accounting Department.

"Wake up, Nicolls!" he muttered as he braced himself for the plunge into the stream of humanity flowing outside the Sloan's glass doors. And during his three-block walk to Waymark-Sims, he pushed his way in a very determined fashion past the crowds that hesitated on corners.

In Arnie Berman's office, he realized that it might have been more efficient to concentrate on a story for Arnie that might explain the Sloan's snooping into Martin Henderson's affairs. "It's like this, Arnie," he began untruthfully. "This Henderson is one of the heirs to a trust that we administer. His co-heirs are minors."

Berman nodded his bald head understandingly. Ken went on, "Well, the story's this. Some funny business had come up—about dissolving the trust, that is, and the kids—they're young boys—make us feel a little uneasy."

Again Berman nodded. Ken continued, "So, we want to find out a little more about Martin Henderson's affairs, without setting up any formal checks. And since he's a customer of yours, I thought that maybe you could fill me in on some of the details. . . ." It was a lame finish.

"I see it all," Berman said, in measured tones. "The Sloan wants to know all about this guy's business with Waymark-Sims—all his stock and bond movements for the last six months, which is a breach of professional confidence. And, the Sloan doesn't want to tell me why. Right?"

Ken flushed under the older man's sardonic gaze. "I'm not as stupid as I look," Berman continued mildly. "But of all the stories! My God, it would be a damn funny thing if the Sloan had to come to Waymark to find out about a man's business affairs."

"Arnie," Ken began . . .

"What's the matter with you? In love or something," Arnie selected a cigar then pushed the box across his desk to Nicolls. "Now what do you really want to know?"

Ken told him. He nodded then said, "Well, I have most of it here. Henderson's been riding pretty high. Started out with about thirty-five thousand dollars, in Raytheon. Got out at the high about a year ago with a tidy profit, went into Thiokol and Hertz, with some Ford. He was doing all right." He looked up at the intent Nicolls. "Then, he committed suicide."

"What?"

"He started getting smart. Convertible debentures. Buying bonds with bank money. He started pyramiding; put up twenty dollars and got the banks to lend him eighty to a hundred dollars. He had about seventy thousand of his own—and by working in convertible debentures, he could play with over three hundred thousand dollars."

Ken frowned in concentration. "But Waymark-Sims wouldn't do that for him, would it? . . ."

"Not for a million dollars," Arnie said. "We wouldn't touch it with a ten-foot pole. No, what happened was that Martin took the profits that we made for him out—or almost all—we still hold a little Remington-Rand and Fairchild for him. At any rate he took his marbles over to Amos Grant—they do these collateral loans, you know. I met Bill Staley who told me all about it."

"You mean that Henderson took all his profits, and started borrowing to build a roll to play around with convertible debentures," Ken said.

"Well, he could have gone into the commodity market," Arnie said sarcastically.

"It's a good way to make a lot of money," the trust officer in Ken admitted, "and lose it. I wish we could find out what he bought," he added in a cautious tone of voice.

Arnie eyed him tolerantly. "Well, my friend, so long as we don't have any more fairy stories about little kids and the Sloan, I'll be good to you. I called Bill just after you called this morning."

Ken leaned forward eagerly. Arnie blew a lazy smoke ring, smiled blandly, then said, "He put half into Firestone convertibles, and the other half into IT&T. Some three hundred thousand dollars, altogether."

"My God!" Kenneth exclaimed. He did some rapid mental calculations. "He made a fortune." It certainly was more than enough to explain the Waverly Place apartment.

"Right," Berman agreed. "But, having learned how to make money easier and faster than the professionals, he went on . . ."

"And . . . ?"

"And put damn near a half a million dollars into Stevens Tools, International Fruit, and Collins Chemicals."

"Into the bonds?" Ken said, incredulously.

"Into the bonds," Arnie said. Both men fell silent. In his mind's eye, Ken could see the weekly bulletins that Walter Bowman prepared for the trust officers; at the bottom, was a list of what the Research Department thought were the least desirable stocks in the market. On this select roster, Collins Chemicals and Stevens Tools had appeared with regularity; Ken knew that International Fruit had lost twelve points in the last month.

"And that's the stock price," he thought aloud.

"Yes indeed," Arnie said in satisfied tones. "And with the bond price pegged to the stock price . . . And with somebody else footing over 80 per cent of the price . . ."

"Wow!" said Kenneth inadequately.

"He's had a call on the Stevens Tools already. And both Collins and International Fruit are damn near it. The banks will sell him out unless he can raise enough to bring his collateral up to what it was."

Kenneth nodded in agreement. "We don't think that those stocks have much of a chance."

"They don't." Arnie regarded the lengthening cigar ash, delicately tapped it into the ash tray, then commented. "If he gets through the next two weeks without doing anything worse than losing every cent he's got in the market, he'll be lucky. I hope he's got a lot of money somewhere."

Kenneth knew that he owed the good-natured Berman

some information; he produced a suitably expurgated version of the Sloan's real interest in Martin.

"My God!" said Arnie Berman. "Murder." He thought for a while. "I always did distrust those elegant boys. He was in here one day last fall wearing a silk vest."

They agreed that a man who wore silk vests was capable of almost anything.

As he made his way back to the Sloan, Ken thought of his interviews with Martin Henderson at the Pavillon ... And the apartment on Waverly Place. That languid, cosmopolitan air hid not only a Framingham, Massachusetts, background, but what must be a desperate concern about money. It was very deceptive indeed.

"The information's on your desk," Miss Todd said as he entered the office.

"What information?" he asked, momentarily blank. "Oh yes, Logan." Jane's uncle had indeed put Jane out of his mind.

He picked up the neatly typed schedule, studied it for a moment, then, with no change of expression, reached for the phone.

"Mr. Thatcher free for a moment, Miss Corsa?"

"Let me check, Mr. Nicolls. . . ."

"Thatcher here."

Ken told John Thatcher about Martin's financial hole.

"I thought so," Thatcher said. "More or less inevitable that he'd be a fool, but I didn't think that he'd be that big a fool."

"No, sir," Kenneth replied.

"What's the matter with you?"

"Nothing, Mr. Thatcher," Ken replied. "And the other thing. You were right about Logan."

"What about Logan?"

"About its being open. They closed it down from seven in the evening until two in the morning. Then they got two runways cleared, and three planes got out for Chicago and the West Coast. By that morning planes from the west were landing."

There was silence on Thatcher's end of the line; Ken went doggedly on. "That means that it is possible— remotely possible—that Jane Schneider could have flown from Boston to Buffalo and back. Her alibi is worthless."

There was an explosion—apparently of laughter; "Good

Lord, Nicolls, will you stop acting like a moonstruck calf."

"Well, I didn't really . . ." he began.

"Now stop this nonsense about the girl," Thatcher interrupted. "That's very interesting about Martin Henderson." He paused a moment in thought, then went on. "You'd better come in to see me after lunch. I think it's time that I get out to Buffalo. Today or tomorrow." He rang off somewhat abruptly and once again Kenneth sat at his desk. Drawing stars on a pad of paper.

This time, he was interrupted by the shrill of the phone.

"A Miss Schneider to talk to you, Mr. Nicolls."

"Put her on, Miss Todd."

"Ken, is that . . ."

"Jane . . . Jane, darling . . ."

In the outer office, Clare Todd replaced the receiver: "I told you so," she congratulated herself.

15: REGULATORY AGENCIES

By Tuesday afternoon John Thatcher was pursuing his inquiries at the Buffalo Club. The Buffalo Club may be an unlikely place to investigate the death of a man whose head has been bashed in, but it is an extremely reasonable place to discover a good deal about Buffalo Industrial Products Corporation, or, in fact, almost any American profit-making institution. In its hushed, opulent reading room, therefore, John Thatcher found himself engaged in measured conversation with Bryant Cottrell, the Vice-President of the First National Bank of Buffalo who had acted as liaison with the Sloan Trust Department for thirty years. Cottrell spoke with the caution that made him so eminently well suited to bank and trust work; the fireplace cast waves of heat through the room, with an occasional cascade of embers lighting the shadowy corner in which the two men sat over their drinks. Outside, passers-by walked head down into the wind from Lake Erie that was whipping fat snowflakes onto the already deep snow that banked Delaware Avenue. John Thatcher felt sleepy.

". . . not that we have much information on Schneider," Cottrell was saying. He frowned disapprovingly.

"Yes, I had gathered that," Thatcher said somewhat acidly; he had already spent an hour in conference with Cottrell; adjourning to the Buffalo Club had improved the locale without materially speeding the pace of the conversation.

"Nevertheless," Cottrell continued, "unless something unforeseen—quite unforeseen—occurs, it seems that Schneider's wife and children will stand to inherit some 10 per cent of the outstanding stock in Buffalo Industrial Products."

"How much is it worth?" Thatcher asked.

Cottrell took his glasses off and began to polish them in a deliberate, obviously routine, gesture of temporization.

"We really don't know exactly. There hasn't been any immediate reason to request inspection of the BIP accounts until Robert Schneider's estate is settled."

Thatcher's growing impatience, however, was noted and Cottrell deemed it wise to unbend: "Weissman and Weissman—they're the lawyers for Michaels, you know, and they handle all the firm's business—have told me, quite unofficially, that the Schneider share is in the neighborhood of $60,000." He reached for his glass and took a sip of sherry. "Of course, now that the firm is going public and planning a very considerable expansion, this will grow very substantially." He permitted a frosty look of approval to cross his face. "Very substantially," he repeated.

"And have you been in contact with Mrs. Schneider about a lawyer?"

"Certainly not, Thatcher. She maintains no account with us, and we have no interest . . ."

"I want her to have good advice," Thatcher interrupted.

Bryant Cottrell looked as though he would like to remonstrate. "Yes," he said. "You told us. I've spoken with Linkworth, but you'll have to clear it with Mrs. Schneider. I'm not quite sure that I really approve of using the bank's counsel this way."

John Thatcher's attention appeared focused upon the fireplace.

"I am not sure that I approve either," he murmured.

Cottrell shook his head slightly; he was not comfortable with business associates he could not tyrannize, but he knew full well that it would be useless and foolish to try to dictate to a vice-president of the Sloan. He was about to voice a mildly phrased caution, when Thatcher again addressed him. "Of course, what I really want to do is to find out more about Robert Schneider. I take it that you haven't been able to find out much about him."

"Only the information that the police made public."

"Yes, of course, the police. I spoke to Captain Self, you know." Thatcher knew that he was being deliberately provoking: Cottrell was the kind of man who would dislike being associated with the police simply on principle.

"Oh," he said in place of the admonitory lecture he would have liked to deliver.

"What I really would like," said Thatcher, "is a long talk with this Self. And I don't need you to tell me that that's out of the question."

Surprisingly Bryant Cottrell, again polishing his glasses, looked up. "I don't see why," he said calmly. "Not at all impossible. If you want to talk to anybody on the Buffalo Police Force, Thatcher, I think that we can arrange it. In fact I know that we can arrange it. Mind you, I don't say that I advise it, but I certainly can arrange a meeting."

"You surprise me, Cottrell," Thatcher said truthfully. "I should have thought that the First National would be too rarefied to have police contacts."

"It is. I, however, am a regular contributor to the Election Fund of the Western New York State Republican Party. And have been for a good many years."

"Buffalo isn't a Republican stronghold is it?"

"Far from it. Erie County, however, is . . ."

"And you can get cooperation? Tell me, Cottrell, do you look upon your political activities as an investment in professional . . . no, don't answer that. I think that the less I know about this, the better."

Cottrell permitted himself a thin, triumphant smile. "I think perhaps that you're right. Will you excuse me for a moment while I make a phone call?"

So, instead of dining in East Aurora with the Cottrells, John Thatcher found himself, that evening, sitting in a small cheerful restaurant across the booth from Captain Peter Self. Taxiing out what appeared to be the whole length of Delaware Avenue to make the appointment, he had been pleased with the turn of events. Now, however, as he did something less than justice to an excellent steak, he found himself wondering how the man sitting across from him felt.

Peter Self was resigned. Less placid men might have felt hot resentment at being called away from a rare evening at home by the mayor's office and instructed to cooperate with "a New York big shot" who was obviously meddling in what did not concern him, but Self looked upon this as one of the occupational hazards of being a policeman. He was waiting, somewhat guardedly, for the first suggestion of a fix to explain that no matter how high and mighty the Sloan was, it couldn't cover a murder. But until that proved necessary, he was prepared to discuss the Schneider murder case in fairly frank detail; he knew, as the mayor's office knew, and as Bryant Cottrell knew, that this meeting was so far off the record, that for all practical purposes it was not taking place. He signaled the waiter for another beer.

"No, the papers aren't giving it any more play," he said. "In a way, it's a good thing. They were just about driving that wife of his crazy." He looked at Thatcher. "She's your client, isn't she?"

"Not exactly, Captain Self. We are acting for her sons, who have become heirs to their grandfather's trust. But actually we have no real interest in the question of criminal proceedings."

Seeing that Self looked somewhat puzzled, Thatcher tried to explain. "The real truth is that I have been very much worried by the whole setup. A man who stands to inherit something like $100,000 disappears for years. Then, just as we succeed in tracing him—" Thatcher smiled inwardly at the grandeur of his euphemism—"we find he has been murdered. It doesn't feel right to me. I want to be very sure that the Sloan isn't being used—as party to fraud, if nothing else."

Self nodded in comprehension. He was fair-minded enough to see that if he were a trustee, he too, under the circumstances, might develop an unbankerlike interest in murder. Thatcher continued: "Then it appears that the

126

other heirs to the trust all thought that they would stand to benefit considerably if Robert Schneider died. If nothing else, we want to free them from the . . . ah, taint of suspicion. And, of course, protect the interests of the boys."

"We checked them all out after you got in touch with us," Self volunteered. "It was more a matter of routine than anything else, because we've got plenty here in Buffalo to keep us interested. Arthur Schneider was in the Mayflower in Washington at one-thirty, so that lets him out. The other one . . ."

"Martin," prompted Thatcher. "Martin Henderson."

"Well, we don't seem to have any verification of his alibi, but we don't have any verification for most of our alibis. That damn blizzard."

"What about Grace . . . Mrs. Walworth?"

"We know all about where she was, and what she was doing," Self said with a flicker of what might have been amusement. "She's clear too." He paused for a moment, then continued, choosing his words with care. "You know, Mr. Thatcher, when they said you wanted to talk to me I thought it was going to be to ask for special treatment for these people. Or Mrs. Schneider. Now it sounds more as if you're trying to make a case against these people."

Thatcher nodded and smiled wryly; his first impression, that Self was no fool, was indeed correct.

"I suppose that to a policeman, this sounds incorrigibly foolish," he said. "But I just have so many doubts about the whole business that I don't trust anybody. I suppose that what I really want to do is to be convinced that none of them had the remotest possibility of killing this Robert Schneider before I can be easy in my mind."

With more animation than was usual to him, Self again nodded. "Yes," he said, "yes, it's a hell of a thing, isn't it?"

Thatcher raised an interrogative eyebrow. Self went on: "The feeling—the hunch—the smell that something is wrong. I get it and it drives me crazy; because unless you have proof, it doesn't do you any good at all. But I know what you mean. You get a kind of . . ."

"Presentiment," supplied Thatcher.

"Hunch," Self said firmly. Both men smiled. Self went on in what Thatcher was quick to sense was a more relaxed and friendly tone of voice. "I'm not going to be able to help you much in clearing any of these people. We've ruled out your Arthur and Grace on the grounds that they were a long way away from Edward Street, and this Martin Henderson because it's not really likely."

"He's in very serious trouble about money," Thatcher said.

Self put his glass down with a decided gesture. "Well, I'm going to look into his comings and goings again, then, but the trouble is that all we're going to have is another loose end. So far it looks as if nothing is impossible. We can't rule anybody out."

"Take the wife," Self said. "I don't really think that she drove a ten-year-old car through the worst snowstorm of the winter to come in from Batavia, bash her husband's head in, then turn around and drive home. But I have to keep her in mind because it is remotely possible. It isn't turning into . . ." he thought a moment for the word, "into a neat case."

Thatcher studied the menu with care trying to think of the areas where he could get useful information from Self.

"Is this love nest angle really true, or is it a creation of the press?" he inquired.

Self gave an eloquent grunt of disgust; "Love nest! He was sleeping with another man's wife . . ."

"The mystery woman?"

"She's no mystery," Self said sourly. "We know all about her. And her husband. She's the woman who was there that evening—the one who brought the wreath, the one who fits the nightgowns. We know that." The distaste in Self's voice for some reason reminded Thatcher of Tom Robichaux; he must remember to point out to him that sleeping with another man's wife constituted a love nest. Aloud, he said, "Do you think she did it?"

Self stirred his coffee in an absent-minded way. "It's like this Mrs. Schneider—only in reverse. I sort of think that she might have killed Schneider, but I can't prove that she was there. I can't prove that she's the mystery woman. And I don't see any reason for killing him." He frowned in concentration. "I'm going to keep after her, but I don't think I'll find anything. They were careful. Had good reason to be."

128

Thatcher drank his coffee and considered Self's statement. "I suppose the husband is in the clear."

"He was in Montreal, at a dinner given in honor of the Governor General of Canada," Self said bitterly.

"My God!" Thatcher responded.

"And after dinner he played poker with six security analysts," Self added without sarcasm. "I think we can assume that they were not covering for him."

Thatcher began to see more clearly what Self meant when he said that the case was not neat. "Do you think he knew about his wife and Schneider?"

"You know, I just don't know. They're . . ." Self apparently thought better of what he was going to say. He stopped abruptly. "The whole thing is crazy," he said finally. "Then there's this mystery object. That's what the papers called it. A blood-crusted mystery object."

"What was it?" Thatcher asked, remembering vaguely some reference to it in the press.

"I wish to God I knew," Self said. "You know there wasn't much blood, no more than a small thin pool which had dried and crusted by the time we were called in."

Thatcher continued eating his apple pie. Somehow a small thin pool of dried and crusted blood had become a matter of only academic interest. Self continued eating, then said, "Well, our lab men pointed out that something small—about one and a half inches by two and three-quarter inches—had been lying in the blood for several hours, then removed. They could tell by the coagulation—sort of saw the outline. Nothing you could see with the naked eye, but it's definite enough. And they found paper fibers."

Self glared at his coffee. "And of course that's really torn it."

"It means . . ." Thatcher began.

"That the murderer hung around the apartment for several hours after he—or she—brained Schneider with a book end. Or came back to take this mystery object. Or maybe somebody else came. It must have been something important."

"Doesn't that make it easier to check on your other suspects?" Thatcher asked.

"Hell, no!" Self said, with a sort of suppressed vehemence. "That night was a blinding blizzard and nobody can prove where they were for the whole night. The wife, the people he worked with . . ."

"What about them?" Thatcher interrupted. "I mean how did they feel about him?"

"Old man Michaels didn't like him. Nobody did, as far as I can see. But I guess they all needed him."

"He wasn't trying to move in on the company, was he?"

Self put his fork down, and looked up cautiously. "It's possible," he said. "But not likely."

"He had 10 per cent of the stock already, as part of an option plan," Thatcher commented. "The rest of the stock is in the hands of the Michaels family, isn't it?"

Self was still unimpressed. Somewhat ruefully, he said, "We all ride our own hobby horses. You think of that sort of thing. I think of sleeping with other men's wives. But it's possible that they're connected." He held his coffee cup out for the passing waiter to refill. "It could all fit in. Stan and his daughter own the rest, with Roy Novak—the son-in-law—holding 20 per cent in his own right."

Thatcher watched the waiter refill his own cup. "This Novak is in charge of the financial side of the business, isn't he?"

"Yes," said Self.

"And he's just gone to Montreal, hasn't he, to see about licensing arrangements."

Self sat expressionless, not because he did not want to discuss this aspect of the case, Thatcher guessed, but because he was old-fashioned enough to dislike talking about a cuckold. He did not press him, but turned the conversation from the Schneider case to Buffalo weather. It lasted them through the coffee.

As he waited for his change, Thatcher reviewed what he had learned from the big man sitting opposite him. It had been a useful evening, certainly preferable to dining with that fool Cottrell. But it was not so useful as it might have been.

Grace apparently was definitely cleared, John Thatcher mused. Too bad. She would have made a fine murderess, unregretted, he guessed, by most people. What was it that caused the intensely serious Captain Self to smile at the recollection of her alibi? He made a mental note to find out.

It occurred to him that it would be courteous to inform

Self of his plans. "I'm going out to visit Mrs. Schneider tomorrow," he said. "I'll be interested to meet the woman who married this man."

"Now there's a woman I can't help feeling sorry for," Self said readily. "She seems to have gotten stuck with a prime bastard." There was no doubt that the warmth in his voice was not elicited by his pity for Kathryn Schneider but by his disapproval of Robert Schneider.

"Yes, that's the key to the whole thing, isn't it," Thatcher replied. "The kind of man that Robert Schneider was. His family—back East—doesn't have a good word for him. But it's a little difficult to pin them down—to find out exactly what there was about him that made so many people loathe him."

"And made somebody murder him," Self added. He had started to rise, but sat back again. "I can tell you a little about him. One way or another, I've talked to almost all the people who had anything to do with him. He had a lot of faults—but most people do. His wife complained that he neglected her—but hell, so does mine. He wasn't easy to get on with at the shop, but a lot of people have trouble at work. No, these aren't the things that made people hate him. They're just the things people talk about."

Thatcher again revised his opinion of Self upward. "What was it that was so wrong about him?" he asked.

Self glanced at him, suspicious of mockery, then deciding that Thatcher's interest was sincere, answered, "Well, the way I see it he was just like a smart little kid. He was so conceited that he couldn't think about anything but himself. That's bad enough but—again just like a little kid—he liked to do little things to show off. He did little things to show people like Stan Michaels . . ."

"And Roy Novak?"

"And everybody," Self amended firmly. "To show them he was smarter than they were. He liked to get people upset. It made him feel big. His wife told me he was the kind of man who never had time to think about his own son—he was so wrapped up in his work. I don't believe that," Self stopped again in search of the precise way to explain what he meant. "You know, there aren't many people like that in this world."

"Damn few," Thatcher agreed. "You mean the kind of

people who live and die for what they're doing at the office and don't care about anything else."

"Well, Schneider wasn't one of them," Self said. "Don't get me wrong. He was a hard worker, all right. But you just take a look at that Edward Street apartment. Built-in furniture, hi-fi—all of it taking a lot of time and money. No, he noticed a lot of things, all right. He just was playing a game—showing off to that poor stupid woman that he was an important man."

Thatcher thought for a moment; this was a new view of Schneider. It sounded reasonable.

"The same way that he had an affair with the boss's daughter and his partner's wife . . ."

Self hesitated for a moment, then said, "Sure. To show them how clever he was. How much smarter he was. He liked to remind old Stan Michaels how much they needed him. That's it, he was conceited and selfish."

"And you think he pushed somebody too far? By showing off?"

"Hell, I wish I knew," Self said heavily. "It's possible, you know. He showed off once too often, and somebody just exploded." He looked at Thatcher, almost with shyness.

"You know," he said, "people get fooled pretty easily. Just because this guy didn't talk much, a lot of people didn't see that he was showing off. We see a lot of that kind, you know. Only it's mostly murderers, not victims. But if this Schneider goaded someone into killing him, it comes out to about the same thing. Funny, isn't it?"

Thatcher nodded somberly.

"I've really made a speech, haven't I?" Self said as he heaved himself out of the booth.

"A pretty good one, I think."

16: CLOSED ACCOUNT

The First National, inspired by its eagerness to please, provided Thatcher with a car and driver for his trip to Batavia the next morning and he had ample time to review his evening with Captain Self in the light of his approaching interview with Kathryn Schneider.

He was by no means dissatisfied at the result of his dinner with the phlegmatic policeman, although any tangible benefits were difficult to isolate. He had achieved his visible purpose, of course; he had wrapped around Kathryn Schneider the mantle of power and money, and he could rest assured that she would now be treated with impeccable consideration and impartiality. But five minutes with Peter Self had convinced him that this would have been the ultimate issue in any event. The great danger had been a premature arrest and Self was not the man to be premature in anything. His cases would never go to the District Attorney until they were watertight and foolproof despite the tactics of any defending counsel. A good deal more heartening, however, was Thatcher's conviction that no hysterical and ladylike schoolteacher could have sustained repeated questioning by Captain Self if she were guilty. He was now fully confident of Kathryn Schneider's innocence, and he strongly suspected that Self was too. Self's interest in the ramifications of the Schneider clan had seemed a little too genuine to be entirely attributable to civility. Self had even reciprocated with a little information of his own, an action obviously not characteristic. A good man, thought Thatcher approvingly.

The car suddenly decelerated as it swung into a side street and the driver leaned forward to study the house numbers. Thatcher remembered that Kathryn Schneider had sounded reassuringly calm when he had spoken to her on the phone after breakfast. They should be able to get through their business quite rapidly if she could concentrate and supply him with necessary details.

"Here we are, Mr. Thatcher," said the driver, pulling into the curb before a small shabby house. As Thatcher emerged from the car, the door of the house opened and a woman came out onto the porch. She had obviously been watching the traffic, waiting for his arrival.

"Oh, it's so kind of you to come, Mr. Thatcher."

"Nonsense," lied Thatcher bracingly, "I had some business in Buffalo and this trip is no trouble at all."

She ushered him into the tiny living room, installed him in the largest chair, and offered him a variety of refreshments. He accepted a cup of coffee as the easiest way to stem the tide of hospitality, knowing that she would not be comfortable unless she had something to fuss with. She returned almost immediately with a tray and seated herself on the couch. As she poured, he noticed the thinness of her wrists and the raised veins in her hands. A woman old before her time—these were not the signs of her recent worries but of years of strain and anxiety.

"I realize that you must be having a good deal of trouble planning your future, Mrs. Schneider. You should know that I spoke with Mrs. Henderson's physician before I left New York, and she is sinking rapidly. It can only be a matter of a few weeks at the most."

"Mrs. Henderson?"

"Mrs. Henderson is your husband's aunt. When she dies the trust funds will be distributed. It is now reasonable to assume that this will happen within the next three weeks."

"Then the boys will be all right, no matter what happens to me." She spoke wonderingly, as if it were impossible to contemplate a situation in which her first concern must not be directed to the vulnerability of her sons.

"Financially, yes." Thatcher spoke with intentional crispness. It was his experience that dealing with the details of adversity was not only necessary but also helpful in reducing adversity to manageable proportions. "But there are still a good many other problems. Have you engaged a lawyer?"

"No. Fred—my brother-in-law—tried to persuade me, but I don't like his lawyer and I don't know any others, so—"

"Very well then," Thatcher interrupted ruthlessly. "If you approve, I have undertaken to arrange something for you. Captain Self and I had a talk yesterday night before I came out here. It's clear to me that he has no immediate plans for an arrest. Speaking quite personally I doubt if you head his list of suspects, but that's beside the point. In my opinion, matters have not reached the stage where you need a criminal lawyer. But you do need legal services for handling your husband's estate and your sons' inheritance. The First National Bank has spoken with their outside counsel—Gray, Bettinger, and Linkworth—and Mr. Linkworth has agreed to handle your affairs upon your request. He will be in a position to obtain any additional

134

legal services if the need should arise. What do you think?"

"That's wonderful. But Mr. Linkworth's charges? I don't think I can afford . . ."

"You can now. Most of the charges will come out of the estate and the trust. I am leaving you Linkworth's address and phone number. If you will call him as soon as I leave, he will inform Self that he is acting for you. Self will then notify him if he wants to question you further or anything of that sort. If there is any suggestion of an arrest, and let me emphasize that that is an extremely remote possibility, Linkworth will employ someone who specializes in criminal matters. To be precise, he will hire William Denton, who is the most prominent criminal lawyer in Erie County. You understand?"

Kathryn Schneider nodded dumbly. She was feeling somewhat breathless. After years and years of carrying her burdens herself and having only her brother-in-law to criticize, nag and suggest, it was extraordinarily soothing to have this strange decisive man come in and briskly bark out plans to her, pausing only for formal signs of agreement. It was overwhelmingly simple to allow herself to be swept along and relieved of all necessity for decision.

"Now, the best thing you can do after you have called Linkworth is to forget completely about the possibility of arrest. There is nothing more you can do in that direction, and you have a good many other problems that require attention. It is wise," he added pontifically, "to direct your energies where they will do the most good."

Kathryn was moved to protest at this suggestion that she simply shrug off the threat of being charged with murder and turn her mind to really important problems.

"But what about the boys? I know they'll have money, but they're only seven and nine. Who will take care of them? I can't just forget about them!"

"That's the next thing I want to discuss. Linkworth, of course, will go into this thoroughly and he may have other suggestions. Your sons will require a formal guardian. Do you know if your husband made any arrangements?"

"Bob? But what arrangements would he make?" she was totally dumfounded.

"Well, he was their father and there was no legal

custody agreement. There might be a guardianship clause in his will."

Kathryn spread her hands in a hopeless gesture. "You don't understand. Bob didn't care about the boys. I doubt if he remembered their existence. He hasn't seen them in seven years. In fact, he has never seen Donny—the younger boy—at all."

"He sounds like a strange man," said Thatcher sympathetically. He was delighted that Kathryn Schneider had been induced to talk about her dead husband voluntarily. It had seemed all too probable that she would not refer to him at all.

"Yes, nobody really understands how strange. For some reason, I have been able to think of him much more calmly and reasonably since he's been dead. Before, I was always so resentful and hurt that everything he did seemed directed against me. He was the one who was unreasonable and—yes, inhuman—but underneath I felt that it was I who had been a failure. If I had been a better wife, if I had succeeded in ever understanding him, then I thought all that happened would not have happened and our marriage would have been a success. But now I know, he was the same with everybody, and nobody could have had a normal marriage with him because he just wasn't normal."

"Indeed?" murmured Thatcher encouragingly.

"Yes," said Kathryn, her eyes focused on the distance, "he quite literally never thought about anybody else at all. I don't think they had any existence for him unless they stood in his way or could help him. And then they were just objects to be removed or used. I have wondered recently why he ever married at all."

Thatcher, however, realized that she had just given the answer herself. He could imagine a younger Kathryn, a rounder, softer, happier Kathryn, whom Robert Schneider had seen as an object which could contribute to his comfort. And when the object insisted on turning into a human being with the demands and needs of a human being, he had undoubtedly watched the removal of the object from his life with profound relief—if he had not engineered Kathryn's departure deliberately. No, it seemed all too probable that the Robert Schneider who was being described had never given a second thought to his wife and children once they had taken their blessed departure. Meanwhile Kathryn was continuing, in a reflective, dispassionate tone.

"It upset me more because I was the only person who was really close to him. But his attitude was the same to everybody. It wasn't that he was basely inconsiderate as I thought for so long. It was much worse than that. He was supremely indifferent, totally uninterested in anything that was not Robert Schneider." She gave a little shudder, as she returned to the present and to the realization of Thatcher in her living room. "I'm glad he's dead," she concluded with simple sincerity.

"There are not many people like him. The only thing you can do is forget and return to the world of normalcy."

"Yes," she smiled for the first time. "But you see why there's no question of his having made any provision for the boys."

"It seems very clear. But what provisions did he make in his will?"

"He didn't make a will."

"What! Are you sure?" Thatcher was aghast.

"Yes. Captain Self is still looking. He thinks Bob may have had a safety deposit box nobody knew about. There may be a box, but I'm sure there won't be any will. I tried to talk to Bob about one when Allen was born, but he wouldn't listen—he just wasn't interested."

"Good heavens! And you haven't hired a lawyer? You'll have to see Linkworth as soon as he has an hour free. There will be intestacy proceedings and the sooner you start them the better. You will want to have yourself appointed administratrix. Then we come back to the problem of guardianship. My suggestion is that we have a joint guardianship composed of yourself and the Sloan Guaranty Trust. That will simplify the problem of handling the trust income and any advances of trust principal, if that should be necessary, and we can take charge of their business affairs generally. In the unlikely event that you should be arrested we can step into the breach and arrange for their welfare."

"A bank?" Mercifully Kathryn seemed more preoccupied with the impersonal nature of her sons' guardian than with the prospect of arrest. She was beginning to turn her mind to details. Thatcher's treatment had been a success.

"Oh, yes, we do it quite often. If there are any relatives, your sons could stay with them, but a bank officer would be charged with supervising their upbringing."

"Yes, there are Fred and Ellen. The boys are with them now. I didn't want them to be here with an investigation going on into the death of their father."

"Very natural. That should present no difficulty then"— Thatcher refrained from suggesting that most relatives are not reluctant to take in two small boys who have an assured income of respectable magnitude—"and it's an eventuality unlikely to materialize. Tell me, do you have any idea what kind of an estate your husband left?"

"Yes, from the way Captain Self spoke, I think Bob left nothing except a 10 per cent interest in the company he worked for. And I never knew that he had that. The few times that I spoke with him he made it sound as if he had nothing except his salary and that he was spending every penny of it. I expect he was too. He liked expensive things, and there were always women in his life." Kathryn's lips closed firmly as she made the last statement. There was no possibility of information on this point. Discussion would clearly not be welcome and probably fruitless; Kathryn was the sort of woman who would deliberately cultivate ignorance about the sordid details of her husband's extramarital affairs.

"Well, the 10 per cent interest will probably present problems. You and your sons will share it—it's one-third and two-thirds, I believe, but Linkworth will be able to tell you—and you may not want to hold the stock. It was different for your husband who was a working partner in the firm. In your present situation you will probably want to sell out."

"How much do you think 10 per cent of that business is worth?"

"I have no idea. It will depend a good deal on whether the other holders want to buy you out. If you wish, I can have someone from the bank sound them out. In the meantime, our office can make an assessment of the reasonable worth of the company."

"Oh, yes, if it wouldn't be too much trouble. I'd like to know how much we can count on. It may make a big difference. We might be able to move to a better neighborhood. I don't like to think of the boys growing up here."

"No trouble at all." Thatcher noted with approval that she was speaking in terms of a joint future for herself and her sons. "We can arrive at some estimate. The actual sale, of course, will have to be delayed until after probate proceedings. But there shouldn't be too much delay with a surviving wife and children. If you would accept the advice of someone who has had a good deal of experience, Mrs. Schneider, you should turn your mind to practical considerations. As soon as you know the extent of your income, you will probably wish to make some changes in your manner of living. You should start to think about reasonable alternatives so that you can make decisions when the time comes. I am sure that you want to do everything to ensure your sons' future."

"Yes," said Kathryn, "you're right. I'm afraid I haven't been thinking very clearly these past few weeks. You've been so helpful. Everything seems much simpler now, and I can't tell you how grateful I am to you for coming out to see me."

She rose with her guest and impulsively stretched out her hand.

"Nonsense. It's been a pleasure." Thatcher took her hand and patted it gently. "I know you've been through a trying period. But it's time to put that behind you and deal with the future. Good-bye, and don't forget to call Linkworth immediately."

Thatcher emerged from the house to find a vacant car standing in the street under a light dusting of snow and a few flakes leisurely drifting downward. He looked up and down the street, and his driver came hurriedly out of the drugstore on the corner where he had been keeping watch.

"Ready for the airport, Mr. Thatcher?" he asked as he started the engine.

"Yes, Ben, I'm through here."

But twenty miles later the snow had thickened to a dense, obliterating curtain, and the car radio in one of its moments of intermittent reception announced that Western New York was preparing to receive four to five inches of snow. Clearing skies were expected that evening.

After all, mused Thatcher, three o'clock in the afternoon was an awkward time of the day to arrive back at his office—too late to get anything done, but too early to call it a day. Certainly not worth-while taking off in the middle of a snowstorm when he could wait a few hours and travel in comfort. Far wiser to call the airport and find out what the situation was. He told Ben to take him downtown to the Statler instead. He could always pick up the airport limousine there if there was an unexpected break in the weather.

It was just as well that he had rearranged his plans because the airport was prompt to tell him that they had rearranged theirs. The one o'clock flight to New York had been grounded by snow in Detroit. Departure from Buffalo was not expected until four o'clock. There would be no seats for New York until that time.

Thatcher congratulated himself on his foresight as he headed for the dining room with a clear conscience. He could employ some unexpected time in Buffalo very usefully.

17: QUICK POSITION

With Thatcher in Buffalo, Charlie Trinkam assumed nominal direction of the Sloan Trust Department; nominal because senior trust officers are jealous of their independence—and prolific of suggestion.

"I'm afraid I can't quite go along with you on this," Everett Gabler was saying with great precision as he handed Trinkam the draft of an agreement with Hoffman Brothers. The agreement was a slight variant of a document that both Trinkam and Gabler drew up hundreds of times each year.

"Well, Everett, tell me your objections," Trinkam said with insincere geniality. Everett did. It took forty minutes and centered around a change from "60 per cent of all proceeds" to "not less than 60 per cent and no more than 60 per cent of all proceeds."

"Fine, fine," Charlie said. "We'll have that typed up ..."

"I'll want to see a copy of the final draft," Gabler said quickly.

It took some effort for Trinkam to keep the smile on his face. "Sure, Everett, sure. We'll send it around tonight. And thanks a lot."

Old lady, he thought as Gabler left.

Playboy, thought Gabler.

Trinkam had barely settled himself at his desk when his secretary rang through with a call from Phil Cook in Research.

"I'm sorry, Mr. Trinkam, but we won't be able to get that Bolling report to you until tomorrow or the day after."

"What do you mean, tomorrow!" Charlie expostulated. "I've got to have it tonight at the latest!"

"No can do. The fourth quarter figures won't be available until tomorrow at the very earliest."

"What!"

"Sorry," said Cook unrepentantly, and rang off.

Trinkam glared at the phone. He drummed his fingers for a moment, then grasped the receiver again. "Hello, put me through to Walter Bowman ... hello, hello! ... well, put him on right away ... This is Charlie Trinkam ... I don't care if he is in conference, I have to ... oh, hello, Walter? ... Now listen, what the hell is this about the Bolling report? ... Now, Walter, I don't want to ... no ... no ... Listen, here, Bowman ... yes ... yes ... Well, call me back then."

It was at this juncture that his secretary entered to announce that a Martin Henderson had called, that he was demanding instant action of some sort from the Sloan, and that he wanted to talk to the man in charge.

"For God's sake!" Trinkam burst out. "Get Nicolls in here! I don't know how the hell we're supposed to get any work done around here with everybody chasing after this damn Schneider business. And I want you to ring Walter Bowman back in exactly fifteen minutes ... and type up a copy of the Hoffman contract and send it to Gabler." He took a sharp turn around the office and returned to find Ken in the doorway.

"Oh, it's you, is it?" he said ferociously. "Well, you'll be

141

glad to know that just now, when we're up to our ears in work, you are going to be no use to us at all. You're going to take care of this damn fool Schneider business."

"Something new, Charlie?" Ken asked easily.

"How should I know?" his harassed superior replied. "Look, Ken, call this Henderson jerk and keep him out of my hair, will you. I've got more than enough to worry about as it is. Now get out of here and let me work."

Ken was glad to go. And there was something new, as he discovered when he returned Martin's call.

Hilda Henderson was dying.

The news had been disseminated by the Schneider tom-tom with its customary rapidity, and Arthur was in New York for the double purpose of presiding at the deathbed and talking turkey with Thatcher. Ken apologized for Thatcher's absence, which he discreetly described as a "short business trip," and found himself being pressed to join the two men for a short talk.

Left to his own devices he would have returned an unhesitating refusal. Martin's financial irregularities left a persistently sour taste in his mouth, and he strongly doubted his own ability to maintain the proper degree of camaraderie. Furthermore, the introduction of Arthur into the gathering almost certainly presaged a nasty round of bickering which he had no desire to witness.

The fact of the matter was that Ken, having placed Jane on the sleeper to Boston last night after four eminently satisfactory days, was inclined to view the delights of bachelor life with some skepticism; at the moment, he asked nothing better than an opportunity to court Arthur's favor. This meeting promised no such opportunity. However, in view of Thatcher's insatiable appetite for details concerning the Schneiders, he steeled himself to do his duty.

An hour later at Waverly Place he found himself, as he had foreseen, an uncomfortable third in a rapidly shaping family quarrel.

"It's a pity that Thatcher's out of town," Martin said for the second time as he stared morosely into his glass. "As soon as he finds out about Mother's condition, I'll insist that he give us some sort of timetable on the distribution of the trust."

"Well, well," Arthur replied, "he's supposed to be back

tomorrow. In the meantime Nicolls has given us a very good idea of how long the formalities of settlement usually take." He directed an encouraging glance toward Ken, who shifted awkwardly and responded with a smile of suitable gratitude. His relationship with Martin Henderson and Arthur Schneider had undergone a reversal.

Arthur, having received him in his home and accepted him in the light of an escort for Jane, was now prepared to extend to him a certain good-natured tolerance. Martin, however, was in the throes of a monumental fit of irritation. Impatient with everybody, annoyed with Thatcher, and furious with Arthur, he was barely able to play the civil host to Kenneth. His temper had not been improved by the discovery that Grace had told Arthur about his offer to purchase his stock.

"What business has she got running to you? Are you her keeper? If she wants to talk about it, why doesn't she talk to me?"

"Nonsense, Martin. It's entirely natural that Grace should come to me for advice. If she sells her stock, she will have to consider reinvesting the proceeds. She wants to know if she won't be better off staying with the firm."

"You mean she wants to know if there's any chance of wheedling a raise in dividends out of you. Come off it, Arthur, and stop playing the head of the family. She isn't going to you for advice; she's trying to blackmail you by threatening to sell out to me."

Arthur's lips tightened with annoyance. "Don't be childish!" he snapped. "Every investor wants more income than he's getting. Characterizing that as blackmail is simply indulging your taste for the theatrical." He cast a look of jaundiced disapproval about Martin's apartment. "You might just as well say the same thing about your efforts to have your salary raised. And for the record, I will not tolerate any increases, either in salary or dividends, until we're in a position to afford it."

"And when will that be?" asked Martin nastily. "The way things are going, I'd be better off to sell my preferred and clear out altogether."

"If that's a threat, then go ahead. It's a matter of complete indifference to me what you do. All I ask is that you make up your mind. Good God, Martin, try to be reasonable! You're the one who's pressing for an immedi-

143

ate distribution and, I might add, hanging over your mother's deathbed like a ghoul."

"Dammit! Arthur, don't ring that change over me. You know how things stand between me and Mother. I'm not going to turn sanctimonious just because she's dying."

Martin was now striding around the room in a fine fury, glaring down at Arthur who maintained an icy rigidity in his chair, watching the performance with obvious distaste. In the corner, completely ignored by the contestants, Kenneth was adding some soda water to his glass and wearily wishing himself elsewhere. Only blood relatives, he thought, could exacerbate each other quite as successfully as these two were doing. Either it was some curious and antisympathetic result of kinship or, more simply, the product of years of experience. He found himself wondering what it was like when Grace joined the act, and they had the complete three-ring circus. Probably the effect would be diluted by the inevitable creation of factions. Besides, Grace seemed to have a genius for playing one man off against the other.

"Nobody's asking you to be sanctimonious," snapped Arthur. "Although you might try to observe the common decencies. But, as that doesn't worry you, there's no objection to talking about Hilda's estate. You will inherit all the preferred stock and about fifty thousand from her in addition to a hundred thousand from the trust. On the one hand you've told Grace that you want to buy into the company with it, and now you tell me that you want to sell out. Make up your mind!"

"I'll make up my mind when I'm good and ready," said Martin sulkily from the corner of the couch where he had thrown himself. "What's the rush? I don't even know exactly how much Mother's estate will come to, after taxes. I like to know where I stand," he ended weakly.

Arthur looked at him curiously. It was obvious that Martin rarely suffered any doubts at all as to where he stood, and his elder cousin smelled a rat.

"Have you found an outside buyer for the preferred?" Arthur asked sharply.

"No," growled Martin and then he grinned maliciously, "but that doesn't mean that I'm not looking."

Kenneth, in sudden comprehension, realized that this was a deliberate attempt to mislead. Of course, what had happened was very simple. Martin was getting calls from the banks on his convertible debentures and, if things didn't improve, his entire inheritance might be swept away in the desperate attempt to remain solvent. But Martin had no intention of letting Arthur know about this and, it was extremely unlikely that Arthur, with his tidy standards and well defined lines of conduct, could conceive of such unparalleled irregularity and financial folly. The scope of Martin's disaster rendered him immune to discovery—by Arthur, that is.

"Do as you like, by all means, but you owe it to Grace not to lead her on. She has more than enough to worry about at the moment without mythical offers from you. Her financial affairs are getting worse and worse— Rowland seems a complete loss from that point of view and has heavy expenses in addition—and now she has to worry about the police questioning her. For a woman of Grace's sensitivity, it's all very difficult. Although, God knows, she could be more reasonable about it," he added testily.

"I'm sure Mrs. Walworth has no cause to be upset," intervened Kenneth in a misguided attempt to speak soothingly on a neutral topic. "These police checks are merely routine and don't indicate any real suspicion of murder."

There was a sudden hoot of laughter from the sofa. "That's not what's worrying our Grace," burbled Martin. "She's as safe as houses. A neighbor came in and saw her at midnight—the perfect alibi."

"But then, why—" stammered Kenneth.

"Martin, for God's sake!" thundered Arthur furiously.

"She was dead drunk. Our little Grace hits the bottle on those long lonely nights in Washington," sang out Martin happily. "Nothing public, you understand. Everything in the best of taste, complete privacy preserved, and only the family need know. Just a small blemish on the Schneiders' Washington front."

Kenneth was genuinely sickened, not so much at the disclosure as at Martin's unholy glee in making it. It did, however, explain a good deal about Grace and seemed to be the only fact of any interest which he would have to report to Thatcher. It was therefore duly noted.

"The choice part is that Grace is so worried about the

police finding out," continued Martin on a slightly more sober note, "when, if I know my Washington, that neighbor has already spread the news to every house in Georgetown."

"You're disgusting, Martin. Can't you find any better way to amuse yourself than gossiping about Grace?"

"She makes me sick. So damn superior with her patronizing offers to consider selling me her stock, these complaints about her dividends—who the hell does she think she is? Little Miss Perfection? She's a fifty-year-old lush who spends too much."

"You're not so perfect yourself, Martin. One of the reasons Grace can't live the way she used to is that we've had you making a mess of things. Before you sell out, you'd better think where you'll find another firm that will pay you thirty thousand a year to sit around planning the décor of your apartment and losing contracts."

"Oh, it's me that's losing contracts, is it?"

Issue had clearly been joined, and there would be no more side excursions into the affairs of Hilda and Grace. Each man was furious and expressing it in his own way. Arthur signified his control by lowering his voice, a useless gesture in view of the fact that his articulation had quickened to the point of slurring one word into the next. Tiny white lines showed around his facial bones in contrast to the unattractive red flush which had crept over his face and neck. Martin was once again on his feet, frankly shouting with rage.

"Let me tell you, Arthur, that if you go on running that mill as if you were outfitting the Union Army with cardboard shoes, you can expect every firm in the business to walk right over you."

"The walking didn't start until we let you open that flossy office in New York. Nobody expected you to have the energy to go out and look for new contracts, but I did expect you to be able to hang onto customers we've had for fifty-five years."

"What do you expect me to sell? Antique methods and high prices? If you listened to me and made the slightest effort to modernize, we wouldn't be slipping from first place to bottom of the list."

"If I listened to you, we would have lost every customer we had and every penny to boot! What did you do when

146

one of our biggest customers threatened to stop ordering? You couldn't even be bothered to get out of your chair and go and see them. I had to go and now we've got a new contract with them."

"And what the hell do you mean by going out to Wisconsin without telling me? I'm in charge of sales. You stick to your mill in Massachusetts and keep your nose out of my business!"

"This is my business. If you think I'm going to stand by and watch you wreck the work of eighty years, you've got another think coming. I expect to hand this business over to my son in better shape than I found it. If the only way I can do that is by getting rid of you, then I can do that too. But if you're going to run sales, you're going to do it the way I tell you to and that isn't going to mean sitting around too bone-lazy to save a twenty-million-dollar contract."

"So you think you can get rid of me! You'd ruin yourself if you did. Ask anybody who's seen that plant. Ask Grace, ask the bank, ask Nicolls . . ."

Both men turned to look at Nicolls as a thunderous silence filled the room. Kenneth smiled weakly at being suddenly recalled to their attention and wondered what in God's name was the tactful thing to do. Arthur was covered with confusion as he realized that an outsider had been witness to his outburst of temper. Martin, moved by a totally reflexive response, went to the bar and suggested another round of drinks. Obviously this was his panacea for any social crisis.

"Not for me, thank you," answered Nicolls. "I have to be getting back to the office."

"Nonsense," growled Arthur in some embarrassment. "You mustn't let this scene bother you, Kenneth. I am extremely sorry that we've brawled in your presence but you shouldn't make too much of it. Martin and I don't always see eye to eye about managing the business, and we've both lost our tempers before."

"Yes," said Martin, handing Kenneth a drink which he was obliged to accept unless he was prepared to make an issue of it. "Everybody's nerves are on edge right now, and Arthur and I usually have to have a row before we can decide on any new policy anyway."

"It's not that I'm saying we couldn't do with a few

changes," said Arthur in mellowed tones. "I would like to put some money into research now that we know what direction we want to go in—mass production and precutting. And I realize perfectly that, even if we were willing to go on relying upon skilled labor, the supply of trained craftsmen in this field is rapidly dwindling and won't be replenished. I just don't want us to go in over our heads on expenditure, and I don't want to cut Grace's dividends. She's having a hard enough time, and, after all, the purpose of a small family firm is to support the family."

"All right," Martin grinned. "I'll go along with that, so long as I'm included in the definition of family. Grace shall have her dividends and no kicks from me."

Kenneth marveled at Grace's position in the family. She seemed to him uniformly unpleasant. She was relentless in her demands, perfectly prepared to deal with either man behind the other's back, perpetually hysterical, and, it now appeared, a grave social handicap. But the one question on which complete accord could be achieved between Martin and Arthur was the necessity of providing Grace with an income. Grace knew how to play her hand.

"What's more, Arthur, I'll admit that you were right about Wisconsin Paper and Novelty," Martin added handsomely, making his amende honorable. "I ought to have gone out to Beloit, instead of trying to handle it from New York. When I got their letter saying they weren't going to renew, I was so stunned I couldn't think straight."

"Well, well, that's over and done with now," said Arthur, with an uncomfortable glance at Kenneth as if unwilling to reopen the subject of their recent quarrel. "The important thing is that we've got a good chance of getting them to sign a bigger contract than ever before. If we can get just one more like that, we'll have enough extra earnings to subsidize a research program."

"Well, that's not going to be easy unless we can satisfy people we're in a position to increase production substantially. But I'm seeing a man from West Virginia Pulp and Paper this week."

"Good," said Arthur approvingly. "I've brought down some statistics on our production for the last quarter which you'll want to see."

And as the conversation now threatened to become

severely technical, Kenneth felt he could take his leave gracefully. No attempts were made to detain him this time, but his departure was marked by the excessive cordiality due a guest who has been badly treated. Martin repeatedly assured him of a warm welcome whenever he felt inclined to drop by, and Arthur, clapping him fondly on the shoulder, promised to look in when he came to the bank to see Thatcher.

Finally making his escape, Kenneth felt a wave of relief as he mounted the steps to the street. He turned toward Eighth Street and mulled over the recent interview as he walked along. Curiously enough he was not thinking of it in terms of his duties as a trust officer. He was thinking that, if he was to suffer all the disadvantages entailed by admission to family quarrels, maybe it was time that he began to enjoy some of the advantages of a relative too. Perhaps he should plan to spend the weekend in Framingham.

18: CONSOLIDATED STATEMENT

In Buffalo, John Thatcher was already finishing luncheon and having his coffee before he interrupted his idle appraisal of the crowded dining room of the Statler to examine his own motives. An elderly bus boy side-stepped a group of diners who had unexpectedly pushed their chairs back to stand up and mill about in the way of the scurrying staff, an indifferent *maître d'hôtel* leaned against his service desk and watched the waitresses swinging in and out of the kitchen—when a sudden inner voice spoke somewhat severely to John Thatcher: "You want to go out to Buffalo Industrial Products yourself, to see the people that Schneider worked for."

He considered the truth of this with amusement.

"Do you want anything else, sir?" a waitress asked deferentially. John Thatcher liked to think that it was force of character that got him good service; in fact, it was because he looked like a good tipper.

"No thank you," he said, pleasantly if absently. "The check please."

It was forthcoming promptly. He left it on the table, tossed a bill over it, edged his way past another group milling this time around a table that was being cleared, and headed for the telephone booths in the lobby.

"You can always tell the really good ones," the waitress said as she stuffed a five-dollar bill in the pocket of her apron. "Money doesn't mean a thing to them."

Bryant Cottrell was surprised to hear that Thatcher was still in Buffalo. He thought, although of course he couldn't be absolutely sure, that he might be able to contact Stanislas Michaels and arrange an interview. This afternoon? Well, of course, that was very short notice, and it might develop . . .

"Try," said John Thatcher tersely.

And Bryant Cottrell did try. Within half an hour, Cottrell's secretary called back with a message: "Mr. Michaels expects you at three-thirty. Car will be ready at three o'clock." He retrieved his suitcase from the baggage room, read the *Times* in the lobby, and at nearly three picked up his coat and hat and strolled out to the street.

He waited no more than a minute or two, when the First National's impeccably polished Chrysler arrived.

"Hello, Mr. Thatcher," the driver greeted him as he jumped out to open the door for him. "They told me you want to go out to Lackawanna this time."

"That's right, Ben," Thatcher replied, settling himself in the back seat. He looked around the whitened city; the snow was now falling thickly and it was bitterly cold. People on the streets were bundled up against the biting wind, and Thatcher thought that there were fewer cars than usual on Delaware Avenue.

"How's the driving going to be?"

Ben dismissed the weather with a lordly gesture, as he slammed his door and started the big gray car. "We've got chains on now, so it won't make any difference."

The drive to Lackawanna was spent in a detailed comparison of the merits of chains and snow tires.

"I mean, when you really need traction, you've got to have chains," Ben said authoritatively as they drove along the Skyway Drive at a pace suitable to the dignity of the First National Bank and the Chrysler.

Thatcher nodded; he liked to talk to specialists. Someday, Walter Bowman would lecture him about snow tires, and one part of his mind stored Ben's observations. The other part, however, was concerned with Buffalo Industrial Products.

For once, he thought, watching the grimy stacks of the Bethlehem Steel plant drift by, his position could be straightforward and businesslike. And truthful, if not completely so. He was going to find out what the Michaels family's position would be if Kathryn Schneider wanted to sell the interest in BIP that she would presumably inherit. A perfectly reasonable reason for an interview and, he reminded himself, he must write Bryant Cottrell and tell him the results of the fishing expedition.

"Here we are, Mr. Thatcher," Ben said, as he pulled into the driveway of a long, shedlike building. "BIP."

Buffalo Industrial Products had not yet reached the level of conspicuous affluence which creates landscaped marvels and carpeted noiseless waiting rooms, furnished with Danish contour chairs and one luxuriant pot of tropical foliage. Lackawanna, as a whole, seemed due for an industrial face-lifting. Thatcher walked up a driveway through a cluttered delivery yard; as he entered the building his ears were assaulted by a heavy rumble of machinery. Sitting at a scarred desk in a hallway, rather than in a waiting room, there was not a goddesslike young woman with exotic make-up, but a middle-aged woman wearing a cheap maroon sweater to ward off the chills that came from the opening of the front door. She looked mildly surprised when he interrupted her typing to identify himself and explain that he had an appointment with the president of the firm.

"He's the third office down the hall," she said, returning to her typing. Thatcher understood this to mean that he should proceed, without waiting for preliminary buzzings. He went.

At the third office door down the dingy hall, Thatcher paused in uncertainty. BIP also dispensed with such niceties as name plates. He knocked, and opened the door.

Stan Michaels, clad in a blue work shirt with rolled-up sleeves, was talking to a young woman. He looked up, and said, "Come in. You're Mr. . . . ."

"Thatcher."

The bull-chested man shifted heavily in his chair. "People at the First National told me you want to talk to me about something. Schneider's common stock, I guess they said." He waved Thatcher into a straight-backed chair. No nonsense about taking his coat off, Thatcher noted with appreciation.

Michaels in fact was not even looking at his visitor.

"Mr. Thatcher and I have business, Jeannie," he said meaningfully.

"I know you do, Pa, you just told me," the tone of voice was discontented. "And I told you that I'm staying. I've got my interests to protect too."

"Jeannie," he said in a pleading voice. But the young woman, who appeared to be set on disagreeableness, turned to Thatcher who sketched a half-rise. "How do you do, Mr. Thatcher. My name is Jean Novak. Mrs. Novak." She was built on generous lines like her father and was, Thatcher guessed, about thirty years old.

"How do you do?" he replied. "I won't be interrupting you for long."

"I've got plenty of time," she said with a twist of her lips, and a sharp look at her father who looked heavily disapproving.

"Splendid," said Thatcher heartily. He was not prepared to let shrewish young women set the tone of his conversations. Jeannie Novak gave him a look of dislike.

Thatcher turned to Michaels. "Now, Mr. Michaels, I think I need not take too much of your time. Perhaps Mr. Cottrell did not explain . . ."

"Didn't explain a damn thing," Michaels said, not in anger but as an additional bit of information.

"No," Thatcher said. "Well, it is a little complicated to discuss by phone, but the situation is roughly that I represent the Sloan Guaranty Trust Bank. Of New York," he added, but Michaels merely nodded. "We are acting as trustees for the heirs of Robert Schneider in another matter. Mrs. Schneider has asked us about the possibility . . ."

"Mrs. Schneider," Jeannie Novak said with loathing. "She's got a nerve asking anybody for anything."

"Jeannie," her father said, in a warning tone of voice. "What do you want to find out, Mr. Thatcher?" Thatcher watched him clench and unclench his fists in what must be a gesture of impatience. Or fear. Both Stan Michaels and his daughter were taut with . . . was it fear?

Jeannie Novak had risen to her feet and was staring out the grimy window; Thatcher wished he could see her face. "It's a question of Robert Schneider's holdings of your common stock," he began, but Michaels interrupted him with a slap on the desk.

"I knew it was a mistake," he grunted in a spurt of anger. He talked to his daughter's back. "I told you and that smart husband of yours that we shouldn't have let the stock out of our hands . . ."

"How would you have kept Bob otherwise?" the daughter said, turning to face him. "How far could we have gotten without him during the last few years. Who was going to get us the Wisconsin Paper and Novelty Contract?"

Michaels looked at his daughter with an unreadable expression on his face; then his features softened and he shrugged.

"O.K., baby, O.K." He again turned to Thatcher who responded to the dumb inquiry in his eyes, rather than any spoken question. "I think we may be at cross-purposes," he said. "What I want to do is find out your interest in acquiring the stock that the boys . . ."

Jeannie Novak gave a strangled snort. Thatcher went on with some severity, "Robert Schneider's children will, presumably, inherit . . ."

Again, Jeannie Novak interrupted him, this time with a sharp question. "Presumably," she snapped. "What does that mean?"

Thatcher looked at her with a grave courtesy that hid his growing interest. Her vague sluttishness, her petulance and selfishness were very much what he had been led to expect of the "mystery woman," the woman who deceived her husband and betrayed an obviously doting father— with Robert Schneider. What he had not expected was the vein of shrewdness blended, he would guess, with acquisitiveness. She showed a good grasp of the business; she had instantly appreciated his guarded reference to the confusion that surrounded Robert Schneider's estate. She was obviously in a state of suppressed hysteria; but her mind was working at top speed.

Aloud he said, "Apparently Robert Schneider died intestate, Mrs. Novak. Without a will," he added in response to an interrogative rumble from Michaels. "At least, Captain Self tells me that the police haven't been able to find one. That means that the courts are going to award his estate to his wife and his children . . ."

"It isn't fair," Jeannie again said, this time between clenched teeth. "Oh damn him, damn him."

"That's no way to talk," her father said reprovingly; then, in a clumsy attempt to divert Thatcher's attention from this outburst, he added, "He's just doing his duty when he comes around and asks a lot of questions."

"You know I don't mean that stupid cop," she said furiously. "And don't pretend that you don't. I mean that bastard Bob. Robert Schneider," she added in what Thatcher took to be a humorless parody of his own precise voice.

"Jeannie!" her father shouted in an agony of apprehension.

But she was not to be stopped. "After all we did for him," she spat. "Took him off the line. Made a big man out of him. Gave him his big chance. Then he leaves things so that his kids, his lousy kids . . ."

Thatcher watched the performance. Jeannie Novak might have been having an affair with Robert Schneider, but she certainly gave no sign that she was deeply moved by his death. Or rather, that his death had left her with a sense of loss. On the other hand, she did seem to feel the loss of certain material advantages keenly. She was continuing her shrilly pitched lament.

"My God, you can't trust anybody. After all we did for him."

"Maybe too much, huh Jeannie?"

Thatcher and Michaels, who had been staring helplessly at Jeannie, both jumped at the new voice. In the doorway was a tall thin man, who put down a suitcase, carefully shut the door behind him, and entered.

"Roy!"

Stan Michaels lumbered to his feet. "Roy," he repeated thankfully. "My God, it's good to see you. I'm going crazy." He glanced at Thatcher, and hurriedly added, "Paul Reardon and I have been on the phone to Beloit half the day. Oh, this is . . ."

Again John Thatcher identified himself. Roy Novak

exchanged salutations with him; he did no more than glance at his wife with a cold "Hello, Jeannie." She watched him through narrowed eyes as he turned back to Thatcher.

"Of course I've heard of you, Mr. Thatcher," he said in a level voice. "What's your interest in BIP?"

Again Thatcher explained that he was acting in the interests of Robert Schneider's children.

Roy Novak heard him out in silence, exchanged a long look with his father-in-law, and said, "I think we'd have to say that we want a little time to think it over, Mr Thatcher."

Michaels nodded approval. "Yeah, we've got a lot of things—details and stuff—that we've got to settle pretty soon."

Thatcher was interested in learning what those details were, but he saw that he might just as well cut the interview short. Roy Novak was not likely to reveal anything.

"I thought that you would want time to think it over," he replied, "but I was in Buffalo on business, and I wanted to put the facts before you." He rose, then deliberately added, "By the way, is Schneider's death going to have any effect on your going public?"

Both Novak and Michaels stiffened with suspicion. Thatcher raised his eyebrows, then explained the Sloan's connection with Robichaux and Devane. Novak nodded, but Michaels continued to look wary.

"I'm safe, Mr. Michaels," Thatcher said with a small smile. "I've heard a lot of confidential financial information in my day. Nobody has ever complained that I can't keep a secret."

Novak expelled a breath, smiled dutifully if coldly, then, after another quick glance at Michaels, said, "Well, that's one of the things that Stan and I are going to have to thrash out this morning."

Michaels capitulated. Deciding that Thatcher was trustworthy he said, in a heavy confiding tone, "Can't deny that losing Schneider is a blow. We sent Roy here right on from Montreal to New York to talk to those people. We're all going to have to do a lot of hard thinking about our plans."

"You're right, Stan," Roy started. "We're really . . ."

"Well!" The word was like an explosion. Jeannie Novak, who had been silent, again stood up, trembling with rage. "I like that. *You'll* make decisions, will you? And you'll sit down with Stan and decide what we're going to do, will you?" She drew a deep breath, sat down, then answered her own questions. "Like hell you will! From now on, Roy Novak, you're not running the show, ordering me around. From now on, you're going to pay a little more attention to what I want."

"Now, Jeannie," her father said in a placating voice.

"We'll talk about all of this later," her husband said colorlessly. "We have a lot of things to talk about."

John Thatcher could almost feel Jeannie Novak's contempt for her husband. His clerkish superiority, his cold, authoritative voice, his prim correctness must have been unendurable to her at any time. Now, however, it flicked her into a sort of frenzy.

"We have a lot of things to talk about, do we? Well, you old lady, don't think that you can take that tone of voice with me. Ever again." She gave a grim smile. "And don't look at me as though I'm something you wouldn't pick up in a bargain basement. I know all about it . . ."

Roy cut in coldly, "I don't know what you're talking about, but this isn't the time to bring out . . ."

"You don't know what I'm talking about," she crowed. "Oh, no, you don't. You lousy, two-bit . . . murderer!"

She confronted her husband and father who stared at her in undisguised horror. John Thatcher stood rooted. He might have been a piece of office equipment for all the attention she payed to him as he swept on.

"I know it, do you hear me, I know it. I've got the proof that you did it, you lousy killer. You didn't know that you left proof, did you? Well you did, you smart bastard. No, you were flying straight to Montreal, weren't you? Well, I happen to know that you stopped by Bob's apartment. And I can prove it. Do you hear me, I can prove it. So don't you take that damned smug tone with me." She stopped, white-faced and trembling.

Her father recovered himself. "Jeannie, you should be ashamed. Roy's been a good husband to you . . ."

"Good husband!" she mimicked contemptuously.

He came around the desk and put his great, work-scarred hands on her shoulders and shook her roughly.

"Don't be foolish. The police have cleared him. They know he was in Montreal. He didn't kill . . ."

"Your lover," Roy said icily. Michaels looked at him sharply, started to say something, then thought better of it. For a moment there was silence. Thatcher looked at the three protagonists. Emotion had stripped all concealment from them. Michaels looked agonized, Roy Novak embarrassed and disdainful. But certainly not guilty.

And Jeannie Novak looked stupefied by emotion. She stared dully at her father; she looked at her husband who met her long look. She was drained—and, thought Thatcher, genuinely surprised.

"The police cleared Roy?" she repeated mechanically. Then slowly she began to cry; first with tears coursing down her ashen face, then with great racking sobs. Her father cradled her comfortingly against his shoulder.

Roy Novak was white-faced too, but characteristically he turned to Thatcher with a ghastly smile. "I'm sorry we've subjected you to this," he began.

Thatcher, a man who liked his emotions decently veiled, murmured meaningless phrases aimed at expressing sympathy and understanding as he strode to the door. He looked back for a moment, debating the propriety of taking formal leave of Stan Michaels and his daughter. Then, frankly appalled, he turned on his heels and fled.

Thus making his second mistake in the investigation of Robert Schneider's murder.

19: CHAIRMAN OF THE BOARD

Sinking thankfully into the back seat of the Chrysler, John Thatcher expelled a sigh of relief as he watched Ben expertly guide the car out of the yard and onto the road. Away from Buffalo Industrial Products. A lesser man would have mopped his brow. Vice-presidents of the Sloan Guaranty Trust are out of training for hysterical scenes. It had been at least ten years since he had dealt with anybody who approximated Jeannie Novak's uninhibited, coarse vitality. He was sheltered, he realized.

"Thank God," he murmured aloud.

"Pardon?" Ben said.

"Nothing, Ben. I was just talking to myself."

Ben preserved a sympathetic silence; a number of the passengers he ferried for the First National talked to themselves. "These big businessmen," he often explained to his wife, "they got a lot on their minds."

It was nevertheless necessary to interrupt.

"Back to the Statler, Mr. Thatcher?"

"What . . . oh no, Ben. I think we'd better head for the airport. I brought my bag along."

While Ben respected the important matters that occupied the minds of the important men he drove around, he had a very low opinion of their common-sense grasp of everyday facts. He rubbed the windshield and peered through it. The skies were still ominously darkened and fat snow flakes were sticking to the car although he had brushed it very carefully as he waited for Thatcher.

"Doesn't seem reasonable to expect that the planes will be taking off today, Mr. Thatcher," he remarked mildly.

Disturbed in his review of the scene he had just witnessed, Thatcher irritably hitched himself forward and looked out the window.

"Doesn't it ever stop snowing in Buffalo?" he asked testily.

"Only during the heat waves," Ben replied, wheezing happily at a serviceable joke.

Thatcher smiled dutifully, sat back and did a little rapid calculating. A return to the Statler would almost certainly entail an evening spent in the company of Bryant Cottrell; a trip to the airport might, at best, yield a plane to New York, and at worst, some hours spent in the terminal. In his present mood, it seemed the lesser of two evils.

"Let's take a chance on the airport," he said decisively.

Ben nodded, kept his opinion of the wisdom of the decision to himself, and concentrated on finding a turnoff to Genesee Avenue.

By the time they had arrived at the airport, however, it seemed that his pessimism had been ill-founded; the sky was lightening, very slightly, and, more important, it was obvious that some planes were leaving Buffalo. Their muffled roar was the only evidence; clouds hid them from the ground.

Thatcher sent Ben and the First National Chrysler on their way with suitable thanks and gratuities, dismissing Ben's offer to wait and see what happened.

"No thanks, Ben, if I can't get a plane, I'll get a taxi back to town."

The moment Thatcher entered the terminal, however, he wondered if Ben's head-shaking had not been wiser than his own decision to risk getting a flight. The building was packed tight; small groups of people, gesturing, expostulating, and pleading with languidly bored ticket clerks, were lined against the counters. There were what seemed to be dozens of dirty, small children who were cranky with lack of sleep. The great majority of air-age travelers, however, were either sitting down or standing propped against a wall, in apathetic anticipation.

Periodically, a grotesque parody of the human voice rose above the din of small noises that filled the terminal, and everybody listened: "Flight 600, SuperCoach from San Francisco to New York, with stops at Denver, Chicago and Buffalo, scheduled to arrive at 5:45 will not arrive until seven-o'clock." "Departure of Flight 302, non-stop to Boston, scheduled for five oh-two, has been delayed until further announced." "Will passenger Brown, American Airlines Flight 505, please report to the ticket counter?"

After each announcement, there would be a small eddy of activity; four or five people in the corner would groan, a soldier would get up and stride nervously about, somebody would walk out of the waiting room. Most people, however, would check their watches and continue to wait.

It was, Thatcher noted, almost steamy in the terminal, in contrast to the intense cold outside. Yet most people still wore coats and scarves. They were prepared, at a moment's notice, to board a fast-moving vehicle, and soar to distant points; in the meantime, they sat and waited.

Thatcher edged his way to the tail of the long line that coiled accusingly in front of the ticket counter. Within seconds, the line had lengthened behind him, and he was uncomfortably sandwiched in. He stood patiently; the line did not move—there appeared to be some sort of conflict at its head—but, although his plane was scheduled to depart in fifteen minutes, he could not persuade himself

159

that there was any hurry. He resigned himself to a long wait.

". . . it's all very well, and good for this sort of thing. But why can't they tell you, when you call up that the planes are going to be this late? . . ."

"I know, I know. I drove in from Erie, and it would have been much more convenient. . . ."

Thatcher turned idly; camaraderie engendered by common discomfort had drawn two women behind him into vocal attacks on the airlines. The first, a firm-looking middle-aged woman who might have been a nurse, continued with no more than a momentary nod at the contribution of the second, a faded blonde.

"Of course it's nothing to them," she said. "I've waited for as much as four and five hours for planes, sometimes. . . ."

The line shuffled, but did not move forward; battle was drawn at the ticket counter.

An elderly man with a choleric complexion unexpectedly entered the conversation behind Thatcher. "I," he said, investing the word with significance, "I have given up expecting anything at all from the airlines. Would you believe it, last Thanksgiving, I was removed from a plane from Boston to Buffalo—although I had gone to some pains to be sure of having a reservation for the holiday. And do you know why?"

Nobody had any suggestions to offer.

"Because," he said with heavy sarcasm, "because on the busiest weekend in months, the airlines ran out of gas in Buffalo." The audience, eager to break in and describe some outrage the airlines had perpetrated on them, gasped insincerely, and prepared to speak, when he repeated, "Ran out of gas. Would you believe it?"

But the nurse was not going to be put off. She was, Thatcher saw with some amusement, used to giving vent to her irritations. It was apparent, moreover, that while she was firm she was not a gifted raconteur. Held captive by the line, Thatcher and his fellow sufferers—and he was now convinced she was a nurse, used to dealing with listeners rendered immobile by broken bones—were treated to a detailed, and boring account of her last trip to California.

The elderly gentleman stared ahead; the faded blonde looked embarrassed.

Thatcher checked his watch; it was not quite five o'clock. The altercation at the ticket counter had apparently been resolved with mutual recrimination and mistrust; a sharp-featured young woman with a brief case fairly snatched a ticket and turned away from the desk.

". . . so of course I wired my mother—she's ninety-two, and in really marvelous shape for her age, but ninety-two is ninety-two—and my brother-in-law and sister to meet me at Midway Airport. Since I was going to be in California for at least six months, and wouldn't be able to go to Chicago with them for Christmas, it was really worth-while, although they had to drive up from Gary. . . ."

Thatcher shifted his weight; he let his mind wander over the Schneider case. Had his trip to Buffalo clarified anything? He frowned slightly; at least there was no doubt that Kathryn Schneider was quite innocent—and that of course was the bank's prime interest.

". . . then this stupid voice talking in the plane—personally I'd be happier if they just flew the airplanes instead of trying to be radio announcers—well, he announced that we were going to land at O'Hare airport instead of Midway. That's at least thirty miles from Midway. . . ."

The line gave a little lurch forward, an expression of the dumb impatience of the crowd, a gesture of irritation. Thatcher put his brief case down for the fifth time; he would check it through and be free of the nuisance of carrying it if he had to wait any length of time. His thoughts again reverted to this afternoon's scene. Jeannie Novak, he was convinced, was perfectly capable of murder. But although it was apparent that her father was terrified that she might have killed Schneider, Thatcher was convinced that she thought her own husband guilty. And Roy Novak was apparently cleared by the Buffalo and Montreal police. He certainly looked self-confident.

Thatcher, inching forward again, this time nudged the brief case along with his foot, rescuing it from a small boy with an ice cream cone who was hovering perilously close to it.

". . . and of course I was crying. After all, I counted on

seeing my family for that hour, and I was going on to the Coast. Well that . . . that snippet was very unsympathetic. Very unsympathetic. Mind you, if I had been a man, she would have been all over me. Hostess, humph . . . But when I calmed down, and I can tell you it was not thanks to her. . . ."

"I have proof." Another voice, firm and strident, echoed in Thatcher's ears. What sort of proof did Jeannie Novak have? Proof that her husband, who had been in Montreal, murdered her lover. Was it sheer hysteria? Thatcher thought about the voice—triumphant and venomous. What could elicit that in Jeannie Novak?

". . . and of course they won't let you call, even when it is all their own fault. So there was no way I could get in touch with my family. Of course as soon as we landed— and we had over an hour on the ground—I tried to call Midway. But you know what they're like on the phone. As far as my family knew, I never was in Chicago at all. . . ."

The nurse made the mistake of pausing for dramatic effect; her audience seized the opportunity. Both the elderly gentleman and the blonde started:

"Exactly. Why, I called them specifically today, and asked . . ."

"No use calling them at all, I always say. . . ."

John Thatcher was next in line to the ticket counter when he had a sudden insight. Jeannie Novak, he was sure, would use the word proof in a simple, nonmetaphoric sense. She had the kind of fundamental simplicity that would look upon proof as something specific . . . something concrete . . .

"Ticket sir?" an infinitely tired voice requested. He produced his ticket; the clerk went through complex motions involving rubber stamps and pencils before returning it to him.

"Is the plane late?" Thatcher inquired.

The clerk eyed Thatcher with exaggerated patience, then said, "It's leaving in about an hour and a half. You'll be called, sir."

Thatcher eyed him with equal distaste. "Well, then, I think that I'll check my brief case."

The clerk looked at the eminently portable brief case, then up at Thatcher. An impertinent, offensive and inappropriate remark died on his lips.

"Yes, sir," he said. Scribbling the ticket, he handed Thatcher a baggage check and waited for him to move.

"If you please," said the nurse stridently as she elbowed him aside.

"Pardon me," muttered John Thatcher. He looked at the baggage check, then, as he moved along the counter he looked back at the firm-voiced nurse.

He then stood stock still—to the irritation of four stand-bys who were convinced that by keeping in motion their chances of getting on a plane were improved—and explored the idea that had just come to him.

It needed testing. He quickly formulated a plan. Part one would be a call to Captain Self . . . No. That was part two. Part one. . . .

He looked around the terminal thoughtfully. The staff behind the ticket counter looked more vacuous than usual; trying to edge up to the counter would provoke a storm of protest.

He surveyed the waiting room; like all such facilities it was inconveniently arranged so that incoming traffic was immediately added to the confusion before the ticket counters.

From the main room however stretched two corridors. Disconsolate strollers would disappear up them, then return. Thatcher headed for the corridor on his left; it led to the baggage checkroom.

On the right were the rest-rooms; on the left, three blue doors, labeled, "Flight Room," "Pilot's Room," "Traffic Room." And under each sign was the additional information: "No admittance."

Thatcher raised an eyebrow, tossed a mental coin, then without knocking opened the door marked "Traffic Room."

Three men were sitting in front of a long, paper-covered table, piled high with graphs and charts. The windows of the room faced the field, but any worry Thatcher had about interrupting vital processes was dispelled by the appearance of the men. They were in shirt sleeves, and obviously occupied in nothing more important than drinking coffee from paper cups.

One of them, a bullet-headed blond with a crew cut, looked at the intruder; with a touch of Texas in his voice he spoke: "Can't you read, Pop? No admittance. That means you."

John Thatcher prided himself on the fact that, no matter what the provocation, he never lost his temper. It was true. There were, however, occasions when he allowed himself the luxury of what some of his colleagues on the Street referred to as "a show of force."

"My name," he said in an icy voice, "is John Putnam Thatcher. I am not only a vice-president of the Sloan Guaranty Trust, but a member of the board of directors of American Airlines." He paused briefly; the three men sat mesmerized, like rabbits in front of a cobra. Texas' mouth was slightly opened, Thatcher noted with some satisfaction. None of these men was capable of checking on the truth of his claims, and he could, after all, prove he was with the Sloan. He continued with cold deliberation.

"I have been willing to put up with a good deal of incidental discourtesy in the last half hour, but that is attributable to the emergency weather conditions. I am prepared to overlook it. Now, however, it has become a matter of some urgency that I get certain information from the airlines. I propose to get it; either you find out ... or tell me where I can get the information. Quickly."

Texas stiffened as the last word was barked out; one of the other men, leaped to his feet. "Yes, sir," he said in a frightened voice. "Yes, sir. Just tell me—us, what it is you want to know."

Thatcher favored the group with a long look of appraisal, that visibly shook them. Then, tossing his coat negligently over a chair, he frowned, and began. "Now listen carefully. I am interested in flights in and out of Buffalo. On the night of Friday, the thirteenth of December. ..."

20: ACCOUNT RENDERED

The flight from Buffalo to New York took off at seven o'clock but John Thatcher was not aboard. Upon leaving the traffic room armed with sufficient information to galvanize even Self, he had implemented point two of his program. The subsequent descent of Captain Peter Self upon the Buffalo Airport has gone down in the annals of American Airlines history. He tore the place apart. The files were gutted; phone calls buzzed forth to Wisconsin, Buffalo Industrial Products, and the Statler; grim-faced employees of the police department took down depositions, administered oaths, and sealed up documents to be shipped to the Photostat Division; and the unfortunate airport flight master was hauled away from a dinner party at the Lafayette (where he was scheduled to address the Junior Chamber of Commerce on "The Effect of the St. Lawrence Seaway on Buffalo's Future as an International Port") to be relentlessly catechized by an enraged police officer.

When Thatcher finally boarded a plane at nine o'clock, Captain Peter Self was seated on Jeannie Novak's sofa for the last time. It had been apparent to Self from the moment he entered the room that, as far as Jeannie was concerned, the battle was over. His telephone call to BIP had been received by Stan with undisguised relief. The older man had agreed that it was time they all had a talk together and asked him to join them at the Novaks's house. Jeannie was produced by her two male relatives and grimly ensconced in a chair, where she now sat, a picture of sullen discontent, flanked on either side by her grimly disapproving father and husband.

"All right, so I went to see him. He was alone in town, and I was going to ask him to spend Christmas with us. There's nothing wrong with that," she whined.

The air was heavy with disbelief. She stirred uneasily as the silence prolonged itself.

"And what time was it when you got there?" asked Self.

"It was around eleven-thirty. It took me a long time to get there on account of the snow," she said defiantly.

"You were carrying a Christmas wreath?"

"Yes, I just happened to pick one up that evening."

"Well, tell me what happened in your own words."

"I went in the side door to the apartment house. It was quicker that way. I walked up the stairs and knocked on the door. There wasn't any answer, so I went in. The door wasn't locked." She looked at Self expectantly, but he didn't ask her whether she had a key. He already knew that she did, and he was not prepared to waste time on that now. He was thinking what kind of appearance she would make in court. The jury wouldn't like her, but she was such a transparent liar that it was quite easy to know when she was telling the truth.

"Go on," he said quietly.

"The living room was empty. I called, but there wasn't any answer. I started to look around. The study was the last room I went to. He was there—on the floor—there was blood—his head—" her voice started to rise, and she pressed a handkerchief to her mouth. Stan leaned over to put his hand on her shoulder.

"Jeannie, honey, take it easy. You've got to tell Pete."

Roy Novak looked at the two detachedly. He made no attempt to touch his wife or speak to her.

"I'm sorry, Mrs. Novak, but you'll have to go on. You'll feel better when it's all over."

"I leaned down to see if he was still alive. When I touched him, he was cold. But there was some cardboard in the blood next to his head. I picked it up before I realized what it was." She was now very white, and her hands were twisting her handkerchief convulsively. "It was an airplane baggage check. I knew Roy was supposed to be on a plane. He had ideas about Bob and me. I thought he had gone to see Bob and lost his head. I might have known better," she added with a sudden flicker of contempt.

"And what did you do with the check, Mrs. Novak?" asked Self..

"I put it in my purse and ran away as fast as I could! Did you expect me to go to the police with it? I was protecting my husband," she protested with self-conscious virtue. Roy Novak's thin lips twisted in a grimace of disgust. Stan Michaels made inarticulate and embarrassed noises.

"Of course," said Self expressionlessly. It was as good a story as any for the witness stand. "But what did you do with the baggage check afterward?"

"I kept it. It's here now. I was going to give it to Roy."

Self exhaled slowly. Who would have thought it? This stupid and disagreeable woman had had one moment of good sense. She had not destroyed the one piece of solid evidence.

"Would you mind getting it for me?" he said very gently, "and then I'll be on my way. I have a lot to do."

It was the next afternoon before Self was able to call Thatcher in New York and tell him that the baggage check had been retrieved, that the airline had searched its records, and that photostats were even now on their way to Buffalo. Their ultimate destination—a file folder now labeled *State V. Schneider*.

Thatcher frowned as he hung up, asked Miss Corsa to send Nicolls into his office. He was still undecided when Kenneth entered and he waved him to a seat.

"The murder of Robert Schneider has been solved, Nicolls. The police have enough evidence to go to trial and a warrant has been issued."

"Good heavens, sir! Did all this happen while you were in Buffalo?" Nicolls, like every one else in the trust department, had heard from Miss Corsa that Thatcher had arrived at the office promptly that morning, only to spend the day gazing out the window and repeatedly alerting his secretary for a phone call which he expected momentarily from Buffalo Police Headquarters. Thatcher, in a fit of abstraction was a novelty for the trust department and the staff, while amusing itself with sundry speculations about September love or embezzlement, agreed he should only be approached with great caution.

"Most of it happened yesterday. All things considered, it might be wise if you were to go to Framingham. You may be needed there. It's only decent ... yes, Miss Corsa, what is it?"

"It's that Mr. Schneider again," said Miss Corsa in the tone of one washing her hands of the situation. "You saw him last time without an appointment, and I thought you might want to do it again. He says it's important."

"Hmm, that certainly is awkward. You'd better show him in. I see no reason why we should be embarrassed," he ended firmly.

Kenneth looked at his superior in bewilderment. Thatcher had advanced this *non sequitur* with the air of one making a highly reasonable statement. But it was too late to ask why anyone should be embarrassed, for Arthur Schneider was striding buoyantly into the room.

"Now, I won't take much of your time today," he began as soon as the round of greetings was over. "I've come from the hospital. Poor Hilda has just died, and I stopped in to let you know that you could start to draw up the papers immediately. It will be a relief for Grace that . . ."

But Thatcher held up an imperative hand suddenly and took command of the conversation.

"Before you go any further, it is only right that you should know that I just received a telephone call from the Buffalo Police. They have found the baggage check which you left behind in Robert Schneider's apartment and they have checked with the airport about your stopover. I expect that you will be arrested before the day is out unless you leave for Massachusetts instantly. Even there it will only be a matter of time."

When Thatcher finished this extraordinary speech, Kenneth turned expectantly to Schneider, prepared for a flood of indignant outrage. But Schneider was sitting perfectly motionless in his chair, and only the rise and fall of his chest as he fought for breath indicated the extent of his shock. Nothing could have made Thatcher's accusation credible so effectively as Schneider's reception of it. Arthur Schneider, whose joviality, irritation and anger were always freely and loudly expressed, sat silent for a long time before he spoke. He sounded very tired.

"It's always been a matter of time. I never expected to get away with it, you know," he said emotionlessly. "I just wanted to see my family once before I was arrested. But they never came to arrest me, and then I began to forget that it really was a murder that I had committed."

"But, you were in Washington!" Kenneth had finally found his voice, which sounded strangely melodramatic after Arthur Schneider's quiet monotone.

"Not until later." Schneider smiled at him calmly. "It's really quite simple. We were grounded in Buffalo. I wanted to talk to Robert about the Beloit contract. So I called him from the airport, and he agreed that he would be at home. I took the limousine because there weren't any taxis. Later on after—after I had killed him—I ran back to the Statler and took the limousine back to the airport. They were just announcing the departure of my plane. There was a slight clearing in the weather then, and they were getting a few planes out. It was about ten o'clock then. They don't usually close down airports for an entire day, you know. They open them up whenever there's a break."

Kenneth gave a sudden start. He remembered that Thatcher had made this point when he was discussing Jane's alibi. Could the old man have been thinking even then of Arthur Schneider? He looked suspiciously at Thatcher, but there was no sign of triumph there, nothing but polite receptivity. Meanwhile Arthur Schneider was continuing his story in the same exhausted monotone.

"I don't think I was in Buffalo for more than two and a half hours. On the plane all I could think of was getting home and explaining to Josephine—that's my wife—what had happened. I didn't want her to hear the story from anyone else. But then the plane was rerouted and we didn't go to Boston. I thought about going to Grace, but I couldn't put her in the position of having her brother arrested in her house, could I?" Arthur looked appealingly at Thatcher for confirmation.

"No," said Thatcher slowly, "you couldn't do that."

"But nobody had arrested me by the next morning, so I took the train to Boston. It was only when I got home that I realized that everybody thought the plane had gone directly from Chicago to Washington. I ought to have remembered that the airlines don't usually mention unscheduled stopovers, even to the people who are waiting. I knew it wouldn't make any difference in the long run, but it gave me some time with my family, and that was all that I cared about."

"When did you realize that you'd lost your baggage check?" asked Thatcher.

"What's so important about the baggage check?" said Kenneth. He was afflicted by a sensation of unreality. In part this was due to the enormously sympathetic image projected by Arthur Schneider. Never had he seemed so attractive as now, when he was confessing to a brutal murder. Kenneth shook his head and concentrated on the answer.

"It was the mystery object in the pool of blood," explained Thatcher kindly. "It must have fallen out of your pocket," he went on to Schneider, "and then the blood coagulated around it."

"I saw that in the Buffalo papers. After a week, I couldn't stand the suspense any more, so I went to the Boston Public Library to read the accounts. There wasn't anything about my baggage check. In fact, there wasn't anything about me! It was all about a liaison with a woman who carried a Christmas wreath around. I decided I must have lost the claim check someplace else, and it was safe to put in a request for my luggage."

"Yes, the police now have the luggage check and also a copy of your claim, identifying the luggage as yours."

"It was bound to come out," said Schneider fatalistically. "It's curious, but the people I care for the most have all made it inevitable. Josephine, who was the first to notice my missing baggage and insisted I do something about it, and Jane, poor child, who couldn't resist the temptation to tell her funny story about my flight home from Chicago—you remember," he said, turning to Kenneth, "she told it to you that time you came to us in Framingham, and even Grace, who wanted me to go with her to the Public Library where the librarian would have been sure to remember me as the man who had asked for all the Buffalo papers the week before. But what I don't understand is what happened to the claim check for my luggage. If I dropped it in Robert's apartment, why didn't the police find it right away?"

"Robert was expecting a woman that night. She came a few hours after you left. She found the body and assumed that her husband was the murderer. So she pocketed the claim check, thinking it was evidence against her husband, and left without giving the alarm. When she found out that her husband had an impeccable alibi, she delivered the check to the police." Thatcher felt that it was only tactful to gloss over his own activities in the discovery of this evidence. Fortunately it did not seem to occur to Schneider to question Thatcher's intimacy with the police in Buffalo. This removed one embarrassment from a conversation already rich in social awkwardness.

"It's just like Robert to be involved in a sordid affair with a married woman," said Schneider censoriously, with a return to his old manner. Kenneth silently marveled at the outlook which could take murder, but not adultery, in its stride.

"I'm afraid that he was a remarkably unpleasant man," mused Thatcher.

"You could not fully appreciate his unpleasantness without having met him," said Schneider. "It's why I killed him, of course," he went on in a conversational tone of voice.

"Because he was unpleasant!" Kenneth was outraged. "But surely, sir, there was some other reason."

"The contract, Nicolls," said Thatcher. "Surely you've realized that it was the same contract that the mill in Framingham was losing and that the mill in Buffalo was getting."

"But I still don't see—"

"Let me explain," interrupted Schneider. "After I stopped in New York to talk to you both about the trust, I went on to Beloit to find out why we were losing the contract. I thought it was some incredible imbecility on Martin's part. But no, they explained that this man, Robert Schneider, had a new process and he seemed capable of steering it through the pilot runs. I knew at once that it could mean the end of us, and I was sure that it must be our Robert Schneider. After all, I'd just been talking with you about him a few days before. It was exactly the sort of thing his father was always fooling around with, but his father could never get it to the production stage. If the process was successful, and it was handled by any other firm, we would have to go into bankruptcy. I knew then that I would have to talk with Robert."

"Did you intend to do it then?" asked Thatcher curiously.

"No, of course not. The plane was supposed to be non-stop. But when the opportunity arose, I went to see him. I explained to Robert very carefully the implication of his discovery and what it would mean to the family firm. I also explained to him that the trust was coming to an end, and he could count on a hundred thousand dollars. Then I made him an offer—it was an extremely generous offer. A very large salary, more than he was getting at Buffalo, and the opportunity to buy into the firm with his capital."

"What did he say?" asked Kenneth.

"He didn't really say anything about my offer. He just

started to think out loud. I don't believe I can explain it to you. He was totally indifferent to my presence, totally uninterested in everything I had told him about the family business. He was calculating how he could use the hundred thousand to bring pressure on somebody called Michaels, get himself a controlling interest in Buffalo Industrial, and then build it up to the point where he could run every other firm out of business. You understand, he was planning to use the money from the Schneider family trust to ruin the Schneider family. I think that I could have stood it if he had just said no, or if he had explained that he was committed to the Buffalo firm, or if he had just bothered to be polite. But he didn't notice my existence at all; I just wasn't important enough to his plans for him to pretend, even though he was planning to ruin me and my family. Then I must have picked up the book end and hit him. The next thing I knew, I was standing there, still in my hat and coat—"

"And gloves," interjected Thatcher.

White-faced and incurious, Schneider stared dully at the banker.

"You didn't leave any fingerprints," explained Thatcher.

"I never thought of that," said Schneider. "I never really thought at all. Suddenly I was standing there, looking down at a man whom I had just murdered." Schneider shook his head slowly as if to clear his thoughts. "The next thing I remember I was running back to the Statler through the snow." Arthur Schneider brought his story to a close in a mildly astonished voice as if he still could not entirely credit his conduct in Buffalo. It was noticeable that there was not a particle of remorse in his voice. He saw the shock on Kenneth's face and explained calmly, "All I wanted to do was to save my family."

"You succeeded," said Thatcher after a short silence. He, at least, had absorbed whatever shock he felt at Arthur Schneider's crime a good twenty hours earlier. "You got back your contract, and you have saved your family."

"Yes," Arthur sounded slightly amused. "Martin thinks I got that contract back through personal adroitness; he still hasn't realized that the people in Beloit just wouldn't trust the Michaels firm to carry out Robert's process. They were afraid of bugs. And if Martin is really on his

172

toes, I suppose he will be able to do well enough with the firm to have something to hand over to my son. But, all this is going to have very little to do with me. My efforts are over." He leaned back in his chair and shut his eyes.

"Nonsense," said Thatcher firmly. "You should do what you planned to do from the start. Go home and tell your family. It will be less of a shock coming from you. You mustn't stop thinking of them at this point. And, if you go to Massachusetts, that will delay your arrest long enough for you to take legal advice. I realize that you're tired, but, in all probability, you will have a good long time to rest in the future."

"You mean you don't think I'll be given the death penalty," said Schneider detachedly.

"Almost definitely not. There is nothing to show premeditation. The prosecution will probably confine themselves to a charge of second degree murder."

"I'm not so sure that I'd prefer that," said Schneider thoughtfully. Nicolls wondered where Thatcher had acquired all this erudition on the law of homicide. Probably boned it up at night since all this started. The duties of a banker certainly seemed variegated.

"It is not a question of what you prefer," responded Thatcher austerely. "It is a question of your duty. You should go home." The words were a clarion call to Schneider. After all, the expression of unpleasant actions in the terms of duty was a concept very familiar to him.

"Yes, of course. It is the only thing to do. I wonder," he hesitated, almost shyly, before addressing Nicolls, "I wonder if you would care to come with me."

Kenneth started visibly as the significance of Schneider's request came home to him. Arthur could not have asked him more plainly what his intentions were with respect to Arthur's daughter. Murderer or no, Arthur Schneider remained invincibly Victorian and invincibly New England.

Kenneth hesitated for only a moment. "It would give me great pleasure," he said with the formality suitable to the occasion.

It was almost as if the two men had sealed some sort of pact for the protection of the Schneider women.

Thatcher watched them go out together, shoulder to shoulder. He wondered what Kenneth and his prospective father-in-law would talk about on the plane.

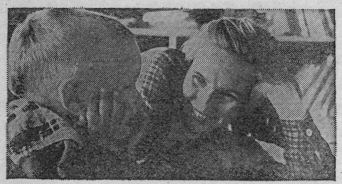

Today they're playing word games.
Before he's five, he can be reading 150 words a minute.

HOW TO GIVE YOUR CHILD A SUPERIOR MIND

A remarkable new book tells how you, yourself—at home—with no special training can actually add as much as thirty points to your child's effective I.Q. . . . how you can help him move ahead quickly in school and enable him to be more successful in an education-conscious world.

Best of all, your child can achieve this early success without being pushed and without interference with a happy, normal, well-adjusted childhood.

GIVE YOUR CHILD A SUPERIOR MIND provides a planned program of home instruction that any parent can start using immediately. *You will learn:*

1. How to awaken your child's inborn desire to learn.
2. How to teach your child to read.
3. How to help your child streak ahead in math.
4. How to give your child the power of abstract reasoning.
5. How to increase your child's effective I.Q.

At all bookstores, or mail coupon today.➡

LOOK FOR THESE GREAT POCKET 📖 BOOK BESTSELLERS AT YOUR FAVORITE BOOKSTORE

THE PIRATE • Harold Robbins	
YOU CAN SAY THAT AGAIN, SAM! • Sam Levenson	
THE BEST • Peter Passell & Leonard Ross	
CROCKERY COOKING • Paula Franklin	
SHARP PRACTICE • John Farris	
JUDY GARLAND • Anne Edwards	
SPY STORY • Len Deighton	
HARLEQUIN • Morris West	
THE SILVER BEARS • Paul E. Erdman	
FORBIDDEN FLOWERS: **More Women's Sexual Fantasies** • Nancy Friday	
MURDER ON THE ORIENT EXPRESS • Agatha Christie	
THE JOY OF SEX • Alex Comfort	
RETURN JOURNEY • R. F. Delderfield	
THE TEACHINGS OF DON JUAN • Carlos Castaneda	
JOURNEY TO IXTLAN • Carlos Castaneda	
A SEPARATE REALITY • Carlos Castaneda	
TEN LITTLE INDIANS • Agatha Christie	
BABY AND CHILD CARE • Dr. Benjamin Spock	
BODY LANGUAGE • Julius Fast	
THE MERRIAM-WEBSTER DICTIONARY (Newly Revised)	